DYNDAER

Book 2

The Kaelandur Series

Thrice Nine Legends

Joshua Robertson

Acknowledgement

For the few who have found significance in the sprawling ramblings of an aged man, and against their better judgment, decided to put another log on the fire.

There once was a time when the gods were gods without question. When men were men without example. When heroes were only the frivolous dreams of lurid mortality. It was a time when truths and untruths were indistinguishable, hatred and love were equally excusable, and life and death regaled all of humanity in the same breath. Myths of old were realized and legends were born from the very dust man was formed of, to be told and retold until the grace of time altered them beyond knowing or forgot them completely. Still, some tales were preserved deep within the hearts of mankind, for reasons that could not be fathomed. Perhaps bearing the fruit of some profound truth or kept alive merely by the strength of the men who lived them. Some tales would never be forgotten.

Table of Contents

Prologue	**1**
Chapter I	**12**
Chapter II	**21**
Chapter III	**32**
Chapter IV	**43**
Chapter V	**59**
Chapter VI	**67**
Chapter VII	**75**
Chapter VIII	**84**
Chapter IX	**91**
Chapter X	**101**
Chapter XI	**111**
Chapter XII	**121**
Chapter XIII	**129**
Chapter XIV	**138**
Chapter XV	**146**
Chapter XVI	**155**
Chapter XVII	**163**
Chapter XVIII	**174**
Chapter XIX	**185**
Chapter XX	**191**
Chapter XXI	**199**
Chapter XXII	**208**
Chapter XXIII	**215**
Chapter XXIV	**223**
Chapter XXV	**233**
Chapter XXVI	**241**
Chapter XXVII	**246**
Chapter XXVIII	**256**
Chapter XXIX	**265**
Chapter XXX	**278**
Chapter XXXI	**283**
Chapter XXXII	**288**
Maharia **Prologue**	**304**

Thrice Nine Legends Saga

ANAERFELL*

The Kaelandur Series
MELKORKA*
DYNDAER*
MAHARIA**

Short Stories
STRONG ARMED*
WHEN BLOOD FALLS*
THE NAME OF DEATH*

Additional Works

THE HAWKHURST SAGA*

**Published by Crimson Edge*
***Forthcoming by Crimson Edge*

DYNDAER

Book 2

The Kaelandur Series

Thrice Nine Legends

Joshua Robertson

Prologue

Age-old promises kept Dorofej alive. At the outset, he could not say how many years had passed. Time and space were distorted in the realm of the dead, but the stint had not caused him to stumble in his walk. Upon returning to Aenar, even after a thousand years, the Highborn found the world had not changed. Men were still enthused by power and gain, leaving sagacity to those who retained ideals but had nothing to show for it. Still, he had his promises.

"Another storm is coming. We should find shelter." Sulanna Maelthirren spoke in the tone of a true diplomat. Her voice was terse, yet gentle. At one time, she might have been found within the fastened bodice of a noble. Now, she wore the strapping armor of a soldier.

In the preceding months, Dorofej found Sulanna had the knack for speaking her mind, whether one wanted to hear it or not. Even now, her words served as a fair warning when considering the dimming light that gave shadow to the Hyaendi Hills.

The middle-aged man who led them responded. "Nowhere to go out here but forward."

Thunder rumbled overhead.

Dorofej disregarded the imminent storm. His companions were far more interesting. Sulanna and Alden had inadvertently educated him about what he had missed during the past millennia when he had been traversing the Netherworld.

Sulanna tightened her cloak, her brown hair falling against her cheek. "There is no chance of reaching Eldhaft this eve, Alden. We are over a hundred leagues out. Be sensible."

Alden gazed over his shoulder, letting the horse guide him. "Sensible? The only cover you will find out here is your horse's ass. Look around you. There is nothing but dirt and grass, woman."

Sulanna glowered at the warrior.

He pressed, "Besides, we have nearly reached the outer bounds of the Svet territory. I'd rather not spend another night risking our necks sleeping in the lands of the centaurs."

The belly of the sky was gutted, adding weight to his words. Rain pattered down into small puddles around the clopping hooves of their horses. Their stamping reminded Dorofej of the centaurs. He had learned the Svet were nearly slaughtered to extinction by the Northmen in past years. The thought still made his stomach upset. The centaurs may have been fierce, but it did not discount their goodness.

Sulanna centered herself on her mare. "These are their Holy Lands, Alden. You cannot hate them for protecting what is rightfully theirs."

"I can hate what I wish. The savages should have been cut down years ago. Maharia was given to the Anshedar."

"Given? Men took Maharia by force, slaughtering thousands."

"With the blessing of Svarog."

The woman tilted her head, squinting at the man ahead of her. The spear on his back bounced in rhythm with his horse's clopping feet. "Do not bring your god into this."

"You cannot ignore Svarog forever."

"I'll acknowledge the gods when they do something worth acknowledging." She shot back with irritation.

"Svarog will see to His children, my sweetness." Alden spit harshly and then licked the driblets of saliva from his lip. "Listen, I will not be sleeping on the ground tonight. My frame is too old and my ass cheeks too wrinkled. Riding this gelding for weeks has likely caused what little hair I have left to fall from my head."

To make his point, the warrior threw back the olive-colored hood of his cloak. His receding hair sparsely covered his scalp, covering just the tips of his thin ears.

A chilled wind advanced from the rear.

Dorofej held his black robes and watched Alden. The warrior had no less hair than when they had left Tamarri, but even in the failing light, Dorofej could see the scabbed cuts along Alden's arms. The blemishes joined many scars, which staggered his wrinkled skin; some were fresher and deeper than others.

Sulanna did not stumble over her words. "I do not see any gods helping us, Alden."

The man swiftly pulled his hood over his head, seemingly frustrated for not getting the hoped for reaction from the woman. Alden spoke again, but this time his words were directed at Dorofej. "What do you have to say about this?"

Dorofej adjusted his hood, to keep his tufts of red hair dry. He could not agree with Sulanna, who had no belief in the gods. Nor, could he side with Alden, who had a misconstrued understanding of them. "I say, there is more than one god by far."

"That isn't the question, Dorofej." Alden spat again.

"It wasn't? Oh, I do apologize. I must have been distracted by the rain, yes?"

"You are kidding me?"

Sulanna scoffed. "Leave the boy alone."

Dorofej grew silent again, taking the advantage of his dark robes to slink back into the darkness.

"Fine. I'll let it be, but he is not a boy. He is a young man and should learn to speak his mind once in a while. He cannot spend all of his time with his nose in a book," Alden muttered. A few seconds later he added, "We will press forward until the storm lets up or we find shelter."

The lightning flanked them, snagging the sky, as they meandered west. The jagged earth was layered in small patches of greenery through the muddied soil with tall grasses stretching in every direction across the swells in the land. With each step forward, the rain only thickened.

In the many leagues that passed, as the hours of darkness further set, there was no disrupting the melodic tune of raindrops, besides that of the horses' hooves stamping through the mire. Hill and hill again, they traveled over, rising and falling in their saddles.

"For honor, for glory," Alden uttered in a whispered prayer. Dorofej barely heard the words against the metallic sound of Alden's belt knife sliding from its scabbard. Even in the dark, Dorofej saw the loosened bracer hanging from Alden's forearm, and the sharpened blade slicing through his sensitive flesh.

He had to turn his eyes away.

Dorofej had learned the warrior cut himself as penance and would not stop until he felt he had brought glory to Svarog. Dorofej had attempted to explain to Alden the nature of the gods, of Svarog, but the attempts were futile. In time, he discovered Sulanna had spent the better half of a decade attempting to convince Alden of his irrationality. It did not do any good. The man was beyond help. Of course, this was not Svarog's way. Nor was this the way of the Anshedar. This was Alden's way.

The Highborn did not look again until he heard the blade return to its holding. Alden's blood washed away with the downpour, dripping from his fingertips.

Sulanna interrupted Alden's continued prayers, which had given undertone to the falling rain for the past mile. "I do not understand why anyone would hide this relic here in the North. Maybe the old Anshedar who Ivarr speaks about buried it, during the War of Shayol Domier."

"The War of Shayol Domier, Third of Frost, Month of Falling Leaves, 124 CE, it was, when demons last walked upon Aenar," Dorofej's whistled from the rear, welcoming the conversation. He was eager to take his mind off of Alden's life-threatening pastime. "That battle was leagues to the south. Further than either of you have traveled, yes?"

"The mysterious, all-knowing Dorofej," Sulanna mocked. "There surely is some use to those books but I was not asking for a history lesson."

"Sweet Sulanna, through history we find the road to our destiny, yes?"

Sulanna turned to him sharply. "Either of you men call me sweet again, or any variation of, I will run you through personally."

Dorofej tittered with amusement.

Sulanna bit her bottom lip and tried again. "Seriously, what of the relic? Any ideas as to what we are looking for exactly?"

"We are searching for what is called *kaelandur*, yes?" Dorofej said. "The power to bring the demons back to Aenar, it possesses."

Sulanna raised her eyebrow. "And what exactly is this *kaelandur*?"

Alden coughed, finally joining the conversation. "No one knows."

"Then why were we sent after it?"

"Would you like to ride back to Tamarri and ask, my swee—"

"Alden means to say we do not know, yes?" Dorofej flashed his white teeth in a smile with the break of lightning, interrupting the balding warrior.

Sulanna glared at Alden, nearly reaching for her belt knife to follow through with her threat. She grimaced. "I certainly cannot imagine what would be buried in these hills."

Silence ensued.

At the bottom of yet another hill, a small, wooden farmhouse seemed to rise magically from the earth. The dark clouds lightened, though the rain continued, giving enough light to roughly see the terrain. A faint glow of a lantern's light radiated from a second-story window on the eastward side of the building, barely casting an outline of the diminutive home. A tattered fence of thin branches shaped the land around the place. Strangely enough, the structure stood alone with no outbuildings for livestock or farming equipment. Oddities such as these briefly slipped through Dorofej's mind, but was forgotten in anticipation of a warm fireplace.

The barking of dogs erupted into the night air, announcing their arrival. A small smile lifted on Sulanna's face. "I stand corrected. It seems your god has finally decided to do something worthwhile."

Alden ignored the sarcasm. "Something does not feel right."

Sulanna heatedly pushed back the soaked strands of hair from her eyes, attempting to regain a bit of composure. "Are you suggesting we refuse the mercy of your god?"

"Svarog does not simply give mercy to those who ask. We may be fools to seek sanctuary at this farmhouse."

"We are fools to sit here in a downpour discussing this nonsense," Sulanna barked with frustration. "We have been traveling in the rain for hours."

Alden met her unblinking eyes in complete wonderment. "There is something amiss, Sulanna."

"You are amiss, Alden," Sulanna retorted.

Alden frowned in defeat. "You are going to get us killed."

Dorofej followed them down the hill, watching the noble woman sitting high on her horse as though the edge of any sword was too dull to leave a mark on her throat.

Dark shapes distinguished to be the barking dogs ran towards them. There was a mutter from Sulanna indicating there were two in number. In a matter of seconds, the animals sprung over the fence and were next to them.

Even in the heavy rain, it was easy to tell these were nothing but ordinary dogs. The three riders ignored the mutts snapping around their heels and at the legs of their trained mounts. A couple measly dogs were not threatening.

Drawing near, Dorofej could see shadows through the window bouncing off the walls from a lantern's light. The shaggy animals jumping about his feet continued to snarl and yap, creating a great ruckus. Though, the booming voice of a man caught his attention as the narrow door at the front of the home opened.

"Jorwarg! Worlack! In the name of Marheena, stop…!"

The silver-haired man who stepped out into the rain appeared at least twenty years older than Alden. His face was wrinkled and unkempt with coarse patched hair that could not rightly be called a beard. He wore a white shirt with the collar untied and short brown trousers. Once seeing the riders, he froze barefooted in a mucky puddle of rainwater, holding his bulky body up with a fat branch in one hand. In his other hand, a lantern hung from his fingers swaying as his staff settled itself in the loose sludge.

In a moment of silence, Alden and Sulanna stared wide-eyed at the older man as he did back at them, his mouth crooked with his jaw dropped. He could have very well been the oldest man in the world.

Dorofej tugged back the hood of his robes. He was uncertain whether the man's words regarding Marheena had been a curse or a prayer. As if understanding the unknown, the yipping dogs became eerily quiet, and trotted off around the back of the house.

Sulanna introduced them. "I am Sulanna Maelthirren and these are my companions, Alden Forgaaf and Dorofej Creighton. If you would be so kind, we seek shelter from the storm."

Dorofej nodded at the made-up surname he had given himself upon returning to Aenar. Fortunately, it had been accepted by strangers with little question about its origin.

The stranger's brow wrinkled as though he were seriously distressed by Sulanna's words. His expression hardened, lips curling into a sneer. "Bohumir is my boy! You cannot take him from me."

Sulanna loosened her long knife from her belt. "I do not know any boy named Bohumir. We simply need a place to rest for a few hours."

"Bohumir Mager? You know Bohumir Mager!" The man spouted in laughter, tilting his head backwards.

Alden turned his head sideward to speak into Sulanna's ear. He was loud enough that all could hear him. "He is mad."

"Maybe not," Dorofej muttered.

She ignored them both, nudging her horse a step closer. "These rains do not show signs of stopping anytime soon…"

"Curse you!" The man croaked, his laughter abruptly ceasing with a sinister gaze resting on Sulanna. "Curse you and the foul rain!" Then, under his breath as if asking a question, the man spat, and whispered feverishly.

Dorofej leaned forward to try to grasp the words. They sounded ancient, familiar.

The lantern flying towards Sulanna's chest stole away his concentration. He watched as she dived from her horse, avoided the object, and landed in a grimy puddle.

The man reacted before Dorofej or Alden had a chance. He bolted to Sulanna's side with his staff raised over his head. In no way did the movement appear to offset the older man's balance. Sulanna, who acted more on impulse than anything else, rolled out of the away to avoid certain death. Then, with a quick sweep of her leg, the she took the aggressor off his feet.

He landed with a thud, the staff bouncing far from his grasp. His white shirt was dirtied, covered in both rain and mud. With a bestial snarl, he spun onto all fours like a rabid animal and rushed the noble woman again.

Sulanna cried out. She scurried backwards to regain her footing, fighting to pull her dagger from her belt.

From the side, Alden had dismounted from his gelding. With expert timing, he stepped forward and kicked the charging man sending him sprawling backwards once more. The old man clamored in the mud. Alden did not waste any more time, lifting his spear and pointing the tip at the fallen foe.

"Find salvation in this life or the next, it is your choice," Alden sneered. Sulanna pulled herself to her feet, finally yanking her dagger from her belt.

The man rolled over in the mud, gasping and wheezing. The white shirt was barely hanging on his body, torn down the front, staying in place with caked mud. He glowered, trying to stand, only to slip to his knees again. Alden kept his gaze on the man, allowing the stranger to stand erect.

He shifted his full attention to Alden and his spear. He spoke in huffs, "Marheena will smolder the lot of you!"

None of them had a chance to respond.

The stranger spun around the spear with inhuman dexterity. He had not taken more than three steps before Sulanna flung her dagger, the blade sinking into his neck.

Blood spurted to the sound of his horrific, gurgled scream. With a jolt, he staggered, crawling back toward the entrance of his home. His blood mixed with the moist earth.

"No," Dorofej inhaled. He raised his gaze from the dying body to see a small boy in his sleeping garments standing in the doorway. The boy did not return the look, but instead stared in shock at the dying man who had fallen near the doorstep.

"Father..." the boy was barely audible through tears.

The man struggled, raising his arm towards the boy, who rushed to him. The son fell to his father's embrace, weeping uncontrollably. The father cupped his hand on the young boy's cheek, and in a curdled moan stammered, "Bohumir, my son. Come with me."

With his remaining strength, the old man pulled a dagger from the back of his belt. In a moment too quick to respond, the father sunk the blade into his son's chest. The father crumpled in a heap, lifeless. The son spurted blood from his mouth, his face aghast in bewilderment.

"Dorofej!" Sulanna cried, running to the boy's side.

He threw himself off the horse and ran to the doorstep, his eyes locking on the copper blade within the boy. He knew it well. "Take the dagger and quick, you must be." Dorofej kneeled, peeling back the eyelids of the boy called Bohumir.

Sulanna jerked the dagger from the cavity of Bohumir's chest. Dark red blood spewed from the wound. "Save him!"

"His spirit has not fled from the body. Time there may be." Dorofej was delicate in his movements.

Dorofej caught sight of Alden, who was kneeling in the mud a few yards away with his bracer dislodged. His belt knife was clutched in his left hand as he cut another gash into his forearm. It may have been a third cut, possibly fourth. He could not tell from the overwhelming amount of blood streaming down his arm. The old man's prayers to Svarog for forgiveness were choked and difficult to understand. His words were suffocated through gasps for breath, through tears and mucus. The warrior was lament with grief.

He spoke to Sulanna, "Go to Alden."

The Highborn's hands touched Bohumir, covering the wound. Blood flowed freely over his steadied hands. A glow of red and yellow glowed beneath the boy's skin as Dorofej manipulated his craft, the *Koldovstvo*, ever ancient and powerful.

From the corner of his eye, Dorofej saw Sulanna rush to Alden. She grabbed him, screaming, all noble equanimity was lost. "Stop this, Alden! No god is worth this!"

Alden shouted back. "Let me go, Sulanna! I must save him with my sacrifice!"

"No, Alden," she pleaded. "Think for yourself."

"You must let me go. I must do this."

Sulanna clutched the powerful man's arms in defiance.

From the depths of his gut, Alden bellowed. With merciless strength, he picked Sulanna off the ground and flung her to the side. She spiraled into a roll, slamming her face hard against the wet ground. Mud splattered into her eyes and covered her hair.

Determined. Gasping for air. She rolled against the sludge.

Dorofej winced, knowing he could not help. His task was too important.

Alden cut himself with more intensity. His prayers were screams. Pleas. He was going to kill himself.

The boy suddenly twitched beneath Dorofej's trembling hands. The black mage cried out, "He will live!"

Alden dropped the knife, his arm shreds of flesh hanging from bone. "Praise Svarog! For the Kingdom and glory."

Dorofej joined Sulanna in the mud, knowing not else to do, and wept.

Month of Falling Leaves

Third of Frost

1350 CE

Chapter I

"Stone the crows! Is your name really Branimir?" Drak Ghas clicked his tongue. The Kras clenched his red fingers around the handful of twigs inside the leather pouch. The smooth, shortened sticks poked upward over the lip of the leather giving view of the strange carvings on the end. He continued with a wide grin. "Did you know we were freed by a Kras named Branimir Baran?"

"I did hear something about that," Branimir said from the opposite side of the table. He wrung his hands together to calm his nerves. He could not tell this stranger, here in Ojenir, the truth. Instead, he played dumb. "What had this *Branimir* done?"

Drak pulled the twigs from their pouch. His voice was jarring, giddy with glee. "Branimir saved our kind from the *Kadari*. Those evil mages once kept the Kras as slaves—in the Dyndaer—at Shayol Domier, a thousand years ago and more."

The *Kadari* had seemingly destroyed any record of the Highborn after their victory at Shayol Domier. Bran doubted if anyone knew the mages had once been called Highborn.

Drak shuffled the many sticks in his hands.

Branimir realized Drak was gawking at him, possibly looking for a reaction. He forced his lips to part. "That *is* something."

"It is," Drak agreed. "My grandfather was among those freed; the same is true for most Kras who live here within Ojenir. You are lucky to have come from another place and born free. Where did you say you were from?"

Branimir hesitated, scanning the underground cavern called Ojenir. The Kras city bore no natural light. Without torches or lanterns, the cavern was but a chasm of blackness for all living creatures, save the Kras. "Across the ocean."

"You traveled across Strega's Deep? I have never known a Kras to go far from their home. Though, I admit I have always thought about going on an adventure." Drak dipped his head and pressed on with his story. "Did you know these mountains, the Hrani Highlands, are said to be named after Branimir's father?"

"That," Branimir moved his hands to rest against the leggings of his trousers, concealing his grin, "that is *really* something." He found himself amused that he had been remembered over the course of a millennia. He would have never thought a slave from Melkorka would be considered a celebrated hero in the modern age. He had been written into history and was not yet dead.

He felt Drak's eyes on him again and had to look away to keep from beaming. The cavernous chamber, beneath the Hrani Highlands, had little movement from its inhabitants on the other levels. Night had settled beyond the rocky walls about an hour before he had arrived. Somehow, Drak had taken it on himself to give him a warm meal and welcome.

In many ways, Ojenir reminded him of the Kras city of Illuard, within the Crags of Kazimir, where he had traveled a lifetime ago. That is, with the exception, Ojenir was not in ruins.

The hollow of the cave was a wide-open space with an area in the center for mining, and small workbenches to cut sediment from any stones found by the diggers. There were a few burrowed holes in the rock or makeshift mudhouses lining the walls, suitable as sleeping quarters. The place was anything but civilized compared to the outside world.

Tunnels lined the expanse of the circular, rocky dome, leading deeper into the Highlands. Branimir almost expected demons to rush from the burrows as they had at Illuard.

He shivered, but nothing ominous emerged from the depths.

"Will you be staying long?" Drak asked. "I know you have only gotten here, but it would not be hard to find an extra den. I have an extra bed inside, if needed." Drak pointed to the mudhouse behind the stone table they occupied. "We have never had another Kras visit before. I would be glad to hear about your home across the sea."

"No thank you, Drak, is it?" Before the other Kras could answer, Branimir added, "It was only by chance I came to Ojenir. I might stay for the night, but no longer."

"Where are you heading? Winter in Maharia is wicked. It is hardly the time to be traveling on the road."

Branimir shifted his gaze to his small hands. "The cold does not bother me much." For a moment, his mind wandered to the many centuries he had spent in the Netherworld. The experience had hardened him, but time did not flow the same in the realm of the dead. Where his mind had grown wiser, his body had remained ever young-looking. Of course, there was no way he could tell this stranger, or anyone else, what could not be explained.

"Are you alright, Branimir?" Drak asked.

He scraped his teeth against his cracked lips, giving Drak his attention. Branimir knew he would never again taste the acidic breath of the Netherworld. Yet, scarily enough, he found some days he longed to return to the place he had traversed for a thousand years. For three years, he had drifted aimlessly across Maharia without any particular place to go. The frozen wastelands of the dead were still more familiar to him than Maharia or the Hrani Highlands.

"Yes. I will be just fine." Branimir said. "Were you not going to tell me my future?"

"Ah." Drak shifted on the stone rock, widening his eyes at the twigs in his hand. "Stone the crows! I nearly forgot about the rune staves. I suppose you have finished your supper." Drak fiddled with the twigs, eyeing Branimir's empty bowl on the table. The Kras said, "These were passed down from my father, who taught me the secrets of *div-i-nation*."

Branimir smiled as the friendly Kras struggled to say the word. "And, where did your father learn it?"

Drak knit his brow.

Branimir did his best to not grin. "I am sorry, but I have never before heard of this talent."

"My father never told me," Drak said.

"Okay," Branimir straightened himself on top of his own rock, "what do I need to do?

"Nothing," Drak said. "I just throw them in the dirt and then I tell you what the sticks say."

"The sticks talk to you?"

Drak angled his eyebrows over his black-filled eyes, looking seriously at Branimir. "They are called rune staves, not sticks—and yes. Do you always ask this many questions?"

Branimir smiled. "I have been told I do."

Drak clicked his tongue, rubbing the twigs between his red hands with fervor.

"Alack!" Drak squealed hurling the twigs to the cavern floor.

Branimir jumped at the sudden exclamation while Drak hurriedly stooped over to examine the rune staves.

After steadying his heartbeat, Branimir crooked his own neck in trying to make some meaning of the weird black scratches on the wood. Most of the staves were faced down, hiding the markings, but there were a few that were exposed.

"Oh, my," Drak whistled. "Yes…oh my, my, my."

Branimir tightened his lips to keep himself from making a comment on the usefulness of Drak's mumblings. He did not want to offend the stranger, who clearly took this rune-reading business very seriously.

"You will never find love, or peace, or riches in your lifetime," Drak started. His finger was on the edge of his pointed nose, tapping it while concentrating.

"Ha!" Branimir slumped on his rock. "Perfect."

"Hold on," Drak narrowed his eyes, glimmers of black flashing, like jasper. "You will soon be traveling into the frigid cold with a man. No something more than a man—he is coming for you."

Branimir felt his eyes widen. "Are you talking about the future or the past?"

Drak was off his stone and on his knees, drawing closer to the scattered twigs. His pointed ears twitched like the staves were actually making a sound, which only Drak could hear. "The rune staves only tell the future."

Branimir shoved his hands into his pockets to keep them from trembling. He bumped into something buried in his pocket. With recognition, his fingers skimmed the soft surface of the bluish moonstone, the *Ojenek*.

He had found it at Illuard within the Hall of Gravels, the *Eevaltti*, when he was still a slave to the Highborn. Now, he always kept the precious relic close. The gem allowed the holder to speak and understand any tongue; *Ojenek* was as much a part of him as his own hand. It had always given him an unexplainable comfort.

He took a deep breath, calming his nerves.

"There is more," Drak jerked his head to stare at Branimir. "I have never seen this…"

Branimir turned his head, reaching for his pack of extra food and his cowl. "I must be going." Despite being comforted by the moonstone, he did not want to stick around at Ojenir any longer. He did not want to know what else these rune staves said.

Drak reached out and clutched Branimir's arm, holding tight. "Stone the crows! Your life, and your death, is somehow connected with the gods, Branimir. I know it sounds ominous, but the death rune is leaning against the rune of the gods."

Naturally, Drak would know the word *ominous* but could not say *divination*.

Branimir stood, throwing his cowl over his head. "I don't know what you are talking about, but I don't plan to die anytime soon."

Even Branimir was surprised at the smooth tone of his voice.

"You must be Master Branimir," a shrill voice acknowledged from the rear. "There is a man waiting outside the gate. He specifically asked for you—by name."

He turned around to face another small, crimson creature. "Who?"

The Kras shrugged. "He did not give his name."

Drak tried to gather all his sticks. "A man has come to take you on an adventure."

"I don't think so," Branimir trailed off. His mind riddled with confusion. He did not know anybody.

"If you would please come with me," the messenger said. "We would prefer the man not tarry outside of Ojenir."

"Wait for me," Drak said. "I must go with you on this adventure. I want to know more about the meaning behind the rune staves."

"I think it would be best if you stayed," Branimir frowned. Recalling his manners, he bowed his head. "Thank you for the meal, Drak. It was nice meeting you."

Without waiting for a response, he turned to follow the messenger. He was led away from his stone seat and through a tunnel to the outside. As he walked away, he heard Drak yelp for him to wait, scrambling to put the rune staves in the pouch.

The breeze rolling through the Hrani Highlands hit Branimir before he reached the exit. The coldness reminded him of the Netherworld's frosty ether. He tightened the red cowl around his shoulders to keep himself from shivering and exhaled. The misty vapor fled his lips, dissipating into nothingness.

The moment he could see the frozen dirt of the Hrani Highlands, the Kras messenger said his farewells and turned to go back to Ojenir.

Bran bobbed his head and followed the clatter of a horse's hooves against the ground. He no more had stepped outside the tunnel before a familiar voice called out with a heavy accent.

"Branimir Baran, yes? Too long, it has been."

Branimir halted. He gaped at the red-haired man atop the dark horse near a ridge. The two had not been affected by the passing of time while in the Netherworld together, but since returning to Aenar, Branimir had felt the impact of age on his body. He swore his knees creaked whenever he stood. He noticed little change in the black mage though.

"Dorofej?" Branimir nearly cried, his eyes watering in the breeze. "You have come back for me?" The Highborn looked almost as youthful as he had at Shayol Domier a millennium ago. His hair was a bit longer, and there were a couple of extra lines around his eyes, but he was still a young man. It could not be possible unless…unless, he had found the Ash Tree, again.

"My dear friend," Dorofej beamed, his brow unruffled with reassurance. "Over, our adventure is not. I must call on your service once more, yes?"

Branimir's chest tightened in a mixture of fear and excitement, no longer worried about the foretelling of the twigs.

"It has been three years. What has happened? Did you find what we sought?"

Dorofej did not hesitate, revealing a copper dagger from his cloak. He held it outright over his horse's head with a firm grip. "Something worse, I am afraid."

"*Kaelandur!*" Branimir gasped in recognition. "It's not possible. I watched you cast it from the *Tower of Eresh*. The dagger was left behind, forever lost in the Netherworld!"

Dorofej flared his nostrils. "As it should have been, yes? Yet recovered somehow and carried back to Maharia, *kaelandur* has been. We can speak on the road, but time is fleeting. Come with me, you must."

"What a pigsticker," Drak piped up next to Branimir, appearing from the tunnel behind him. The Kras's eyes were glued to *kaelandur.*

Branimir jumped, frowning at Drak. "What are you doing out here? I said not to come."

"And, I said I am coming with you."

Branimir grunted. "No, you most definitely are not."

"Yes, I am. The rune staves say you will have the greatest of adventures. Alack! Your name is already marked for greatness, *Branimir.* If anything, I must come with you to tell your story."

Dorofej spoke with amusement, "Let him come, Branimir. I say, we could use a guide, and the Kras would know Maharia well, or at least have a greater knowledge of its history. Besides, an extra hand may be helpful, yes?"

"Anything you need to know, I could tell," Drak agreed.

Branimir gave a side-long, scrutinizing glance at Drak, and spoke to Dorofej. "What is happening?".

Dorofej answered, "You have seen it too, yes? Rumors of the dead spilling over from the Netherworld, there are; a place for them to find rest, there is not. Rumor, there is, that Wolos, the Horned God, has been slain. I say, if true, the Likhyi will come."

"Huzzah. I said you walked in the footpath of the gods. *Div-i-nation.*" Drak slapped his hands together and flashed his crooked teeth. "I will fetch us ponies."

Chapter II

Branimir did not own a weapon, armor, or really anything useful when considering the dead were *spilling over*, as Dorofej indicated. His pack had a few pieces of dried meat and unleavened bread atop an extra set of clothes. From the looks of it, Drak had brought even less.

"What are the Kras doing with ponies?" Branimir murmured, fearful of startling his tan mare. He gripped onto the yellowish mane, his fingers warmed by the thick strands of hair. He sat only a few feet above the ground with his body slanted in the small saddle. He was certain he had never ridden an animal before in all his life.

Drak, who rode next to him, bounced on his pony like it was an extension of his bottom. "What do you mean?"

"I mean, Kras are quicker on their feet and do not tire easily. Why would you own a pony for riding?" Branimir asked.

"Oh," Drak shrugged, keeping his dark eyes on the path ahead, "we do not ride them often, unless the snows are too thick or the road is too long. And the snows will be deep soon enough."

Branimir scrunched his nose. "But where did you get them? How did you train them?"

Drak laughed out loud, patting the neck of his black pony. "We did not train them. We traded stones for them last year with men from Hleduk. These are Dukeson ponies from the far north. Trained, short, and sturdy." Drak clicked his tongue, and continued, "We mostly use them to pull our wagons to Halderon when we go trade at the market. I don't like trading stones, but these ponies were worth it. We have to make a living. Don't you have ponies across the ocean?"

Branimir had not yet traveled to the coastal city of Halderon, which he knew to be located on the other side of the Hrani Highlands. In the past few years, he had mostly circled through the inland villages and cities. Branimir responded to Drak, keeping to his lie. "No, we have no ponies across the ocean."

Wanting to avoid a discussion about his origins with Drak, Branimir slowed his mount. Allowing himself to fall behind several paces, he focused on trying to learn how to maneuver the animal. Straightening his back, he clung to the pony with his knees, and pulled at the reins softly to redirect when needed.

To help ease his tension, Bran spent many miles focusing on his breath, watching the patterned air mist in front of the edge of his pointed nose. Soon, he found it was not as difficult to ride as he might have imagined. Relaxing, he watched the terrain around him, knowing he could see better than Dorofej in the dark. The Highlands had a thin layer of frost in some areas, but mainly, Bran saw hardened red rock and discolored foliage.

The first real snowfall would be coming soon.

Half the day had passed and Ojenir was well behind them when Drak whistled through his teeth. He wiggled his pointed nose against the cold wind. "I should formally introduce myself since we will be spending time together. I am called Drak Ghas, son of Figkor, son of Callux."

Dorofej dipped his chin. "Dorofej Creighton."

Branimir was speechless, not remembering Dorofej to ever have had a surname. Either he finally remembered it, or he had made it up altogether.

He was not sure Drak would be sticking around for the entirety of the journey, especially if he had anything to say of it, but he followed Dorofej's example. "My name is Branimir Bar—" He stopped, remembering Drak's familiarity with history and the Kras. "Branimir Barthor." He lied.

Dorofej glanced over his shoulder with equal surprise.

Drak did not seem to notice. Scratching his hair, black and frayed, from beneath the gray linings of his hood, he said, "Pray tell, where are we going, Anshedar?"

"An Anshedar, I should not be considered," Dorofej said. "I am Highborn. And to Cavell, within the Dyndaer, we are riding."

Drak gasped. "You are *Kadari*?"

"No," Dorofej said. "I say, considered among the *Kadari*, I will never be."

"Then, what do you mean by Highborn?" Drak whispered, trying to make sense of the word. "And why do you talk with that silly accent? I have never heard anyone talk like you before."

Dorofej's forehead crumpled.

Branimir answered, reiterating what he had come to learn in the past few years. "Highborn is an old word once used to describe the *Kadari*. The mages used to be respected, but long ago, there were men…" Branimir thought of Kinhar Sayan and Falmagon Sej, the Highborn Long-Walker, "…who craved power and—" Branimir, suddenly serious, turned to Dorofej for help.

Dorefej picked up on the pause and continued the thought, "And the blessing of Dahz the Lightbringer, these men sought, to acquire said power. These men destroyed what the Highborn were meant to be, they did."

"You know the *Kadari* then?" Drak responded, lifting his nose to look at Dorofej.

"From Maharia to Kalamaar, I have heard mentioning of the *Kadari*, yes? In the past thousand years, gifted the world with vast death, the *Kadari* have. I say, I know them well, better than most. The first to seek power and immortality, they are not; and the last to pay with their lives, they will not be."

Drak's mouth was wide open. His feet bobbed on either side of the pony. "Alack! Aren't the *Kadari* keeping demons at bay on the other side of the world?"

Dorofej rubbed his chin. "I say, heard such rumors, I have. Whether true or not, time will tell."

"Did the *Kadari* make the pigsticker you are carrying about?" Drak asked.

Dorofej hummed in response.

Branimir gulped, his throat dry. He struggled not to blab the tale of him and Dorofej right then and there. A thousand years had passed since *kaelandur* had been removed from the world of Aenar and taken to the Netherworld. Branimir wanted to know why it had been returned to the north, to Maharia, and who was responsible.

"Dorofej, what have you learned since we parted at Strahil?" Branimir probed, again, fiddling with the reins of his pony. His red fingers were already chilled, but it was nothing he could not withstand. He had spent a lifetime and more in the frozen Netherworld. The winter in Maharia did not compare.

Dorofej peered at Branimir from beneath his black hood. He considered Drak before answering, "Little, I am afraid. I say, the past years have been spent with the Crimson Sun at Tamarri in attempts to learn what the world has become."

"Crimson Sun?" Drak repeated under his breath.

"And what has the world become?" Branimir turned from Drak, disregarding his widened eyes and twitching ears.

"You heard the tales, as much as I, or any other who listens, yes?" Dorofej said. "Dragon-men and skin-switchers continue to clash in the north, the *Kadari* spreads their reign here and in the east, and warring races in the southern deserts expand toward Maharia, yes?"

"I have," Branimir agreed. "But I also heard whispers of the Crimson Sun and what they do; though, I did not know you were with them. Aren't they sellswords who mostly do business for the *Kadari*?"

Dorofej laughed, cheeks red from the cold. "I say, I have forgotten what you have become. A servant no longer and again, you never will be."

"You were a slave? I thought you were born free." Drak intruded leaning over on his pony. "Were the *Kadari* your masters?" Drak ogled and then hissed, "Or Dorofej?"

Branimir avoided the question.

Drak may get caught up in Dorofej's rhetoric, but Bran knew better. He had spent enough time with the Highborn to know when he was being sent on a wild goose chase. Praises and poppycock was Dorofej's way of swaying a conversation.

"That is not an answer, Dorofej," Bran said.

The black mage smiled. "Keep the enemy close, I thought I would."

Branimir pressed, "And, in doing so, what did you learn about *kaelandur?*"

Dorofej grew stone-faced, glancing sideways at Branimir and exhaled. Dorofej acquiesced, "In 1348 CE, Ivarr Gauthus, the now standing master of the Crimson Sun, directed myself and two others to find *kaelandur* for the *Kadari*."

Branimir gasped, gripping the saddle. "This man, Ivarr, knew *kaelandur* by name?"

Dorofej dipped his head. "Indeed, but tell him of its discovery, we did not. Alden Forgaff and Sulanna Maelthirren, my companions, had the same opinion as myself to withhold *kaelandur* until the truth of its wanting was learnt. Luckily, motivated merely by money, not all sellswords are."

Branimir recognized the riddlesome words of his friend, and demanded, "How did you convince them to keep the secret? How could you trust them?" He could only think that Dorofej had revealed all to this man and woman: his age; the Ash Tree; the Netherworld; and the history of *kaelandur.*

Dorofej rocked in his saddle. "Oh, dear Branimir. I am a man of erudition, yes? I say, I am known to have an uncanny and unhealthy fascination for knowledge."

Branimir snorted, catching sight of Drak, whom was gawking at them as though they were from another world.

Branimir smiled, knowing they were.

The Kras must have taken the gesture as an invitation to join the conversation. "Did you find out why Ivarr wanted the pigsticker?"

Dorofej, again, hesitated before replying. "As I said, the *Kadari* commissioned him to find it, yes? Know why the *Kadari* wanted the dagger, the Crimson Sun does not."

"Is Falmagon still alive?" Branimir screeched louder than he intended. He had to pull on the reins to keep the pony from jutting forth through the mountainous terrain. When he finally gained control of the animal, he considered kicking himself for uttering the Highborn Long-Walker's name in the same vicinity as Drak.

"We cannot be certain, yes?" Dorofej said simply, but the Highborn could not hide his grimace. "Yet regained Melkorka as a stronghold, the *Kadari* have, so time we may still possess, if we are quick. Cling to hope, dear Kras; hope the *Kadari* know less than we know and remain at Melkorka, yes?"

"Time for what?" Drak squinted like he was trying to see through Dorofej. "What do we know? What does all of this have to do with the gods and Branimir?"

Drak clearly attempted to match his understanding of his rune staves with the information he was being told.

Dorofej dropped his head in defeat. "Correct, you may have been, Branimir, to leave this Kras at Ojenir. He is as tireless in his questioning as you once were, yes?" Dorofej exhaled noisily.

Branimir smiled, mocking Dorofej's speaking pattern, "*I say*, fair questions, are they not?"

"Some, yes? Though, unaware of the significance of the inquiry, you are," Dorofej frowned, seemingly unaware of the joke Branimir aimed to make. The black mage tapped his fingers on the saddle, and finally making up his mind, he resumed, "Time to recover a boy, we have. A boy, who I have hidden away, called Bohumir…Mager."

Branimir stopped his pony on the path with a jolt, comprehending the importance, and history, of the name. Mager was the last name of the *Eretik*, a dark magus, whom the Highborn had executed at Melkorka.

Snowfall began to descend down from the heavens, settling atop his pony and the rocky terrain around them. He scarcely noticed. "Dorofej, could it really be?"

"Afraid, it is true," Dorofej said, laying out the measure of their journey. "Bound by the same bloodline as Nedezhda, our quarry is, and through death affixed to *kaelandur*, he might be. I say, the *Kadari* will want him as desperately as the copper dagger."

Half the night had passed when Dorofej stopped them to rest. The red rock of the Highlands rose on either side of them with only a few scattered trees. Branimir hoped there would be enough timber to make a fire.

He slid sideways from his saddle, missed his stirrup, and clumsily bounced on a single foot away from his pony. His animal stood, unaffected, nuzzling against the snow for something to eat.

If Dorofej or Drak had noticed his near collision with the lightly powdered ground, neither said a word.

Branimir cleared his throat and tightened his cloak while steadying his feet against the slick ground. "Do you have any grain for the ponies, Drak?"

The other Kras, already down from his mount, gritted his teeth and looked at Branimir with pause. He blew air between his teeth, giving the clear answer, and said, "Marry! I forgot."

"No matter," Dorofej said. "Plenty of grain, I have, until we reach Cavell."

"Oh, good," Drak said.

The Kras from Ojenir started to loosen and unfasten the straps across his pony. Branimir attempted to mirror the action with hopes to remove the saddle from his own mare. His cold fingers had difficulty trying to manipulate the hardened leather.

Drak talked while he worked. "Cavell is a dangerous place to be traveling this time of year. There are only two towns with Northmen in the Dyndaer: Ariadne and Cavell. Folks in Halderon say the men who live in either place are a bunch of boobs."

"What?" Branimir faltered. "A bunch of what?"

Drak casually looked over his shoulder. "Boobs. You know—chumps, fools, dupes."

"Um…" Branimir looked to Dorofej, who he could see broadly grinning while ducking behind his horse. Bran hesitated before replying. "Why would they say that?"

Drak did not miss a beat. "Because of the number of cities that have turned to ruins over the years. There is *Shayol Domier*, of course, and *End'augh*, and *Undril*. The last Ariadnean city before they built Ariadne was *Garain'l*. There is some question as to whether the Northmen really lived there. No matter, the place is now home to the dead and who knows what else."

Low murmurings came from Dorofej, but Branimir could not make out the words. He watched the Highborn pull his saddle free from the back of his dark horse.

Branimir racked his memory. He knew of Shayol Domier, but the other cities were a mystery. They must have risen and fallen while he was in the Netherworld with Dorofej. "Why were so many cities lost? War?" asked Branimir.

Drak scratched his head. "That is right. You are from across the ocean and do not know these things like I would think you would." Drak removed the saddle from his pony, laying it on the ground. "War has had its place, but more so, the Dyndaer is a cursed place with many sorts of creepy crawlies. I hear they are as thick as the trees, but I know little of what they're called. I guess it would be hard to keep a city if there were always beasts running through the streets."

Branimir swallowed. Once more, he expected Dorofej to respond or give some sense of comfort. The black mage retrieved a grain bag for his mount, and no longer appeared to be listening to Drak.

Drak continued, "I have heard folks in Halderon say the ruins are grand, maybe even built with magic. We know Shayol Domier was built with *Kadari* magic, but who would have built the other ruins? No one really has ever said."

Thinking of the *Kadari* at Shayol Domier halted Branimir from trying to loosen the straps. The mages, who once would have been called Highborn, had built a suitable stronghold in the Dyndaer. Branimir remembered Shayol Domier to be far more impressive than Melkorka. Knowing as much, he wondered why the *Kadari* would have withdrawn back to the Seven Islands, to Melkorka.

Drak approached Branimir with a smile, stepping between him and the horse.

"Here," he offered, "let me get the saddle for you. It can be tricky if you haven't done it before."

"Thanks," Branimir said.

Drak slackened the leather strips when Dorofej absently said, "Branimir, firewood needs to be gathered, yes? Freezing through the night, we should try to avoid."

"I will see what I can find," Branimir said.

Drak pulled the saddle to the ground with a grunt. "Let me go with you, Branimir. I would like to help."

Branimir led them to the few scattered trees. The two had only gone around thirty paces when Bran found several dampened sticks beneath the slush. He knocked each broken branch against his foot to loosen the wet snowfall, and then placed them under his arm. Drak circled around him to discover more buried wood.

"I'm curious," Drak whispered so quiet Branimir had to strain to listen to him, "why did you come looking for wood as soon as Dorofej said? Why didn't you tell him to get it himself?"

Branimir turned his chin in surprise, clamping his jaw shut to keep from huffing. The question was bizarre. He shifted his gaze from Drak to Dorofej, who moved to feed the ponies with the extra grain.

"That is an odd thing to ask," he replied, tightening his grip on the timber under his arm. Considering his thoughts, Branimir glanced around the Highlands. Then, as if realizing the truth of it, he said, "It is nighttime. Dorofej cannot see in the darkness like you or me. I can find the wood in half the time."

"That may be true," Drak nodded. "But earlier, Dorofej had said you were no longer a slave. What did he mean by that? I tried to ask before…"

"I know you did," Branimir said, stopping to nibble on the end of his lip. He could feel himself fidgeting while he stared back at Drak. "I am not a slave, Drak. He and I have been through a great deal together. I doubt there are any in the world who could say as much."

Drak slid another branch under his small arm. "Like what?"

"Like what?" Branimir echoed. The words were faint under his breath. "We haven't the time for me to tell all our tales."

The doubtful tone Drak responded with put Branimir on the edge of his heels. The Kras spoke hesitantly, "No time? It will take several weeks to journey to Cavell. We have all the time in the world to tell stories."

Branimir shook his head, and tried to respond how Dorofej might. He answered the original question with a question. "Why do you want to know?"

The other Kras continued to scoop up sticks, not realizing Branimir had stopped to watch him. Drak spoke at length. "Marry! I don't know. I am curious, I guess. You are marked with greatness, according to the rune staves. I could have a better idea of where you are heading if I knew where you had been."

Branimir's mind raced to change the subject. He had no interest of telling Drak about his adventures in the Netherworld. He interjected, "I had a friend who was curious like you."

"What was his name?"

"Mojmir," Branimir answered. Although he brought up the subject, he did not want to see Mojmir's red skin and single black bulb staring back at him. He pushed away the image of his one-eyed friend from Melkorka. The Kras had died as a result of his loud mouth the same night in which Branimir's real adventure had started.

Drak balanced the wood in his hands, suddenly turning about. "What happened to him?"

"He had his neck snapped," Branimir said, "for talking too much." He saw Drak's noticeable gulp before turning his back. Branimir kept all emotion out of his words, ending the conversation. "Now, let's go get the fire started."

Chapter III

Twelve more days had come and gone since Ojenir with little excitement. Drak had slowed in his persistent questioning, while Dorofej and Branimir had conceded to staying hushed about the road ahead. The urgency of their quest remained, but Branimir found himself with more questions than answers about the nature of their charge. He could only wait until he had an opportunity to speak with Dorofej alone.

The Hrani Highlands to the north had grayed once Dorofej had guided them into the dark woods of the Dyndaer. The trees were five times thicker than their ponies, towering around them with the space in-between filled with corroded, wilting hedges and speckled undergrowth. Vines snaked between the boughs above, the ends hanging inches above the ground or buried under snow. If ever there had been a path through the Dyndaer to Cavell, the road was hidden in the wintery weather.

Branimir lay on his back within the Dyndaer wilds. The layered snow beneath his blanket was hardened against his back, unaffected by the radiant heat from the fire. He half-listened to Drak throw his rune staves against the forest flooring. The other Kras mumbled under his breath while the sticks clacked and smacked together.

He did his best to ignore the sound with his head resting against his pack. He watched white flakes spin down from the crown of branches above him. Besides the small fire flickering, almost failing near his feet, the forest remained as dark as Ojenir. Though, for Branimir, being a Kras, his eyes gave him clear sight.

A thousand years ago, Branimir had walked through the Dyndaer in the heart of winter, the same as now. Bran would have never thought the Dyndaer could have become so much darker in the elapsed time. Where the forest had been enigmatic then, the ambiance had become more fear-provoking than ever.

Dorofej rustled from under his hood, raising his voice in the darkness. "Another stick I hear clattering and snap the twig in two, I will."

"The gurgling mire makes it too difficult to sleep," Drak said, turning around from the other side of the fire. "And, they are called rune staves, not sticks."

Dorofej raised his head, propping himself up on an elbow near Branimir. He blinked irritably at the Kras. "Keep at it and called firewood, they will be."

Drak grumbled, clutching his twigs to his chest. "It's too noisy here to rest."

"Do stop your sniveling, yes? I say, if you are upset by the noise then go and tell the swamp to shush."

"Marry! I was simply saying," Drak faced the Highborn with a scowl. "You do not have to be bad-tempered about it."

Dorofej snorted. "You wanted to come on an adventure, yes? Be glad the bog is only blubbering and there are no beasts dragging you beneath, you should." The Highborn pulled his hood over the back of his ears and laid back down.

"What beasts?" Branimir shivered, watching Dorofej with sudden interest. Drak had mentioned creatures roaming the Dyndaer when they left Ojenek, but Dorofej had not said a word. The Highborn always had his secrets.

Drak stood. "I told you this forest is full of monsters."

Branimir looked toward the mire on one side, and the half-frozen river they had been following on the other. "I cannot think of any monsters I know in the Dyndaer, save the Vucari."

"Spoilt since our last coming, this place has been. The Vucari abandoned the Dyndaer for good reason, yes? A wisdom unknown by men, it is." He paused to sink further into his wrappings. "In the Dyndaer, vili and bagiennik; bluds and mylings; you will find." Dorofej reshuffled, again, against the ground, twisting over onto his side.

Branimir could make out the tufts of red hair sticking out from his hood. How could he lay so calmly after saying such things?

Drak seemed to have a similar mind, no longer giving any sign of resting. He scanned the trees around him. "Stone the crows! Mylings are the worse," he shook his head, "but what are those other *things*?"

Dorofej murmured, near napping, again, "Nymphs and fays. Imps…and wights. The fire keeps them away…yes?"

Branimir shuddered, scooting closer to the flames.

Drak stood. He turned his neck, inspecting the trees and twitching his ears at the nearby mire. With droplets of sweat swelling on his forehead, he looked to Branimir and pursed his cracked lips.

"Suppose, I can gather more wood for the fire."

Branimir could only nod.

Drak scuttled off.

The ponies nickered, followed by a whinny from Dorofej's horse several feet away.

Branimir realized he could not sleep either. "Dorofej?"

The Highborn grumbled.

"Being back in this place is unreal, like I am dreaming, or in a story." Branimir picked at his fingernails, staring into the burning logs. The Highborn had not moved, or even given a sign of listening, but Branimir needed to talk.

"Do you ever think of Melyena and—" Bran tried to recall the centaur's name, who had come with them to protect the Ash Tree so long ago; the mighty Svet, who had been slain by the ruthless *Kadari*. "Asgrim." He finally said. "I hate that I cannot remember names like I think I should. Though, how much can a mind hold before it begins to forget? We have lived more lives than most, even since Nedezhda. I had thought the tale of the *Eretik* had been finished, especially after seeing you cast *kaelandur* from the *Tower of Eresh*." Branimir bit his cheek. "I almost want to go back to see the tower. I want to know the place is as I remember it. The Netherworld really was something, wasn't it?"

He continued to ramble, paying no mind to anything else. "Mm. But tossing the dagger into the abyss should have been the end. And now, the tale has begun all over. Are we meant to live this story again? Maybe…maybe this story will not be quite the same."

Branimir shook his head, his chest tightening, overwhelmed with emotion. He tried to think of something else. Snowflakes skidded down from the treetops, catching his attention. "Do you remember when we last came here? It was the same time of the year; the first snow had just fallen. By what chance would we enter the Dyndaer during the course of winter, again? Maybe we are actually dead, and caught in some vortex of time and space, reliving a nightmare."

Branimir laughed at the thought. The flames flickered against the wood, pressing heat against his cheeks. "I keep thinking about the cold here in Aenar compared to the Netherworld. I guess nothing will ever compare. Even more, I cannot help but think this place, Maharia, feels deader than the realm of the dead. Is that strange?"

"It is not," Dorofej said.

Branimir lifted his head, seeing Dorofej sitting upright, listening intently. His hood was pulled back, revealing his full features, including his flaming hair and wide nose.

"A longing for lost memories, I, too, have found." Dorofej averted his eyes. "The fascination for what cannot be attained guides us toward our charge in life, yes?"

Branimir scrunched his face. "What do you mean?"

"Most measure the worth of something based on constructs of good or evil, justice or corruption, and beauty or defilement, yes?" Dorofej rubbed his hands together, warming them near the fire. "Each paradigm is a puzzle, and the definition of each differ from era to era, yes? A riddle for the living, it is. But an infatuation with puzzles, the dead and the gods, have not."

Branimir said, "Because, they have the answers?"

Dorofej shook his head. "Because, answers to these questions, there are not. I say, there is no gamut to be measured. These questions were created by men; not gods. Hard to understand, I know, for the living have not the scope of immortality. Bound by time and our flesh, we are, yes?"

"Why, then, did you bring me back to life in the Netherworld? Why did you not let me die as I should have?"

"Should you have?" Dorofej elevated his eyes, cheekbones lifting in a warm smile. "Time does not make me any more of a god than you, Branimir. Value in healing the ailments of others, I have found, yes? Whether false or otherwise, my talent with *Koldovstvo* may grant me admittance into Thrice Ten Kingdom, yes?"

Branimir matched Dorofej's smile. He could not remember when the Highborn had ever spoken of life beyond death, in a thousand years, and specifically never had talked of reaching Thrice Ten Kingdom. Bran had grown accustomed to thinking Dorofej would never die, and live forever.

Dorofej must have picked up on his unspoken thoughts, "We must all die eventually, yes?"

From the brush, Branimir saw Drak rushing towards them. The Kras shimmered against the backdrop, telling Branimir that Drak was invisible, blending in with his surroundings. The skill was only known to the Kras, to disappear when needing to stay safe, but a Kras was unable to hide from the perceptive eyes of another Kras.

Still, Dorofej's attention was caught in a similar way. He watched the patterned footprints appearing in the snow, nearing the illuminated area of the fire.

Drak skittered towards them, talking before materializing next to Dorofej. "Alack! Something is coming through the brush behind me."

Branimir barely made it to his feet before a bellowing voice boomed, "The pint-sized bastard went yonder."

With Drak at his side, Bran retreated. At the same time, a hulkish giant smashed through the scrublands, cracking the base of a tree in his wake.

Branimir first thought the huge man was a Bukavac, a frozen behemoth from the Netherworld. His mind hastily painted sporadic memories of battles at Melkorka, and Kalamaar, and the Netherworld before dissolving into nothingness. He quickly discovered this giant was not a demon.

The tyrant appeared more humanoid his with tannish skin, dark hair shaggily hanging over his ears, and piercing blue eyes. More than anything, the giant seemed to be an oversized Anshedar.

The oversized man looked directly at Dorofej and the two Kras standing in the firelight. The giant stopped, steadying his uncovered feet in the snow, and yanked a large two-sided axe from the strapping of his back. He gripped the handle in the meaty grasp of his two six-fingered hands.

"He is not wearing shoes," Branimir whispered in surprise. The giant should have been freezing, but seemed unaffected by the cold.

"Bah! I found two foul half pints and a Stuhia, by the looks of it. You know him, Eisliev?"

Stuhia? Branimir had no way to place the word, but could only think the giant was speaking of Dorofej, who clearly was *not* a half pint. The Highborn, who had found his way to his feet, pulled the black hood over his head to better conceal his reddened hair.

"What in the Nine Lands, Tyr," a heightened voice snickered, with undertones like Dorofej. A flash of red robes surfaced through the brush while an unseen man attempted to push his way around the giant. "You are going to alert every living thing in the Dyndaer with your ruckus. The Stuhia do not travel this far east, and if they did, we do not inherently know one another. I have never met such a boorish swine."

The man, called Eisliev, barreled around the growling Tyr, who kept his eyes on Dorofej and the Kras. Eisliev carried a torch, wearing robes as red as Dorofej's were black. He shoved on Tyr unsuccessfully with irritation, standing just beneath his chest, and lastly smacked the giant in the forearm with the back of his hand.

The bare-chested brute shoved him back, without looking, sending the robed man sprawling to the ground. "Ah! If you are looking for a fight then jump upon my blade and your death thereafter, Eisliev. I have no interest in hearing your blabbering squall."

Eisliev grunted, somehow keeping his torch from being doused. He flung himself back up from the ground and approached Tyr with a sneer. His own hood had fallen back giving full sight to his long, reddened hair and light eyes.

Branimir raised his eyes to Dorofej for direction, but the black mage acted equally surprised by these mens' sudden appearance.

A third voice, unhurried and balanced, redirected them, "Enough, the both of you. What have you found, Tyr?" An Anshedar, covered in an array of greens and grays, who carried his own torch, stepped from the tree line on the opposite side of Tyr.

Branimir first noticed the impression of the head of a horse imprinted on the iron breastplate glinting beneath the flaps of his cloak. The swordsman had a long piece of sharp iron hanging from his belt within a decorated scabbard.

"Teodor Bacheva," Dorofej finally acknowledged, sounding comforted. "A long way from Tamarri, you are?"

Teodor gazed at them, and then rushed to dip his chin to the black mage. He dropped his resting hand from hilt of the long sword at his belt. "Dorofej Creighton, whatever are you doing here in the Dyndaer? Ivarr has been asking of you for many months now." Dorofej clicked his tongue. Before he could answer, Teodor said to Tyr, "Put your weapon away. He is with the Crimson Sun."

Bran bit his tongue, recognizing the name of Ivarr, who Dorofej had said was the master of the Crimson Sun. According to the Highborn, Ivarr also had been responsible for sending Dorofej to find *kaelandur.*

Tyr relaxed, easing the weapon back into its holding.

Eisliev, however, tightened his hands into fists and took a step toward them. On impulse, Branimir reached for a dagger from his belt. When his hand swiped at nothing, he gritted his teeth in frustration. He had traded them for food and supplies weeks before reaching Ojenir.

Dorofej answered Teodor, "I may ask you the same question, yes? I say, did Ivarr send you to the Dyndaer to find me?"

The Anshedar dawdled, "Not hardly. Ivarr sent me to complete another assignment for the *Kadari.* It is a simple task of retrieving a young lad who has eluded them. Nothing too difficult." Teodor shrugged.

Branimir straightened his back, seeing Dorofej's jaw drop at the mention of their intentions. These three were also seeking Bohumir Mager.

Teodor said, "I would have liked for Ivarr to have given the task to you, or even Alden and Sulanna, but you all have been gone from Tamarri for many months."

"My sincerest apologies, Teodor. Still been seeking the relic the *Kadari* sought, I have, and distracted by other matters, I have been."

"Weren't you sent for that relic several years ago? You and I had returned signing a treaty at Mabek when Ivarr gave you the job, right?" Teodor asked.

"A few years, it has been," Dorofej agreed.

Eisliev took another stepped forward, practically glaring at Dorofej. Branimir could not ignore the look of contention from the red-haired man.

Teodor replied casually, "Indeed. Your service to the Crimson Sun has been remarkable. Ivarr talks about you like you are some legend from the stories."

Branimir thought he heard the undertones of jealousy in the Teodor's voice.

Dorofej cocked his head, and scoffed. "Trust in you equally, Ivarr must, to send you after a helpless child, yes?"

"Is that sarcasm?" Teodor laughed, and went on. "If I recall, the relic you were meant to find was not in the Dyndaer. The *Kadari* reported it was buried in the Hyaendi Hills."

"An impressive memory you have." Dorofej flashed his teeth, lying, "After several months, other options, I thought I might consider."

"I am certain Ivarr will be glad to know of your reconsideration," Teodor replied with a sly smile.

Dorofej matched the expression.

Eisliev, suddenly interjected, as though he had finally gained the courage to speak, "Time seems to have treated you well, Dorofej, is it?" Eisliev curled his lip. "How long have you been away from Lairhein? It is rare to find a Stuhia this far from home."

Branimir noticed Dorofej swallow air. "Long enough," he answered.

"What did you say your surname was?" Eisliev pressed.

When Dorofej did not immediately answer, Teodor answered, "Creighton."

"Creighton?" Eisliev repeated with doubt, and then accused, "I am not familiar with the name among the Stuhia bloodlines."

"And, you are?" Dorofej asked, suddenly full of fire.

"Ah," Teodor elevated his voice, "Eisliev Kluk and Tyr Og have recently joined the Crimson Sun."

Eisliev glared at Teodor for a moment, and then turned his gaze back to Dorofej

"How pleasant," Dorofej murmured with less enthusiasm. He smoothed his robes, focused on Teodor. He changed the subject. "Listen, since I am here, I would be glad to fetch the lad, yes? You can be on your way back to Tamarri."

"No," Eisliev nearly shouted, his voice echoing through the trees behind Branimir. "We will be taking the boy to Melkorka."

Drak sprang back at the outcry.

"Eisliev," Teodor cautioned, lifting his hand.

The red mage curled his lip, but said nothing more.

"A bit late on the offer, Dorofej. We hope to arrive at Cavell by morning." Teodor said casually

"If you don't get us lost again," Tyr added with a smirk.

Teodor frowned, ignoring the giant. "Perhaps, you—" The man dipped his eyebrows at Branimir and Drak, peering in the dim light, though he were trying to identify what they were exactly.

Drak filled the blank, "Kras."

"Of course," Teodor said with a nervous laugh. "Send them back to their home, and return to Ivarr. He will be eager for you to explain your absence."

"Heading another way, we are," Dorofej replied, forcing a smile at the opposing group.

"I see." Teodor tensed. "Should I report to Ivarr for you, then, when I return?"

Dorofej pushed his teeth outward, doing his best to maintain the phony smile. He looked like a half-brained horse. "I say, do whatever you must, Teodor. Best of fortune on your journey, yes?"

Chapter IV

The next few minutes were a blur. In one moment, Branimir was watching Teodor, Tyr, and Eisliev tramp off into the Dyndaer, and then Dorofej was kicking snow over the fire, shouting orders.

"Follow the river to Cavell, they will," Dorofej said. "Make haste. Ready your ponies, you must. I say, we will reach Cavell and find Bohumir first, yes?"

"How do you plan to get to Cavell without following the river?" Drak squealed. The Kras dashed by the fire to start placing his bridle on the animal. "Alack! We will get lost."

"Hope we do not," Dorofej said.

A few moments later, Branimir's tan mare scrambled behind the other mounts. He clung to the pony, bouncing inches off the saddle, barely staying atop. Ahead of him, the black mage led them through the thick trees. The bog bubbled wickedly alongside them.

Branimir almost considered forsaking the ponies, knowing he and Drak could likely run faster than the creatures. Though, with foresight, Bran was also aware he would exhaust himself long before the mount would lose wind. So, he held to the reins and mane of his animal, and bolted after Dorofej into the Dyndaer.

"Gah!" Dorofej shouted, hunkering down on his horse, slapping its hind quarters with the reins in one hand while holding a torch outright with the other.

"Can you see?" Branimir called out. He hoped Dorofej did not lead them straight into a swamp. Branimir was certain the Highborn could see no more than a haze of shapes and shadows rushing on either side of them.

"Well enough," Dorofej cried.

Drak squealed from either fear or amusement, galloping right in front of Branimir. After a short time, any sign of the river leading directly to Cavell disappeared entirely behind them.

For almost an hour, they were hard-pressed, making their way through the Dyndaer without saying more than a few words. At last, thinking they had made up enough time moving west and south to get past the other group, Dorofej slowed.

Branimir's pony huffed and snorted.

"Climb off of her, Branimir," Dorofej instructed, breathing heavily himself. He dismounted from his black horse. "Breathe for a moment, we all must."

"We will be lucky if we are not totally lost," Drak said, gasping for air. "Hard to keep any sense of direction in the Dyndaer. We could be near the ruins of Shayol Domier at the rate we were going. I bet we looked like a bunch of boobs speeding in between the trees."

Branimir shook his head at Drak's choice language.

Dorofej whipped his torch around. "Similar to anything boobish, we are not." He cleared this throat. "Shayol Domier is further to the east and south, yes? Overshot our mark, we have not."

"How do you know?" Branimir asked, while Drak twisted his face at Dorofej.

"I say, look at the trees, Branimir," Dorofej said. "Many have been cut, leaving stumps between those fully grown, yes? Harvested for the buildings, and homes, and palisades, they have been."

Dorofej was right. If Branimir had taken the time to look around, he would have noticed the mangled remains of many chopped trees. Though, the crown of limbs that thatched the ceiling of the forest was as concentrated, if not moreso.

Drak's pony whinnied. He did not bother to shush it, but instead counseled Dorofej and Branimir. "You should know people in the Dyndaer do not think well of the *Kadari*. Saying anything about them or—"

"Told you, *Kadari*, I am not," Dorofej interrupted.

"I know," Drak said, "but any talk of Dahz the Lightbringer should be kept to yourself. The Dyndaer is different than the rest of Maharia. The folk here worship Czern, the Gray-Clad."

"So, they hate the Lightbringer?" Branimir clarified.

"Mostly yes," Drak replied, "and anything to do with the *Kadari*."

"As dark as the Dyndaer is," Branimir pondered. "I can see why the people would respect the God of Darkness. Yet I wonder…"

Dorofej tilted his head with interest.

Branimir continued, "Why don't the *Kadari* take the Dyndaer as they have the rest of the north? Their stronghold had once been here—the Ash Tree, too. From what I have heard, the *Kadari* have forced people to worship Dahz all across Maharia. Why not do the same here?"

Dorofej raised his eyebrows with matched curiosity.

"Well, most would tell you the *Kadari* are locked in a battle at Melkorka against demons," Drak explained. "The storytellers say the monsters came after Wolos was killed. I heard the Netherworld has no more room for the dead."

"Isn't that only a rumor?" Branimir asked, looking to Dorofej uneasily. He had seen the numerous dead scouring the frozen wasteland of the Netherworld. At the time, he had thought it normal.

"It is," Dorofej said, wrinkles forming at the edges of the Highborn's eyes.

Drak rubbed his chin, looking southward. "Ariadne is another possible reason. The city is said to be greater than Gaetana." Branimir recognized the name of the capitol city, home of the nearest King. Drak went on, "In Halderon, folks say Ariadne is time-honored, for over five-hundred years now, birthing Aenar's greatest hero-warriors. Not only were the soldiers from Ariadne critical in the final wars with the centaurs, but they are still called on again and again to fight battles for the Northmen."

"*Hero-warriors*," Branimir wondered for a moment. He then added, "How do they keep the *Kadari* out of the Dyndaer?"

"They don't. Not really," Drak said. "The *Kadari* need the Ariadneans for them, especially now, against the desert people."

"In other words, the *Kadari* don't oppose Czern because the Ariadneans fight their wars," Branimir finished. "Do the kings and queens of Maharia have no say?"

Drak scrunched his shoulders. "From what I know, the *Kadari* controls them. What can simple Northmen, or even Kings, do against magic?

"Plenty," spouted Dorofej.

"I wonder what the *Kadari* would do if the Ash Tree were in the Dyndaer," Branimir said.

"Oh, they would attempt to convert Ariadne, for sure," Drak agreed. "Some Kras at Ojenir repeat the stories of their old kin. Of course, there are none left who remember the Ash Tree being in the Dyndaer, but I have heard of how the *Kadari* once fought the Vucari over their difference in belief. All that is left are the stories."

Branimir thought to mention how it all was more than a simple story, but decided against saying anything.

Drak said, "War springs the quickest from those who have faith in gods, even the peaceful ones. It is likely why our people worship nothing."

The words left Branimir speechless. He had never considered why he did not worship like most. In hindsight, he figured there was little difference, whether forcibly enslaved to men or blindly following the gods. In either case, he would have no freedom. The thought mortified him.

Drak gradually added, "You know, there is another reason why the *Kadari* might leave the Dyndaer be." Drak's voice was almost wistful while sharing his knowledge. "I forgot about the Lilitu. They have built seafaring, trade cities all along the edge of the Dyndaer. Any destruction within the forest would surely upset their market on the coast and spur them to war, too."

Branimir's mind raced to place the name. "Who are the Lilitu?"

"Alack! I know you come from across the ocean, but how could you not hear of the Lilitu?" Drak crooked his neck. "The Lilitu have been in Maharia since the beginning of the Third Age. They come from the south, from Haemus Mons. Our people trade gems with them often in Halderon."

Branimir asked, "Why would the *Kadari* be afraid of the Lilitu?"

"Their sheer size," Drak said. "Even when counting the *Kadari*, the Lilitu exceed the Northmen fifty to one."

Dorofej said, "Expanded greatly, the world has."

"When compared to what?" Drak raised his eyebrows in confusion. Before either Dorofej or Branimir could respond, Drak threw up his hand to stop them. "Wait. Something is moving in the clearing ahead."

Dorofej swiftly flipped his torch upside down and pressed it to the earth to squelch it. "Branimir," he whispered, "see what stirs, yes?"

Branimir reacted, becoming invisible to all who might be able to see him, save Drak, who directed the ponies back.

He had become familiar with the scout and report routine when traveling with Dorofej in the frozen wasteland of the dead. The tactic had kept them from many skirmishes which might have left them bloodied or worse.

Branimir zipped ahead, his feet lightly crunching against the snow. The sound was hardly audible, even to his ears; however, the footprints he left in his wake were unavoidable. The surrounding swamp bubbled and gurgled nearby, swollen against the blackened earth. He considered the bizarre swamp babbling in the Season of Frost while he advanced.

The moment slowed.

Branimir took two steps into the clearing and stopped dead in his tracks. He goggled at a young, dark-haired boy, likely ten-years-old, who held a torch to inspect a woman dangling from rope by the neck. The corpse hung from a straight branch, swaying to and fro. The limb from which she was attached to creaked. Her face was grayish-blue, barely observable through her mangled, golden hair.

Branimir had seen many dead bodies in his lifetime. He guessed she had been dead for the better part of the afternoon.

The boy climbed carefully up an adjacent tree for a better look. His torch flickered from the ground below, cackling against the snow. He took his time, unhurried, without worry.

A brown horse whinnied from behind the boy, burying its nose into the snow, searching for fresh grass. The animal's reins sagged against the ground.

"Bohumir Mager!" An aged man in a fancy jacket shouted from the opposite side of the clearing. The boy sprang from the tree, falling to the mush below. "Czern's breath! What are you doing?"

The child recoiled from the dead body, bright blue eyes wide with horror in the faint light of his torchlight, but clear to Branimir. His leather boots slipped in the snowfall that covered the ground, but he steadied his feet. The boy gawked at the older man hesitantly, lifting his hands innocently.

"I didn't kill her, Lamont. I found her like this," Bohumir's voice trembled. "Please, you must believe me."

Lamont eyed the child, angling his thick brow, as if appraising his worth.

The boy shouted, "Lamont, please! There's no need for your sword."

Branimir jerked toward the man in the fancy coat. True enough, he held a short, heavy sword in his hand. The single-edged blade curved slightly at the end, looking more like a farmer's tool for harvesting the crop than a warrior's weapon.

"I am not going to kill you, you looby," Lamont snorted. The gray-haired man stepped closer, shaking his head with disbelief. "You really think anyone would believe you'd have the strength to hang a grown woman, boy?"

"Well…" the boy stammered.

"Climb back up there and cut her down," Lamont ordered. He tossed his sword at the boy's feet.

"I say, what has happened here?" Dorofej's voice rumbled across the space of the clearing.

The man, likely a noble, jolted at the sound. He observed the black mage and then the weapon he had thrown. When Bran materialized in front of Dorofej, the boy and man both took a noticeable step backwards.

"Who are you? What are you doing here?" Lamont asked, stepping nearer to the boy. Bohumir shifted his own gaze toward the sword.

"Lamont Dthais," Dorofej eased, "leave the sword alone, yes? Familiar with me, you are. It is I, Dorofej Creighton."

"Dorofej," Lamont crooned with a relieved sigh, pushing his chin forward and squinting his eyes, .Is that really you? I hardly recognized you in this terrible light. Why have you come back?"

Bohumir stared at the black mage.

Dorofej hummed, ignoring the older man. "The girl hung herself, yes?"

Lamont answered, measuring Dorofej with his eyes. "I truly do not know. Lady Nitalia went missing and now, here she is."

"Lady Nitalia?" Dorofej's eyes slightly widened.

Branimir shifted his feet with discomfort.

"Yes," Lamont whispered. "The Count's daughter disappeared this morning. The whole village has been searching for her."

Her golden hair and bluish-gray nose caught Branimir's eye again. He had to turn away.

Lamont continued, "Czern's breath has been exceedingly dark these past months. The people of Cavell are on edge, plagued with superstition."

Dorofej said, "I say, darker times are coming, lest I can take Bohumir with me. This is the boy I had left in your care, yes?"

Lamont adjusted his jacket, frowning. "It is."

"You are one of the men who came to my father's house," Bohumir glared at the Highborn. "Where is the woman who killed him?"

"I am, yes," Dorofej said. The black mage side-stepped the second question. "Saved you once, I have, Bohumir, and again, I must. I say, you need to come with me."

Lamont tightened his jaw. "An explanation would be welcomed, Dorofej. When you left Bohumir, I did not expect to see you again. The boy has just begun to settle here. What is the meaning of all this? I had meant for him to take over my business someday, and provide care for my daughters."

Drak suddenly piped up, joining them, "They have a pigsticker—"

Dorofej hushed him. "I say, the less you are aware, the better, it is. Best for Bohumir gather his things and we be gone at once, yes?"

"No," Bohumir said. He reached down gripping the handle of the falchion in his fist. It was off-balanced in his hand. He barely could lift the blade from the ground. "I am not going anywhere with you. This is my home now, and my family."

"Here, you have lived," Dorofej said, "but your home, it is not. And I imagine neither was the Hyaendi Hills, yes?"

The boy jerked his head toward Lamont uneasily.

Dorofej shifted in his robes, saying, "Saved you after your father stabbed you, I did, and not for you to ignore reason when it is plainly given to you, nor raise a sword against me when I aim to help. Come with me, you must, or die, you will."

"That is hardly a thing to say to a boy," Lamont protested.

"The truth, it is," Dorofej replied.

Drak's eyes widened. "Alack! Put the sword down."

The boy shuffled toward Dorofej, dragging the sword behind him.

"Enough." Dorofej used *Koldovstvo*, the ancient magic, pulling the sword through space and time from Bohumir's hand and into his own.

Bohumir cried out as the weapon was yanked from his hand.

"Marry!" Drak bawled. "Pray tell, how did you do that? I thought you were not *Kadari*."

"*Kadari?*" Lamont wondered, scanning Dorofej with wide eyes. "You worship the Lightbringer?"

"No, and no, again," Dorofej said.

Lamont grunted, second guessing himself. "I don't want to know what this is about, Dorofej. Let's cut down the Princess and return her body to the Count. Afterwards, you can do as you wish with Bohumir."

The Highborn tossed the falchion back to the ground in the boy's direction.

"As you say, Lamont." Bohumir said, retrieving the sword with less fervor. Bohumir began to climb back up the tree.

Branimir watched uncomfortably. The hanged face of the girl was twisted, either from the strain of lack of breath, shock of what she had done mid-drop, or the sudden snap of her body lurching towards the ground. Her lifeless blue eyes matched the tenor of the expression.

"Hurry up with it," Lamont said crossly, "I said to cut her down."

Bohumir hoisted the sword against the rope and sawed through the hemp with a few quick movements, causing the threads to split. The body clamored to the ground.

Branimir held his breath. The Princess reeked of urine and feces.

Lamont, who seemed unaffected by the stench, heaved the Princess over the saddle of the horse. Bruises and rope marks lined the neck. The head fell awkwardly.

"Her spine is broken," Drak said, making a face.

"Commonplace in hangings, it is," Dorofej said, clearing his throat. "Drak, gather our horse and ponies, yes?"

When Drak returned, Lamont handed the reins of their horse to Bohumir. "You can lead the horse back to town."

Supper had passed by the time the five of them reached the dirt path outside of Cavell. The small hamlet was nestled within the Dyndaer, awkwardly wedged between the river and the woods. Branimir first noticed the looming towers of the stone castle on a small rise.

A single sentry at the open gate approached Lamont, an unusual hammer strung across his back in leather fastenings. The path beyond the gate was lit with torchlight.

Lamont stopped several feet from the guard. "Good evening, Ignac."

The guard called Ignac tilted his head. "And to you, Lamont. Who have you brought with you?"

"Dorofej Creighton of Tamarri. Branimir Barthor and Drak Ghas of Ojenir," Dorofej answered for him, luckily remembering Branimir's false surname.

Drak shifted his weight when realizing Branimir had been included in being from Ojenir. Branimir caught his eye with his own and shook his head to indicate to keep his mouth closed. Drak looked down at his feet nervously.

Ignac tilted his head. "I did not realize the Kras ventured from Ojenir, unless trading in Halderon with the Lilitu."

"Much is unknown of the Kras, yes?" Dorofej thinned his lips.

"I suppose," Ignac said. "Lamont, what news of Lady Nitalia? Count Frantisek has been waiting eagerly in the Great Chamber for hours. He has barely moved since sending out sentries this morning."

Lamont nodded towards the horse. There was no way to hide the body from any who took a simple glance. The girl was easily identified with her blond locks hanging toward the dirt. "Lady Nitalia Frantisek is dead."

Ignac's jaw dropped, seeing the woman slung over the horse. He likely was cursing himself for not noticing when they had approached. "We should not waste any more time. I will lead you to the keep, Lamont. Right this way."

The guard led them through the gates where several armed men dwelled in the shadows. The men stepped from their post momentarily to stare at the dead girl as the horse carried her by them. Her name was whispered.

Ignac led them through the dusty streets, past open taverns and closed shops. Home fires burned in the village of Cavell, the odor of stewed pork and breaded stew creeping out of the chimneys with gray smoke. Branimir's stomach rumbled at the smell despite him eating only hours ago.

Few men hastily moved through the streets and lighted a few torches to accompany candlelit windows. Though, they halted their chore when they noticed the Princess slung over the back of the brown mare. Without doubt, rumor would flood the streets before reaching the castle wall.

Lamont broke the silence. "I am surprised to see folks still meandering about this late. Why have the taverns not closed down?"

"The village has been on edge with the disappearance of the Princess, Lamont," Ignac said. "Keldron decided to keep his place open a bit later. Seems half the town has gone there to drink and who knows what else. We have increased the number of sentries."

"Are you expecting trouble?" Lamont asked.

"Not especially," Ignac said, looking back at Nitalia's body, "but once they hear the Princess is dead…" he glanced around the streets, "…or see it. Who knows what will come."

Dorofej interjected, changing the subject, "I say, have any others passed through tonight?"

Branimir winced, knowing Dorofej was asking about the three from the Crimson Sun. He, too, had wondered if Teodor, Tyr, and Eisliev had arrived in Cavell yet.

"None," Ignac replied with caution. "Are you expecting more companions? You should know Cavell is not used to many travelers, especially during the winter."

Dorofej shook his head. He slipped back into their walking formation without another word.

The road was practically desolate from the main gate to the opening to the keep. The walls were elevated only a few feet above the city wall. The arch leading into the keep was simple with the wooden portcullis strung up. Two more guards stood idly at the entrance, barely noticing the line of men before they had passed.

Branimir stepped closer to Dorofej, recognizing how unaware the guardsmen acted. He guessed the edifice of the hamlet had been built more for display than defense. Perhaps, the people did not fear battle or war with other nations—not in the Dyndaer—but what of the beasties Dorofej had mentioned earlier.

At the steps leading up to the wooden, double doors of the keep, Lamont left the girl's dead body for Ignac to tend. He walked up the stone steps with Bohumir and Dorofej at his heels.

Branimir and Drak followed.

The Great Chamber had a fire pit in the center of the stone floor. Branimir noticed he did not feel much heat from the pit. The temperature in the chamber was only a hair warmer than outside. There were no windows in the room. Only a hole in the ceiling allowed the smoke to escape from the room.

The lord and lady's chairs had been situated on a small rise beyond two long tables on either side of the fire pit accompanied by wooden benches. There was another smaller fire pit near the throne chairs. Sconces lining the stone walls held torches on both sides, separated by embroidered cloths of purple, red, and black hinting at the history and lore of the royal family and Cavell.

A man dressed much like Lamont entered the room and announced the noble family, "Count Vlaskhorn Frantisek and Countess Maja Frantisek."

The Count and Countess entered the chamber from a stone staircase near the rear of the room, and approached their thrones. The husband and wife appeared exhausted, slouching in their step, stricken with concern. Maja's eyes were especially puffy and bloodshot, telling Branimir she had been crying. Her blonde strands were halfway pushed into a bun atop her head with loose ends hanging. The mother of Lady Nitalia did her best to remain poised and placid.

Branimir did like the others and bowed his head. He did not lift it again until the couple had taken their place at the head of the Chamber.

Count Frantisek loosened the pin that held his purplish cloak across his shoulder, letting it fall to the throne behind him. Leaning forward over his plump stomach, he eyed the three men and Kras. He blinked several times with his oversized blue eyes, finding confusion in the presence of the strangers. "Lamont, I was told you had news regarding my daughter. Has she been found?"

Lamont nodded, contorting his face. "She has been found, Count."

"Where is she?" Countess Maja's lip quivered.

"I apologize to tell you, but Bohumir found her hanging dead in the forest," Lamont swallowed. "These travelers, and myself, came upon the scene shortly after he had discovered her."

The Count did not move.

"Nitalia!" The Countess covered her mouth in horror. She looked at Bohumir. "Poor boy." As if not knowing where to direct her sadness, she dropped her face to her hands. She held the position, heaving, choking on her own breath.

The fire crackled as the members of the Great Chamber stared empathetically at the Countess. None, including her husband, had the words to comfort her.

Finally, Maja stood from her chair, unable to regain her composure. She stumbled from the room from which she had come.

Count Frantisek attempted to speak, but had to stop, suddenly coughing into his fist. Bran thought it was possible he was holding back tears of his own. Clearing his throat, the Count sat up in his chair, and said, "Lad, what were you doing in the Dyndaer? I do not recall giving instruction to go beyond the wall, even to find my daughter."

Bohumir sniffled. "I thought, when she was not found here, I should check the forest. I am sorry for not asking to go."

Vlaskhorn clenched his fists, his voice winding into a growl. "If only you would have gone sooner…" He took a deep breath. "Still, you were wiser than any other. Tell me what you know." He shifted his gaze over his shoulder to where his wife had retreated. "Anything that may bring some comfort to my wife."

Bohumir stiffened, keeping his hands firmly pressed to his sides. His boyish hands shook against his pant legs. "I went to find Princess Nitalia after lunch. There were tracks in the snow not far from the gate, and I followed them to a clearing. I found the Princess hanging from a tree. She was… already dead when I got there. The others," Bohumir lifted his hand at Dorofej, Branimir, and Drak, "arrived soon after."

"What else? Were there any other footprints in the snow?" The Count rumbled, "This does not sound like suicide."

"There were no footprints besides her own," Bohumir said. "Count, there is nothing else to tell."

"I see," Vlaskhorn swallowed, "then, can someone explain to me, why strangers appear at the same time of her death? It is the Season of Frost. It is strange to see visitors this time of the year."

Dorofej pulled his hood back. "Business for the Crimson Sun, we have, Count. I say, their work is not bound by the weather, yes? By happenstance, passing through Cavell in these dark times, we are."

Lamont nodded in agreement. "Count, I am afraid it looked as though she had taken her own life. I understand this does not provide much comfort."

"It does not provide anything. Czern's breath! There is no reason why Nitalia would hang herself." The Count's anger came without warning, any calmness in his tone disappeared. "You may be a member of this court, Lamont, but I will not accept your ineptitude. You will investigate this crime, and you will be thorough."

Branimir instinctively stepped back from the throne. He had not realized Lamont was a noble among the court.

The Count continued in his rage, "Someone must have murdered my daughter. I want them found!"

Lamont whispered, "As you wish, Count."

Chapter V

The sound of flutes and cellos drifted through the street from the main tavern in Cavell. Branimir half-listened while leading the mounts behind him. The entire populace of the village might as well have been relishing in the hubbub of debauchery, storytelling, and dancing.

Drak skipped and pirouetted in the streets in step with the melody, humming to himself. His red, pointed ears twitched while flapping his brown cloak about with more jollity than the rest of them combined. If Drak had been affected by the conversation with the Count, he did not show it.

"What are we going to do?" Lamont groaned, leading the company away from the Count's home. He looked over his shoulder nervously, his wrinkled face hanging in despair.

"Do nothing, we will," Dorofej muttered. "I say, there is no time to deal with the witlessness of Counts, especially those who wish to seek a murderer when there is none to be had. A charge of folly is given to senseless men; the burden we carry is of greater consequence, it is."

"I don't know it was really suicide," Branimir said. "The Princess would have a hard time hanging herself from the tree alone. And why go to all the trouble? She could have just as easily hung herself in her own chambers."

"Bah! Matter, it does not," Dorofej argued.

Lamont's jaw dropped. "You are suggesting one man's charge is greater than another? Who are you to gauge the tasks given to men? My station demands I investigate this death, Dorofej."

"Go and investigate, if you must," Dorofej said. "I say, the Princess's death has nothing to do with us. The time, we have not."

Something cold struck Branimir's cheek. He lifted his head upward, feeling another bit of wetness against his shoulder. He stopped Dorofej from engaging with the man. "This is not the time to argue theology. We need to be away from Cavell."

Gentle rumbles of thunder echoed in the distance, stopping all but Drak's gambol. The other Kras continued to listen to the harmony from the nearby tavern, tapping his feet against the hardened, dirt road.

"Thunder in the winter," Lamont peered at the overhanging trees, a mixture of sleet and rain dribbled quicker from above. He whispered, sticking to his accusation, "You have upset Czern with your words, Dorofej."

"Ha!" Dorofej laughed, scratching his head. "Find meaning in things which have none, men always will." Dorofej turned to Bohumir. "Time, it is, for you to come with us."

Bohumir shivered, lifting his hands to touch the cold pellets of ice that fell. "Can't we wait until morning?"

"Best, we do not," Dorofej replied.

"I agree we need to leave," Branimir said, "but the boy is right. We won't make it far in the slush. We will be looking for shelter in an hour. Let's get food in our bellies and rest, and leave before first light."

Drak nodded, orienting toward the tavern. "A piping hot bowl of soup would be nice."

The sleet increased, almost to the frequency of rain. Dorofej frowned. "Very well. Drak, take the horse and ponies to the stable boy, yes? Then go with Bohumir to gather his things. Return when finished, you must. In the commons of this tavern, Branimir and I will wait."

Drak's head sagged, dancing subsided. "Stone the crows! The Kras aren't slaves any longer. I am sure Bohumir can find his way back. I am hungry."

"A matter of slavery, this is not," Dorofej said. "I say, talk to Branimir alone, I will, and without your pestering questions."

Drak's face twisted into a pout, hurt by Dorofej's candor. Reluctantly, he took the reins from Branimir.

The boy, however, continued to argue. "I can sleep in my own home and meet you in the morning. Give me time to say goodbye to my sisters and Lamont."

"No. Return at once, you must," Dorofej waggled his head. "Lamont, see it is done, yes? Under our watch, Bohumir must remain."

"Whatever you say, Dorofej. Clearly, you are going to do what you want." The old man jerked his head in accord. His face was etched in a permanent scowl.

Dorofej nodded idly, his hand resting on Branimir's shoulder. Branimir watched Drak saunter off to take the animals to the stable around back of the tavern, covering his head with one hand. Lamont and Bohumir, recognizing the conversation was at an end, followed after him.

Dorofej leaned forward and whispered hastily under his breath. "Keep an eye open for the Crimson Sun, we must. A great risk to stay here overnight, we take."

Branimir nodded, allowing Dorofej to lead him toward the oak door of *The Stone Crown*. Stepping inside, they were welcomed by roaring laughter and hearty songs playing from the stage. Tankards of ale clashed together as drunkards and tavern wenches danced about between cramped tables. *The*

Stone Crown embodied nothing of the alehouses from when he traveled across Kalamaar during the Second Age.

He looked for Teodor, Eisliev, or Tyr, but no sooner had they stepped through the door of the place then a greasy haired man in his midyears approached with a crooked grin on his thick lips. His black hair was cut short and receding above his forehead. "Humph. Strangers—and a Kras, too? Well, I'll be," he forced himself, as if trying to find the proper words. "Name is Keldron Luben, what can I do you for?"

"Some plum and something to eat with it, yes?" replied Dorofej. "Also, welcoming of a room for rest, we would be."

"Plenty of space upstairs. Most these folk are from these parts, and I'd be wary of those who weren't, if I were you."

"We have also animals sheltering in the stables," Branimir chimed.

"I figured you did, Master Kras," Keldron flashed his teeth. "Wouldn't imagine you would have walked here from anywhere, considering the weather. A few silver should cover your meal and a bit of wine."

Dorofej revealed coins from a leather pouch and dropped them into Keldron's hand. His bag still had plenty of jingle in it when he was done.

Branimir put his hand in his own pocket, recognizing he did not have any silver coins of his own. All he had was his moonstone, the *Ojenek*.

The owner of *The Stone Crown* must have also noticed the hefty size of Dorofej's bag, because he added, "Anything else I can do you for?"

The black mage shook his head, already looking beyond the Anshedar. "Only tell me when the room is ready, you will. Leave us be, otherwise, you should."

Keldron shifted his weight at the direct tone, placing his hand on his belly, muttering something about *strangers*.

Dorofej did not notice. He squeezed through the crowd in search for empty chairs. Branimir hurried to follow, remaining cautious as to not get trampled by the other patrons.

The Highborn steered them to a small round table near the back corner buried in the throng of townsfolk. He signaled the barmaid for drinks before speaking in a low undertone with Branimir. The Highborn jumped straight into matters of strictest importance, realizing their time alone was short. "Remember the pact before parting from Strahil, we made, yes? Know what you have discovered, I must, while Drak and Bohumir are away."

Branimir's eyes locked onto Dorofej's blue ovals, his red tufts falling from his hood once more. After exiting the Netherworld, and learning the Ash Tree was no longer in the Dyndaer, he and Dorofej had agreed to separate in order to determine its location. Dorofej had once expressed the Ash Tree would vanish and reappear to new regions across Aenar, but Branimir had not truly believed it until their return to Maharia. It had been three years since they had last seen one another at Strahil, far northwest from where they currently roamed.

Unfortunately, Branimir had not paid much mind to the pact. He had not found the agreement between them to be of great importance, particularly when *kaelandur* had supposedly been abandoned in the land of the dead. Who would have thought it would have been found? More importantly, *who brought it back?*

The Kras cleared his throat, keeping his voice small by the same token. "Hard to say anything of true worth. The *tree* could be anywhere from the Shade Fells to the Dyndaer, within Maharia or even this place called Haemus Mons."

Dorofej could not hide the disappointment from his face.

"Though," Branimir shared, leaning closer, "after our conversation on the road…I wonder of Kalamaar."

"Kalamaar?"

He wobbled his head. "I find it odd the *Kadari* took Melkorka back as their home when the greater number of people are here, in Maharia. After listening to you and Drak thus far, I find myself questioning the *Kadari*'s motive. Why abandon Shayol Domier, the Dyndaer, and leave Maharia unless…"

Dorofej brightened, "Ah, yes? What ruler, who craves power, rules from a distance? Best to be in the mix of things, it is. The Ash Tree must be back on Kalamaar, or even at Melkorka."

Branimir shrugged, "As strange as it sounds, it is what I keep thinking. There are folks all over Maharia. You would think if it was here, someone would have said something."

"I say, rumors of demons would keep any from looking for it at Melkorka," Dorofej added. "Leaving the power of the Ash Tree for the *Kadari* and the *Kadari* alone, yes?"

"Exactly," Branimir said.

"Given us the advantage once more, your meddlesome mind has," Dorofej hit the table with a cheer. "Glad to have scooped you from Ojenir, I am."

"And, I am glad to be back with you, Dorofej," Bran said, "but I am curious as to how you knew where to find me. We have not spoken in years."

"Old tricks," Dorofej touched his nose, "of which I have told you not to pry, yes?"

Branimir interlaced his red fingers, settling on the chair, feet hanging above the wooden flooring. He thought of the red mage from the Dyndaer called Eisliev, and said, "Did you learn said trick, locating people—or perhaps even objects lost—from the Stuhia?"

Any manner of mirth Dorofej held departed from his eyes.

"We have known one another for a very long time, old friend," Branimir said. He no longer struggled to meet Dorofej's eye as he might have in his youth. He spoke boldly, "I wonder about as to whom or what you really are, and where you have come from. Not truly a Highborn, as you have claimed to be, and plainly not an Anshedar."

"Someday," Dorofej said, removing all emotion from his words, "tell you who I am, I will."

Feeling content, knowing he had gained something, Branimir chuckled, "Do not let the riddle die with you."

A serving girl eventually reached Dorofej and Branimir bringing stew, biscuits, and wine. Whenever their drinks went empty, the girl fought through the throng with her small frame to fill their clay mugs, over and over again.

The evening dragged on, and as expected, the storm outside intensified.

After about an hour, the clamor in *The Stone Crown* elevated as the musicians changed their tune from a small stage on the opposite side of the room. Branimir had heard the song, *The Gal from Garain'l*, sung on the streets in other cities, telling the story of a woman who was said to haunt the ruins of the lost city of *Garain'l* in the southern Dyndaer.

He bobbled his head, mouthing the first couple of verses while sipping on his wine.

'Though the gal from Garain'l did not chide; she had lied, about the silver strung,

When evening comes in Garain'l, hear men mull, pay the toll, from her neck she hung,

Alas, a comely gal comes, who lost her head; she is dead; O' poor Garain'l.'

The pangs on the windowpanes and patters on the roof accompanied the instrumentals resounding off the walls. Folks continued to play from song to song with little intermission. After a time, none in the tavern seemed to care enough to make requests—their bellies were too full of alcohol.

Branimir felt tipsy, but not so much he would forget his list of questions he had reserved for the black mage. "At

Melkorka," Branimir started, "Nedezhda had told Kinhar she had been dead for years but only moments had passed. But when we were in the Netherworld, time stayed the same for us. Why?"

Dorofej rocked forward, pressing his finger to his lips, having the sense to not blather to a room full of strangers all that was known, but still he said, "The passage of time flows differently for the deceased than for the living, yes? *Here* and *now* is assembled so the living can have meaning, it does. In death, find *before* or *after*, you will not."

Branimir put his hands to his ears, cupping them to hear Dorofej better, thinking the action would help him understand what he heard. "How do you mean?"

"Deviate from the narrow path, time does not, for the living. We live and die, yes? Straight line." Dorofej jutted his hand forward, his arm straight. "But for the dead, *everywhere* and *nowhere*, time is, at once. A jumbled mess for them to make sense of, it is."

Branimir scrunched his nose.

Dorofej waved his hand. "An example, I will provide." He lifted his tankard. "Time for you and I is like the plum contained, *unwavering*, in this mug, yes? For those not living—" He paused, swooping up the drink; and then, after swigging a mouthful—to make his point—spewed it out at Branimir.

The alcohol splattered and sprinkled Bran's face, his clothes, and the table.

Branimir blinked, gawping at Dorofej's exposed violet-stained teeth. The effects of his own wine fled his senses.

Dumbstruck, he wiped the purple liquor from his face with a fixed stare. Whatever other questions he may have had were forgotten.

"I get it."

The black mage erupted into laughter, throwing his head back and pointing at the Kras, while wine driveled down his lip and pointed chin.

Chapter VI

The night deepened. Another hour may have passed, and Drak and Bohumir still had not returned. Many patrons had left the tavern, calling it a night, but overall, the place had maintained its elevated din.

Branimir had found his mirth again and chortled alongside Dorofej, who amalgamated with the rest of *The Stone Crown* in rancorous laughter.

"Remember the time we were sneaking through the halls of *Heshayol*," Branimir said, holding a hand halfway over his mouth, "and I heard the hissing you could not."

"Stop it." Dorofej rocked forward in his chair, his face growing pale. His hands slapped down on the table. "Time after time, you bring this up. If I could forget about *Ososcica* for the rest of my life, soon enough, it would not be. And likely, I would forget, if you would stop talking about it."

"Never have I seen such a big snake," Branimir wiggled his eyebrows, continuing, "nor have I ever heard you shriek so much like a woman."

"Branimir, snakes are serious business," the black mage warned, tightening his cheekbones to hold back his own smile. "Killed us both, *Ososcica* would have."

"Should I imitate the scream?" Branimir chortled, hardly hearing Dorofej. "I am not certain my voice can get as high, but I will try."

"Nine Lands, Branimir," Dorofej said with a shake of his head, "in real danger, we were."

Branimir pointed at Dorofej, keeping his grin. "The danger was tenfold after your display of girlish tenor. How long did we have to run from the demons you drew our attention to?"

Dorofej puckered his brow, running his hand through his red hair. "I say, more than a day, it was."

"More like a week." Branimir opened his mouth to silently imitate Dorofej's scream, bobbling his head back and forth for an added touch.

Dorofej good-humoredly swatted his hand toward Branimir before leaning back and gulping another mouthful of plum.

"Evening, mind if me and my friend take these seats at your table?" a bulky, black-bearded man said throatily, tapping on the table near Dorofej. "Seems they are the only chairs left in this place."

The man took Branimir off guard, stifling his chuckle from his and Dorofej's conversation. The man who spoke had more muscle on him than a centaur with arms thicker than Branimir's body.

Of course, the comparison was an exaggeration, but the Anshedar was robust, nonetheless.

The Kras swallowed, eyeing the thick, polished breastplate, made of something other than iron, bronze, or copper. Branimir had never seen a metal so shiny. The material used to forge the protective covering also had been used to create the oval shield and the half-moon, bladed axe hanging at his waist.

Dorofej leaned back, less impressed. "Expecting two more, we are. I say, reason for the additional chairs, it is."

The man plucked a chair away from the table and plopped down. "Too easy. We will only stay until they arrive. I have been on the road far too long and my belly is aching for some ale." As if he were making his point known, he saluted them with his mug. "The name is Adamus Ebordon from Ariadne." He unexpectedly roared out to the tavern almost knocking Branimir from his chair in surprise. "All you remember that name! Tis not the last time you will hear it!"

Branimir found his smile again when none in *The Stone Crown* so much as turned in their direction. Though, he could not help but wonder if this was one of the *hero-warriors* Drak had talked about from Ariadne.

A woman, unlike any Branimir had ever seen, emerged from the crowd and occupied the remaining chair. The bow slung over her shoulder, and the quiver on her back were the last things Branimir noticed. She was shorter than most Anshedar with an oversized head, a scrawny neck, and a sickly, thin frame. Yet her skin, smooth and colored a reddish brown, darker than Branimir, caused him to lean toward her. A sash, red as blood, hung across her shoulder, angled over her small chest.

She sat with her back stiffened and chin jutted forward. Pushing long black strands behind her ears, she introduced herself, "Hanna Bretka, daughter of Briv, from Danduher in Haemus Mons." She sloshed her mug onto the table after taking a gulp.

"Branimir and Dorofej," Bran said, "And, excuse my asking, but what are you?"

Her eyes swelled like an owl, a circular black center and the rest filled with a cerulean orb. The colored ring twinkled like the *Ojenek* in his pocket. "What do you mean *what* am I?"

Adamus and Dorofej merged in laughter.

"Kras," she said. "I am a Lilitu. How would you not know my kind? The Kras frequent trade with the Lilitu in Halderon."

Branimir rubbed the back of his neck with a crooked smile, and meekly shrugged. He could not take his eyes off of her.

"*What are you?*" Adamus repeated, wiping a tear from the corner of his eye. "Best thing I have heard in two months. Having you travel with me never tires, Hanna."

"Glad to please you, Adamus," Hanna muttered, rolling his name off her tongue. "Is this why we detoured to Cavell? I thought we were aiming for debauchery, not expanding on our alleged *friendship*."

Adamus waved his hand. "Do not be sour. We are going home. I will see my sister, and you will rejoin with your *nest*. Our part in the war is over."

"We do not have nests," she scowled. "They are called colonies."

"War?" Branimir perched from his mug. "What war?"

"Must you blab our history to every passerby who shares a table with you?" She spoke in a monotone, without emotion.

The bearded man gulped down his drink, and raised it toward the passing serving girl to fill it once more. After she filled the mug to the brim, he said, "You were paid, as was I, to fight at Raybin, lest we would not have gone. We did our part and received our papers. The battle was lost; but the people are safe. There is no shame in going home."

"I did not say there was shame, but the war is not over," Hanna said. "I am a *Rudhira*, a warrior. The war is never over."

Dorofej interjected, "You are speaking of the war with the desert people, yes? Among their ranks, you were?"

"Mm," Adamus grunted. His hand touched the top of his axe, grinning wider when he realized it was intact. "We fought for the Gaetanaen Kingdom for two years, and dismissed after the Uvil took the field."

"And, you call that winning," Hanna said.

"I am not dead, am I?" He lifted an eye to Hanna. "If you are so bent, then go back."

"When the coffers are refilled, I might," Hanna took another drink and Adamus received another from the barmaid. "Fighting without payment is a fool's task. Most true when fighting for the Anshedar, who fight without any sense."

"You rely too much on the fellow soldier," he said. "Your people will never know glory."

"Glory is a concept for the poor," She scoffed, sipping at her drink. "Consider the fact your people will never know victory."

Adamus glared at her under bushy eyebrows, and downed his mug in a single swoop. He signaled for the wench once more.

"Dorofej," Branimir tapped his fingers on the table, changing topic, "we need to go, and leave these two to their drinking. Drak and Bohumir have been gone too long."

"Right, you are, and well said," Dorofej agreed, guzzling the rest of his drink, before adding, "But the way is blocked, if noticed, you have not?"

"What?" Branimir hissed, turning in his chair, his leg smacking the edge of the table. "

At the opening of *The Stone Crown*, Branimir saw the red mage, Eisliev, and then a second later, the Anshedar from the Crimson Sun, Teodor. If the two men were inside the tavern, it could only mean the giant guarded the road outside.

"That must be what has kept them," Branimir said out loud, "but whether Drak and Bohumir have been found remains to be seen. Come, Dorofej," Bran whispered, almost forgetting about Hanna and Adamus, "what do we do?"

"Hidden here for a short time, we are," Dorofej settled lower in his chair. The Kras caught sight of Eisliev's light eyes skimming by them. "But leave at any time, you are able, Branimir."

"I am not going to leave you," Branimir said. "I am not a coward."

Adamus, who had found his mug refilled, stayed attuned to their conversation. He leaned inward. "Hanna and I can create a bit of a distraction, if tis required for you to duck out."

Dorofej raised his eyebrows, contemplating the offer, "I say, how many silver to divert the two near the tavern door?"

"What is your *price*, Hanna?" Adamus said, pressing his lips together as though his teeth would burst through.

"Ten silver," she said, finishing up her drink, and pulling free her bow. The offer was so quickly given Branimir almost wondered if she had prepared a number before sitting down.

"You shared your table freely. Besides, I like to receive my payments in loyalty and friendship," Adamus downed his drink once more, most of it dripping down his beard.

"Whether too generous or too drunk, you are, I cannot say," Dorofej slapped the table, sliding ten silver to Hanna, "but in our debt, you will be; loyalty and friendship abound."

Adamus said, "Heh, generous or drunk? I imagine I am a bit of both."

"You speak only to the Anshedar," Hanna clinked the coins together. "Our deal is satisfactory, unless I die, and then I'll expect double." The Lilitu, who had called herself a *Rudhira*, did not so much as crack a smile.

Branimir had to admit he was shocked by the emotionless attitude of the woman, who seemed motivated solely by the pursuit of coin. More surprising was how solemn she was about wanting the silver.

The Ariadnean narrowed his beady, gray eyes. He stood from the table, wobbling slightly from the alcohol. Bran watched him while burying his own drink. It was thick and burned his throat.

"Hanna," Adamus said. "Keep an eye on my back, will ya?"

"I have been paid, haven't I?"

Adamus murmured in agreement.

Branimir stooped down as Adamus stumbled by him toward Teodor. Hanna shifted around the table to where Adamus had been sitting.

Teodor talked to Keldron, unaware of Adamus approaching fast. Teodor's hand rested on the sword hilt. The horse head inscribed on his breastplate stayed partially hidden among the greens and grays.

Adamus stormed forward, pushing Teodor to the side and getting in Eisliev's face. He garbled, breathing fumes, "If you grew a beard half as long as mine, you would still look like a wench. Never disfigured a woman before, but suppose I gotta rip a belly open."

"Stand back," Keldron said, stepping between Adamus and Eisliev, arms crossed over his chest. "Do not have me call the guards."

Adamus did not hesitate. He planted his right fist across Keldron's jaw. The man fell flat to the floor, unconscious.

Gasps of surprise and nervous laughter echoed.

Eisliev glared, his light eyes smoldering beneath his red bangs. "Find somewhere else to meddle."

Adamus struggled to stand. Branimir was sure the poor man was inebriated, namely because it took him three wild swings to reach the axe at his side and shield on his back.

Branimir tugged at Dorofej's dark robes "Better make haste while we are able." Dorofej thanked Hanna, who waved him off and nocked an arrow.

The two of them twisted and turned, ducking behind the people who circled to watch the commotion.

Somewhere, outside of Branimir's sight, Adamus let out a roar. The sound of clashing weapons echoed, giving the suggestion Teodor had pulled his sword.

An arrow zinged.

Branimir and Dorofej sprung into the streets of Cavell.

Chapter VII

Within *The Stone Crown*, Branimir could hear the clamouring of screeching voices, tables crashing, and chairs being thrown. He stumbled away from the tavern with Dorofej muttering offhandedly at his heels.

The outside cold tore into his bones, worse than it had before, whirling down the main street of Cavell from the north to south. Faint lights of lanterns, hanging on either side of the snow-covered road, were blurred to Branimir with his Kras vision. He teetered forward to take a gander between the closed shops. The plum had taken its toll. The world spun around him.

Branimir sucked the icy air into his lungs. When he exhaled, his breath erupted as a misty vapour. "We should not have drunk so much."

"Fortunate, we are," Dorofej said, joining Branimir in looking either way. "The Ispolini is nowhere to be found, yes?"

"The what?" Branimir finally mumbled when realizing Dorofej's words had no connection with his own.

Dorofej hiccupped, "The giant, Branimir. Also known as an Ispolini, from the far west, beyond the desert and the Shade, he is."

"Ah," Branimir sighed, rubbing his temples and recalling the oversized mercenary with the Crimson Sun. The giant had been called Tyr Og. The name sounded like a guttural grunt. "Is there anything you do not know, Dorofej?"

"Certain, there is," Dorofej laughed. "And, tell you, I will, when I recall what it is."

"Dorofej. Branimir." Drak shouted, making his way to them from down the road. The Kras clutched his cowl, running with a weird waddle, while slipping on the frozen ground.

Bohumir, who faltered several paces behind, tried to keep pace with the faster Kras. The boy gripped his own pack in his hand.

Dorofej raised his fist at them, shaking it with force. "Waiting for hours, we have been. I say, where have you been?"

"Alack! If I were any bigger, I would have dragged the boy back sooner. He took his sweet time gathering his things." Drak looked pleadingly at Branimir. "Are they still serving food?"

In response, the door of the tavern banged open, and several patrons flooded into the streets. Drak looked pass Branimir, horrified, as the men and women began screaming for the guard. Their cries were coupled with a piece of wood, which may have been a stool leg, busting through a window and into the streets. Several tankards—some still holding ale—followed. Then, without warning, a man was tossed through the open space. He howled in shock and slammed into the frozen ground with a hollowed grunt. Inhibited by alcohol, he shakily rose to his feet and stumbled away from the place as quick as he was able.

Branimir froze, ogling with the others, dumbstruck, while the man, too, screamed for the sentry.

"What did you two do?" Drak asked in exasperation.

"We didn't do anything, but I don't think you'll be eating here," Branimir said, "Teodor and Eisliev are in there."

"Here already," Drak blew out his cheeks and whined. "Stone the crows!"

"I say, fetch the horses," Dorofej said, "and one for Bohumir too. Make haste, you must."

Branimir spun around for the stables when the door to *The Stone Crown* burst open again. Any hint of intoxication Branimir may have felt moments ago fled from him like shadow from flame.

More townsfolk ran from the tavern, springing into the streets. Nevertheless, to his dismay, calmly stepping through the hoard of men and women, emerged Teodor, sword in hand, his iron breastplate gleaming. Teodor yanked an arrow from his left arm and tossed it on the ground. Ignoring the dark blood coloring his shirt, he cast an eye over the scattering people. His nostrils flared and eyes narrowed, taking only seconds to pinpoint Dorofej and Branimir on the road.

Following directly behind him, strode Eisliev drenched in his red cloak, the hood pulled over his long fiery hair. His face was completely hidden beneath, but the wind carried the growl that escaped his lips. "I have waited too long for my revenge. I will not be stopped now."

The racket from within the tavern grew louder. The brawl inside continued, accompanied with whooping and hollering. From the sound of it, the place was being torn apart.

"Allow them to have *kaelandur*, we must not," Dorofej instructed at a whisper, "Nor slay Bohumir!"

"What? Kill me?" The boy's gaped. "Czern's breath!" He grabbed at Dorofej. "Why would you say that? Who are they?"

"Bohumir Mager, is it?" Teodor guessed. "You will be coming with us, lad. And Dorofej," he sneered, "do you think yourself clever? You can consider your contract, and all future contracts with the Crimson Sun expired."

Bohumir clenched his jaw, using the black mage to shield him from the assailants. Dorofej pushed Bohumir behind him protectively with his hand.

"Saddened by the revelation, I truly am," Dorofej said, "but part our separate ways, we must." He bowed his head, placing his other hand on Bohumir's chest to guide him backwards with him. "The boy, you cannot have. Consider the earnings from the *Kadari* forfeit, yes? Understand the impact of his deliverance, you do not."

"No," Eisliev shouted over the noise in the streets, "you do not understand. Give me the boy! I will have my revenge on Dagmar Kaligula."

Branimir twisted to Dorofej, his mind muddled. "Who is that?"

Dorofej took a step back from Eisliev. Branimir thought he saw fear in the black mage's eyes. His mumbled words were quiet. "A name long forgotten, that is."

"Who is it?" Branimir earnestly repeated. Dorofej could not have responded if he had wanted. The main road became even more chaotic.

"Tyr," Teodor hollered, disregarding Dorofej's speech, while suspiciously looking at Eisliev from the corner of his eye, "bring me the lad."

Bohumir cried out, likely shaking more from fear than the cold, "What is going on?"

Tyr lumbered into the street from the shadows adjacent to the tavern. Those making their escape cried out when seeing the towering frame of the giant. Likely, none in the Dyndaer had seen an Ispolini before. Tyr was a stone tower, etched with muscle from foot to forehead. His flesh seemed unaffected by the cold from his bare chest to his bare feet. His only attire were his dark trousers and the angled, leather belting which held the battle axe on his back.

His towering frame caused many of the patrons to screech and run in the opposite direction. Tyr removed his weapon from the latching on his back, holding it at the ready in his massive six-fingered hands.

The boy's face fell at the sight of the giant. "Nine Lands."

Branimir lunged in front of Tyr as the Ispolini started across the road to grab the boy. "Stop. You don't know what you are doing."

Tyr paused for a moment, considering the words. He looked back to Teodor.

However, Eisliev gave the order. "The boy, Tyr."

With a growl, Tyr moved forward again, lifting his battle axe threateningly toward Bran. "Step aside, or I will cut through you, half pint."

Branimir braced himself for the giant's death stroke.

A gust of wind blew past Branimir spiralling his cloak around him. The blast struck Tyr in the chest, sending him reeling backwards. Branimir nearly fell to his knees as the ground shook under the weight of the massive Ispolini.

"Tyr," Teodor shouted as the brawn of his party fell. He spun on Dorofej, who had delivered the simple display of *Koldovstvo*.

"I say, I do not wish to fight, but a choice, you leave me not," Dorofej pleaded. "Let us be, Teodor. Take these men from here."

Teodor scowled, speaking to Eisliev, "Take the quarry."

"Branimir, fall back," Dorofej shouted, eyeing the red mage.

Branimir had not the chance to move before a woozy feeling washed over him. He felt as though something had struck him, an unseen energy, but he could not place it. The thought slipped away.

His stomach churned, pain surfacing in the pit of his belly, and creeping up his chest and throat. Another thought rebounded against his skull, forced into his thinking, *too much plum*. He could not believe the lie; it came to him like a voice across a great distance. Inside his head, he heard his own scream in defiance. No sound came from his lips.

The street dimmed temporarily. His hands moved like spiders through the air to grip his head with aim to clear the clouded feeling swelling into his ears and mind. From somewhere, he could hear battle echoing, but he was blind to the world around him.

"Branimir!" a voice cried, aloof and far away. He thought he knew the voice, but he could not place it.

Memories of the Netherworld danced in his mind. Flying, demonic Skyrz flew from nothingness toward him with their sharpened claws and fanged teeth. They had not only been at Illuard but also across the frozen wasteland, where Marheena ruled over the dead. The little beasts were the size of bats with horned skulls and spindly forelimbs. He could not let them suck his blood.

From somewhere, a dagger had found its way into his hand. He did not think he had his weapons any longer, but here they were. He could not deny it. He could not think about it fully. The Skyrz were coming. He swung madly.

For a moment, the scene disappeared and he was back in the streets of Cavell. A stone the size of Branimir's head flew over him. White dust powdered the air.

Drak grabbed Branimir's arm, pulling him back from wherever he had been. "Stone the crows! Stop this, Branimir! What are you doing?"

"*Mojmir*," Bran believed before remembering Drak's face. He held his head, stumbling to stay on his feet. He felt faint. Something hard was held against his head, clasped in his hand. He lowered his arm and jerked back when seeing a dagger between his fingers, dripping with blood. It did not look familiar. This was not a dagger he had ever owned.

He lifted his eyes to Drak. The Kras clutched his arm where his flesh had been cut. Red seeped through his fingers.

"I cut you…" Branimir gaped. "How did I get this weapon?"

"From him," Drak winced, pointing behind Branimir. "You stole it from his boot after he saved you from the giant's axe. You stabbed him in the leg, and then I pulled you back. That is when you cut me."

"No…" Branimir twisted to see Adamus battling against Tyr. The Ariadnean had his smaller axe lodged against the battle axe of the Ispolini. Even at a distance, the stench of ale lurked off the man's long, black beard like manure from a horse's ass.

Adamus bellowed from his gut, throwing Tyr back, an inner rage unleashed. Branimir gawked at the blood oozing from the man's thigh. Tyr slid back on his bare feet, surprised at the strength of the human. The giant released his own primitive roar. The battle axe crashed down toward Adamus again and again, deflected and met with equal ferocity.

Scooting back, Branimir looked to Dorofej for an explanation. The black mage could give none. Dorofej stumbled, intoxicated, doing what he might to avoid Eisliev's magic. Stone and fire was flung through the air at his friend.

Bohumir, the poor boy, crouched fearfully behind Dorofej.

Branimir gripped the curved dagger in his hand, still feeling sick. Ahead of him, Eisliev snarled. The red mage peered over his shoulder at Teodor, who had fallen. Branimir counted two arrows in his chest and one in his skull.

"The haze in your eyes went away when he fell," Drak said, answering the unspoken question. "I think it distracted the Stuhia."

Hanna, the Lilitu, a ghost in the shadows, had turned to fire arrows at Eisliev, the Stuhia, who Drak referred. She crouched near the tavern wall, releasing arrow after arrow like a true warrior. Yet the Stuhia from the Crimson Sun swatted away her arrows with *Koldovstvo*, while continuing to attack the drunken Dorofej.

"Come on, Tyr," Eisliev shouted. "Finish this."

The giant slammed a fist into Adamus, reeling the Ariadnean backwards. And still, Adamus advanced at the Ispolini.

"Get the boy to safety," Branimir said, feeling the weight of the dagger in his hand, as though it were the first time. He made eye contact with Eisliev, and glowered.

"But are you alright?" Drak asked.

Branimir tried to say he was fine, but he could not form the words. Eisliev's light eyes caught his own and burned into him, again, striking him with some unseen magic. Bran sputtered, vomit burning with ire in his throat. Sourness filled his nostrils.

His feet carried him across the dark, frozen battlefield, but soon, he no longer recognized Cavell. The demons of the Netherworld chased him. Four-legged, wolf-like creatures, known as Dreka, rammed their goat horns at Branimir. The grey, wrinkled skin clung to their gaunt frames. Thin lips stretched back displaying rows of teeth on the tops and bottoms of their bloodied gums.

Branimir tumbled, swinging his weapon and feeling it tear through flesh as easily as a hot blade through frost. For a moment, he may have heard Dorofej's riddlesome voice— no, his cry—but Branimir had not the time to listen. He had to scramble, and sneak, and stab.

And stab. And stab. And stab.

The urgency of the battle and the demons thumped inside of his head.

"Stop!" A familiar voice, again, cried in desperation.

Crimson splattered his vision as his dagger cut through skin once more. Blood dripped from his blade.

Pain stung his leg, but it was quickly forgotten as demon after demon lunged for him. The Dreka were ever persistent in their attack. He spun, and twisted, and disappeared to avoid every demonic beast soaring through the air, vicious teeth aimed for his throat. They would not reach him. For a moment, he thought he saw a flash of Hanna's wide eyes, but they looked unfamiliar. Treacherous. Evil. Besides, his dagger was already cocked behind his ear and he felt incapable of restraining himself.

With a growl, Branimir let the dagger fly, the blade slamming into his target. Blood spurted from the gash in the chest…of the Lilitu.

Cavell rushed back to him as Hanna fell to her knees, clutching the hilt of the weapon protruding from her torso. Branimir collapsed, his hand hurriedly finding two sharp arrows lodged in his leg.

Drak shrieked.

Branimir turned in time to see Tyr smack the Kras from his path. Adamus, only feet away, bled from his side and his leg, twisting in pain against the ground, near dead. The fighter fought to stand.

"Hanna." Branimir could hear Adamus's strained whisper.

Dorofej also writhed on the ground. Blood oozed from his black robes where a dagger—Branimir's weapon—had pierced him multiple times.

"Glad your mind magic does not affect me, Eisliev," Tyr grunted, picking up the whimpering Bohumir in his oversized hand.

"The guard are coming," Eisliev said. "Grab Teodor's body and let's go."

"What about them?" Tyr asked.

"Let them bleed out," Eisliev said, touching his face tenderly. His skin had aged considerably through his use of *Koldovstvo.* "We have what we came for. This boy is the key to Melkorka. Patrician Sej can have him as long as I can have Dagmar Kaligula."

Falmagon!

Chapter VIII

The Great Chamber had been eerily quiet for several minutes while they waited for Count Vlaskhorn Frantisek to come into the room. The mood within the keep had changed little since the previous night. If anything, the gloom feeling had intensified following the battle outside of *The Stone Crown.*

Branimir stood erect with his knees locked, unwilling to look at any of his companions. He ignored the purple, red, and black tapestries hanging around the room, shadowed by the failing light of the firepits. He could not focus on the throne, where the purplish cloak remained from the previous night. Instead, he felt trapped in his own mind, doubting what he had seen, and doubting what had happened.

He wanted to go back and save Bohumir. He wanted to be able to fight against Eisliev's magic, and battle alongside his allies instead of against them. He wanted too much, all at once. He fought hard against his emotions. He did not want to cry.

An oak door creaked open from the corner. Count Frantisek walked to his throne, as he had done the night before. Sitting forward, the noble man stared at them for several minutes, tapping his pudgy fingers on his round belly.

"They worship Czern, remember? He is going to hang us all," Drak said, slanting over to murmur in Branimir's ear. The Kras may have been talking to Bran since they entered the chamber. He could not be for certain.

Branimir tensed his shoulders, trying to recall what Dorofej had taught him about the gods. Something about the living making gods seem more good or evil than they were. "I don't think so, Drak."

"What if they learn you are not from Ojenir? Why did Dorofej say you were? Why can't they know where you really came from, across the ocean?" Drak, who stood next to him, quivered where he stood, stealing frightful glances at the Count. His fingers fiddled with his brown cloak, pulling at the fabric.

"Calm down," Branimir said between clenched teeth.

Bran lifted his eyes to Dorofej, who watched the Count with intensity. The black mage stood proper with back straight and chin up. Branimir could see the dried blood caked across his robes from the many wounds he had received from the dagger in Branimir's hand.

Dorofej had not wasted much energy in fighting Eisliev, but he had used *Koldovstvo* excessively while healing himself, Adamus, Hanna, and lastly, Branimir. He had been wise in healing only what was fatal for each of them, leaving the minor bumps and bruises.

The Highborn, if he was really a Highborn, had absolved Branimir's actions, saying there was no fault when considering Eisliev's wicked magic. Dorofej said he did not know the source of the Stuhia's mind magic, but was certain Bran had not been at fault. Adamus and Hanna, who now stood with them, had also exonerated him after given an explanation.

Branimir could not forgive himself.

As if reading his mind, Drak said under his breath, "Let it go. It is done."

Branimir exhaled. His gaze shifted momentarily to the dagger returned to Adamus's boot. He never wanted to touch the dagger again.

Ignac, the guard from the gate, shooed away those who had helped escort Branimir and the others into the Great Chamber. He stepped around the center firepit and the Count acknowledged him.

"What is the meaning of this, Ignac?"

Ignac dipped his head, "I received a report of a *scuffle* in the streets. Those here were found at the scene. Presented are Dorofej Creighton of Tamarri, Branimir Barthor and Drak Ghas of Ojenir, Adamus Ebordon of Ariadne, and Hanna Bretka of Danduher."

"A peculiar group of travellers." The Count pulled at his black beard, eyes still swollen from crying over his dead daughter. His eyes rested on Dorofej. "He and the Kras were here last night. When did the others arrive?"

"The guard at the gate reported they also arrived yesterday evening, Count," Ignac answered.

The Count continued, speaking to Dorofej, "You said you were here on business for the Crimson Sun, right? Was this event associated with that business?"

"Yes, it was, Count," Dorofej said, "but Adamus and Hanna were there only by happenstance."

"I see," the Count tilted forward until he was stopped by his round stomach pressing against his knees. "You claim you do not know them?"

"Beyond name, I do not, Count Frantisek," Dorofej said.

"How many dead bodies were there, Ignac?" the Count questioned, resting back in his chair. He seemed to believe what Dorofej shared.

Ignac answered, "None, Count. There were traces of blood outside of *The Stone Crown*, but no bodies were found."

"Hmm. Tell me, were these men responsible for the hanging of my daughter?" Vlaskhorn turned his attention fully on the guard.

"No, Count."

"Did they kill anyone?"

The guard fidgeted. "I am not aware—"

"Have you lost your sense?" He hissed. "My wife and I are in mourning, planning a funeral instead of a betrothal, as we should have been," Vlaskhorn wheezed. "I am beginning to wonder why you have disrupted this chamber, Ignac. You are testing my patience."

"According to witnesses, Lamont Dthais's boy, Bohumir, was abducted as a direct result of the conflict," Ignac explained.

"The boy who found Nitalia?"

Adamus cleared his throat. "That *is* interesting."

Branimir saw Hanna elbow him in the side before the warrior could say anything more.

"A citizen of Cavell has been captured, which requires a report to the King in Gaetana. These five have the details," finished Ignac.

"I am aware of my duties," the Count breathed. "Next time, try starting with the pertinent details."

Ignac found his composure again, responding at the same time, "Yes, Count."

"Of interest, there is nothing, Count," Dorofej interjected, but the Count silenced him.

"I do not want to hear from you, Dorofej. Your riddlesome accent hurts my ears. Let me hear from one of the Kras. Their reputation for honesty supersedes that of the *Kadari*."

"*Kadari*, I am not," Dorofej snapped.

"You work for the Crimson Sun," Vlaskhorn accused, spit flying from his lips, demonstrating anger at having his direction ignored, "who offer service to the *Kadari* more than any other. Dorofej, you are an associate, whether you claim to be or not. Let it be known those who follow Dahz, and their associates, have no voice in Cavell."

Branimir tightened his jaw, remembering Drak's warning about the people in the Dyndaer and their hate for the *Kadari*. The Kras from Ojenir had been accurate in his assumption.

"A weak argument, you have, when your brother, the King of Gaetana, also holds allegiances to the *Kadari* and the Lightbringer, yes?" Dorofej said, his eyes icy.

The Count's face darkened, "I said I will hear from the Kras. Don't open your mouth again, Dorofej."

The black mage grumbled.

Drak scooted further behind Dorofej and Adamus making himself hidden from the pungent eyes of the Count.

Branimir sighed and stepped forward to speak with the Count. He would prefer to speak than allow Drak to talk at any length. "What do you want to know, Count Vlaskhorn?"

"Plainly, I want to know why you have come to Cavell and what happened outside *The Stone Crown*," the Count said.

"We came here to protect Bohumir. Last night, we failed to save him from those who took him," said Branimir. The truth seemed simple enough to share.

"See, the Kras is able to tell me exactly what I can report to the King. Simple. Eloquent. Now, why did the boy need protected," asked the Count, "and, why was he taken?"

Branimir grinded his teeth, but did his best to keep his eyes locked onto Vlaskhorn. Dorofej had told him they were working for the Crimson Sun, so Branimir could not imply Teodor, Eisliev, and Tyr were with the same organization. At the same time, Bran could not speak of the *Kadari*, the Ash Tree, and he surely could not say anything about *kaelandur*.

He reached for a less noble response. "My apologies, Count. We never did ask. The silver promised in finishing the job satisfied our curiosity."

The Count did not directly scorn Branimir, but stated, "I would not think any greater of the Crimson Sun or the foul

Kadari. They make claims to the Lightbringer, but hold corruption in their hearts as well as any other." Vlaskhorn shifted in his seat, waving his hand out toward the Chamber, but speaking of the Dyndaer and Cavell, "Here, the God of Darkness, the God of Sacrifice, appreciates and understands who we are as living creatures. We are imperfect, flawed; and we are loved and accepted as such."

"Glory to the Grey-Clad," Adamus hear-heared, marking him as the only true follower, coming from Ariadne.

"Yes, glory to the Grey-Clad," Vlaskhorn repeated, nodding with respect to the so-called hero-warrior. "I welcome your openness, Branimir, is it?" He waved at Ignac. "They have committed no crime in Cavell; no more than any drunkard who brawls nightly at *The Stone Crown*."

"Keldron was beat unconscious by Adamus," Ignac tried. "There must be more to the story."

"The man was hardly beat," Hanna said, plain-faced. "It was a single punch." She said her words so matter-of-factly Branimir almost laughed, nearly forgetting his misery.

"You probably did him a favor," Vlaskhorn smiled for the first time since Branimir had met the noble lord. "Still, I think it is best none of you tarry here any longer. Ignac, you have their horses readied and waiting at the edge of town. I want all of you gone within the hour."

"Thank you. We will, Count," said Branimir. The others echoed his sentiment and assurances of following his word.

Ignac lifted his hand. "One more thing." He pulled coiled piece of paper from his pocket. "A letter arrived for Dorofej a fortnight ago. I admit, I do not know the message was fully transcribed by the courier. It is about as puzzling as your tongue."

Dorofej lifted his eyebrows with interest.

"Since when do you withhold mail, Ignac," the Count said. "Give it to him."

"The letter is signed by Sulanna Maelthirren, a noble name from Eldhaft," Ignac said, "and it reads: '*We have the artifact. We wait in Ariadne.*'"

"Maelthirren?" the Count raised an eyebrow. "You have strange friends, Dorofej. Be warned, there are no roads to Ariadne from Cavell. The safest pathway is the river, and it is frozen solid this time of year."

"What does it mean?" Branimir looked to Dorofej, whistling between his teeth.

Dorofej turned his head toward the north, as though contemplating giving chase to Bohumir. His head fell to the floor, speaking softly, "Safe or not, a way to Ariadne, we must find."

Month of Slaughter

Fourth of Frost

1351 CE

Chapter IX

The ice from the forked river creaked and shifted under the dimming rays of sunlight. Branimir listened to the sound absently, focusing on the golden orb shimmering through the thinning canopy of branches. He could not remember the last time the sky had been clear of clouds. In the two weeks since leaving Cavell, he had seen little more than a dark grey and milky white haze through the limbs above.

Though, now, as long as they kept to the river's edge, the sky stayed in open view. He took delight in the beams warming against his face, smiling for what felt like the first time in forever.

Dorofej's horse plodded alongside his pony with the rest of the group meandering in the front. Branimir shifted his gaze from the sun to the black mage, pondering their situation. He stared for some time before finally saying in a hushed tone, "You know, I suddenly realize you never asked me where I have been the past few years."

Dorofej kept his eyes forward, fixated on the backs of Adamus, Hanna, and Drak. Branimir saw the wrinkles around his eyes deepen before he responded. "Searching for the Ash Tree, as we said we would at Strahil, I assumed you were."

"True. I did for a while," Branimir admitted. "Though, being a Kras is not any easier in this world than it was in the last. I drifted from place to place, having to rely on the kindness of others to survive."

"Stones and gems from the Netherworld, you had collected, and sell them, you could have," Dorofej said with a sigh. "Elected to hold onto them and hide them, you did."

"How did you know that?" Branimir asked. "Or, are there more secrets to be kept from me."

Dorofej half-heartedly grinned, giving Branimir the sense it was not genuine. "Held onto *Ojenek*, you always have. Selling your stones, even for food, would be against your nature, yes? I say, you found a way to survive, yes?"

"I did find work in Gavlok for a time," Bran replied. He rubbed his fingers together nervously, wondering if he had just given away the location of his buried treasure.

Dorofej hummed, "I say, what did you do there?" His tone gave the indication Branimir had told this to him before, and was simply entertaining the story.

Branimir shivered. Of course, Dorofej was not interested in his shiny stones. No, something else likely perturbed the man. The thought unexpectedly crossed Branimir's mind that Dorofej might be angry about what had happened in Cavell, despite him saying Branimir was forgiven.

Suddenly, he remembered something of importance from the night in Cavell. He remembered what the red mage, Eisliev, had said. "Who is Dagmar Kaligula?"

Dorofej turned his head away, eyebrows angling with annoyance. "I say, that is not a topic I wish to discuss with you, Branimir," he objected, flaring his nostrils. Branimir thought it may have been the most direct Dorofej had ever been with him. The tone gave him chills. The black mage relaxed his voice, likely realizing his harshness. "Tell me, at Gavlok, what did you do?"

"Very well," Branimir anxiously said, and then continued at length, "I worked as a serving hand at a tavern called *The Oaken Bard*. At times, I would perform for the folk by throwing knives. After half a year or so, the owner told me people talked about my dagger tossing all the way in Eldhaft. He said someone would likely come and talk to me. I got scared and left before anyone had the chance."

"A good thing, you did," Dorofej said idly. "I say, it may have been someone from the league of thieves. And, being a thief rarely ends well, yes?"

Branimir shook his head in agreement. He would be ashamed to admit he had stolen, more than a handful of times, when his stomach would not quit growling.

Afraid to continue the conversation, or admit to anything he may have done, Bran turned from Dorofej.

Ahead of him, Adamus and Hanna steered them toward Ariadne with Drak bouncing on his pony at the center. Branimir had been surprised the Ariadnean and Lilitu had joined them, particularly after he had nearly killed them both while under Eisliev's control. Luckily, Adamus continued to talk about friendship and loyalty, and Hanna had been more fascinated by his fighting style than vindictive. In addition, Branimir had sworn not to touch any of their weapons, especially Adamus's dagger. The last bit had been Bran's decision.

For a good many hours, the lot of them carried on along the river. They swapped riding and walking to allow the horses to rest when needed. The river winded and bent, heading south, with ice chunks mashing into one another or with the surface frozen altogether. Hoarfrost covered the ground. Nothing melted.

In time, Drak complained of hunger and they stopped to eat meat and unleavened bread. The supper shushed his mouth and his stomach; and then, they rode onward again.

The day passed and dusk came. The sun eventually dipped below the trees, taking its warmth with it. The cold wind that followed from the north not only chilled Branimir through his cloak, but also his skin. The strong breeze pitched along the surface of the adjacent frozen river, adding to its bite. He did his best to ignore the frigidness.

Inhaling the cold air through his nostrils, Branimir expanded his lungs. Mile after mile, frustration poked at his gut. He admitted the feeling had been with him since riding out from Cavell. He could no longer contain his worry, and turned to speak to Dorofej again. "Are we going to leave Bohumir be? I did tell you what Eisliev said. He is bringing the boy to Falmagon?"

Dorofej, who had been leaning over his horse, stroking the mane and whispering in contemplation, pulled himself upright and looked down to Branimir. "Yes, you told me what Eisliev said, and forsake the boy, we will not. I say, what would make you think we would abandon what we had set out to do?"

Branimir heaved a sigh of relief before continuing. He had been beating himself up for days and had chosen to say nothing. "Because, we ride to Ariadne at the direction of your letter when Bohumir has been taken the other way?"

"To Melkorka, yes, Bohumir is being taken," Dorofej agreed. "Though you must think why Falmagon wants the boy, yes?"

Branimir turned his head back toward the way they had come. He had not thought of asking what Falmagon—or the *Kadari*—would want with the bloodline of Nedezhda Mager.

The black mage hummed in his throat, rubbing the neck of his mount. "A fair question, is it not?"

"It is," Branimir said, moving his eyes back to the Highborn, who he certainly did not believe could be called a Highborn any longer. No, the man had been called something else at some time in history. Branimir wondered if Dorofej was a Stuhia like the man named Eisliev. "Why does Falmagon want the boy?"

A moment of silence passed before Dorofej finally rubbed his prickling red beard. "Uncertain, I am. But I can only guess they try sacrificing the boy to gain more power, yes? I say, old rituals requiring magical weapons, there are."

"That is terrible!"

Dorofej smiled. "Except, *kaelandur*, they would require to see it done, which we hold. So, time, we have, yes?"

Branimir felt a knot in his throat. "I hope you are right."

"I say, the *Kadari* are likely scheming more than a simple sacrifice, yes?" Dorofej said. "So simple, nothing ever is."

Drak clearly eavesdropping, leaned back in his saddle to be heard. "I could use my rune staves and attempt to find more answers."

Dorofej's eyes flashed, glancing at Drak over his shoulder. "Helpful, it might be, when we make camp."

Drak beamed, bouncing excitedly in his saddle.

Dorofej leaned toward Branimir, saying in a quieter tone, "To Melkorka, we will travel after Ariadne. Until then, be comforted, yes?"

"I will try. But what are we after in Ariadne? The letter from Sulanna mentioned an artifact. You said she and Alden were with you but also the Crimson Sun. What did she find for you?" Branimir questioned.

Dorofej looked to Drak ahead of them, and then placed a finger to his lips. "The time for questions, it is not." He adjusted his black hood, and again, faced the road.

Branimir writhed with the response. He and Dorofej had wandered the Netherworld for a thousand years, and still the black mage kept his secrets. He hoped the reaction was due to Dorofej realizing Drak could hear them.

The Kras were known for their excellent hearing.

Night had set when they stopped to build a fire. Among the five, setting camp did not take long.

After they had eaten, and fed the mounts, Drak assembled them all around the fire. He waved his hands with encouragement. "Gather around, gather around," He pulled the rune staves from his pack and out of their leather holding. "Dorofej, let us get started and find what answers we can about the *Kadari*. Now, to use *div-i-nation*, I need to know what question I am asking."

Dorofej did not have an opportunity to respond.

Hanna stopped him. "Hold on, Drak. Where did you learn to read rune staves?" Hanna scooted away from the Kras, her oversized eyes wider than ever. The *Rudhira* adjusted the crimson sash over her shoulder.

Adamus raised his eyes from his burly eyebrows, and grunted. "Let him be, Hanna."

"The only people I know who use runes to tell the future is the Uvil. Their fortune-telling is wicked," she said.

"The desert people?" Branimir clarified, placing the name of the Uvil.

"Yes," Hanna said. "The future should stay where it belongs. Trying to predict what will happen is unwise."

"Ha!" Drak laughed. "My father taught me, and I have been telling futures for years. There is nothing evil about this."

Hanna winced. "The Dyndaer is enigmatic enough without playing with dark magic."

Branimir peered through the flames. "I don't understand. What are you scared of?"

"I am not scared; I am vigilant. Looking into the future suggests we should have no concern of our actions," she explained. "To think we know what will happen may cause us to worry unneedingly or to have false hope. Or, worse yet, you may indirectly create this prophesized future because you think you should."

"You are overthinking, Hanna," Adamus defended Drak, again. "Czern oversees the Dyndaer. He will not frown on fortune-telling or lead any astray. He is likely the only god who understands the nature of men."

The Lilitu shook her head. "Your God of Darkness is not as longstanding as the Dyndaer. No matter what Czern values, this wood holds greater evils, more powerful than him."

"Like what?" Drak asked, shaking under his skin.

"We cannot know everything," she responded. "There is a time and an order to all things. There are rules, and one of those is not to consider the future. The Dyndaer is an aged place, and we cannot say what all has happened here over the past millenniums."

Branimir swallowed. He knew some of what had happened in this forest. Though, he asked the question anyway. "What do you think has happened here?"

"Who can say," Hanna said. Her vagueness was paired hastily with her next statement. "But my people know the Uvil once meandered through the Dyndaer, even before the Northmen, long, long ago."

"I don't know anything about desert people in the Dyndaer," Drak said. His trembling had not subsided. "Why did they leave?"

Hanna leaned closer to the flames. "The desert people go from place to place based on their divinations. I would guess something drew them away from this place, and if that is true, I would say it is worth heeding."

Adamus grunted. A stick had found its way into his hand and he poked it into the fire. "Even I am surprised by the weakness of your argument, Hanna. If fortune-telling led the Uvil from the Dyndaer, there seems to be all the more reason to use their magic and see what they may have seen."

"Unless their magic elicited unwanted attention from the evils already here," Hanna argued. "Such curiosity may lead you to your grave."

Adamus snorted. "I am going to die anyway. I might as well do it on my own terms."

Branimir squirmed with uneasiness. He looked to Dorofej, who added nothing to the conversation.

"You are just trying to scare me," reasoned Drak. His sticks clinked together in his hands, while he stared wide-eyed at Hanna.

Hanna's oval eyes remained emotionless, looking at the Kras across the fire. She waited.

Drak licked his cracked lips, rolling the rune staves in his hands. The twigs clacked and clicked between his fingers. Then, after making a final decision, he shoved them back into the pouch. "Another time, eh?"

Branimir did not miss the glare which arose from Adamus. The Ariadnean only took a moment before tearing into Hanna. "For years we have stood by one another, Hanna, and still, you shame yourself by shaming other cultures and their practice. Do you have no honor? What would your god think of this?"

"My god is a goddess, Adamus," Hanna said with absolution, "and the Mother would bless me for sharing wisdom with the world. Informing lesser beings of the danger of their actions is not shaming. You forget—the Lilitu were not created like the Anshedar or the Kras. We were born from the union of gods, not their imagination."

"No honor," Adamus repeated.

"Your definition of honor is echoed in the vain applause of men," Hanna said, slowly clapping her hands together three times, mockingly. The dryness of her tone made the fire feel wet. She dropped her hands back to her lap. "I have no need for mortal praises. Honor comes to me from the Mother."

"Who is the Mother?" Branimir asked, steering Adamus's wrath from unfolding. He admitted he was intrigued by the Lilitu and their peculiar culture. He had never heard of a place in the world who shared this strange belief. He wondered if all races in Haemus Mons worshipped this Mother.

Drak, who had stuffed his sticks away, answered, "The Mother is also called Lillith. The Lilitu lore says Lillith lay with the great spirit, Anu, and bore the Lilitu."

"It is not lore, Drak," Hanna said. "It is the truth of our people. We are the children of Lillith and Anu."

Branimir's mind swarmed with questions about Lillith and Anu. How were they created? Where did they come from? How did they align with the pantheon of gods in Maharia? To his memory, he had never heard of either in the history of the old world or the new.

Before Branimir could ask anything, Dorofej piped up, changing the topic, "I say, how much longer until we reach Ariadne?"

"'Tis a bit more than a week on horseback. Just have to stay along the river," Adamus said with aggravation, keeping his eyes from Hanna. "The road has been quiet, surprisingly, but tis not natural. I had expected a few more snags."

Hanna lay her small bow on the ground. "There will not be any snags, Adamus. Don't start your naysaying already."

The mood around the fire turned for the worse as Hanna's voice trailed off. Several minutes passed before the Lilitu slanted her head toward Adamus, and said, "No reason in waiting until tomorrow to say something."

Adamus snorted with discomfort. He glared at her from beneath his bushy brow.

"What needs to be said?" Branimir asked. Dorofej and Drak, equally bewildered, stooped forward.

"'Tis the time of *Koricern*," Adamus pronounced, "the celebration of the longest night of the year, a tribute to Czern. Tis a blessing to pay homage to our ancestors during *Koricern* and my own are buried at the ruins of *Garain'l*."

"Why would you bury your dead at a ruins?" Branimir wrinkled his nose.

"'Tis sacred ground, Branimir," Adamus said. "This is a tradition of my family for generations."

Branimir, realizing he may have struck a chord, retracted his statement. "Your family?"

Drak added, "I have never heard of any Anshedar, or even any Ariadnean, doing this."

"I said, it is a custom for *my* family," Adamus boomed, a threatening tone on the edge of his voice. "*Garain'l* is only a few days ride from here." Adamus reached to touch his axe and then the shield on his back. "I am not asking any of you to come."

Dorofej dipped his chin. "Trekking into the Dyndaer wilds would cost us more than time, I am afraid. Wish you the best, we will. I say, to Ariadne, we must hurry, yes?"

"It is settled then," Adamus said. "Hanna and I will part paths with you in the morning."

"As long as you pay me what is owed, Adamus. Do not forget our agreement." Hanna narrowed her large eyes.

"I would not dream of forgetting," Adamus forced a smile under his black beard. "You will be paid when we reach my sister's in Ariadne."

Hanna turned her head to the rest, satisfied by the answer. "Ariadne is built directly on this river. Keep following it south and you will have no trouble finding it."

Branimir hoped she was right.

Chapter X

Branimir woke to the sound of rummaging. He tried to fully awaken, humming softly in his chest. He yawned wide, and then sputtered uncomfortably. He heard Drak stir next to him with a half-snort and whimper.

Branimir kept his eyes closed and reached out to find his bedroll, and found nothing. Irritated, he cleared his dry throat. An itch coursed beyond his tongue, subdued from breathing the cold air throughout the night. He coughed and hacked while rubbing his eyelids. They felt frozen to his upper cheeks.

The noise he had heard lingered and then carried on with more intensity. With some work, he struggled to open his eyes and realized morning had not yet come. Dark greys still painted the sky.

The bedroll he had been searching for lay several feet away beyond his feet. Branimir grunted with a weak voice, reaching for the blankets. He was answered by a guttural uttering.

The scuffling and shuffling halted.

He wrenched his head around the campsite to discover the source of the sound. Dorofej, Adamus, and Hanna slept, bundled beneath their blankets, and Drak snored all the louder. And then, there was something else.

Branimir froze.

Lingering over the top of Hanna lurked a hideous thing comparable to Branimir in size and breadth. It crouched with glowing, bulbous, yellow eyes locked onto Bran across the short distance. Its corroded skin had mold growing at the bloodied edges, globbed up in rolled spurts from neck to knee. The extra flab of skin did not make the creature look so much fat as it did malformed.

The thing gurgled in its chest, demonic eyes lustrous between its oversized round ears.

Branimir's scream came as a silent bawl, his throat too dry to alert the others.

The beastie, the thing Branimir could not name, leaned toward him, taking a delicate step, soundless against the sleet-covered moss. Its fingers scraped, clacking together, advancing footfall after footfall in a hunched ball. With its back curved, the monster lifted one arm ending in clawed fingers—more claw than finger—and pointed at Branimir with deep interest.

"Eats it."

Branimir choked, forcing the wail to finally escape. He sprung to his feet, reeling backward from the thing.

He was too late. The imp pounced, soaring through the air with its claws extended. The hooked fingers dug into Branimir's back, legs wrapping around his chest. He shrieked in pain; the knife-like nails tore into the muscle beneath his shoulders.

Tears swelled.

Yellow eyes, round and filled with animosity, clouded his vision. The beast's teeth gnashed, using its hold to direct Branimir backward. He stumbled, unable to direct his feet or even fall to his knees. His feet etched backwards where he knew the frozen river awaited. Horror filling the cavity of his chest. He jerked his head away from the gnashing teeth. Putrid breath, like death, opposite side of yellow-caked gums flooded his senses.

"Eats it."

The imp grew heavier against his torso with the claws seeming to tear deeper into his muscle. He staggered, toppling nearer the ice.

"Help!" he managed to cry, again.

A meek war cry resounded, followed by something striking the creature. Branimir hobbled back several steps from the impact, his foot crunching against the edge of the riverbed.

"Get off," Drak squawked, raising a stick to hit the imp another time.

"Stand aside," Adamus grunted, grabbing the Kras and lifting his axe. Drak moved hastily before Adamus sliced his blade into the fat rolls of the monstrous beastie. Blood spewed. More blood than what one creature should have within it.

Branimir's legs weakened.

The imp howled, rocking headfirst, screeching in Branimir's face.

"Eats it!"

Branimir felt warm blood trickling down his back against the bottom seam of his britches. The beast clung onto him all the more, claws cutting through muscle from back to chest, causing him to wobble onto the ice.

Adamus fell his axe, again. This time, he chopped the weapon directly into the imp's skullcap. The creature's brains splattered, eyes dimmed, and it dropped from Branimir.

He wheezed with a snivel, falling sideways onto the solid ice. He tried to roll to solid ground but could not budge, his back muscles torn to shreds.

"Branimir!" cried Dorofej, dashing to him.

Adamus reached Branimir first, throwing his weapon to the ground. He scooped Branimir from the river and rushed him to the hardened ground. "A myling. The imp would have killed him for sure if we had not woken."

Hanna spoke little by little, "His injuries will take weeks to mend. Any herbs for healing will be impossible to find in the hoarfrost. Dorofej can you use your magic as you did at Cavell?"

"He would die long before reaching Ariadne," Adamus agreed, holding his head gently.

Bran's back itched and prickled, throbbed and stung. He felt light headed, sleep pulling at his senses. He tried to focus on something, anything. At the angle he lay, he could see the myling, as Adamus called it, swollen against the ice. It had grown twice the size it had been with the fat rolls now bulging and filled, instead of folding over one another. There were several arrows sticking out of the imp from where Hanna must have struck it while it had attacked him.

Blood oozed from the punctured wounds.

"The thing sucked his blood through its claws?" Drak asked.

"Fed on his blood, it did," confirmed Dorofej. His voice sounded a lifetime away. "And, unquestionably heal him, I will. Now, step back, and give me room to work, you must."

"A nasty creature," said Adamus.

"Indeed," Hanna stated, "but where is the Branimir we saw at Cavell, who nearly butchered us all? He came at us like a warrior then, but here, he showed no more prowess than a sheep."

"Leave him be," Adamus boomed. "This could have happened to any one of us."

"You should have left him your knife," she concluded.

Hanna's words stung Branimir's ears as Dorofej loomed over him. A familiar red and yellow glow flooded Dorofej's hands as he reached for Branimir's body.

Branimir convulsed before Dorofej's hands touched him, feeling his insides stitching themselves back together, skin weaving together. Like bristles against his back, he itched and shivered, feeling *Koldovstvo* creep through his body. He whimpered and jerked again, sensing an itching from the back of his spine to his skull. Dorofej was mending him; it was the same as when Branimir had fallen to the Netherworld ages ago.

Once more, the black mage had kept him from certain death.

After an hour, Branimir had fully recovered and Dorofej's healing talent with *Koldovstvo* had been acknowledged, again, by the others of the party. By first light, the campsite was packed and they were prepared to ride off.

"It has been quite an eventful morning." Adamus circled his horse around to face Dorofej, Branimir, and Drak. "I suppose this is where we say our goodbyes."

"Ah," Dorofej hummed, "actually, with the tumult this morning, forget to request to join you, I have."

Drak almost fell from his saddle. "You want to go to *Garain'l*? What about Ariadne?

"Ariadne, we will go," Dorofej assured, "but something in *Garain'l*, there is to be seen. By happenstance, crossed paths with Adamus, I do not think we have, yes?"

"Are we speaking again of fortune and fate?" Hanna gleaned from the top of her mare.

"Call it whatever you wish, Hanna," Dorofej said, adjusting his hood. "I say, accompany you, we would like, if you would have us. The road is difficult, yes?"

Branimir cowered. He had partly looking forward to parting from the two, particularly Hanna.

Adamus pulled his beard, staring into the wilds of the Dyndaer. "I would not turn you away. There are worse things than mylings at *Garain'l*."

"Yes," Dorofej gritted his teeth. "Aware of the dangers, I am, Adamus."

The first several miles were uneventful. Branimir rocked in the saddle on his pony's back. He stayed in the hindmost position behind the other four with Hanna and Adamus leading the way to the ruins of *Garain'l*.

The company journeyed southeast, away from the river, and back into the deep of the Dyndaer. The path had become pitch-black within an hour with Branimir and Drak scanning the trees for movement. Hanna, no more hindered by the dark than the Kras, rode at the front. Adamus and Dorofej carried torches in the middle.

Branimir's mood had turned increasingly sour since the campsite. He wanted to bury himself in his cloak and hide from embarrassment. Not only had he nearly killed the lot of them at Cavell, but now, he had been helpless against the myling.

"Branimir," Drak said, drawing out his name while, at the same time, slowing the pace of his pony. He spoke to him in a child-like way, chock-full of concerned innocence, "are you going to be okay?"

"I will," he fibbed, turning to stare at anything else. Bran had fought demon after demon in the Netherworld. He should have been able to face the myling with little dispute. If only he had a weapon, he could have proven himself. Instead, Hanna's comment about him hung on his mind. *Sheep.*

Branimir tightened his jaw. Maybe he should have kept Adamus's dagger.

"You are brave," Drak awed, "like the *Branimir* from the old tales." He did not detect Branimir's discomfort. "If I had a myling jab its claws into my backside, I would forever be scarred. I would be afraid to carry on living, and you have climbed back on your pony and strode back into the Dyndaer."

He cringed, feeling the myling's claws ripping through his flesh. "Have I?"

"Oh, yes," Drak said. "You have made it look easy. If it were not for the dried blood on your back…and clothes, I would never guess you had almost walked the Nine Lands."

"Thanks," sighed Branimir.

"If Dorofej had not been there to save you with his magic, you would be dead," Drak scratched the edge of his hooked nose, black eyes widening for emphasis.

The statement stung Branimir. He suspected he would have died many times over if it were not for the black mage. Maybe, he was not a hero after all.

"Drak," said Branimir, turning his tone cold, "can we ride in silence for a while?"

"Marry!" Drak grinded his teeth to his cracked lips. "Did I say something to sadden you, Branimir?"

"I will—"

"Simargl!" Hanna shushed, sliding off her mare and whipping her bow from her shoulder. "Keep your mouths shut."

"What?" Drak asked, raking the Dyndaer with his black orbs. "I thought they were myths."

"There is very little that is myth," Branimir said, elevating his head. He heard the low rumble ahead, which he would have picked up on earlier had Drak had not been talking. He searched the thick trees.

"Whoa," Adamus pulled on his horse's reins. Dorofej did the same, and both men climbed down from their mounts, retreating from the way they had been heading.

"Just our luck," Adamus mumbled, pulling his shield from his back and the axe from his belt. His torch dropped to the ground. "First the myling, and now these curs."

Drak hissed between clenched teeth. "Alack! Why are we getting off the horses? You plan to outrun the beasts on foot." He rocked on his pony as though he were debating whether to join the others on the ground.

Branimir tensed his throat, holding his breath, finally noticing the three giant, black wolves called simargl. He followed suit and climbed down from his pony. The wolves ambled lazily in the direction they had been riding.

He gaped at their size, which were comparable to the frozen Bukavac of the Netherworld. The monstrous beasts had leathered wings etching from their longhaired backs, and stood taller than the horses. The simargl's head was bulkier than Branimir and Drak combined.

Drak squealed, falling off his mount and landing with a thud to the ground.

The three simargl abruptly lifted their heads, cream-colored eyes focusing in their direction.

"Nobody die," Hanna said in her no-nonsense tone.

Branimir could have sworn she looked in his direction.

"Reassuring, you are," Dorofej snorted, throwing down his torch, and casting a light above them with *Koldovstvo*. The action hastened the next moments.

The simargl sauntered between the trees, large paws marring the layered snow. The oversized beasts kept their webbed wings tucked, while pacing wide to encircle their prey.

Branimir shuddered. Again, he found himself at the mercy of the fighters around him to protect him—to save him. He was incapable of fighting against these beasts.

A loud bark signaled the wolves to advance. The first leapt forward through the trees while the other two dashed to either side. Hanna loosened arrow after arrow, striking the wolves in the cheek, neck, and head. The animals whimpered, and slowed, stumbling in their attack, but still, they came.

Adamus moved in front of the rest to face the lead simargl. He held his shield upright to prepare for the impact of the charging animal. As the beast neared, Dorofej touched *Koldovstvo* and loosened fire to the simargl's fur. Flames erupted and the beast howled, stumbling with a snarl. All the same, the beast propelled itself into the much smaller Anshedar. Adamus rocked backwards, shield—shining silver—vibrating from the impact, sending him tumbling back across the ground, head over heels. Any lesser substance would have cracked under the impact. Again, Branimir questioned its crafting.

The thought was brief as Branimir found himself face to face with a snapping row of sharp teeth. The wolf-like creature lurched forward to take a bite, and Branimir dodged the attack. He quickly rolled forward under the beast, and then, realizing the danger, jerked sideways between the front and back paw to avoid being squashed.

Bran bounded to his feet and ran pass the second simargl, who leaped at Dorofej.

"Alack!" Drak twisted away from his pony which the third simargl tackled, wings spread with fangs sinking into its neck.

Adamus shouted something unintelligible and charged past Hanna again, his shield thrown to the side. The fighter hurdled by Dorofej, who used *Koldovstvo* to jump through space and time to avoid certain death. Adamus reared his axe with immense potency. The blade caught the edge of the simargl's cheek, tearing through the thin membrane and splattering blood.

A yap of anguish hummed and the black beast whipped its head from the impact. At the same time, a roar from the second softened; Hanna rapidly unleashed several more arrows into its skull. It crumpled to the snow, eyes blackening.

The first, injured from Adamus's axe, drowned out the dying animal with a bark, and snapped at the Anshedar once more. Adamus stepped back, defending his unprotected arm.

"Over here!" Branimir screamed, rushing forward and peddling backwards again.

The simargl turned toward the Kras snarling. It had barely taken a step when Adamus raged forward, swinging the axe upward and cutting into the throat of the beast. The wolf gurgled, juttering to snap at the man, before falling over and bleeding out.

Adamus roared with victory. The shaggy black hair and beard nearly covering his triumphant expression.

Hanna turned her attention on the remaining simargl. It howled as she buried an arrow under its eye.

"One more," Dorofej cried. "Adamus!" The black mage flashed white light into the eyes of the dark-furred wolf, blinding it. With a haughty thrust, the Anshedar hastened forward and crushed his axe into the temple of the simargl. The silver blade slashed through the flesh like fire through frost. It dropped without much more than a whimper.

Adamus ripped his blade free, brought the axe down again at a downward angle into the neck.

Branimir panted for air, whirling to face Dorofej. The black mage had a patch of gray in his red hair.

"What is your axe made from?" Drak cried.

"Steel." Adamus answered, cleaning it on the hide of the beast. "Glorious steel from the south."

Branimir gawked at the size of the simargl. "How much further until we reach *Garain'l*?"

Hanna smiled. "Oh, Branimir, we have only begun."

Chapter XI

Two days passed and the forest had become more subdued. Branimir spent most of the time in his own head, captivated by the events at Cavell and with the myling. He tried to forget his failings, but the thought would not escape him. Even if he wanted to forget, Drak would not let him.

Even last night, Drak had challenged his wits while they had been keeping watch.

"Do you think there are mylings at *Garain'l*?" Drak had asked. Branimir had noted Drak spent more time frightening himself to tears than doing anything else, whether or not they could hear the bawls of beasts in the surrounding wild.

"Whatever comes will come," Bran said. Through talking to Drak, he had realized he was angrier at himself than afraid. "We must trust Dorofej knows what he is doing."

In truth, Drak's constant worrying reminded Branimir of how he had once been. He had changed in the Netherworld, long before returning to Maharia. Now, the eerie sounds here had no more effect than the grating dead there.

"Stone the crows! Why put so much trust into him, Branimir? He hasn't told us why we are going to the ruins, or even Ariadne for that matter. We left the boy we were meant to save, and now, he is going to be sacrificed" Drak debated.

"Not without *kaelandur*," Branimir argued.

Drak retorted, "We hope."

"Dorofej has his secrets," Branimir had finally responded, assuring himself more than Drak. "He will tell us more when it is time."

"You said you were not his slave."

"And, I am not," Branimir said.

"You do his will, follow him wherever he goes, and ask little to no questions. That sounds like slavery to me," Drak contended.

"It can also sound like faith," Branimir had argued.

Drak whistled between his teeth. "You talk as though we are all slaves."

"Maybe we are," Branimir had concluded. "It could be there is only freedom in death."

"Not if Wolos is really dead," Drak said. "If that is true, then we will all be slaves to Marheena, trapped in the Netherworld."

Bran ended the conversation, saying, "Maybe freedom doesn't exist."

Morning had come, and Branimir could not shake his and Drak's conversation. He did not want to be a slave, and he did not want to die. The thoughts lingered with him throughout the day.

As of now, they had skipped the midday meal, and quickened their pace for *Garain'l*. Adamus promised they would reach the ruins before long.

Bran walked alongside Dorofej's horse, keeping his gaze fixed to the snowfall that patterned the landscape. Even with the thick awning of trees, stopping the white fluff from collecting on the forest floor was impossible. Branimir's leather shoes sunk into the slush, freezing his feet and toes. He told himself he had been through worse, and still he suffered.

"Do you want your turn?" Drak asked, bouncing atop the pony. The Kras swayed with a tune in his head, one which he always seemed to have. He had more giddiness in him than what any creature should carry about.

Branimir scowled, keeping his head down. For the past couple days, he and Drak had taken turns on the single pony after the other had been lost in the skirmish with the simargl. In truth, the two could ride the pony together, but Branimir did not want to share the small saddle.

He finally said, "I would prefer to walk a bit longer."

When Branimir had traveled with the Highborn from Melkorka to the Ash Tree, he had found purpose in being among them. He had led them to Illuard, saved them from the clutches of the centaurs, and led them across the frozen river near Shayol Domier. He had given the Kras the courage to find freedom. He had been a hero.

But why was he here? He was supposed to be a warrior and a hero, not a liability.

Through the shadows, without any noticeable landmark except tree next to another tree, the company continued to create their own path. Adamus, who led them, would share songs of Ariadne, and from distant battlefields. His words often enchanted Branimir, rescuing him momentarily from his self-doubt. Adamus sung with a deep baritone, at a slow pace, which seemed to bring peace to the shadows of the Dyndaer.

Lost is the large mountain,
Beside the river swift,
Within a joyless wood,
O death has come for me.

To grind the iron blade,
Kneel to the crown of stone,
Fell hero; warrior,
O death has come for me.

The words gave Branimir chills. He could only guess the words were an ode to Czern, speaking of the crown of stone and sacrifice.

Branimir settled his hand in his pocket to touch the *Ojenek*. Feeling the smooth surface of the stone comforted him.

Ages had passed since he had relied on the magic of the moonstone. Then again, in a world where trade connected kingdoms and culture, folks were persuaded to learn new languages. Even now, he journeyed with an Anshedar, Highborn, Lilitu, and Kras; and they could all speak to one another without constraint. Bran wondered if he would ever need the gifts of the *Ojenek* again.

"Branimir, my friend, you have not been yourself for many days, yes?" probed Dorofej, dipping down from his black mare. "In your mind something is disturbed, yes?"

"It is nothing," Branimir said, distancing himself from Dorofej's horse, but only slightly.

"I say, *nothing* is temporary, yes?"

Branimir frowned. "I don't know what that means, Dorofej."

"Fades quickly, *nothing* does, and soon, what is *nothing* becomes *something*," Dorofej expounded, rubbing at his half-grey, half-red beard. The stubble had grown out to a full beard with his casting of *Koldovstvo*. At this rate, the black mage would kill himself before they rescued Bohumir. Bran wondered at Drak's suggestion as to whether they should have joined Adamus and Hanna on the trip to *Garain'l*. It may have been wiser, instead, to pursue the lad, or at least gather whatever Dorofej wanted in Ariadne.

"What is your point?" Branimir griped.

Dorofej whistled between his teeth, giving an air of annoyance. He breathed slowly and enunciated each word to make sure he was well heard. "I say, my point is pouting, you are, and no one pouts about *nothing*."

Branimir turned his head further away. He fought against the urge to make claim that he was not pouting, even when the truth was he most definitely had been. After a time, he turned back, and the truth came forward, "I do not want to die, Dorofej."

"Ah, brave you are to admit to say what most would fear, yes?"

Branimir sniffed, his nose numb. "I do not feel brave."

"I say, none of us truly want to die, even with the promise of something greater. Clear to me, it is," said Dorofej, "broken, one must be, to want to abort the blessing of life."

Hanna turned her enlarged head to join the conversation. "You claim every life is a blessing. Since when are all of us created to find joy? What of those who suffer from their birthing til their passing, finding no time for reprieve? The message you are presenting is false."

"There is no joy in war," Drak agreed. "Those who survive it leave with less of themselves than when they started."

"What do you know of war, Drak?" Adamus snorted. "Most men don't truly find what they are made of until they go to war."

"Not only war," Hanna insisted, "whatever point Adamus aims to make. But what of the starving or sick? The unloved and misused? The dull-minded and broken? I would think it better to end their suffering than expect them to find joy when there is none to be had."

Dorofej grunted. "Speak as though sorrow is pressed on you by another, you do."

"'Tis true," said Adamus, his voice flattened after being disregarded by Hanna. "Misery and blessing comes from the gods. It guides men to complete their charge so they may find rest in the Thrice Ten Kingdom."

"The common belief, it is," said Dorofej, responding to Adamus. He tugged at the scruff on his chin, as though he had forgotten the feel of facial hair and had missed its absence. He said, "Have the gods have come from Iriy, or the heavens, or some other place, and came to you with an unexpected windfall or woe? I say, I think not. Despair does not come from anything outside of the self, but from within, yes?"

Dorofej's suggestion that the gods might swoop down to speak with the living caused Branimir to laugh. He had once told Branimir that Iriy was the city of the gods found within the Shade Fells in the far west; though Dorofej claimed he had never been to this mystical place.

"I don't understand what this has to do with Branimir talking about dying, but," Drak said seriously, "the gods would not speak to us. They might have folks close to us cause pain or happiness—to teach us what we should learn."

"I would have never thought to hear such wisdom from a Kras," supplied Hanna in her even tone. "Yet the way to the Beyond is not easy, and its blessings are withheld only for the strong. If you want to have eternal life, toss aside the weak and persevere with the blessed."

Branimir gaped. "You mean kill those weaker than yourself."

"Not necessarily kill," Hanna narrowed her eyes. "But can the weak really live? Truly not. Best to give them a better chance in their next life. You would not fear death if you were strong."

"What madness! There is nothing that guarantees another life." Branimir shook, from either fear or fury. "And who here is weak, Hanna?"

"It has yet to be determined," she answered.

Drak, who must have felt similarly snubbed, said, "You are the one fighting with a teeny bow. You are no stronger than me."

Branimir covered his mouth with both hands, taking notice of the weapon, half the size of what a normal archer would carry.

Hanna stayed serene, saying, "I will let my actions speak for my strength. Can you say the same, Drak?" Her red sash caught Branimir's eye as Drak looked away. Hanna's point could not be missed. She had proven herself in the battle at Cavell, against the myling, and the simargl. Drak had done nothing of consequence in any battle. Hanna continued her lecture, "I am a warrior of the Lilitu. I am a *Rudhira*. I was born to fight. I succeed or I die, and I am not dead."

Drak gulped, lowering his own offset, blackened eyes to the back of Dorofej.

"There are other gifts besides fighting," Branimir said, attempting to convince himself more than the others. "Do you not think of that when measuring a person's worth?"

Hanna kept her eyes on the road. "Your argument is an old one, and I will tell you what I tell Adamus. Worth is calculated by many things: knowledge, influence, and utility."

"She is speaking in riddles," Drak mused.

"I am not," Hanna said. "Let us consider the value of your people. The Kras are one of the longest living races in the north, and hold historic knowledge, but they do not use it to their advantage. What the Kras know is not used to govern or manage battles or control trade, but is squandered on their pursuit for gemstones or to craft trinkets."

Drak sniffed, and squeaked, "What do you have against shiny stones?"

"Nothing," Hanna said, "when it lands a hefty profit and rises my people to greater prosperity."

Branimir felt *Ojenek* in his pocket. He could not imagine giving away the moonstone for something as meaningless as silver. The same was true of his gems buried back at Gavlok. Ridiculous. "What of influence?"

"Influence?" Hanna awed with amusement. "The Kras have no influence on any civilization. The people are not motivated by politics, war, religion, or any other thing that motivates the world. The Kras may very well engage in trade but only to endure, and not to thrive. They only give away the jewels they must part with to make enough to survive, do they not?"

Again, Drak fidgeted on his saddle. "And why should we hand over the stones we discover in the soil? They are ours." Branimir smiled at Drak's argument, similar to what he had thought himself.

"I would be ignorant to encourage you to change," Hanna said, "but your lack of influence speaks to your lack of utility and your ultimate annihilation. The Kras serve to add flavor to the marketplace with their ornaments, but their role otherwise is undefined. In fact, I would argue the Kras could disappear entirely from Aenar and very little would change in the course of the world."

Not having the words to dispute Hanna's allegations, Drak said with a snivel. "You're a boob."

Adamus nearly slipped sideways from his saddle. "Don't be cross, Drak."

"You're saying we are useless," Branimir concluded quietly, "because we do not force others to bend to our will?"

Hanna replied, paying no attention to Drak, "You do not have a will for others to bend toward."

"Seems to me," Branimir considered, "the world has enough pokers in the fire."

"A common viewpoint for the weak. They minimize the value of power because they cannot obtain it." Hanna settled with satisfaction. "Also, why the Kras will never thrive. The race would better serve another as slave than to be left to their own devices. The Kras have talents wasted because they are too ignorant to know how best to apply them."

Branimir scowled. "You think the Kras would better be slaves again than have their freedom?"

"Ah, I remember they were slaves once, were they not?" Hanna must have realized she struck a chord, but went on, "I saw how you were used by the Stuhia at Cavell. You fought better under his mind control with his magic than I have seen from you at any other time."

"I say, that is enough, Hanna." Dorofej choked.

Hanna stayed stoic, though she were reading from the most boring of stories. "Do not fret, Branimir. Most of the northern races are equally useless. Freedom is a gift for those worthy, and truth is, most are not."

Adamus growled. "Hanna, you need to be more careful with your words,"

"Indeed," Dorofej said louder.

"You separate the north from Haemus Mons, even suggesting the desert people are superior," Adamus disputed in his deep baritone. "'Tis they who have been advancing into Maharia and slaughtering my people. I hardly see how that is commendable."

"The mark of a person's virtue does not match his or her greatness. The path of power is not decorated with honor; and decency does not win wars. Nor is value found in integrity or morality. The question of utility lies in whether or not what one can offer is greater than another."

"You misjudge the Anshedar. May I remind you that you have fought for us in the war against the desert people," Adamus said.

"I fought for the Anshedar because the desert people do not pay sellswords," Hanna said plainly. "Do not misjudge my actions as allegiance."

"So, you believe the Uvil are the greater race?" Adamus challenged, his grimace hidden beneath his black beard.

"Don't you?" Hanna shifted her bulbous head toward the hero-warrior, and almost grinned, for what would have been the first time. "Our greatest fighters in Lilitu cities carry their weapons, which we won in battle. Even you are carrying their shield and steel on your back."

While Adamus bit his tongue, Branimir combed the trees for movement, and ignored Hanna. He knew he would feel better about the journey if she were no longer with them.

Chapter XII

Garain'l materialized, shrouded in shades only a hair lighter than the rest of the forest. The stone archways were corroded and laced in creepers, coiling and curling around the molded grey edifices. The few towers, constructed from ancient wood, had collapsed into dilapidated piles of mush or sunk into the expanding marsh snaking through the ruins.

The vinegary odor poked at Branimir's senses. He pulled his cowl over his nose, scanning the white flakes that painted parts of the ruins.

"Stone the crows! Are there treasures buried here?" Drak straightened on the pony, smacking his lips. The Kras scanned the shapes of broken statues and half-raised buildings emerging from the puddled muck.

Branimir shivered, seeing the besmirched edges of snowfall. "I do not think I would want to go searching for silver or stones here, Drak. You would find yourself falling into hidden bits of swamp, and drown before you could find solid ground again."

"Which is why tis best to leave the horses here. We can't have them bolting into the bog." Adamus dismounted, directing his horse to the nearest tree, and tying him off. "Follow me on the old footpath until we reach the burial ground. Fiends, likely mylings, lurk among the swamp and the buildings from time to time."

"Then, why did you come here?" Branimir shivered.

"Tradition," Adamus said. "'Tis custom to pay respects during the *Koricern*. You came of your own accord."

"If it is a tradition, where is everyone else?" Drak asked.

"I told you," Adamus explained, "'tis tradition of my family, passed down through our bloodline only."

"How long will we be here?" Drak shivered, looking across the ruins.

"I would not risk staying more than a night," Adamus said. "We will complete the sacrifice and make headway toward Ariadne in the morning."

"Sacrifice?" Branimir whispered in confusion. He thought of Bohumir.

"Best not to tarry too long, yes?" Dorofej slipped from his mount. The black mage's calmness caused Branimir to grow in concern.

"What is it, Dorofej?" he urged.

"As I feared, lingering among these stones, something ancient does," Dorofej forewarned. "Not quite a part of this world, it is not. I say, I fear it—"

"Come out with it, Stuhia," Hanna demanded, her feet crunching against the snow. "Demon, devil, or something more?"

Dorofej raised his eyebrows, and angled them over the bridge of his nose. His brow had become noticeably bushier since the simargl. In short time, Branimir thought he may be speaking with the old man he had known at Melkorka. "Too dangerous to fully know, it would be, but a Likhyi, methinks. Though, the power of the spectre is weakened, still held at bay by the Ash Tree, it should be."

"A Likhyi?" Drak scratched the thinning hair on top of his head. "You mentioned the name back at Ojenir, but I have never thought to ask of its nature."

"I have not heard of this *thing,* though many dangers creep within *Garain'l,*" Adamus responded.

Branimir realized he, too, could not answer the question of the Likhyi. Beyond what Dorofej had recently said, Bran had only heard it mentioned by Nedezhda at Melkorka, years ago, when she vowed to release the Likhyi.

"Clear, it is not," Dorofej tried to explain, "but ancient, it is. I say, there are some who claim the Likhyi are older than gods, or may even be gods themselves from a time before time."

Hanna cleared her throat. "You are talking about an epoch when the world was still being formed. It is when the first magics, called the *Runista,* were made, in a time prior to our creation. We tell stories—tales known well by the desert people—of primordial wraiths who warped this world, who had been trapped by the current gods in a place between this world and the next. Our people have often thought the Mother wants to free them again."

Branimir scratched his head. "You are talking of your goddess, Lillith? How does the Lilitu god fit with the gods of the Anshedar?"

Drak said, "Did I not say before? Lillith is the same as Marheena for the Northman, or close enough."

Branimir's jaw hung. "The Frozen Goddess of the Netherworld! No, you did not tell me. You mean the Mother is the Seamstress of Nightmares."

Drak, who did not seem to understand the implication, mashed his lips together and sluggishly nodded.

Adamus had a similar expression, eyeing Branimir with caution.

Branimir wailed, turning to Dorofej for help. "Say something to her. We cannot stand here and support a follower of Marheena when the aim is to let loose wraiths into Aenar. This is why Nedezhda came for the Ash Tree a thousand years ago! There must be reason why these old gods, the Likhyi, were trapped."

The forest fell quiet for many seconds after Branimir's lamenting. Dorofej said nothing. The black mage simply looked around at the company in contemplation.

Adamus spoke first, like he was joking, "The Kras do know their history, don't they? We have heard of the Ash Tree in Ariadne but it is more myth than history. Some say, it is somewhere within the Dyndaer. But Nedezhda? I know nothing of that name."

The Lilitu women's eyes were exceptionally round, her tone also elevated with a hint of humor. "Maybe this Kras is different from the rest. Motivated by something, indeed; though, poking at me would be ill-advised, Branimir."

Branimir puffed his chest, finding his strength returning. He would not be threatened. "I am nothing that you think I am."

"The old gods," Drak paused, rubbing his chin in deep thought, offsetting the tension, "were entombed to give us life. All of us. The Kras have told the stories for centuries, even before Shayol Domier. I had heard the stories from my grandfather growing up about how the essence of the old gods were encapsulated into the Ash Tree to give birth to the living. I have never heard them called Likhyi before, but to free these…these Likhyi…you would have to have something strong enough to destroy the Ash Tree."

Kaelandur, Branimir thought.

At least Drak was beginning to understand the seriousness of the situation. Branimir moved to clasp his hand on Drak's shoulder, almost screaming, "And you," he pointed his finger at Hanna accusingly, "want this to happen. You want Marheena to kill us, don't you?"

Adamus moved to intercept. "I do not see why you are attacking Hanna. Tis the gods who have a better understanding of the cycle of things than the living. Czern teaches us that we are imperfect. We cannot hope to fight against the gods. If our time on Aenar is done, tis done. If the Likhyi must come, then let them come. If the gods wish the Ash Tree to be destroyed, let it be destroyed."

"Life is about the perseverance of the mightiest," Hanna echoed a similar sentiment as the hero-warrior from Ariadne, holding her ground. "Lillith, or Marheena, as you would say, will see to her will. The Mother will do what must be done."

Branimir's body shook with fury. He felt Drak wince under his grip, but he could not believe what he was hearing. "Dorofej, say something to this. The world will crumble around these two and they will watch it happen without even lifting a finger. Dorofej! Why have you said nothing?"

The black mage grumbled, adjusting his robes, nodding his head at Branimir.

"Each of us have our own reasons for doing what must be done, yes?" Dorofej staggered his words, having less poise than Branimir generally found in the ageless Highborn. "Difficult to believe, it is, Marheena, or any deity, acts with accordance, or interest, of the nature of men, yes? Men have motivations. Demons have motivations. Even my horse finds motivation." Dorofej patted the animal softly against the cheek. "But not the gods. Reverence in the gods is found—not for what they have given or what they have taken—but because of whom they are, yes? I say, reason for their being and their doing is not for me to consider."

"So, you will do nothing, too?" Branimir asked in shock.

"Say that, I did not," Dorofej whistled. "I say, as I have said before, Branimir Baran. I am but a man—"

"Branimir Baran!" Drak yelled. "Dorofej, why would you say that when his surname is Barthor?"

Branimir cowered at the lapse.

"Yes, yes, yes," Dorofej waved off Drak, finishing his thought. "I am but a man and I have no interest in dying. Bohumir must be rescued, the Ash Tree must be protected, and the Likhyi must be withheld, but first Adamus has a grave to consecrate, yes?"

Adamus adjusted his weapon and shield, nodding with respect to Dorofej. The black-bearded man turned and led the way into *Garain'l*. Hanna followed behind him, averting her eyes from Branimir as she passed by, and Drak pulled from his hand to take his place in the solitary line.

"Go on, Branimir," Dorofej said. "We can speak more of this later."

Bran sighed and headed into the ruins. Dorofej trailed behind him.

Garain'l gave the impression of being trivial at the front arch where the horses remained, but the girth of the place was greater than anticipated. The shallow light from Adamus and Dorofej's torches gave them minimal sight while Hanna, Branimir, and Drak peered through the trees and structures for any sign suggesting the fiends of which Adamus had spoken skulked. Several times, Adamus asked Dorofej to cast light into the darkness of the Dyndaer and had been refused. The black mage spoke of the importance of saving his power.

Nothing stirred.

The pathway twisted from time to time, covered with debris of broken limbs and cracked stone. Vines and branches lay half-buried in the snow like snakes on the surface of water. In some areas, the bog ran alongside the makeshift trail, overwhelming their senses with the stench. Adamus moved slower in these areas to assure his footing was never misplaced. Slipping into the muck would have left any of them damp, and likely would have played negatively toward their already sour tempers.

At one point, the company reached a shattered stone building of sorts across the footpath. Instead of going over or through, Adamus elected to double back and take another path to the burial ground. He welcomed the Anshedar's sense of caution. Bran could not ignore the intolerable sense of distress that stayed with him as they moved through *Garain'l*.

They had passed by another curve in the path when Drak broke the silence.

"Look there," the Kras rustled, stopping suddenly in front of Branimir. He pointed across the mire through the trees toward one of the many structures.

Adamus halted the group, lifting his hand, "'Tis too far to see, Drak. What moves?"

Branimir looked in the direction Drak pointed and saw nothing. The building bowed near the flattened top, stones jutting from their holdings in several places. The opening in the front was hollow without a door without any movement inside.

"Simargl?" Adamus asked.

"No," Drak replied, "something strange, green and ghost-like. It was there and wasn't there, floating when it moved. The thing drifted into the hole on the side of the building. It was a woman, I think."

Branimir shuddered at the bizarre description. Dorofej shook his head unknowingly.

"You think it was the gal of *Garain'l*, like from the song?" Drak cringed, tightening his pointed nose.

Hanna said, "Whatever it was, if it was anything, is gone."

"Something was there," Drak declared, rising on his tiptoes.

"Doubts you, no one does, Drak," Dorofej said. "Best we move with haste but silently, yes?"

Adamus grunted in acknowledgement and drifted forward again, almost crouched. Those behind him maintained a similar station and tiptoed across the wet snow. Branimir watched the doorway of the building until he could not see it anymore.

At length they came to a sharp bend and turned left to a series of stone steps leading down beneath three archways. They were adjacent and parallel to one another, and amazingly, each were still intact. Adamus took the lead beneath the archways. The snow swirled around their feet from piled drifts on either side of the discolored stairs.

When the stairway ended, a building, a shrine, set in between two trees loomed. Green gunk painted the greying rock which formed its bulky structure. Branimir halted behind those in front of him, mesmerized by the magnificence of the building's height and thickness. A statue, marked by a man with a crown and scythe, stood, as though keeping guard, on either side of the shrine.

"An image of Czern, it is," Dorofej identified with a rise of his hand, and a pull at his beard.

Adamus turned to face them, and said, "I will enter alone and pay respects to my fallen kin. Please, make camp here and I will return by morning."

None protested, but Branimir noticed Drak shift uneasily at the request.

As the dark-bearded warrior disappeared into the shrine, Branimir could not help but want to know what was inside.

Chapter XIII

The deep, singsong voice of Adamus rumbled from the deeps of the shrine behind the campfire. The words were indistinguishable, but the hum of song teased Branimir's ears. The tune was lovely and cavernous, profound and arcane, and he pined to know the words.

Instead of tiptoeing into the place he had been asked not to go, he leaned toward the fire. His body had numbed to the point he had forgotten the biting cold. Now, with the fire cackling, warming him, Branimir was reminded how chilled he must have been before making camp. He enjoyed the moment.

Drak spent the last hour standing in the far corner by two stones, throwing his rune staves against the ground and mumbling under his breath. Hanna had disappeared somewhere nearby to keep watch, saying something about scouting the area. Dorofej had disappeared shortly after without a word. Branimir could only guess he was off looking for whatever he had come here to find.

Before long, Drak kicked at the ground with frustration and joined Branimir at the fire. His sticks were gathered in his hands. "I cannot seem to make anything of what the rune staves are trying to tell me."

"What do you mean?" Branimir said, wringing his hands over the flames.

"My mind is mush," Drak said. "I throw the rune staves down but I cannot hear anything."

Branimir smiled. "I forgot they could talk to you."

Drak scowled at the remark. The red-skinned Kras plopped down on his bedroll, dropping his hands and sticks into his lap. His dark eyes blazed in the flickering light. "I might be too tired."

"You can try again tomorrow," Branimir encouraged, still not certain whether there was anything to the rune staves. "Drak, did you really come with us simply because of the sticks?"

"Marry! I keep saying they aren't sticks." Drak scrunched his nose at the question. "And, yes. The rune staves said you would do something great, and along the path of the gods, remember? I haven't forgotten."

"Well, we are beside a shrine of the gods," Branimir mused.

Drak looked up at the statues of Czern. "I had thought it might be something a bit more than listening to an Anshedar sing in a tomb."

Bran pointed at the sticks. "Do you really think those *things* tell the future?"

"I do. Why are you asking me this?" Drak wondered.

Branimir shrugged. "When we first met, and you read my *fortune*, you had said something that troubled me. I have not been able to get it out of my head."

Drak blinked with confusion.

"You told me that I would never find joy," Branimir went on. "I can't help but think the rune staves might be right, mainly when I think of these past several weeks."

"Oh." Dorofej shuffled out from the shadows, rejoining them near the fire. He appeared disgruntled, despite his words. "We have shared pleasant times together, yes? I say, do not sum up all arduous times to be grievous."

"I was only telling you what I was seeing," Drak explained. "I did not mean anything by it."

"All the same, your words have stayed with me," said Branimir, scooting over to make room for Dorofej.

"I say, Hanna did warn us that we may create our own future by thinking that we know what to expect, yes? Emotions can create your reality if you are not careful," Dorofej softened his gaze.

Drak sniffed through his nose. "The rune staves tell what will happen. Branimir cannot change it, no matter how he feels about it."

Dorofej furrowed his brow. "Know that for certain, we do not. Regardless, whether our paths are fixed or not, we choose how we walk them. Dangerous, it is, to find comfort in sadness. Leads only to more sadness, it does."

"I like that thought," Drak granted, and then grinned wide. "Feelings are unseen and untouched by anyone or anything. Fate cannot tell you how to feel."

Branimir held his face, pondering the wisdom of the two. "Telling yourself how to feel seems easier to think about than to do."

"Such is the task of the living, yes? I say, our minds are riddled with grand ideas and limited enthusiasm to see it done. Driven towards the things we wish to avoid, men are. Drink, does the drunkard; fight, does the warrior; and on and on, it goes."

"Is it not what they want?" Branimir asked.

Dorofej lifted his eyebrows. "What do you want, Branimir?"

"I want…" Branimir may have never thought about the question before. He had always been entertained with trying to survive, the question of *what to live for* was beyond his knowing. Yet when taking a moment to think, the answer was not hard to come by. "I want happiness, Dorofej."

"What we all want, it is, and also the drunk, the warrior, and any other, yes?"

Drak, who had still been holding his rune staves, slid them back into their pouch. "I wonder what you are driven to do, though?"

"Flee!" Hanna's voice thundered over the sound of anything Branimir might have said. The flash of her reddish brown skin rushed between the trees fifty feet away. "Get Adamus! Flee for your lives!"

Branimir stared in bafflement, hearing barking resounding in the distance. The sound was too familiar. Drak sprung to his feet.

Dorofej's eyebrows came together arcing over his wide nose. He shouted back. "What is it?"

The Lilitu woman skidded into the camp, covering the distance. "Has the chill stolen your senses? I have seen Drak's green ghost. And simargl have picked up our scent!"

"I told you I was telling the truth," Drak hollered.

"What was the ghost?" Branimir asked.

Hanna lifted her bow as though she might smack them all, including Dorofej, who stood dumbfounded. "This is not the time for questions. For all I know, it is the Likhyi. Now, come! We cannot win a battle here."

Dorofej halfway nodded, the sounds of the simargl echoing through the ruins. Battle was going to be upon them in moments.

"Branimir, fetch Adamus, you must," Dorofej directed, rubbing his head. "Found what I needed to find, I have not." He looked around the ruins expectantly. "Something hidden here, there is. Douse the fire, we will, with hope they stay clear from us. Make haste."

Hanna could be heard arguing with Dorofej as he skidded toward the steps, nearly falling. Steading himself, Branimir rattled down the slick, stone stairs. With every step, Adamus's song intensified, but he did not have the time to enjoy the words.

"Adamus," he screamed.

A putrid smell touched Branimir's sensitive nose. He gagged and pressed forward, reaching the bottom. The disheveled crypt had skeletons and half-rotten corpses flung about the underpasses, running in either direction. It appeared whomever brought the bodies had thrown them down the steps, or had simply piled them in several disorganized mounds. Despite the smell, the bodies looked as though they had been sitting for some time.

Branimir's stomach roiled. In the Netherworld, he had witnessed many *dead* things, but they did not carry the smell like the corpses here. He could ignore the lifeless eyes and decayed flesh collecting in piles. He could even overlook the rodents—despite the cold—who tore skin from marrow and gnashed. But the smell was unbearable.

The barking from above ground had turned into growls and roars. He had to hurry.

A torchlight flickered in one of the many directions, and Branimir rushed toward the soft, orange glow. He stepped over mangled arms and shriveled stomachs, keeping his eyes focused on the light as much as he could without tripping over the pile of dead Anshedar.

As Branimir neared the door, he heard Adamus continue to sing in soothing, muffled rumbles. But there were other voices too. He barely had time to consider what it meant before he burst into the chamber.

"Adamus," Branimir shouted.

The Anshedar did not respond.

"Oh, son, you have grown strong. I have missed the light in your eyes," said a motherly voice.

Branimir stood, uncertain, in the entry way with Adamus facing a table, his back to him. He stepped forward carefully.

"The way is shut. The *way* is shut. *The way is shut*," cried another.

"More wine," a third begged. "Never have I been so parched."

Laughter.

And, still, Adamus sung.

"Adamus!" Branimir called out, tugging on the back of the man's cloak.

The black-bearded hero-warrior spun from the stone tablet, his eyes rolled back into his head, whites showing, and blood oozing off his lip. He spat, coughing blood into Branimir's face.

Bran swiped his hands in front of him in attempt to block the blood. "Adamus."

"It cannot be," something cried.

Branimir tottered into the table, raising his chin to find three severed heads, one skull with a green light blazing within its empty orbs. The others were half decomposed, looking back at him, with an undead gaze. They circled a pool of blood which had seemingly come from Adamus's cut tongue.

Branimir screamed flailing away from them, and back into the wall.

One by one the heads shrieked, mouths gaping and blackness flooding the room from their opened orifices. As the gloom flooded the room, the energy in the lifeless heads drained and they each returned to death.

"Wha—What?" Branimir tried.

Adamus roared from his chest, convulsing, jerking his head like an upset mule. His light eyes rolled back into their place and he hurriedly wiped the crimson liquid from his lips.

"Branimir," he retched, spitting blood. "Why have you interrupted this time with my family?"

"I—I'm sorry, Adamus. We are under attack," Branimir stammered, staring at what must have been the man's relatives lined on the table. Small bulbs of fire burned in containers between each skull, but the fresh blood is what kept his eye. "Dorofej said to…"

"Czern's breath!" Adamus choked, checking his armaments and staggering toward the door. "Come on."

Bran backed out of the chamber to follow Adamus unsure about the dark magic he had witnessed, and hastily tried to push it from his mind. He did not want to think Adamus to be as wicked as Hanna. Though, perhaps this god called Czern was as terrible as Marheena, no matter what Dorofej claimed the will of the gods were.

Branimir climbed up the steps from the shrine, hearing the grating snarls of simargl. When reaching the smothered fire, he saw the winged wolves flooding in columns from the trees in packs of three and five. There were dozens.

Drak cowered near the steps with their items gathered, cheering at Adamus's emergence from the catacombs. Hanna stood several feet in front of him, her quiver nearly emptied, entombing her arrows deep into the skulls of the beasts. Simargl after simargl fell, crashing and skidding across the hoarfrost.

Dorofej stood beyond them all, protecting the path, casting *Koldovstvo* without restraint. The black mage flung ice shards and spheres of fire, exploding the earth, and pulling trees down atop the backs of the beasts.

Adamus had his axe at the ready, sprinting to Dorofej's side. Soon, his axe rising and falling, hacking through skin, fur, and bones as if it were snowfall.

The dark-haired man called out to Dorofej. "We cannot win this. Move back." He plunged his blade into another razor-toothed simargl with a growl of savagery. Another beast slammed into his steel shield, knocking him back. The Anshedar skidded and twisted, ramming back into the creature. He worked his axe methodically, slashing at every opening, giving no notice to the blood that spurred.

"Leave *Garain'l*, we mustn't," Dorofej said. "I say, something stirs here, yes?"

"Mm," Adamus huffed. "The simargl."

Branimir could hear Dorofej's dissatisfied groan.

"We cannot stay here," Drak shrieked from Branimir's side. "They cannot kill them all."

Branimir knew the Kras was right. The black mage had already aged considerably. Adamus and Dorofej had already begun to inch backwards towards the shrine, overwhelmed by the packs of wolves. Hanna screamed out to them as more appeared further back in the trees.

Dorofej and Adamus hardly heard her warning, shouting back and forth to each other, cutting down as many of the beasts as they could. The craft of *Koldovstvo* lighting up the Dyndaer almost matched the rhythm of the falling axe. Ice and fire surged through the shadowed forest at every shape that stirred.

"I am out," Hanna said, hooking her bow back onto her shoulder.

"Hanna!" Drak screamed, cowering back.

From the side of the shrine, a simargl crashed into the Lilitu, sinking its teeth into her arm and side in a massive bite. Branimir scooted backwards while the simargl picked Hanna off the ground and flung her about. Her body twisted and heaved in between its jaws, from her chest to her midsection; she screeched in agony. With desperation, she struggled pulling on either side of the creature's curled lips. Blood slopped down the side of her body; her innards exposed through the gaping hole of her split skin. With a final rumble, the simargl pitched Hanna to the snow.

Branimir vanished from sight, shouting at Drak to do the same. The beast sniffed at the air, considered the shrine, and then raced toward Adamus and Dorofej with its wings etched behind its back.

He did not care to watch the fate of the beast, his eyes locked on Hanna who wriggled about on the ground in pain. He crept toward her, hidden by his invisibility.

"Help…me," she choked. He knew she did not speak to him. He was not where she could see him. "Adamus…"

If Dorofej caught sight of Hanna, he would spend his years healing her. Branimir was not certain if he could allow it. Hanna worshiped Marheena and Dorofej could not die!

Branimir glanced at Dorofej across the field, hair already whitening, using *Koldovstvo* to protect them all. Indeed, Dorofej would kill himself to save her.

"What do we do?" Drak whispered over his shoulder, eyes tearing while he watched Hanna with his beady black eyes.

Branimir could not look away from Hanna. Her owl eyes were searching for something, anything, and yet, Branimir and Drak were unseen.

"We need to get her away from here," Branimir said.

Gritting his teeth, he scrambled forward and clamped his hands under her arms. With surprise, he began to pull her back across the stone into the catacombs with ease. She flailed her good arm in the air trying to help. She had little strength, floundering hopelessly.

"It is no use," Drak cried.

Branimir ignored the Kras, holding fast until Hanna's stifled cries finally ceased and she lost consciousness. Even though her body went limp, he continued to pull her until she was safe within the shrine at the top of the steps.

Pulsating, he pulled himself away from her body and stepped back.

"She's dead." Drak said.

"No," he blenched. "she is still alive." Branimir stepped away from Drak, shouting. "Retreat, Dorofej. Adamus. Retreat!"

He heard Adamus in the distance. "I told you we had to run. Back to the catacombs."

Dorofej yelled in defeat, and fled with Adamus. The black mage caught sight of Hanna as he neared. "Lost, she is." Dorofej said stepping by Hanna. "No time for sadness, there is. Run!"

"Not quite!" Adamus cried. The burly Anshedar scooped up the woman and sprang into the depths. Branimir and Drak kept to his heels.

Chapter XIV

He tried to find the strength to tear himself away from the stone wall within the chamber. His hands quaked beyond his control. He had placed his hands between his knees to stop them from trembling, and still it did nothing. Dorofej and Adamus hovered over Hanna, the *Rudhira*, gawking at her insides spilling out across the stone table. Her crimson sash was stained with her blood.

"Are we safe?" Drak mouthed softly, sitting next to Branimir. The Kras eyed the dead bodies in the room and the severed heads on the stone table, seemingly distracting himself from Hanna.

"Should be," Adamus said, gritting his teeth. "The simargl are too big to squeeze down here. You could have come down here to begin with and avoided them altogether instead of attempting a stand-off. I told you we should have fled."

"Hanna is dead," Dorofej whispered, stepping away from the body and leaving Adamus alone. Dorofej moved to the doorway and peered into the catacomb. "Other dangers, there were said to be. Hanna alleged she saw the green ghost and thought it to be the Likhyi, yes?"

"She did," Drak nodded. "And we thought to run away. I wonder if the thing will come for us down here."

Adamus turned his head from Hanna's lifeless corpse, and sniffed. "We can leave in short time, if that is what must be done. The simargl are mindless brutes. They attack for play more than anything, and soon something more will grab at their attention."

As if on cue, growling resounded from above.

Dorofej ignored the simargls and said, "First, find what lingers here in *Garain'l*, I must."

Drak shook next to Bran, clenching his jaw between his words. "Is this what adventures are like?"

Branimir frowned, looking at Hanna's corpse. "More or less. Most stories you hear would tell the better parts and ignore the rest."

"I can see what folks would rather hear a story than live it. I will get a fire going," Drak said, tearing up at the corner of his eyes. He moved away to dig about the room to find something to kindle.

Adamus hit the table, and then placed his face into his hands. "Hanna faced legions, steel swords and worse, and only to be slaughtered by beasts. She saved my neck more times than I can count. I should have been there for her."

Branimir looked away. He was glad Adamus could hold himself back. He nearly expected the man to rush back atop for vengeance.

Time slowly passed in the catacombs while they listened to the simargl snarling amongst each other. Drak started a small fire in short time, and soon began wheezing next to the flames, falling asleep in a curled ball. Branimir kept his ears covered, doing his best to clear his thoughts. He wanted to join Drak in sleep, but each time his eyes closed, he could only see Hanna's strained expression, gasping for breath.

Adamus remained in a half-kneeled position leaning against the stone table next to her body and the severed heads of his kin. From time to time, he would splutter or sob only to grumble and groan back into a mumbled prayer.

Dorofej, hair greyed and wrinkles thickened around the eyes, remained at the opening of the chamber. He sat cross-legged in his robes, head resting with eyes open, against the doorway. Branimir did not think the black mage kept watch, but instead wandered among his own inner thoughts. His eyes were glossed over and he hummed to himself.

If Branimir knew any better he may have claimed the black mage was dead, or at least, his spirit had fled from his own skin. His body appeared as lifeless as the dead slinking around the catacombs.

The ruckus of the wolves eventually subsided, and the tomb quieted.

Sleep overtook Branimir. He slumped his head back feeling dizzy with exhaustion. Soon, a dream begun to form, twisted and accursed. The din of battle echoed in his ears. Branimir stood over Hanna. She struggled against him while he suffocated her breath over and over again. Blood spewed and her breath speckled with dark flakes like ashes around his fingertips. All the while, Drak whispered in his ear.

Even in his half-sleep state, he could feel his chest tighten and his feet kick, fighting against what he was doing. He could hear her wails under his hands, begging him not to take her life.

Without warning, the reverie changed. Hanna disappeared and he was back in the catacombs. Near him hovered the green apparition Drak had described, gripping him and shrieking. His ears reverberated with the cries of a thousand dead souls. He fought, contorting his body, trying to see the ghostly face of the undead female. It cried out to him, words jumbled. He strained, crumpling helplessly against the phantasmal spirit.

Branimir lurched, waking from the horrendous nightmares. His scream caught in his throat. He stifled a cough and swallowed. The dryness in his throat burned, but the coldness of his nose caught his attention. The chamber had grown icy since he had fallen asleep, and he realized the fire had been snuffed.

The passing time could not be measured. Adamus slept soundly, hunched over, near the smoking residue of the fire, and Dorofej remained unmoved near the hollow that led into the catacombs, his blue eyes open, but blanketed though he were sleeping.

Feeling as though something were not quite right, he turned toward Drak.

"Drak!" Branimir yelped, scrambling to his feet. He searched the room for any sign of the red Kras, and nothing was found. Drak had gone. "Hurry and wake yourselves. Drak is missing."

Adamus rolled over, rubbing his eyes. His shield grated against the stone. What are you going on about?" The Anshedar's hesitated while Branimir skittered towards the doorway, peering into the hallway.

"Drak?" Dorofej yawned, moving out of Branimir's way. He, too, twisted his neck to look out the doorway. "Gone, he must've, but how did he slink by?"

"He would not be so foolish as to go above ground to face the simargl by himself," Adamus said. "It would be suicide. He must be in the catacombs somewhere."

Branimir agreed.

"I say, why would he run off?" Dorofej pulled himself to his feet. His movements were slow, telling of his lacking nimbleness.

"I don't know," Branimir said. "But he could be in danger. We have to find him."

"Indeed. Leave him in the catacombs alone, we cannot."

Adamus ripped the bottom cloth from his cloak to make a torch, kindling it from the ash while he talked. "'Tis a maze in these tunnels. Even if he wandered off for no reason but to explore, he may never find his way back here anytime soon."

Branimir exhaled. "Do you know the pathways down here, Adamus? I would not want to become lost among the dead."

"Of course," Adamus said. He stepped into the passageway and started off with determination. Branimir followed with Dorofej drifting behind him. "As a child, I spent more time here at *Garain'l* with my family than at my own home in Ariadne. I could walk these tunnels blind if necessary."

"Necessary, it is not, Adamus," Dorofej said.

Branimir thought not to say anything about Adamus roaming around the ruins as a child. Instead, he looked over his shoulder to see Dorofej clench his jaw, his face altering from confusion to an expression of unease.

"What is wrong, Dorofej?"

"Struck me, it suddenly has, a *dream* I had before awakening. Fear, I do, a boding evil is at work."

"I also had a dream that woke me," Branimir said. "I saw the green ghost. It seemed there was something familiar about it, but I could not place it."

Dorofej hummed, the greying beard bobbing over his chest. "Careful, we must be. I say, its evil essence still lingers in the air, foul and malevolent."

"The Likhyi?" Branimir asked, facing Adamus once more.

Dorofej responded. "For certain, I cannot be."

"Is there a difference in sensing this ghost and the dead, or even the Likhyi?" Adamus muttered, looking at Hanna one last time. "Do not cause alarm among us when the situation is already dire, eh? Let us find Drak and be gone from *Garain'l.* I could not bear another among us dying."

Branimir and Dorofej grunted in agreement, and the hero-warrior led them out.

Adamus turned left beyond the staircase that led out from the shrine. Branimir looked toward the path out, and was glad to not see a single, loitering simargl.

As they walked, Dorofej said, "Adamus, hear me when I say, whatever the final outcome of our adventure here at *Garain'l*, it is greater than you and your intention in coming here. Nothing here, did you cause. If you remember, Branimir and I came of our own accord."

Branimir bit his cheek. Dorofej's words were not entirely true. He had brought Drak and Bran here, and with little explanation.

The hero-warrior spun the torch back and forth, illuminating the corpses piled up on either side of the path. "I hear you. Yet the outcome thus far is already more than I wish to bear. Hanna's death will haunt me for the rest of life, no matter how long or short it may be."

"Her death is no more your fault than any other in our company, yes? Tell him, Branimir. The death of friends and more, you have known well," Dorofej said.

"Who do you think you are speaking to?" Adamus barked, not bothering to look back. "Her death is completely your fault, Dorofej. How dare you ask Branimir to support your shallow words."

Dorofej tilted his chin with confusion. "Shallow?"

"Yes," Adamus said. "You demanded we fight a battle we could not win. You would not listen. I have fought many wars for many reasons. I know war, and I know death. I also know glib, and you're full of it."

Dorofej tensed.

"The past is done with," Branimir uttered before Dorofej could retort. "When we are finished we can assign blame, but in this moment, we must find Drak."

Branimir heard Dorofej scrape his foot against the ground behind him, likely stumbling in the dark, or from shock.

Adamus fixed his gaze on the tomb ahead. "Branimir is right. We will talk of this later, if it is even worth talking about."

The three walked in silence for almost half an hour. The tunnels beneath the shrine proved to be a maze. Burial chamber after burial chamber were passed over without any sign of Drak.

"I am not seeing even a scuff mark among the dust," Branimir finally said. "Maybe he did not come this way after all."

Adamus stopped the trek. "Tis likely. Though, the Kras has light feet. I hate to come so far and then turn back when he may be around the next bend."

"True, Kras are light-footed, but not so light as to walk on air," Branimir said. "If he came this way, he would have had to sprouted wings and flown."

A strained bellow, high-pitched and full of torment, abruptly sounded from the path ahead. It may have screamed for help, or it may have shouted nothing at all. Yet the tender lamenting was so heart-wrenching the noise caused Branimir's knees to weaken.

"Drak," he supposed, keeping himself from sprinting ahead. He looked to Adamus apologetically. "Well, either he is ahead, or there is an echo."

"Or, duped by something direr, may befall us," the black mage warned. "Proceed, we must, but with care."

Adamus held the torch outright again. "Your endless foreboding is trying, Dorofej." Despite the words, Branimir took note Adamus freed his axe from its holding before shuffling further down the hallway.

The bewailing of the shrill cry penetrated their ears several more times as Adamus led them through the tunnels. The torturous noise made Branimir cringe in agony. Whether limbs were being severed or flesh was being burnt, he could not tell, but the hubbub emulated with the impression of torture. Branimir felt sickened.

The time spent wading between the skeletons triggered a sensation of nausea, but Branimir pressed on after Adamus. The blubbering wails intensified in duration and length, and though there were no true signs indicating their closing on something tangible, besides sound, Branimir ascertained they were near.

The chamber ahead was dark, and if anything, appeared darker than the veiled hallways of the shrine. The doorway was hollowed like the other burial chambers, but the blackness within was unfamiliar to the Kras. It deepened in pitch unlike anything Branimir had ever seen.

A scream ricocheted. *Drak.*

Dorofej gripped Branimir's shoulder, nearly causing him to scream in response. "What is seen within, you must tell us?"

He juddered, instinctively stepping back, fear crawling up his spine. He did not know how to explain the visage before his eyes, and could only think of what Adamus and Dorofej, and other living things, underwent whenever the sun fell from beyond the horizon. Branimir had never known darkness until now.

"I…I cannot see anything. It is *dark.*"

Chapter XV

Branimir gawped shakily into the abysmal black, overwhelmed with feelings of despair. He had never looked into nothingness before. Though, the stabbing in his gut came from the overwhelming sensation that the nothingness was looking back.

Not in a thousand years had he ever felt this sense of dread. He shuddered from the tip of his crooked nose to his bent toes. His thin dark hairs on the base of his neck prickled. His words flooded from his lips, caught in the breath he had been holding. "I feel scared, Dorofej." He managed to say, turning to the black mage for help. "I can't go in there, even for Drak."

The words brought vomit to the edge of his throat. He had been unable to save Mojmir at Melkorka, and now, Drak would die too.

"I feel it." Adamus forestalled his gaze from the chamber. The beastly man's voice cracked as he retreated a couple steps, trembling. "I have fought hundreds, and now, there is this thought…" The hero-warrior dropped his axe to his feet. His hands balled into fists. "…it is useless."

"I say, pick up your axe, Adamus," Dorofej insisted.

While Dorofej's words were sensible, Branimir knew the tone of the black mage. The broken tenor reminded him of when he and Dorofej had faced *Ososcica*, the giant white snake, who lingered in the halls of *Heshayol*, in the Netherworld. They had lived long enough to laugh at Dorofej's rampant, girlish screaming.

Here and now, Branimir could not laugh.

Adamus bumped into Branimir, stepping backwards again, oblivious to Dorofej. "'Tis hard to admit my dread, but whatever lies in there is neither human or inhuman." His torchlight wavered, the light rescinding away from the darkness, and meandering back toward the passageway from which they had come.

"Please," Branimir whined, "say the word and we will flee. What else could we possibly do?" Words filled his mind and he repeated them, no matter how strange they sounded to him. "A single life cannot be worth our three."

"Hold fast to your wit, you must or you will be bound to this darkness," Dorofej commanded, stopping Adamus with his hand. "Neither of you are yourselves. Leave Drak to his fate here, we must not. No more than leave Bohumir on the dastardly road to Melkorka, yes? Stand fast!"

Drak's screamed filled with the gurgle from inside the chamber.

Adamus clutched his fist around the torch. For a moment, the Ariadnean hesitated under Dorofej's gaze. He finally spoke between clenched teeth. "What must we do?"

"Grab your weapon and be ready for whatever comes, you must," Dorofej inched closer toward the blackness.

"And, what about me?" Branimir asked, thankful that Adamus swiftly scooped his weapon back from the ground.

"If the darkness wanes, you find Drak and pull him free," Dorofej gulped. "And then we flee."

Branimir steadied his breath. His rib cage rattled with every gasp of air, bracing himself against the stone wall. The stench from the bodies at his feet strangely intensified, suffocating him. He did not know if he could grab Drak from the shadows. It may swallow him whole, too. "And, what if it does not?"

Dorofej did not answer, casting light within the tunnel, illuminating all but the gloom within the chamber. His light pulsated in the passageway. "Ancient devil, your name, tell me," Dorofej commanded at the impermeable shadow.

A hissing wind swirled from inside the chamber, shade forming upon shade. The gust blustered against Dorofej, causing his beard and robes to vacillate against his body. No shape formed but a crowing voice cackled, primordial and crashing against them. It sounded more like a god than a devil.

> *'One of the eight who dwell within,*
> *Named the old-dark akin to men,*
> *From nothingness, from earth and sky,*
> *From the Deep returned, called Likhyi.'*

"Likhyi," Branimir gasped, rattled by the eerie voice. His fear could have stopped his heart cold. He felt the sudden urge to kneel to the blackness, but somehow kept his feet beneath him. This spiritual essence held more strength than anything he had ever known.

"I say, the Ash Tree has not been destroyed, and still births life to this land. You have no power here, yes?" Dorofej cried. "Return to your casting. Depart from this place."

> *'Too weak the Ash Tree has become,*
> *When death returned wherever from,*
> *New gods die; old-dark born anew,*
> *What men made, the eight will undo.'*

"Underestimate, you do, the power of the gods, Likhyi. Too great for you to overcome, they are," Dorofej glowered,

"As done in days before our birthing, Marheena, Czern, Dahz, Svarog, Perom—"

'The time for salvation has passed,
The frost falls and fades by fire vast,
The age of the Likhyi returns,
The dark within endlessly churns.'

Drak's whimpering could be heard, but Branimir could not see the Kras beyond the bleakness. Even if he could, it would not matter. He was immobilized by the haunting words, struggling to make sense of their full meaning. The damaged Ash Tree had given the Likhyi enough strength to have some power, but it spoke as though there were a total of eight old gods to be released from the Ash Tree. Branimir could not imagine being in the presence of such powerful beings.

Where the concealed fiend seemed to respond in riddles, or perhaps prophecy, the next few words changed tone, addressing Dorofej directly. The shadows shifted from the depths of the chamber.

O' Dorofej Kaligula,
Ye accursed bloodline cursed Aenar,
Freeing the old-dark from afar.
Embrace sorrow and ever weep,
Now comes the Tree's eternal sleep.

Branimir perked his ears upon hearing the true surname of Dorofej, spoken by the *old-dark* deity, who knew what had long been kept unknown. *Kaligula.* Could Dorofej be a relation to this mysterious Dagmar Kaligula? Unmistakably, Dorofej had kept it secret for a reason, what did the Likhyi mean, saying Dorofej's bloodline had freed them?

The implications haunted Branimir.

"Enough! Unswayed by trickery, we are. Be away, I command you!" Dorofej shouted, using *Koldovstvo* to further irradiate the light against the black essence of the ancient god. The Likhyi screeched in pain, dipping back into the chamber. Branimir felt strengthened by black mage's display of power while the darkness diminished.

Branimir squealed, inching forward. The black mage held great power to withhold the might of a god.

The thought had barely been had when a howl suddenly absconded from the chamber and the Likhyi struck in full force, a haze emanating from the opening and shrouding Dorofej's magic. The colorless gloom flooded the hallway mightier than before.

Branimir screamed at Dorofej, urging him to fight. The black mage thundered in defiance. His hair whitened and the old Highborn Branimir had once known at Melkorka materialized before him. Branimir's howl did not lessen when he realized his friend would keep to his principles, killing himself to save all else. Yet though his magic flickered and waned, the light stayed against the devastating power of the Likhyi, and Dorofej still stood in defiance.

"Branimir!" Adamus's howl echoed from stone wall to stone wall as the Anshedar crashed down next to him, the blade of his axe cutting down, scraping and clanging, near his feet.

Branimir gasped, flinging himself sideways. There, from beyond the grave, lay a drooping corpse with its head split from Adamus's blow. Brains, grey and slimy, spilled across the stone. An exasperated moan escaped the carcass.

Before he could utter a word, the dead rose on either side of him, staggering to their feet. Skin sagging, eyes gaping, and insides spilling outright denoted the undead creatures. Unearthly yowls tremored against Branimir's ears. Chaos filled the catacombs.

Again, he found himself without a weapon in the battle. He could not fight the dead with his bare hands.

Adamus wasted no time. Finding his vigor, he flung the torch behind him into the masses of walking dead, and yanked his shield to his arm.

Dorofej roared with intensity against the strength of the Likhyi. The blackness bellowed from the chamber in waves like fog.

"Destroy them all, Adamus, you must," Dorofej groused, his arms shaking, fixated in place to maintain the energy of the delicate light. "Aid you, I cannot."

Branimir scuttled back, watching the Ariadnean slam his shield into the nearest moaning corpse, smashing it into the stone wall before driving the blade through its skull. The undead fell lifeless once more, and Adamus hurled his bulking frame into another without pause. His axe twisted and fell, carved and plunged, over and over into the army of undead that paraded through the catacombs.

The roars of the hero-warrior resounded. He sprung back and forth on either side of Dorofej with the strength and power that gave him the name of hero-warrior, tireless and true.

Branimir dipped from the reaching arms of another undead, and crouched behind Dorofej. He thought to scream for Adamus's dagger when he fastened his gaze to the leather belt of a fallen body. Four daggers rested in proper clasps near the buckle.

Luck had finally come to him.

He scrambled for the familiar weapons. Yanking them free, he did not look too closely at the bloodied carcass. Instead, he kept a wary eye on Adamus and Dorofej, who cried out mercilessly against their foes. With haste, he shoved two daggers in his own belt for safekeeping. Then, he gripped the two remaining and rose to his full height, hardly reaching Dorofej's waistline.

The mistakes of Cavell and the myling fled his mind.

The tempest from the Likhyi bayed in the midst with winds reeling the span of the underground tunnels, igniting life into all the dead inside. From beyond the immediate hall, the undead screeched and stumbled toward them, tripping over the dead collapsing under Adamus. The comatose creatures gnashed their teeth, bony hands flailing, with eyes hollowed from rot and rats.

Branimir launched himself into battle, comfortable with the dead while holding the daggers; he might as well have traveled back to the Netherworld. He stuck the nearest dagger into a nearby undead's leg, above the knee, and yanked it free. Ducking his shoulder, he avoided the monster's counter, and plowed the second dagger into the creature's gut, emptying its insides. Branimir stooped two steps back, and leapt forward again before the corpse could react. He had to get nearer to kill the creature. His foot found the corpse's thigh, giving him enough momentum to drive both daggers into the undead's chest. The corpse fell helplessly backward, slamming to the ground with a final twitch.

Pulling his daggers free, Bran flipped one to balance the blade between his fingers, and then hurled it into the eye socket of another corpse. He side-stepped, and tumbled, through the dead, slicing and stabbing, until he retrieved his blade from the gory skull.

"Help," Drak's voice rebounded through the bedlam. "Please…"

"Weaker, the Likhyi is becoming," Dorofej festered, the power of *Koldovstvo* dwindling, and the light shaking against the dark. "Claim Drak, you must, Branimir. Hurry."

Dorofej's cry had never been more desperate.

Branimir vanished, starting toward the chamber where the black fog swelled. Still, he could see nothing within, but at least Drak was conscious.

A corpse swayed in front of him, unknowing Branimir had approached him. He moved quick, cutting his daggers through the tendons on the back of the leg of the undead.

The monster crumbled and Branimir pierced his blade through the temple.

"Keep talking, Drak," Branimir yelled, staying invisible. "And I will find you."

"I don't know where I am," Drak snivelled. "I cannot see. I think my eyes have been taken from me."

"It is a dark magic," Branimir said, cutting down another walking corpse with the same method. Ashen blood colored the daggers from the disgusting monsters.

Drak cried out in pain. "Alack! Something has bitten me. Oh, it hurts."

Branimir could only think there was an undead monster within the chamber. He cried out from the doorway of the chamber. "Hold on."

He faced the shadow. And then, with grit, he stepped into the chamber.

No more had Branimir stepped beyond the opening, completely blind, than a green light emitted amongst the magical darkness. A female figure shaped within the burning light.

"The ghost..." Drak cried, curled beneath the apparition with his hands hovering over his leg. Blood oozed from a wound, but Branimir had no time to inspect the injury.

Inches away, crawled one of the undead. The neck looked broken, limply hanging against the shoulder with every vigorous lunge at Drak. The skinned fingers stretched, clawing for its quarry.

Branimir glided across the ground, ignoring the ghost, and plunging the daggers into the skull, felling it in a quick swoop. Drak yelled again, for although he likely had seen Branimir within the jaded light of the ghost, he had missed the monster coming for him.

"Be gone," the ghost screeched, ear-piercing, masking the room in her off-colored light.

At first, Branimir thought the spirit screamed at him, but realized her undead gaze was fixated on the shadow. She spoke to the Likhyi.

Drak whimpered next to him while he stared at the woman, empowered with some power in a realm beyond their own, battling against the ancient god. The power of her essence tore through the Likhyi. An unearthly sound rocked the shrine, and the remaining dead collapsed back to the ground wherever they stood. The blackness vanished and the Likhyi was gone.

Dorofej's white light vented from the doorway, connecting with the spirit's magic.

Dorofej lurched through the doorway, gasping, and barely able to stand. Adamus sprung to his side to give him a hand, stabilizing him against his oversized frame. Yet Branimir still found himself gawking at the woman who floated inches above him and Drak.

What seemed like a lifetime passed and Branimir's memory finally gave him the name he had forgotten.

Erzebeth.

Chapter XVI

Erzebeth Navenka, the skin-switching Vucari, who had once claimed she was from the northern ruins of *Anaerfell*, hovered serenely in the chamber in her ghastly form. She gazed indolently at them, eyes glossed over, lacking any sense of recognition. The brown eyes and dark hair had been replaced with shimmering greens, like emeralds embedded with pale light.

However, despite the difference, the woman was undoubtedly Erzebeth Navenka, who had joined them at Arkaim and traveled to Maharia to protect the Ash Tree, a thousand years ago. She had been missing her hand when she had come with them, punished as a thief by King Merreider Kar—before King Unnvar Grondahl took the throne. Branimir noticed both of her hands were intact in her current form, and as strange as this was, he could only focus on the ultimate fate which had befallen Erzebeth.

Branimir's stomach churned at the thought of her untimely death. She had been captured by the centaurs of the Hyaendi Hills, the Svet, before he and the others had been tricked into…eating her remains. He had done his best to push the memory far from his mind, but upon seeing her, it flooded back in waves.

"I am sorry," he murmured.

Drak kept his hands clasped on his wound and tried to scoot away from the spectral figure. She made no move to stop him.

"Is this the Likhyi?" Adamus doubted, still clinging to his weapon while trying to hold the black mage upright.

"No," Dorofej said, mustache pressed against beard in contemplation. He also recognized her, his blue eyes widening. "I say, how is it you have come to be here, Erzebeth?"

Again, her eyes stared at nothingness, but something moved her to speak. "I have not been called that name for a very long time, but how much time has passed I cannot say. For too long, I have been called the *Gal of Garain'l.*"

"They have written songs about you," said Branimir.

Motionless, she remained. "Do I know you? From what age have you come?"

"You *know* us," Branimir furrowed his brow in confusion. "But you died. Why have you not gone on to the Netherworld?"

Erzebeth drifted downward, her emotionless gaze resting on Branimir. "Ah, I remember now; though, it was so very, very long ago. The Kras from Melkorka, and the Highborn, who is not an Anshedar." She faced Dorofej and tilted her chin. "I refused to cross the Kalinov Bridge into the Nine Lands after my soul fled my body. I am not quite dead; I do not think. Though I am not living either. It was a fate I could not embrace, knowing what I knew."

"You kept yourself from death, even after you were killed?" Branimir choked. "How is that possible?"

"I am a Warden of the Ash Tree. I found the means to anchor myself to this world for time beyond time. In life, I thought I had known about the magic of this world, but in death, there has been new truth. I once believed *Koldovstvo* came from Wolos, and it was the source of my magic. I was wrong. Only the Stuhia and the Highborn use *Koldovstvo.* The magic of the Vucari is not the same."

Branimir interrupted her rambling. "But how did you stay here with your magic."

She hummed. "A tale for another time, perhaps."

Dorofej scrunched his face. "What is it you know?"

Her answer came without pause. "I told you I had lived for many years, traveling across Maharia and beyond. I may have said something when I had known you before about my adventures and what I had seen. I knew the Carian Council in Lairhein, and also the savants at *Anaerfell.* Did I not tell you why I had returned to Kalamaar?"

"Say nothing, you did," Dorofej said, trying desperately to stay on his feet with Adamus's help.

Drak groaned, holding his leg. Branimir noticed, the Kras tried to stifle the pain to hear the conversation. Branimir listened while tearing a strip from Drak's cloak and tying it around his thigh. The bleeding had slowed.

Erzebeth twinkled, fading slightly before radiating once more. She spoke as though she had a story, which she had waited a thousand years and more to tell. "The Second of Frost, 45 CE, I returned to *Anaerfell* after receiving a vision from Wolos. The Horned God had implied the Ash Tree was in danger. He called for the Wardens to return to *Anaerfell.*"

"To speak to him?" Branimir asked. "Since when do the gods come to Aenar?"

"He did frequently," Erzebeth said. "Each and every winter. He came to give blessing to the Vucari and to battle Marheena in the north until Strega would ultimately send her back to the Netherworld. But Wolos was slaughtered at *Anaerfell.* I was there; I saw it."

"You saw the God of the Dead die?" Drak wheezed. "How?"

"I saw two Stuhia fight him in the snows against the mountain," she explained. "I think they killed Wolos, but I cannot say for certain. I don't know if they knew their actions would cause demons to come back from the

Netherworld or the Ash Tree would be threatened, or..." she glanced around the chamber. "The Likhyi would eventually return. I am not even certain either of them knew who the Likhyi were. They had said the intent was to defeat death. I can only think they wanted immortality."

"Why did you not stop them?" Branimir howled.

Erzebeth replied without feeling. "You expect me to destroy those who can defeat gods. I am not great. I was Vucari. I did not hold the power of the dragon-slayers."

"What happened to these two men?" questioned Drak.

"They were imprisoned at *Anaerfell* under the guard of *Lahmia*. Likely, they are still alive, but weak. The Stuhia's blood allows them to be forever living as long as they do not cast *Koldovstvo*," Erzebeth explained. "Unlike the Vucari who change our shape at will but age as the Anshedar would."

Dorofej shifted in his robes. Adamus must have noticed because he finally let loose of the black mage, letting him stand on his own.

Drak held a curled fist again against the ground, swallowing a moan from the pain in his leg.

"I have answered your questions," Erzebeth said. "Now, answer mine before I go. Why have you come here? When we were last together, you were meant to protect the Ash Tree from Nedezhda, but the *old-dark*—the Likhyi—had come here to *Garain'l*. Did you fail?"

"Not entirely," Branimir responded when Dorofej said nothing. He had turned his gaze away from Erzebeth as though he were in deep thought.

"What does that mean? The Likhyi could not be here if their essence was not released from the Ash Tree," she said. "The gods had trapped the eight Likhyi in the Ash Tree to give life to Aenar."

"Part of it withered after it was struck by *kaelandur* but most of it remained intact." Branimir lost sense of who was in the room with him. He was mesmerized by Erzebeth's knowledge, wishing she had shared more with him when they had first met one another. "Though, the last Dorofej or I saw the Ash Tree, it was a thousand years ago at the battle of Shayol Domier."

"What?" Adamus bellowed. "What trickery is this?"

"Huh, you are talking about the pigsticker? And," Drak squawked, "stone the crows! Are you really Branimir Baran, from times long past? How is that possible? How could you have lived so very long?"

Branimir hung his head, realizing his error. The Kras spitballed question after question. There was no hiding who he was anymore. He used Erzebeth's words,."A story for another time."

"What is this thing you call *kaelandur*?" she asked.

Branimir raised his eyes to the green haze, hardly believing the question he was hearing. Though, when he thought hard enough, he remembered Erzebeth had most likely never seen the dagger or heard of it in her time with them.

Adamus and Drak eagerly awaited the response, watching Branimir.

"It is a copper dagger, created by the Highborn to behead Nedezhda Mager back at Melkorka," Branimir finally said.

Adamus said, "The knowledge of the Kras is ever amazing."

"A weapon?" Erzebeth lifted her voice for the first time, in shock. "A weapon was created by the Highborn?"

"Yes," Branimir said. He noticed Dorofej became more uneasy in his dark robes. He stared at the bodies littering the ground of the chamber.

"It must have been crafted with *Koldovstvo* then," she claimed, "or it would not have the power to cut through the Ash Tree. Only magic, gifted by the gods, could destroy it."

Branimir jarred his memory, nodding. "Nedezhda said Jhar, another Highborn, had created the dagger at Melkorka.

I remember her claiming he had crafted it with magic when we were at Arkaim.”

“Where is Jhar now?”

Bran lifted his head, troubled that he had to answer the questions. “He died in the first battle at Melkorka. I watched him fall.”

“You are certain he is dead?” Erzebeth asked.

“Yes.”

Erzebeth now focused her gaze on Dorofej. “Then, he did not create the weapon.”

“Alack! I do not understand what you two are going on about,” Drak mumbled, ridding himself of whatever fear had ailed him before. “How can you be certain?”

“The Highborn are not a natural race of men,” Erzebeth said. “They are born from the union of the Anshedar and Stuhia. The Stuhia, or dragon-men, is where they claim their power; it is where the power of *Koldovstvo* comes from.”

Adamus finally interrupted. “Tis interesting but what does it have to do with this *kae…kae…*this copper dagger?”

“The Stuhia culture forbids any of their kind to create weapons for this very reason. It has been as such since the First Age. Their magic embedded in armaments makes the blade unbreakable with one exception.” Erzebeth kept her eyes locked on the black mage. “It becomes destroyed when the maker is destroyed.”

“*What?*” Branimir shouted. “You mean to say if the Highborn who created *kaelandur* dies, the copper dagger will cease to exist.”

“Yes,” Erzebeth said.

Branimir’s mind riddled. There could only be one other who could have made the dagger. His eyes locked onto the black mage.

Dorofej. It made no sense. There had to be another explanation. Branimir had thought Dorofej to be furious at the creation of *kaelandur*. He had once even ridiculed Falmagon and Kinhar for its making.

There had to be something more to be said.

Dorofej at long last rumbled. "I say, Erzebeth, our quest here on Aenar is not yet done. The Ash Tree can still be saved and the Likhyi will be trapped again, yes? Something worthwhile, you should tell us."

The ghastly figure distended, rising toward the ceiling of the catacombs. Branimir could only guess Erzebeth spurned Dorofej's words. He suggested the information she shared had been worthless to them.

"You are ever wise," Erzebeth said in a mocking tone. "I trust you will find and protect the Ash Tree before further harm will be done. But the Ash Tree is weakening each day and the Likhyi are growing stronger."

"In what way is it becoming weaker?" Branimir wanted to know. "What is causing it?"

She had become emotionless again. "I do not know. I can only feel it."

The Vucari woman had begun to fade.

Drak tried to stand, and fell back down on his injured leg. "Where are you going?"

"To see whether Wolos is dead, and if so, that he is reborn. If you fail, the God of the Dead may be our only chance to defeat the Likhyi, and restore balance," she answered, and then she was gone.

"Impossible," Dorofej grunted, shaking his head at the ceiling where Erzebeth had disappeared.

"'Tis indeed," Adamus said, looking around the room at his companions as if seeing them for the first time. "The conversations had in the past few days have truly come to light. Czern's breath. The two of you are setting out for dark times."

Drak snivelled still, his hands wrapped around his leg.

Branimir ignored the Kras, looking to Adamus, hoping against hope the hero-warrior would join them in their fight.

He was disheartened by the Anshedar's words. "I will lead you to Ariadne, but there we must part ways. My past years have seen too much death, and now with Hanna…" he sighed, shuddering. "I cannot stomach it any longer."

"I say, you are required to do nothing, Adamus Ebordon," Dorofej dipped his head. "Already, learned much at *Garain'l*, we have; and survived, we would not have, without you."

Adamus stroked his beard. "Tis true, I suppose. Many dark things I have seen, especially when fighting against the desert people, but nothing like this. I have to ask, what was said when you and the Likhyi were speaking to each other?"

Dorofej started to open his mouth, but Branimir interrupted.

"I don't understand. What are you asking, Adamus?" Branimir scrunched his nose at the hero-warrior. "Could you not hear them?"

"Hear them?" Adamus lifted his hand. "The two were speaking in some abysmal tongue I have never heard before. Did you not hear it, Branimir? It sounded like a drowning demon, grating as constant thunder. Czern's breath! What was said?"

Branimir fingered *Ojenek* in his pocket, realizing the stone had allowed him to understand the conversation between the black mage and the Likhyi. It did have a purpose after all.

Dorofej returned with a smile. "I would prefer not to repeat such swearwords, yes? I say, let us rest and then leave at once for Ariadne. My artifact awaits, it does."

Month of Ice

Fifth of Frost

1351 CE

Chapter XVII

Branimir blew his breath into his cupped hands, and then tucked them into his red cloak. For three weeks, they had been trudging through the Dyndaer without any sign of Ariadne.

Adamus had guessed the trek to Ariadne would have taken a week or less from *Garain'l*. Though, this would have only been true if they had been traveling by horseback. Sadly, to their dismay, their mounts were found half-eaten by simargl just outside the stone archway. After regarding the gory scene, glazed with guts, they departed from *Garain'l* on foot.

The days and nights soon swam together, giving Branimir a sense of discomfort and disillusion. He could not remember how long they had been walking, or how long ago they had built a fire. He heard Adamus grumble ahead of him, likely having similar thoughts.

Again, he tried to warm his hands against the insides of his cloak, and caught sight of Drak limply lying across the Ariadnean's arms like an infant. Two days ago, Branimir had woken to find Drak feverish and unconscious. Adamus had carried him ever since.

Bran checked on him when he could. Every so often, Drak would wake—long enough to swallow a few snowberries or water—and then he would mumble incomprehensibly and fall asleep again. The last time, Drak's skin had felt hot to the touch, and his heartbeat had beaten so faintly, Branimir had struggled to find it. Dorofej, who had been completely exhausted from his battle with the Likhyi, did not have the magical energy to heal the poor Kras. If they did not reach Ariadne in the next few days, he feared Drak would die from his fever.

Branimir dropped his eyes to Adamus's feet, failing to see any city through the trees.

"Not much further," Adamus mumbled from under his beard. "A bit more."

Outside of his grousing, Adamus had murmured similar sentiments each day while they walked. Branimir gritted his chattering teeth. "We will make it."

Another three hours passed before the towering walls, as large as the trees of Dyndaer, caught Branimir's attention. Torches marked the tops and lanterns were situated around the base of the fortifications. The wall stretched as far as Branimir could see in either direction.

"At last, Ariadne," Adamus said, taking a breath. Drak still lay unconscious in his arms, curled up against his chest and ruffled, black beard. "Been three years since I have seen my sister. I had not thought the war campaign would have lasted so long." The Anshedar swelled his chest and exhaled again. He looked back at Branimir and Dorofej. "I suppose tis nothing compared to what you have lost. I cannot imagine what it would be like, knowing how long it has been since you have been with old friends or family, eh?"

Branimir forced a smile. His face was too frozen to attempt a suitable response. Instead, he said, "What time is it?"

"Tis well past supper time," Adamus guessed. "Likely closer to midnight."

Branimir's stomach rumbled. They had not stopped to eat since…he could not remember when they ate last.

Dorofej sludged forward, the snow crunching beneath his feet, urging them along. For once, he did not appear interested in lengthy dialogue. "Let us find a place to rest and then part ways, yes? I say, you need to reunite with your family, Adamus."

The Anshedar nodded, keeping his eyes fixated on the walls in front of him.

"I say, at least the trees have thinned," the black mage said, leading them toward the lofty gates. "Beginning to wonder if we would ever make it out of the darkness, I was. If it were not for the trees, I would think I was walking through the Netherworld again, yes?"

Branimir half-listened to Dorofej, finding it difficult to keep his eyes off the place stretching along the river. No buildings were raised higher than the walls, but with the gates opened, he could already make out the shops and houses.

Each building had been constructed from the same timber, without any hint of stone, built directly against one another.

"How far are we from Strega's Deep?" Branimir asked, turning his head to the south. He could almost smell the saltwater.

Adamus cleared his throat, uncomfortably shuffling Drak in his arms. "Tis a day, maybe a day and a half, from here on horseback. If you need a boat, there is an Ariadnean port at the mouth of the river, or you can travel further up the coast to a Lilitu city. That is, given nothing has changed while I have been away."

A cold chill swept Branimir's back. Hanna's dimming eyes stared back at him from nothingness. He did not want to face another Lilitu for as long as he lived. "I thought the Lilitu lived on another continent, in Haemus Mons."

"The bulk of them live in Haemus Mons, but the Lilitu have cities all along the coast of Maharia. Our two lands are connected, if you did not know. You will see as much if you plan to sail anywhere. Talastein is the largest Lilitu city to the east, and the largest port city in Maharia. Every boat passes through Talastein before venturing any further."

"What for?" Branimir asked.

"Inspection," Adamus said, repositioning Drak in his arms and following Dorofej through the gates. The handful of guards barely stopped the conversation they were having when they passed by. Branimir could only guess that visitors frequented Ariadne more often than a place like Cavell. The Anshedar continued, "The Lilitu have complete control on trade down here. If they think you are smuggling anything by them, they will take your head and feed it to the fishes."

Branimir gulped a mouthful of air.

"Worry about it, we will not," Dorofej said.

Branimir's feet crunched against the snow. The paths were perfectly squared between what appeared to be blocks of adjacent shops and houses. He noticed the shops were closed, and there were few people on the street.

Dorofej peered around the streets, possibly recognizing how late it was. "I say, we will take a boat north for Melkorka as soon as I have located Alden and Sulanna."

"Tis my hope they are still waiting for you, Dorofej. Ariadne is not the worse of places to hole up, but tis quite bleak in the winter," Adamus replied.

Bran had gotten the impression that the artifact Dorofej sought was important, but the black mage had still given him no indication as to its identity or purpose. He reminded himself to press for the details later, and instead, he asked, "What about Drak? Should we seek out someone to help him?"

"Look for Alden and Sulanna, first, we should," Dorofej said. "Besides, too late to find a human healer, yes? Look for one in the morning, we may."

Adamus grunted. "I agree. You won't find a healer at this hour."

Dorofej added, "But wait for Drak to recover, we must not. We should hurry for Melkorka and find the boy, yes?"

Branimir twitched his nose. He had been saying to pursue Bohumir since Cavell and had argued against bringing Drak since Ojenir. He hoped Dorofej's rationality had not come too late. Bohumir had been gone for over a month now. Anything could have happened to the boy.

"Here," Adamus stopped in front of a wide inn, *Greywood*, pointed towards the sturdy door. "Tis Hoda's place, and she'll do right by you. If your friends are not here, they might be over at *The Scythe and Chalice*, but I would not count on it. Her stewed mutton is worth the silver. Better than Gorg's oat biscuits."

"There are only two taverns in Ariadne?" Branimir asked. He twisted to look at the oversized keep towering above the buildings several streets away.

"No, no. There are dozens, but only two worth mentioning," Adamus grinned.

Branimir suddenly realized he did not want to part from Adamus. He rather enjoyed the Anshedar's company.

His stomach growled. "Well, I am ready to eat something. I am tired of boiling snow and chasing rabbits."

"Come on," Adamus stepped toward the door. "I will help you get settled."

The door closed behind them and the innkeeper waved them to the countertop. The place only had a few late-night patrons left, sipping at their mugs.

As they approached, the woman eyeballed Drak warily in Adamus's thick arms. "Welcome to *Greywood*. Name is Helda and..." she paused, raising her blue eyes. "Adamus Ebordon, is that you?" She pushed her long dark hair behind her ears, staring wistfully at the man.

"Helda," Adamus half-grinned, "tis good to see you. Is Hoda in the back? A bit late to still be cooking, eh?"

The young woman skimmed the tavern for a moment before returning her attention to Adamus. "Died from a sickness last year. I have been keeping up the place."

"Oh! I am sorry," Adamus said, his brow knitting.

Helda ignored the sentiment. "It is good to see you home, at last. Are these friends of yours? Need a room?"

Adamus nodded. "Friends, indeed. It has been a long road and they could use good food and a rest." He looked to Drak in his arms. "And, this one needs a healing touch."

Branimir listened, gladdened to be called a friend by Adamus. He felt pleased, too, that Dorofej had been included. After *Garain'l*, Adamus had said little to Dorofej about Hanna's death, who he had given blame. Something about the urgency of protecting the Ash Tree, and their encounter with the Likhyi, had resolved his accusations.

"I see," Helda grimaced at Drak. "Best keep him from my customers. Take him up to one of the rooms and I will call for Mira, the herbal healer, in the morning."

"Thank you," Branimir blurted. "Thank you for your kindness."

The innkeeper smoothed her apron, and then shooed them toward the stairs. "'Tis not a problem. I'll have a meal waiting when you come back down."

Adamus and Dorofej led the way up the stairs to the room, where they found two beds. After lying Drak down, Adamus left the room and returned with an extra bedroll from Helda. It only took a few moments to situate the room with Drak occupying the bedroll in the corner.

Afterward, Adamus excused himself, eager to find his sister. The farewell was quick with awkward waves. Adamus finally backed out of the room, wishing the best, and skittered away into the city of Ariadne.

Once Branimir checked on Drak again, the two eventually returned to the commons to eat. As promised, Helda had a meal ready as soon as they stepped off the bottom rung of stairs.

Song and storytelling had ended hours ago. Sitting alone in the *Greywood*, Dorofej and Branimir were served intermittently by Helda while she cleaned off tables and stools. Bran hardly noticed. The meal tasted better than anything he had eaten since Cavell, and soon, he had gulped down his stewed mutton and pecan bread. The wine he savoured was stale, but still more flavorful than melted snow. Dorofej ate with equal intensity, drinking three glasses of plum before suggesting they head back to the room to rest.

Branimir knew night would be turning to morning in a few hours. As tired as he was, he needed answers from Dorofej before resting.

He waited until they had reached the room and closed the door. While trying to formulate his question, Branimir checked on Drak, who looked sickly thin. His soft snores were muffled, speaking to what little energy Drak had left. His forehead felt warm, but not nearly as hot as it had earlier that morning. After several days, Branimir hoped the fever might break soon.

The bite on his leg from the corpse had scabbed over. It continued to seep yellowish fluid from the cracks in the hardened shell, but even it looked better. The skin around the mark had darkened against his red skin, but no longer had any tint of blue or green like it had a week ago.

"He will be okay," Branimir said, standing back to his feet and shuffling toward his bed.

Dorofej had not bothered to remove any garments, or even his boots. He simply threw himself down on the bed, bones creaking with the boards beneath. "Hoped they would have had feathered pillows, I did. Suppose there are no chickens to pluck in the Dyndaer, yes?"

Branimir shrugged, clasping his hands together in his lap and sitting down.

"What is the artifact, Dorofej?" Branimir garbled nervously. The alcohol had not jumbled his words, but his wits wavered when bringing up the question again.

Dorofej sat up, eyes bright beneath his bushy, white eyebrows. "Oh, Branimir," he smiled, teeth wide and cheekbones high, "the skull of Moreth, it is."

For what had seemed so secretive on the road from Cavell suddenly was expressed in the most jovial of moods.

Branimir winced.

The answer did not help him understand more. He sat there and blankly looked at Dorofej, who grinned back at him with purple, plum-stained teeth. The black mage clearly was sloshed on wine.

The name sounded familiar but Branimir could not place it. "What are you talking about? Who is Moreth?"

He chortled, "I say, Branimir, your memory is slipping from you. The Patrician of the *Kadari* when we were at Shayol Domier, Moreth was. Fled into the night when Falmagon assumed control, he did, and ventured south into the realms of the desert people, yes? There he learned the ancient, dark arts of *Runista* and acclaimed a power to restore youth without the Ash Tree, and soon after," Dorofej paused for emphasis, wiggling his eyebrows, "lost his head."

"How do you know all of this? We were trapped in the Netherworld for a thousand years."

"*Klukas*." Dorofej said plainly. "An eye on him, I had, and Falmagon. Ha!"

The black mage tittered, throwing himself back against the bed and almost smacking his head against the wall.

Branimir barely remembered the man who Dorofej spoke of, but did remember there being a leader at Shayol Domier so many years ago. It was a fleeting thought and hardly been important to him at the time.

"What is *Klukas*?" At every bend, Dorofej had another secret.

"A place which only the Stuhia can travel, it is," Dorofej said, finally admitting to his true birthing. "A place between this world and the next where the spirit can travel, yes? I say, we, Stuhia, use *Klukas* to scout ahead mostly, but long ago, I discovered the know-how to locate people."

"You can find anyone?"

"Hmm," Dorofej lifted his eyebrows, "unless they know how to hide themselves from the power of *Koldovstvo*."

Branimir gaped. "That is how you found me at Ojenir then?"

Dorofej nodded. "Worried of losing you, I never was, Branimir."

"And what about objects," Branimir urged, "can you find them too? The Ash Tree?"

The black mage shook his head. "Impossible, it is."

Branimir slumped his shoulders. "I don't understand why you hide your secrets from me, Dorofej. You could have said something even before we parted at Strahil. I was worried I'd never see you again." Branimir frowned, shaking his head. He watched his old friend lose himself in drunken laughter "Have you seen Falmagon?"

"For short while, I could," Dorofej said, holding back his snort, "but hidden from me, he has been."

"Why?" Branimir asked. The black mage quickly lost his laugh and scowled, leading Branimir to guess, "Dagmar Kaligula? Is that why? You are a Kaligula, too, are you not?"

"I said," Dorofej blinked. "Talk about Dagmar, I will not."

Bran clenched his fists. "Then, tell me, what are you going to do with the skull of a dead man?"

"Restore my life, I will," Dorofej said, sitting upright again with newfound youth. He admitted. "Of the Kaligula bloodline, I am, gifted with *Koldovstvo*, and more so, the crux to touch the void and the essence of living things. Reach through space and time to steal what Moreth gained in Haemus Mons, I will. His gift of youth I will take on myself, being young again, and then, venture to the Ash Tree, we will."

Branimir's jaw dropped. If he had trouble speaking before, the struggle was now tenfold. "I—I mean, you—the power is…" he took a breath. "You would kill yourself doing something like that, would you not?"

"Close to it, I may," Dorofej shook his head, "but know how to use *Koldovstvo*, I do."

"I thought you were a healer."

"Yes, yes," Dorofej nodded, "and lucky, I am, to have the gift of healing, too, but manipulating the void is in my blood."

He was shaking uncontrollably, pulling the pieces together. "So, at *Garain'l*, you…you knew you would not die? You knew there was a way to be young again once coming to Ariadne?"

"Never does one know whether death will come, but at Cavell, I had hope," Dorofej grinned, "when the Count told me of the letter from Sulanna. In *Klukas*, something at *Garain'l*, I saw. Either Erzebeth or the Likhyi, I think. I say, the time spent there was worth it, yes?"

Branimir instinctively looked to Drak, heaving in the corner, sweating. He wailed with words forming through the high-pitched scream, reiterating his question, "Why do you hide your secrets, Dorofej? Why could you not tell me?"

His smile dispersed. He took a moment, teeth clacking and lips parting. "I say, what has happened?"

"For a thousand years, there has only been you and me, and no one else." Dorofej paled instantly, and Branimir struggled to find his words. "I don't have anyone, Dorofej. I told you I don't want to die, but seeing you die is worse."

"Death has never been welcomed, Branimir, but come eventually, it will," Dorofej drew back, "even for me."

"No," Branimir flinched. "You have saved me time and time again. It is not fair that you can save me, and I cannot save you."

"I say, loss is something we all must learn, yes?"

"No," Branimir squealed. "You don't feel it. You keep me alive. Why? Why do you keep saving me?"

Dorofej swallowed, standing from the bed.

Branimir realized he had answered his own question. He leaned back. "You are afraid, too."

"Go find Alden and Sulanna, I must," he spurted out, lip quivering. He swayed slightly from the alcohol, keeping his eyes away from Branimir.

"Dorofej," Branimir pleaded.

The black mage staggered out the door and slammed it behind him.

Chapter XVIII

Branimir suspected he had not slept more than a couple hours. He had hoped the inn's bed would bring him some comfort, but after talking with Dorofej, he only tossed and turned. Groggily, he sat up on the bed. His eyes burned and his muscles ached. He swung his feet over the edge and faced Dorofej's featherless bed.

Branimir gritted his teeth. The other bed was empty, and from the looks of the unwrinkled sheets, Branimir doubted Dorofej had returned last night.

Drak mumbled in the corner of the room, trying to sit from his bedroll.

"Drak," Branimir said, nearly falling over in attempt to get to the Kras's side, "you are awake."

There was no response.

"How are you feeling?"

The Kras groaned, mumbling again. His hand fell on his head as he collapsed back down to his blankets. Branimir scrunched his nose, smelling what may have been sweat mixed with urine.

"Drak?"

As he approached, he noticed the Kras's hair stuck to scalp, soaked in perspiration. The moisture had seeped into the bedroll, and had also dampened the edges of Drak's clothes. His fever had definitely worsened.

Branimir removed the heavy blankets that lay over Drak's legs. "You are going to be okay. You are going to be okay." Branimir patted him, feeling his forehead. "I will get you some water."

Branimir paused his frantic hands, hovering over Drak in fear. "What did you say?"

Drak's eyelids popped open, eyes wide and blacker than usual, muscles tightening. His mouth popped open and closed like a fish, a strange sound emitting, like the undead moaning in the catacombs of *Garain'l.*

Drak's real voice sounded weak against the raspy wailing. "Please…no."

Branimir could not understand how two voices came from the single mouth.

"Hang on, Drak," Branimir cried. The Kras writhed on the ground, curling into a ball and clutching the bedroll against his chest. Again, his voice rasped.

Bran scooted back on his haunches, the words bellowing out of the small creature like some massive beast. "No, no, no." Branimir whispered to himself. The Likhyi had gotten *inside* of Drak.

Drak breathed heavily, cradling himself by the knees. He rocked back and forth, mumbling while squeezing his eyes shut. Branimir bumped into the bed.

"I am going to get help," he said, afraid to touch the Kras. "I will find Dorofej."

Branimir was up and out the door without bothering to grab his cloak or shoes. He pushed into the hallway, emptied, and rushed toward the stairwell that led into the common room. His feet were like thunder, no matter how small they were, slamming down the staircase and bursting into the wide-open setting where locals and travellers were eating their breakfast.

If the time were not as urgent, he might have enjoyed the scents of porridge, coffee, and fresh biscuits.

Several humans peered at him as he flung himself into the common room, but turned back to their meals without a second glance.

"Master Branimir," Helda, the innkeeper, acknowledged with her hands on her hips, chin cocked with her dark hair pulled up into a bun on top of her head. "There is no need to cave the house in with your stomping about. Breakfast is available whenever you want."

Branimir shook his head. "Where is Dorofej?"

"The bearded gent?" she motioned to the door. "Left hours ago. Spent most the night talking with a couple patrons, and headed out before first light."

"Alden and Sulanna?" Branimir remembered.

"Those are the ones," she grinned. "You know them, too. Well, I imagine you should, but tis not my business to go around handing out names freely."

"Where did they go?" His voice had elevated and several in the *Greywood* turned to look at him and Helda. "Did Dorofej leave me a message?"

"No, no message," she tensed her jaw. "Is something the matter? How is your sick friend doing?"

Branimir grimaced. "Not well. He could use some water, and…" Branimir looked about the room, almost wishing Dorofej would suddenly appear. "Did you send for the herbal healer?"

"I did." Helda widened her eyes, a dark blue like pending storm clouds. "Your friend does not have something catching, does he?"

"Nothing of the sort," he said, hoping he sounded believable. "Drak is not going to make anyone else sick, but I think it would be helpful for him to see someone very soon."

"I am certain Mira will be here as soon as she can. You can always go find her, but tis awfully nippy this morning."

He considered the idea, looking to the door. Drak might be fine in the room, unless someone heard him. Branimir was not sure if he should leave him or not.

Helda turned to return to her customers, grabbing his attention. "I will send her up when she arrives. Again, breakfast is ready when you want it."

He nodded, spinning on his heel. Branimir's stomach rumbled at the suggestion of food, but he could not think of eating right now. He scrambled back up the stairs, but with a lighter step, and pushed through the door to his room.

Drak had not moved from his fetal position in the corner, and seemed to be snoring softly. Branimir cursed at himself for forgetting a mug of water for Drak.

After a few minutes, he thought he should go find this Mira after all. He put on his cloak and boots, and checked his daggers.

He felt *Ojenek* press against his leg. He paused with his foot halfway in his boot. He had forgotten it was in his pocket. The realization rocked him. Drak may have been speaking in the abysmal speech and not regular language. Branimir could not be for certain, but it would confirm the Likhyi had embodied Drak.

Branimir reached for the door handle when it suddenly swung inwards towards him. He stepped back quickly to be met by the black mage, shrouded in his cowl and cloak. Dorofej wasted no time throwing back the black hood hiding his face. The old, wrinkled Dorofej with the white, tasselled beard had vanished, and the young, vibrant Dorofej had returned.

"Branimir, my friend," he cooed, pushing his red strands aside, "Moreth's skull restored me, it has. And now, pursue Bohumir, we must."

"Dorofej!" Branimir balled up his fists, snorting from his nostrils with irritation. "What has gotten into you? You left me alone all night with Drak."

He raised his eyebrows. "I say, gone to find Alden and Sulanna, I had, and found them, I did." He gestured to the hallway behind him. He looked Branimir over. "Going somewhere, you are?"

Before Branimir could answer, a middle-aged man stepped into the room from behind Dorofej. The man's white eyebrows came together arched over the thick arc of his raptorial nose. His head was bald and his beard was as flimsy as the flurries of mountain snow.

His light eyes pierced into Branimir. "So, this is the Kras. Peculiar creatures with their mountains and their stones. You have many secrets, Dorofej, and even stranger friends." He crossed his arms, studying Branimir.

Bran returned the gaze, seeing the falchion hooked to his belt and the long spear fastened on his back. The Anshedar stood a head taller than Dorofej, and although aged, was almost as burly as Adamus.

"Leave the Kras alone, Alden," a woman, who clearly was Sulanna, piped up from the back before stepping into the room. She glanced at Branimir for only a moment, disinterested, and scanned the room. "What is wrong with that one?" She gestured with her pointed chin, cupped by brown hair.

"Sick," Dorofej said, "since *Garain'l*, he has been. Bitten by an undead fiend, he was."

"It is worse than that," Branimir said, staring up at the three who crammed into the doorway. "He has a Likhyi inside of him. I heard it speaking only this morning."

"A Likhyi?" Alden huffed through his hooked nose, cringing his neck toward Dorofej. "An *old-dark*? What is going on here, Dorofej?"

Dorofej paused, staring with intensity at Drak in the corner. The Kras breathed heavily. The sweat dripping from his face glistened, even in the low lit room.

"Yes, tell us, what tale are we stepping into?" Sulanna questioned in her singsong voice. "For the past two years, Alden and I have risked our necks gathering your relics, betraying the Crimson Sun, and from what you shared last night, we have likely marked ourselves as enemies to the *Kadari*. It is near time your secrets are no longer secret."

"Correct, you are," Dorofej cleared his throat, "but if what Branimir says is true, we must make haste for Melkorka. We can speak on the road, yes?"

Alden argued with the Stuhia. "You have shown us a great many things in the past couple years, Dorofej. And, I admit, more times than not, your wisdom has kept us safe. Though if you want our swords on this quest, Sulanna and I need more than faith to ride on." Alden tilted his chin, taking only a moment to swallow. "Now, you told us last night we would need to go to Melkorka, but failed to tell us why. We should not have to wait any longer."

Sulanna elevated her tone. "For once, I agree with Alden. I do not answer to blind faith, Dorofej." She paused, raising an eyebrow at the black mage. "You have traveled with me long enough to know as much."

Dorofej groaned in defeat, looking away from his two companions. "Please do not take my silence over the years for faithlessness, but know you well, I did not. Honest with you, I have not been. The Ash Tree is dying, yes? A long while Branimir and I have spent trying to preserve it, and still, it falters. The only explanation for the Likhyi being freed, it is," Dorofej explained. "I say, Branimir and I have come to believe it is at Melkorka. The fight to save it from annihilation will continue there, yes?"

"Why would you think it is at Melkorka?" Sulanna asked. "No one in this age has heard of the Ash Tree beyond the legend. In truth, you have spoken of it more than any other in the known world."

"Most know too little of the Tree of Life to speak of it," Dorofej said, "but exist, it does. Proof of its existence, I am. Drank from its waters and restored my youth many times, I have."

"It is true," Branimir said. "I have seen it."

Alden turned his gaze to Sulanna, grumbling, "We saw what he did with the skull, Sulanna. There is no reason not to believe him. When we met, I thought him to be just a boy, but he would have had to live several millennia to know what he knows."

Sulanna folded her hands. "I am not questioning his knowledge or his claim, Alden, even if it sounds farfetched. I want to know fighting the *Kadari* is worthwhile. It will be the end of us, you know?"

"Svarog will bless us, Sulanna," Alden said. "If our deeds are righteous, Svarog will bless us."

The woman scowled in response. "Keep your god out of this, Alden. There are no pearly gates waiting for me. If I am going to die for something, I need to know why."

"Listen," Dorofej interrupted, redirecting with a sense of urgency, "Tell me, who is the Patrician of the *Kadari*?"

"Patrician Sej," Alden answered, taking the bait. "It has always been a Sej in my lifetime, and the lifetime of my father."

Dorofej nodded with enthusiasm. "And lifetimes before his, yes? His name is Falmagon Sej, and he has been the only Patrician of the *Kadari*."

"The same man?" Sulanna asked.

"Yes. I say, how else do you think he and the other *Kadari* have maintained their power of *Koldovstvo*—and their youth? The answer is clear, yes? Power over the people of this world, the *Kadari* hold, because their access to the Ash

Tree. Freedom the Likhyi found because of Falmagon's greed."

Branimir cringed at hearing the Highborn Long-Walker's name. He could not believe Falmagon had found the means to stay alive for a thousand years.

"Very well," Sulanna finally said, "but what does that all mean?"

"I say, the world will perish indefinitely if the *Kadari* continue to destroy the tree," Dorofej said plainly. "Stop them, we must."

Sulanna swallowed, lowering her chin for the first time since entering the room.

Alden straightened his back. "Do you need further reason, Sulanna."

Sulanna's face paled indicating the weight of Dorofej's words. She shook her head.

"What about Drak?" Branimir asked, pushing Falmagon from his thoughts. "There is an herbal healer in town. I was going out to find her before you came back."

"If Drak is as you say, help him, she cannot," Dorofej said. "Best to leave him here, yes? Too dangerous for him to accompany us, it will be."

Branimir stammered. "From the start, I said he should not have come, but we cannot leave him without anyone to care for him. He will die."

Dorofej glanced behind him, already speaking, "Death would be a blessing to what he will undergo with a Likhyi under his skin, yes? I say, we must do what must be done, Branimir." Dorofej reached into his robes and displayed *kaelandur*. "Remember what is at stake, we must."

He slammed *kaelandur* down on the table next to the bed. Branimir stared at the copper blade.

"The dagger from the Hyaendi Hills," Sulanna acknowledged, raising her chin once more. "Have you learned of its purpose?"

"Mm," Dorofej nodded. "Always known, I have."

"You lied to us," Alden rumbled, eyebrows rising.

"Forgive me, you must," Dorofej responded. "Created with the purpose to slaughter an evil magus, it was, but has since been tied to ancient prophecies. The talisman for the *Kadari*, and an object capable of destroying the Ash Tree, *kaelandur* is."

"The gods are at play?" Alden mused. "If the *Kadari* held the weapon, Dahz might be able to keep Marheena and the *old-dark* trapped. The dead would pile up in the Netherworld for eternity. But if the Ash Tree is pierced by its blade, the dead will find reprieve in the world of the living."

Branimir scrunched his nose. "I don't understand. If the *old-dark* are released from the Ash Tree, won't they kill the other gods anyway?"

"Marheena would have no choice if the Netherworld is flooded with the dead," Alden explained. "If the God of the Dead is really dead, as people say, there is none to take the souls to Thrice Ten Kingdom. Marheena is inundated with the dead."

"I cannot believe I am even listening to this," Sulanna hung her head. "Even if I were to pretend gods cared about this world, the argument does not make sense. Why would Marheena release the Likhyi if their intent is to kill her? Do the gods not have any sense of self-preservation?"

"Misunderstand the gods, you do," Dorofej swallowed, before reiterating what Branimir had heard many times. "Correct, Alden might be. If unbalance is found, a new balance is sought by the gods. The Frozen Goddess has her part to play in the cycle of our existence. Broken, the sequence is, and fixed, it must be."

"So, we are to die by the hand of the Likhyi?" Branimir huffed. "Is that what you are saying? We should go to Melkorka and destroy the Ash Tree ourselves?"

"No, no." Dorofej pulled at his robe.

"Then, we destroy the dagger?" Alden asked.

Branimir covered his face at the thought. He knew they could only destroy the dagger by destroying the creator, considering what Erzebeth had claimed.

"No, destroy the dagger, we cannot," Dorofej said. "We will stop Falmagon from destroying the Ash Tree, yes? And keep the dagger hidden from the world forever, we must."

Sulanna clenched her jaw, clearly disbelieving the entirety of the story. "I am finding this all difficult to stomach, but I will play along. You are suggesting an eternal deadlock? It seems far easier to find the maker, as the Kras suggested, and slit his throat."

Dorofej gulped. "A month ago, Branimir and I ran into an old friend, yes? Suggested a way to bring Wolos back from the dead, she did. Do our part, we must, and hope against hope she does hers. Balance will be reclaimed, yes?"

Erzebeth.

Branimir lifted his head, having no understanding how the Vucari ghost would accomplish such a feat. Though, if Dorofej truly was the creator of *kaelandur*, it was the only scheme that left him alive. Branimir did not want to see Dorofej dead.

"Very well," Alden consented, while Sulanna grunted nearby, "but it makes little sense to flee to Melkorka while holding onto the very *thing* the *Kadari* are seeking. Should we not be fleeing to the south with the dagger, far from their reach?"

Before the black mage could respond, Branimir interjected, looking to the table, "Where is *kaelandur*?"

Dorofej spun around frantically, while Sulanna timidly asked, "Where is the other Kras?"

"Drak…" Dorofej looked to the door, still standing open. "Invisible, he must be. Branimir, find him!"

Branimir bolted from the room, racing down the steps into the commons of *Greywood*. He saw the front door slam shut as he hit the bottom rung of stairs. Helda's shouts to slow down echoed behind him.

Flinging himself into the wintery streets, Branimir peddled onto the snow-layered cobblestone. People ambled up and down the road in all directions, including the patron who had just left the inn.

The walls around the city blocked the wind, but the cold could not be ignored. Branimir's fingers quickly went numb and gooseflesh pimpled his legs even beneath his trousers. He ran willy-nilly through the streets, pass the *Scythe and Chalice* and several shops of trinkets. Desperately, he looked for small footsteps in the snow.

It was hopeless. Drak, possessed by the ancient devil, had taken *kaelandur*.

Chapter XIX

Dorofej sat against the wall within the small bedroom of the *Greywood*. His eyes were glazed over, as though he may have been sleeping, breathing softly through his nose. Alden and Sulanna stood near him like two sentries guarding a chest of silver.

Bran paced the room nervously, glancing at Dorofej as often as he dared. He had returned to the tavern and had told the three of Drak's desertion. Dorofej had wasted little time in falling into this trance-like state. The black mage had said something about locating the missing Kras with *Klukas*.

Dorofej had talked of *Klukas* just last night. He had said it was a place between the fabric of this world and the next, somewhere only accessible by the Stuhia people. Dorofej had not only used *Klukas* to find Branimir at Ojenek, but had also used it to keep an eye on Falmagon.

Branimir's head hurt from thinking too hard. When had Dorofej lost sight of Falmagon? When they were in the Netherworld? The black mage never did say. If the Ash Tree were at Melkorka, would Dorofej had seen it when he saw Falmagon?

"How long must this go on?" Sulanna said, sitting up from the bed. "He has been like this for hours."

"So sorry the timing is not appeasing you, my sweetness," Alden mocked, leaning against the wall. "Would you like me to send for a fresh pot of tea, or perhaps, a flutist to help pass the time?"

"Oh, please, would you?" Sulanna swooned with sarcasm, raising her voice. She curled her upper lip losing all sense of being ladylike. Her words were iced over, "I don't understand why you continue to mock me. I have not been in my father's house for the better part of a decade."

Alden grunted. "Once a noble, always a noble."

"For all your blathering about the gods and forgiveness, you truly are merciless, Alden," Sulanna said. "And, may I add, you are making a great impression on the Kras, you crabby, old man."

"I am not a god," Alden said, like it gave him permission to be unforgiving He shifted his blue eyes to Branimir and harrumphed, settling back in his chair. He pulled his own belt knife from its scabbard. "Besides, the Kras doesn't have the mind to be impressed or otherwise by what men do. It is not in their nature. The red broods find fascination that men do anything at all."

The claim caused Sulanna to lift her eyes to Branimir as if expecting a rebuttal.

Branimir lifted his shoulders to his cheeks. "It's true." It had been quite some time since he had heard anyone call him a *red brood.*

Suddenly, Branimir caught sight of Alden's left forearm. The deformed arm was laden with scars. The older man did not seem to favour the arm, but the disfigurement was beyond evident. Branimir wondered how he had not missed it earlier.

The coarse skin could only be described as ugly from the elbow to the wrist with indentions and blotches of white daubing his pinkish skin.

Alden took his knife, held it against his forearm, and sliced the blade through the film of flesh. Blood trickled and dropped to the floor.

"What are you doing?" Branimir exclaimed, stepping back nauseously.

Sulanna exhaled noisily and said, "Pay no attention to Alden and his nonsense. Those pockmarks are more from himself than from his enemies. He claims it to be a reminder of mistakes he has made toward his make-believe morals."

Branimir retorted with bewilderment. "But why now? I did not see any mistake."

Alden remained stone-faced, carving another bleeding wound into his arm.

She rolled her eyes, apathetic to Alden's behavior. "He probably didn't say his prayers this morning."

"Not funny, Sulanna. The laws of the gods are not pretend," Alden barked. "You will learn soon enough. Wait until you are judged in the Beyond. Your eyes will be opened to the signs you have chosen to ignore."

Sulanna shook her head. "I don't question there being order to the way things are, Alden, but it's not your way. Even if the gods did create our bodies, they did not do so for us to mutilate them in repentance."

"The body is a simple vessel," Alden said, putting his blade away. Branimir had to look away from the blood. "The real work is done within our spirit. What I do lifts my spirit to greater heights, giving me sanction to enter Thrice Ten Kingdom. Why can you not understand this?"

"Do you not have any duty to lift others up?" Bran asked, almost afraid to enter the conversation.

"Whether other souls make it to the Beyond or not is not my problem," Alden replied.

Sulanna blinked, glancing at Alden's arm before lifting her eyes to the old man. "There are many things I want to understand. But I have no interest in torturing myself."

"You are selfish," Alden said.

"Selfish? You just said you only worried about your own soul," Sulanna mocked.

"You are selfish when it comes to your relationship to the gods. That is the only relationship which matters in the end," he retorted.

"Our relationship doesn't matter?" she challenged.

"Yes, of course," he said, "but it is nothing compared to my allegiance to my faith."

"So much for being humane," Sulanna said.

His throat rumbled. "This is sacrifice, Sulanna."

"It's stupid."

Branimir watched the back and forth in shock. He regrettably brought attention to himself by covering his mouth with abhorrence.

Alden turned his frustration on the Kras. "And, what of you, Branimir? How do you see the gods? What does life mean to you?"

Branimir's mouth dried at the sudden question. He barely thought of these things. He spent most his days trying to survive to the next, not contemplating over the meaning of his existence.

Dorofej stirred, gasping for air and clinging onto his darkened robes. His abruptness interrupted the need for Branimir to respond to the old Anshedar.

"Dorofej." Branimir sprang to his side, putting a hand on the black cloak of his friend. "Are you okay?"

Through heaved breathes, Dorofej said, "Fleeing north by pony, Drak is, making his way for Melkorka. I say, the Likhyi has taken full control of the poor Kras. Little, if anything, remains of the Drak we knew."

"No," Branimir mouthed. "The Likhyi goes to destroy the Ash Tree and gain full freedom."

"I will gather the horses and we will set the pace to intercept him," Alden pushed off from the wall. "The *old-dark* can be stopped. It has little power in the Kras."

"You did not see its power at *Garain'l*," Branimir muttered under his breath.

"No," Dorofej shook his head, speaking over Branimir while catching his breath. "Catch him, we cannot."

"In the middle of winter? In the snow?" Alden fired the questions in disbelief.

"Quite." Dorofej nodded. "Possibly powered by the Likhyi, he is. Make our way south to the shoreline, we must. Find a ship, yes?"

"You want to sail around the bulk of Maharia for the shores of Melkorka," Sulanna reasoned. "You hope to beat the Kras by sea?"

"Another choice, we do not have," Dorofej said.

Sulanna scoffed.

"Come," Dorofej said, pulling himself to his feet, light and agile in his youthful appearance. "With haste, we must move, if we are to outdo Drak."

Alden set out to ready the horses while Sulanna packed his and her belongings. Dorofej sent Branimir to the commons to speak with Helda, since the black mage was unrecognizable in his boyish state. Branimir used Dorofej's silver to purchase rations from the innkeeper.

Within the hour, the four of them were riding out of the wooden gates of Ariadne.

Branimir was nestled on the saddle with Dorofej on a brown horse. Alden took the lead on his darker brown gelding, and Sulanna kept at the rear atop her black mare. They had only made it fifty paces up the snowy path before shouting erupted behind them.

"Dorofej, Branimir. Wait!"

Branimir twisted in the saddle, recognizing the voice of the hero-warrior from Ariadne. "Adamus."

"I am coming with you," he cried, galloping forth on his own black steed. His dark cloak bounced around his strong frame while he quickly gained on their small caravan. He directed his horse in step among their own. Adamus almost fell from his saddle seeing the black mage. "Dorofej, how have you become young again?"

Dorofej smiled, "The artifact I sought has given me the strength for what is to come, yes?"

Adamus bounced his head, his beard waggling. "I had spoken too hastily at *Garain'l.* You must forgive me."

"What of your sister?" Branimir questioned, paying little mind to the inquiring looks of Alden and Sulanna.

"My sister is well and she knows my nature." Adamus avowed, "War is what I know, and knowing your quest, I can't abandon you."

Branimir said, "There is no guarantee of coming back, Adamus. You may never see your family again."

Dorofej nodded. "I say, it is much to ask."

"Please," Adamus held out his hand.

"I have no qualms in having another among our numbers," Sulanna interjected.

"The man seems certain in his conviction," Alden said. "Every blade we can gain is worthwhile, especially one who hails from Ariadne. But does he know the full of what he is asking?"

"Mostly. Share the rest with him along the way, we will." Dorofej clasped Adamus's outstretched hand.

Chapter XX

Branimir inhaled the strong scent of ocean water on the frigid breeze. The horse beneath him and Dorofej stamped through the snow with the other mounts, clamoring toward Strega's Deep. From where he sat, he watched the road along the river. The path was clear from any sign of life, and the snow and trees seemed to stretch for miles.

Dorofej provided Adamus the details regarding Drak and *kaelandur*. After what had transpired at *Garain'l*, Adamus hardly seemed surprised by the information. He had only tugged at his beard and grunted when Dorofej paused in his telling.

After a long day's ride in the cold, and with the promise of reaching the Ariadnean port in the morning, they settled for camp late that evening.

While in camp, the warmth of *Greywood* was a fleeting memory. Winter's chill pierced through Branimir's flesh and touched his bones as if he were without skin. He could only guess the single night of warm fires and hot foods had made the cold seem worse. Yet drops of sweat still slid down the back of his neck, causing his hair to stick to him like a wet cloth. He could not identify the reason for the unwarranted perspiration but found a certain familiarity while sitting near the riverside.

His mind flooded to the myling south of Cavell. The last thing he wanted was another scenario with the impish beasties.

The frozen river bed and the darkened forest were quiet, save the clopping of horse's hooves. Alden had just fed the mounts and made his way back to the small campfire.

Adamus sat near Branimir with his silvery axe across his lap. He must have had similar thoughts as the Kras. "We should stay awake and watch the camp. I'll take the first watch with Branimir."

"I will take second watch with Dorofej," Alden said, removing the spear from his back and laying it behind him on the hardened ground. "We will let sweet Sulanna get her precious sleep."

Adamus, who had picked up on the temperament of the two's relationship, remarked, "Careful, Alden. She is likely to cut off your bits if you keep at it."

Sulanna situated herself with her back against a tree, settling against the hardened ground. "Not like he has ever used them anyway. He'd be more motivated if I threatened to take his sword."

Adamus cackled deep in his chest. "A difficult tossup, to be sure."

A frosty wind sputtered through Branimir's green cloak, flapping it around him. He readjusted the hood over his head with a shiver and scooted nearer to the fire.

Dorofej sat on the other side of him, unmoved by the humor and the cold, looking intently into the fire.

Branimir ignored the Stuhia. The black mage had been quiet for the better part of the day. "If it is this cold on the coast, I can only think how cold it will be on the ship," Branimir said.

Sulanna assented. "It will be miserable."

Branimir leaned back to gaze at the far-reaching sky through the few overshadowing branches above. The trees had thinned considerably through the day, looking less and less like the Dyndaer. The trees had likely been cut, not only to build Ariadne, but also to add to the ships at the promised port ahead. The stars were visible again, distant sparkles. Unlike the others, the world was still visible for his eyes.

His mind wandered. He considered his companions were anything but heroes, and yet, they sought out to claim the title. They had ignored the Count's request to find his daughter's *killer*, lost Bohumir to the Crimson Sun, and had, most certainly, failed Drak. He had seen Adamus meddling in dark magic. He believed Dorofej to have created the very dagger which threatened all of creation. And, according to Alden and Sulanna, the *Kadari*, the most accepted and most powerful leaders in the world, were their enemies. Yet they still ventured forward with the sense that they would do something great, something memorable.

A mild push on his shoulder snapped Branimir from his thoughts, "Don't fall asleep on me. Adamus whispered.

Branimir sprang back to the moment, glancing around the campsite. Dorofej, Alden, and Sulanna had already nestled down for the night. The two men were snoring.

"Sorry," Branimir said. "I was thinking about what makes a person a hero."

Adamus pulled at his beard. "How so?"

Branimir sat up, realizing the hero-warrior from Ariadne, likely had the answers he sought. "I guess I am unsure how to measure heroics. Is it about triumph or defeat?"

"Both and neither," Adamus said, relaxing his hands in his lap. "You do not have to be victorious to be heroic. In the same way, having victory doesn't always earn the name hero. You do what you think is best and leave judgment for the gods."

"What do you mean?"

Adamus answered, "Take the war with Uvil, for instance. When we abandoned the battlefield at Raybin, it had been taken by the Uvil. They had sacked the city, and we had to flee back to Draha."

"The Uvil were victorious," Branimir chimed.

"Sure, they had won the battle; and they continue to win *this* war," Adamus admitted, "but they are not heroes, not to me."

"They must be heroes to their own people," Branimir replied.

"Indeed. That is my point. Tis the same in how we Ariadneans are called hero-warriors by the Anshedar for fighting the Svet in the early wars," Adamus said. "Do you think the Svet call us heroes? No, they call us murderers, rogues, and worse."

Branimir held his head, recalling all he had heard from Adamus over the past month. "So, what does make a man a hero?"

"Being a hero is in here," Adamus touched his chest, "and here." He touched his forehead. "Being a hero is doing what you know needs done, even when standing alone; and when facing defeat, you stay standing."

Branimir thought of his sleeping companions around the fire. "I think we are doing that."

Adamus chuckled. "I would not be here if I did not think so. Now…" he settled back, again. "Tell me about Melkorka."

"That was a very long time ago," Branimir said, surprised by the sudden question.

"But you are the Branimir who Drak thought you to be," Adamus said. "I do not know the history of the Kras, but Drak seemed to think it was important. Besides, tis a tale I would like to hear, and I can think of no better way to spend the next few hours."

The coals of the fire crackled. The snow had melted, skirting the charred wood.

Branimir stood and stepped lightly to gather another log from the pile collected earlier. He took his time, considering Adamus's question. Dropping the wood onto the embers, he watched the sparks dance.

"What do you want to know?" he asked, after sitting cross-legged near the flames. The smoke spiraled toward the tree tops.

Adamus hummed in his throat. "'Tis hard to ask anything specific when I know nothing. Tell me about Melkorka."

"Melkorka," Branimir reminisced, "is a castle built near the Crags of Kazimir on the island of Folkmar, one of the Seven Islands. At one time, I thought it was the grandest place in all the world, but the world has grown. Now I think about it, Ariadne's keep is larger than Melkorka. I have not been there since coming back to Aenar."

"Where were you?" Adamus insisted.

Branimir raised his eyes to the bulky man. "I thought you knew. Dorofej and I were stuck…in the Netherworld." Adamus's jaw fell open, staring hard at Branimir. "We were there for over a thousand years."

Adamus narrowed his gaze. "I am unsure whether to believe you, but it would be a strange thing to lie about. A thousand years is a long time to keep alive… Then again, Dorofej looks nothing like he did at Cavell or *Garain'l*, and I could not guess at your age."

Branimir smiled. "The Kras usually live a long time, sometimes five hundred years; and the Stuhia, it seems, live even longer if they can keep themselves from touching *Koldovstvo*, which is the source of their aging. But time passes differently in the Netherworld altogether. I am not sure Dorofej or I aged a day in the time we were there, even when he cast his magic. We did not really know how much time had passed until we returned here."

"Did you fight demons?" Adamus said incredulously.

Branimir held his smile, looking at the Anshedar's expression. "It would have been hard to escape the dead without killing a few."

"I imagine so," Adamus flashed his teeth, "and even harder to kill what had already been killed. Though, I cannot imagine what it would be like to see the frozen wasteland, and then to return to Aenar. Did you see Marheena?"

"Thankfully, no," Branimir answered, twisting back to the fire. "But the place was scary all the same. Still," he paused, almost afraid to admit what he had thought many times before. "I miss it sometimes. It was surreal being there amongst the demons in the cold. And the *Tower of Eresh* was huge, even greater than Melkorka."

Adamus scratched his beard, a look of puzzlement painted on his face. "I do not know what the *Tower of Eresh* is, but I believe you. I imagine I would be overwhelmed by a place ruled by the gods, even if it were Marheena's abode. I wonder at how much more grand the Thrice Ten Kingdom would be."

"I had never thought of that," Branimir pondered, sucking air in through his cracked teeth. "That *is* something to think about. It is scary to think that none will ever see it again."

"I was thinking the same thing after Dorofej told me the full of what was happening. If Wolos is dead, there is no one to lead the dead to the afterlife. We all will become the pawns of Marheena." Adamus swallowed.

Branimir said, "Were you not speaking to your dead family members at *Garain'l*?"

"Yes," Adamus disclosed, "but I did not know to ask questions of Wolos, and even if I did, the dead don't necessarily know everything because they are dead."

Leaning closer to the fire, Bran warmed his hands. He remembered how confused Nedezhda had been when she returned from the Netherworld. She surely did not know everything.

Adamus added, "Tis sad to think Hanna might be in the Netherworld now, already being warped by Marheena's magic."

Branimir could only shake his head. The thought was something he had not considered at all. "Didn't she worship Marheena—or Lilith—as she called her?"

"In a way, yes," Adamus admitted, "but it did not make her evil, nor did it suggest she should be chained to the Netherworld in death. She respected Marheena for the role the goddess has in the cycle of life and death. Many also find Czern to be evil in nature, who I pay homage, but does that mean I am evil or should suffer indefinitely?"

"Mm," Branimir wondered. "I suppose not."

"I would hope not." Adamus chuckled. "Many think one god to be greater than another god, instead of recognizing each god has its purpose. If one were to not exist, the entirety of the system would fall apart. All would lose their purpose."

"Like Wolos," Branimir said at the simple realization. "I think Dorofej would agree with you."

Adamus glanced offhandedly at the Stuhia. "'Tis the same way we teach men to fight in battle. Stand together or crumble."

Branimir knew not what to say, and Adamus quickly continued as though he had another question he had been meaning to ask.

"Were you always at Melkorka, Branimir? I mean, did you have another place you called home?" He watched Branimir with admiration, intently.

Branimir squirmed a bit under the gaze, but found himself excited by forming a real friendship with the Ariadnean. He had never talked to another about these things besides Dorofej. He was glad Adamus had decided to come with them.

"For a long while, I was a slave to the Highborn and Melkorka was the only home I had known. My people had come from cities within the mountain. I eventually had the chance to visit one of them. It was not what I had expected it to be—to be honest." Branimir rubbed his pointed nose, thinking of *Illuard*. "Melkorka is probably the closest thing to home I have known, but really no place in this world has ever felt like home. Maybe—maybe that is what Thrice Ten Kingdom will be. Do the Kras go there, too?"

A thin smile twisted the lips of Adamus. "I would think so, Bran. Thrice Ten Kingdom is reserved for all living creatures. That is, if we can find a way to restore this imbalance."

Branimir smiled. "Good. I wish the way of things was clearer for us to understand. It is awfully hard trying to figure it out on our own."

"Tis why we have friendship, methinks." The flames finally melted the frost on the wood and wrapped around the log. Smoke rose from the campfire. Adamus continued, "How else can simple men," he glanced to Sulanna with a raised eyebrow, "and women, aim to be heroes. There is nothing which suggests we will be successful, and in the same breath, how can we not be?"

"I think," Branimir gulped, reflecting on Adamus's question, "I think, if history teaches us anything, our success or failure will depend on what we are willing to sacrifice."

Adamus nodded to the Kras, the blazes of the fire reflecting against his blue eyes. "Tis likely it cannot be any other way. But is it important whether we win? Every race looks for meaning in life, discovering their charge. Tis the hardest thing for any to do. But at the same time, tis a struggle we all share. I am saying the real fight is finding friendships, and then, despite it all, holding fast to them."

Chapter XXI

Sulanna's small frame silhouetted against the morning sunbeams. She tenderly nudged Bran's shoulder waking him from sleep. "Come, Branimir. A short road this morning to the Ariadnean port, and then onward to Melkorka."

Branimir blinked several times, taking in the warm sunrays penetrating through the tree line. The light was nearly blinding to Branimir. He shielded his eyes, faintly hearing the drops of melted ice pattering around him.

"Spring comes early this year," Adamus said, scooping up his bedroll from near Branimir's bedside and carrying it to his horse. "This is the warmest morning I remember in months."

"Could not have come at a better time either." Alden grunted in agreement, gathering his own items from where he had kept watch for the remainder of the night. "The warmer the weather, the smoother the sailing will be in the north."

"I, too, had wondered about sailing through ice chunks," Sulanna added, eyeing the frozen river. "I know there is a joke about Alden's god in all of this, but I am too tired to think of anything."

Alden grumbled. "I don't want to hear it. You have slept more than the rest of us."

Dorofej overlooked them, with his hood thrown back, already settled into his saddle. He motioned for Branimir to hurry while Sulanna climbed onto her horse. He looked back the way they had traveled and then toward the riverbank. "I say, Drak rested little during the night. Pushing him, the Likhyi does. We must hurry, yes?"

"Does anyone else find it strange that Dorofej roams the countryside watching people when we think he is sleeping, or is it just me?" Sulanna smirked.

Branimir stifled a chuckle.

Alden picked up his pace, fastening his own pack to the gelding. He swung himself over the animal, pulling at the reins. "Let's not waste time with Sulanna's blathering. We will not sit by while the *old-dark* undoes what the gods have done. This world was created for men, not demons."

Sulanna waved a less than inviting hand gesture at her long-time companion, while gripping the reins with the other.

Branimir gathered his belongings and raced to the brown mare. Dorofej snagged his pack and tied it off. Then, he hoisted Branimir up onto the saddle with ease.

Adamus made his way to the front of the fellowship, guiding his horse with equal eagerness. "Onward then. Let's hope there is a boat awaiting at the docks."

Branimir groaned. He had not realized they might arrive at the dock and find nothing to sail on.

The next hour felt like a year to Branimir as they raced towards the shoreline. The sun seemed to shine all the brighter as the morning lengthened. By the time the wooden buildings appeared ahead of them, Branimir was nearly ready to take off his cloak.

The group of them paused at the edge of the tree line to gawk at the Ariadnean port. A handful of single story wooden homes were built in the open, away from the trees, and fifty yards from the water's edge. Snow drifts were piled against the buildings, plagued by footprints across the terrain.

Branimir noticed a centralized building, slightly larger than the others, but looked beyond it when catching sight of the blue ocean.

Strega's Deep was eternal, stretching beyond the horizon. To the south, Branimir could see more land against the skyline where Saudis Dar, the landmass that included Maharia, extended into the notorious Haemus Mons. Dark trees lined the landmass, even across the waters, where the massive Dyndaer continued to grow. Truly, the forest was immense, extending hundreds of miles.

"It goes on forever," he whispered to himself.

"The gods may bless us yet," Adamus said, not hearing the Kras. He pointed ahead to the docks. "Indeed, there is a knarr in port."

"A single boat," Sulanna said dryly. "It is hardly anything to get excited about. I doubt it could make it to Melkorka without capsizing."

"It'll do," Adamus said.

Branimir lifted his chin above the horse's head in front of him to see the small wooden ship. It sat opposite side of the larger wooden structure. The faering he had traveled on from Melkorka to Kalamaar a lifetime ago had barely fit a handful of men. The knarr, as Adamus called it, was wide and deep, and over a hundred and fifty hands long. It looked to be four times greater than the faerings built a millennium ago.

"Let us just hope their sail is not torn, and the sailors have already loaded their supplies," Adamus added.

Branimir asked. "Loaded supplies?"

"Of course. All boats from these ports are cargo ships," Adamus answered. "The Lilitu in Talastein all but eliminated the trees nearer to the coastline, and they often send for more wood from Ariadne."

"It is going to be difficult to convince a shipmaster to allow five strangers with horses on a cargo ship," Sulanna said. "A knarr usually has enough room to carry the crew and supplies, not passengers. We likely will not be welcomed. We should ride up the coast. Riding to Talastein will take less than a week, and the Lilitu ships are more impressive."

"Still, taking this boat saves time, it does, even if we find another up the coast," Dorofej cleared his throat. "I say, the horses we can leave. Time is of the essence, yes?"

Sulanna did not turn back toward Dorofej, so Branimir could not catch her expression, but her tone was flat. "The pintsize boat, it is."

"Wait," Branimir whispered, twisting to see around the neck of the horse. "What is that?"

He pointed amid the buildings at what appeared to be a water well with a horizontal post fixed on top of two vertical poles. Ropes were suspended on from the center, hanging toward the well. One of the ropes surely held a bucket deep within the enclave, but on the other ropes were…bodies.

"Someone has been hanged," Alden pulled his horse back a couple of steps. "We should have been more cautious approaching this place."

"Ariadneans don't hang their own," Adamus growled, leaning forward to scan up the coast.

"But most Northmen would," Sulanna started.

"The bodies are human," Branimir confirmed, squinting against the bright sun, "but I don't see any movement down there."

Alden patted his horse's neck. "Me either."

He had no more than said the words when the twang of a bow sounded.

"There," Sulanna pointed while the arrow wavered through the air toward them, "from behind the building."

Dorofej reached out his hand, and using *Koldovstvo*, yanked the arrow through the air and straight to his hand, catching it by the shaft. The arrow moved so quickly by

Branimir, he barely had time to flinch in his saddle. Dorofej threw the projectile to the ground behind him.

Adamus offered an explanation, pointing at the red-hooded figure Sulanna had noticed. The individual ducked behind a wooden beam. "Lilitu pirates."

"Cut them down," Dorofej commanded plainly, "and take the ship. We haven't the time for this, yes?"

Branimir twisted in the saddle to object, but before he could say a word, the three Anshedar roared by, storming the hamlet.

Dorofej wrenched the horse's reins and shouted, causing it to take off behind the Anshedar. Bran clung onto the mane of the mare as it crashed toward the shoreline.

They had only made it about halfway when the Lilitu started coming out of the woodwork. A single, brown-cloaked bowman, wearing a red sash, sprung from the side of a building. He fired arrows at them, which Dorofej easily swatted away with *Koldovstvo*. Adamus broke away to run down the bowman. Branimir lost site of the Ariadnean about the time he had pulled his axe loose.

Alden flung his spear into the gut of a second bowman, who had barely pulled back on the sinew of his bow. The Lilitu fell on his back, clutching his stomach. Alden pulled free his sword, the falchion, and pulled his horse to a stop near the water well, dismounting. Another attacker was cut down by the warrior.

Sulanna was more dexterous than Branimir would have guessed. She guided her mare, balancing in a single stirrup on one side while the horse galloped. The move helped her avoid several arrows aimed for her chest. As she rounded one of the buildings, she dove from the mount into another pirate, tackling him to the ground. Her knife sunk into the chest cavity of the Lilitu before it could make a sound.

Branimir watched Sulanna sprint to retrieve Alden's spear while Dorofej sped his mare around the larger building. He directed them back toward the wellspring.

A sound caught Branimir's sensitive ears.

"Let me down, Dorofej," Branimir squirmed. "There is someone inside calling for help."

Unwilling to stop their momentum, Dorofej slowed time with *Koldovstvo*, while guiding the horse. With his free hand, he jerked Branimir from the saddle and released him just inches above the ground. Time wavered.

Branimir's thoughts moved at a regular pace, but his physical body froze, dangling above the ground. The world around him blurred—distorted—with Dorofej shimmering like a wraith.

The moment passed and Branimir fell half an inch to his feet in the snow. Dorofej sprung away, galloping away at full speed as though nothing irregular had happened.

Branimir turned invisible and raced toward the large wooden building. Several voices could be heard crying out with desperation. His hand grabbed the wooden knob and he pushed his way through the door.

An arrow punched through the air above his head. If he had been at a human's height, it would have instantly killed him. Luckily, he held his tongue and pushed forward. His momentum caused him to stumble ahead several more feet and then he slunk to the side, remaining unseen.

He noticed the Lilitu woman with her oversized head, slim neck, and scrawny frame. She lowered the bow that had loosened the arrow, yanking another arrow from the quiver on her back. Her skin was reddish brown—like Hanna. Though, her clothing was colored in blues, including a knotted blue cord that hung next to her cheek.

A male Lilitu, also decorated in blues, spoke in a granular voice. "The wind pushed it open."

She said, "I think not. You saw the men on the hill. You heard the horses. Something opened the door and fled away."

"It could have been the wind," he argued.

Muffled cries behind them distracted them. Three humans, two men and a woman, struggled against their bindings.

The male Lilitu kicked at one of the men. "How hard is it to stay quiet?"

The woman's eyes, wide like an owl, skimmed the room, glancing past Branimir several times. "You telling them to be quiet is not going to make them any quieter. I say, let's slit their throats and be done with it."

"We are not *Rudhira*," The male shrugged, "but if that is what you want, Margya, then just give the word and it will be done. This is your expedition. Though, you will have to answer to the *Arjuna* when we return. You shouldn't even be holding the bow."

The bluish orbs in the center of her eyes glimmered. She dipped her head.

Branimir pulled two daggers free from his belt, and eyed the Lilitu cautiously. He did not know what they were talking about, but he could not let them kill the human captives.

His experiences in the Netherworld suddenly pinpricked his mind, whether he was climbing the *Tower of Eresh*, scouring the halls of *Heshayol*, or tiptoeing within the shadows of *Breyntor Gate*. Branimir generally did not like to think of the warrior he had been forced to become in the Netherworld, but admittedly, the weight and balance of knives were more than familiar to him.

He already knew what he must do. Otherwise, he would not have lifted the daggers to his hands.

The female reached for another arrow, and took a step toward the tied humans. The male captive with his grisly black hair and a round belly struggled to scoot back.

Branimir did not hesitate. He flicked the dagger from his fingers. The blade had no more impaled the Lilitu's skull before Branimir threw a second into the male's chest. The female crumpled. The male stifled a surprised moan, joining his comrade on the ground. Branimir scrambled to him, ignoring his round eyes, and ripped the knife from his chest. He could not fight him when he could not see him.

He slit the thin throat. His hand grazed the blue cord next to the Lilitu's cheek.

Inaudible whimpers came from those bound on the ground. Branimir appeared before them, pressing his finger over his lips. The single story building did not seem to have anyone else within its quarters. He glanced quickly towards the windows, boarded up for the winter. No sign of movement through the cracks.

Branimir used his knife to cut the rope that gagged the round bellied man, and set to work on the bindings on the arms and legs. "Who are you?"

The man sputtered, falling over his own words, "Sefton Jegger. I am the captain of the *Winds Rising* on the dock. We arrived this morning to collect our batch of wood for...uh, Talastein...when these pirates attacked us."

"What about the people of the hamlet?" Branimir asked.

Sefton replied, "The pirates had already killed everyone."

"And, the men of your ship?"

"Killed, too," Sefton swallowed, glancing uneasily at his two companions. "They were good friends, Master Kras."

"Is that so?" Branimir said steely. He sounded fouler than he intended, but after being forced to kill the two Lilitu, he found it appropriate. He sawed at the binds on the other two, the gaunt, bearded man and the light-haired woman, who was nearly as skeletal as a Lilitu. "And, these two? They are from your crew?"

"Yes, Gaewl Farlin and Jelena Moosc. They are both shiphands. Good people...Listen, we owe you our thanks, Kras. If you had not come, we would be food for the fishes."

Branimir grinded his teeth, sighing, "I'm sorry, Master Jegger, if I am upset." He looked to the bodies of the two Lilitu bleeding out. "Taking a life is not something I take lightly."

"And thankful for that, too," Sefton muttered, rubbing his wrists once the rope fell away. "We, ourselves, are simple merchants. We are not warmongers or death dealers."

Branimir retrieved his dagger from the skull of the pirate. He hurriedly cleaned both his weapons on the clothes of the dead.

"Are the rest dead?" Jelena asked. A flicker of fear danced across the woman's eyes.

He nodded solemnly, ignoring the nauseating feeling springing up in his stomach. "If they are not, they will be soon enough"

Sefton heaved a sigh, not missing a beat, "There must be some way we can repay you."

"You can." Branimir locked his black eyes onto Sefton's blue irises. He knew too well what Dorofej would bargain. "We need passage to the north, to Melkorka."

Gaewl was the first to jerk his head toward Branimir at the blunt request.

The shipmaster eyed the daggers as Branimir placed them back on his belt, befuddled by the response. He opened his mouth like he had something further to say, but stopped.

"Sefton," Jelena protested.

The portly fellow silenced her with his raised hand. "No, it is quite alright, Jelena." He bowed his head. "For my life, it is a fair trade, Master Kras. A fair trade. We will take you to Melkorka."

Chapter XXII

"Ahoy, Lady Sulanna!" The corpulent man, named Sefton, shouted from the stern of *Winds Rising*. "We will set sail at once." Sefton gave a wave before disappearing into the bowl of the craft.

Sulanna shouted something inaudible back, and made her way down the dock and onto the knarr.

Branimir watched Sulanna step onboard the ship. On her heels, the black mage nearly ran down the wooden planks, fumbling with his belongings, skittering about in his robes.

An hour had passed since they had taken the hamlet and rescued Sefton and the others. After formal introductions, they cut down the dead from the water well, and laid them out with the slain Lilitu on the frozen ground. There was little more they could do for the bodies without wasting more time. Branimir had been surprised at how little Sefton cared for the dead, assuming some had been crew among the ship.

Sulanna had convinced Sefton to forego his shipment of timber for silver, saving them from loading wood onto the knarr. The woman had pulled several coins from her pouch and placed them in the shipmaster's hand. Sefton had all but agreed to the deal at the mention of silver. Branimir knew little of commodities and their worth, but from the smile on Sefton's face, Branimir guessed Sulanna had paid more than the shipment would have been worth.

Alden had watched the exchange, mumbling something about nobles.

The group of them searched the hamlet and found additional provisions among the houses. With so many hands, the ship was loaded in short time.

Branimir could hear Sulanna, Dorofej, and Sefton talking within the knarr.

"What are you going to Melkorka for?"

"We have business there," Sulanna replied. "Do not worry about it."

Sefton asked, "Do you know the quickest way to reach the place?"

"Follow the coast east and north, you must," Dorofej answered.

Jelena interjected, also from within the boat. Her voice was crisp, accented, "What about the *Kadari*?"

Sefton laughed. "I do miss me some *Kadari*. You mix it up with some soy oil and rice from Haemus Mons. Best raw fish—"

"The *Kadari* are not a type of fish, you fool," Jelena scorned.

"Oh, yes," Sefton chuckled. "You mean the dreaded fish women, who lure sailors into the water to eat them."

"Those are rusalki. You have no idea what you have agreed to do, do you?" Her words were followed by the clamor of wood hitting wood, as though she might have thrown something.

Branimir stood a distance away with Alden and Adamus at the edge of the dock. He had not heard of the rumored rusalki since living on Melkorka.

Alden shifted his pack from one shoulder to the other, glancing at the horse he was leaving on shore. "Something about this shipmaster rubs me the wrong way. Do me a favor and keep an eye on him, Kras."

Adamus grunted in agreement. "I get the feeling he might've been a mule in a previous life. Working his way up, it seems." Adamus looked east. "We still have time to turn back for the coast. Tis safer to swim to Kalamaar than to sail with him. He doesn't even know where we are going."

Branimir said, "Sulanna has already paid him the silver."

Alden lowered his head. "Let us have faith Svarog has guided us wisely. We cannot turn back now. The quickest route is forward."

"As long as you know, forward may result with my axe in that man's skull," Adamus flashed his teeth.

"Master Kras, are we ready to set off? Master Dorofej says to hurry." Sefton raised an eyebrow, peeking over the edge of the knarr again. "I hope the *Winds Rising* is to your liking? I presumed it would be. Ha! I have never had an unsatisfied traveler on my ship. I assure you that this will be a most splendid voyage."

"Czern's breath! He talks a lot," Adamus muttered,

Bran yelled back, "We are coming."

The hull was wider, deeper, and shorter than what Branimir would have imagined from the shore. Surprisingly, they fit more comfortably in the ship than what he would have thought.

Branimir was the only one who could not help row them out to deeper waters. He did not have the strength to manipulate the long oars. The rest grunted and heaved, taking the knarr out to the ocean. In short time, Sefton sprung the woolen sail, colored blue and gold, and the knarr practically sailed itself for the rest of the afternoon.

Sefton steered the boat with a mechanism near the back, and Gaewl and Jelena managed the sail when needed. The rest of them used the space to meander comfortably among each other.

Evening was beginning to set when Branimir caught up with Dorofej alone at the front of the boat. Adamus and Sulanna had joined in a game of dice with Gaewl, and Alden had fallen asleep across one of the plank boards. Sefton and Jelena tended to the boat, or were caught up in their own daydreams.

Branimir sat for some time without saying anything, listening to Gaewl tell stories while they played dice.

"Gebereht, was once a hero of Ariadne," Gaewl said with a hint of excitement. "Had an old friend who use to tell the tale often."

Adamus said, "There is not a fighter alive who has not heard of the legends of Gebereht. He brought more glory to the God of War than any other ever born."

"But did you know he was said to be reborn?" Gaewl challenged. "People say he came back from Thrice Ten Kingdom at the request of Svathevit the Red."

"Why would the God of War call him back?" the Ariadnean asked.

Gaewl threw the dice. "Someone needs to save this world from itself."

Sulanna sighed heavily, muttering something about *god rubbish*.

Branimir stifled a smile.

"Something you want to ask me, yes?" Dorofej said, diverting Branimir from the conversation, and pulling his black hood over his red tuft of hair. The breeze had cooled in the last hour, reminding them they were not entirely out of the Season of Frost.

A great time had passed since Branimir had felt this powerless around Dorofej. In many ways, the two of them had worked together as equals to survive the Netherworld, but here, back on Aenar, Dorofej seemed to be the wiser once more, full of his secrets.

"I want answers," Branimir said. There was a short moment of silence while he waited for the black mage to respond. When Dorofej said nothing, Branimir blurted out what had been most on his mind. "Did you make *kaelandur*?"

"Mm. No longer can I say I did not," Dorofej gazed across the water. "Crafted it with *Koldovstvo*, I did."

Branimir caught his breath, trying to endure the truth which Dorofej said so matter-of-factly. Dorofej had more chances than Branimir could count to admit to creating the copper dagger. And he had never said a word. "Why? Do not tell me, you do not remember."

Dorofej dropped his bushy eyebrows, touching his smooth chin. "Requested to, I was. Though I did not fully know what I was being asked, yes? I say, I did not know demons would come, nor did I know the Ash Tree would be endangered."

His words made Branimir feel a bit better. It was something to know Dorofej was not intentionally trying to destroy the world. "Who asked you to do such a thing? I mean, you had to know it was forbidden for you—a Stuhia—to make a weapon with *Koldovstvo*, like Erzebeth said?" Branimir hissed under his breath, intent to keep attention off their conversation. He peeked over his shoulder at the other shipmates.

None bothered to look in their direction.

Dorofej dropped his hands into his lap, half-smiling at Branimir as though a great joke were being told. "In *Klukas*, a long time ago, I was visited by a woman, yes? Make it, she told me, and it will be called *kaelandur*. Maybe, it was my charge to do such a thing."

"Who was she?"

The black mage's light eyes seemed to glow in the lowering sun, and then he said in a hushed tone, "Why *Marheena*, of course."

Branimir almost screamed, barely catching himself, "Marheena! Why would you listen to the Frozen Witch?"

"Much you do not understand, I know," Dorofej concurred, tilting his head toward Branimir, "despite what I try to teach, yes? Verily, know if it was her or not, I can never truly say, but I believe it to be. And listen to Marheena, I always have. See the power I have—the *Koldovstvo*—she bestows upon me."

"Were you not the one who laughed at the gods coming to speak with men?" Branimir asked in confusion.

"Typical, it is not. But long ago, more frequent, it was," Dorofej said, "as Erzebeth plainly said."

Branimir held his head, slumping over. "But that is where *Koldovstvo* comes from? From Marheena? Do the *Kadari* know? Did any of the Highborn?" Branimir already knew the answer, especially when remembering how Falmagon, and his predecessor, like Kinhar, spoke of Dahz the Lightbringer.

Dorofej shaking his head only confirmed what Branimir knew.

"But…you worship Marheena!" Branimir cried again. He had to let go of his leg, realizing how tightly he was pinching himself. This could not be real.

"Branimir, my friend," Dorofej soothed him, reaching for his shoulder. "She has no more evil in her than you or me, yes?"

He pulled away from the Stuhia, hearing commotion on the boat behind him. With a quick glance, he found his companions, as well as the *Winds Rising* crew were looking at him. Bran had a hundred emotions flowing throughout his body like drops of rain.

He glared at the black mage. "You are wrong. How can the whole world say she is bad, and you argue against it?"

"Because many think a thing does not make it the right thing, dear Branimir," Dorofej said.

"Why compare us to her?" He lowered his eyes to the floor, listening to the creaking boards of the ship. He felt the boat rocking against the water. His voice was barely a whisper, nearly a plea. "Are we the heroes in this tale? Please, tell me, we are the heroes."

Dorofej looked longingly toward the horizon. "That, my friend, is yet to be learned."

Chapter XXIII

Branimir could not sleep. At one time, the rocking of the boat would have caused his stomach to churn, but now, he hardly noticed. The smell of the sea and salt stung his nostrils, and the cold chilled his nose. Though, neither were the reason he stayed awake. Despite his burning eyes, his mind was peppered.

Hanna haunted his thoughts. He had been captivated when he first met her, and then he learned of her worship of Lilith, or Marheena. He almost found himself hating her for worshipping such a despicable god.

Then, to learn Dorofej had followed Marheena all these years, and had said nothing. More than that, Dorofej had created the very weapon which was meant to destroy the Ash Tree and release the Likhyi.

Branimir buried his head in his hands, trying to make sense of it all. Dorofej was his friend. Dorofej had saved him from death more times than he could count. Yet Dorofej revered the most hated goddess in Aenar, and led them to fight the *Kadari*, who spread the teachings of the Sun God, the most loved of all the deities.

Branimir feared he was fighting on the wrong side, but how could that be? They were defending the Ash Tree. They were stopping the *old-dark* from returning to the world and killing the living. Falmagon was the evil one. He was.

Branimir trembled, glancing at Gaewl, who guided the boat on the opposite end of the ship. The man sluggishly gestured for Branimir to join him. He then glanced out across the deep waters, rubbing his beard.

Branimir carefully crept along the boat, passing Dorofej, Alden, and Adamus, over Sulanna, and beyond Sefton and Jelena. Each of them were curled up or sprawled out across the planks of the knarr, breathing steadily. He found himself glad he could see them as clearly as he could with his Kras vision. He hated to think what it would be like to be challenged by darkness like he had faced at *Garain'l*.

"Evening, Branimir, is it?" Gaewl said. "I thought you would be sleeping. Always best to get rest when you can and it sounds like you have a long journey ahead."

"Too much on my mind," Branimir said. He changed the subject. "Where are you from, Gaewl?"

Gaewl pulled at his facial hair again, steering the boat with his free hand. "Born in Mecka, east of Gaetana, up north. It is a decent sized village, but many have not heard of it. My father ran the ferry across the lake."

Branimir felt good hearing about the normalcy of the man's life. He found it pleasant that not every man had to be on epic quest to find purpose in their life. He pressed to continue the conversation. "I see how you might have become a sailor then," he said. "How long have you been doing this?"

"Oh," Gaewl hesitated, "only a few years. Still getting my feet wet, you might say. The pay is decent and it gives me a way to see the world without having to fight with armies. I had heard of the wars with the desert people in the south. I have no interest in that sort of thing."

Branimir bit his cheek. Gaewl was talking about the war with the Uvil. "Adamus fought in the war."

Gaewl looked to the sleeping Ariadnean. "Did he now?"

Branimir nodded. He scanned the sky, speckled with faint stars behind thick, scattered clouds.

The small waves crashed against the side of the knarr harmlessly. "Can this boat really carry us all the way to Melkorka?" Branimir asked.

"Not rightly sure," Gaewl said. "If we keep out of the deeper waters, it might. Though, I hear there are some big fish out here, and even larger ones in the far north. I suppose one could easily topple us over. To make matters worse, we'd freeze to death in the water before we could swim to shore."

Branimir spread his thin lips, showing off his crooked teeth. With sarcasm, he said, "You like to keep things light, don't you?"

Gaewl chuckled, holding a wry grin. "I like to tell it like it is."

Branimir turned from the glimmer in the man's eye. He glanced pass the blue and gold sails of the *Winds Rising*. He could see lights far off in the distance. "What is that?"

"Akothiya, I think." Gaewl squinted. "One of the Lilitu cities along the shore. I am surprised you can see it from here. I can barely make out the lantern lights of the village."

"You have probably sailed this passage a hundred times." Branimir eyed the man, rocking on his haunches. "Is it close?"

Gaewl licked his lips, and then shook his head. "No, no. It likely looks much closer than it is. It is surprising how far a small amount of light can travel when surrounded by darkness."

Branimir considered the words when, suddenly, a shadow passed overhead. Gaewl must have noticed it too, because he glanced at the sky.

"Gaewl," Branimir's voice dropped, standing up from the plank. He clearly could see the stark white beast swoop overhead. Its three crescent-shaped heads twisted every which way to look at them. Bright blue eyes shined on each head, observing the knarr and its occupants.

It was a monster from legends.

An unearthly screech arose from the center head chilling Branimir's skin, stealing away his cry and anything Gaewl may have said. The creature spun in the air, flapping its fibrous wings. The gusts of wind blew Branimir's hood back, and water sprayed across his face. The freezing water felt like icicles piercing his crimson skin.

He gathered his courage. "A dragon."

The scaled monster was enormous. He could fit inside one mouth and not even need to stoop.

The creature swayed and coiled keeping above the craft with its two thin, yet sizeable, wings. The lower half of the beast was slim for the most part, until it erupted into two overly large feet and a massive tail, tucked up against its body.

The monster twisted another head towards the sky, emitting another screech that was hundred times worse than the first one, causing the entire boat to shake and creak under the sound. Branimir clutched his ears instinctively.

The knarr had come alive with movement. Branimir bent his body, hesitant to take his eyes off the beast, to see Sefton standing in the soft glow of a lantern. He held it up into the night to get a better look at the leviathan.

"This drake will eat us alive."

Branimir stared up at the shipmaster blankly.

Directly behind him, the rest of the crew had found their weapons. If any of them had been initially surprised at the dragon hovering above their vessel, there was no sign of it now.

Jelena followed Sulanna to the opposite end of the knarr. "Watch for its firebreath. Better to drown and freeze to death than be burnt alive."

"Wrong sort, yes?" Dorofej educated them, peering at the dragon. "*Lahmia*, the name of this dragon is, and an icebreath, it has. I say, she has a fondness for the blood of children and must think Branimir to be one."

Branimir glared at Dorofej. "I am not a child!"

"Convince me, you do not, Branimir," Dorofej cried. "Convince her, yes?"

Sefton ducked away from the beast. "Why has it come this far south? We are leagues away from the Shade Fells and Lairhein."

"Even further north, she normally resides," Dorofej said, ducking his head.

"And, how do you know all this?" Gaewl asked, cowering behind the steering mechanism.

"The Stuhia are known for their knowledge on dragons," Alden offered.

Lahmia swooped down, slamming her clawed feet onto the edge of the boat and pushing back off into the air. Adamus swung wildly with his axe, missing the dragon entirely. *Lahmia* circled the boat, pounding her wings.

"She is playing with us," Alden said, pulling his spear from his back.

Sulanna eyed the dragon warily. "I am not certain the dragon is here to eat any of us, even the Kras. Dragons are not stupid creatures."

"Not known to be generous either," Sefton said.

"Be ready," Gaewl shouted, holding onto the side of the boat. His warning was only in time as *Lahmia* clawed the mass that held the sail, causing the boat to sway and nearly topple over.

Branimir rolled across the bottom, holding tightly to one of the planks. The others frantically shouted, floundering about the knarr. As the boat heaved to and fro, the fellowship crashed into one another, desperately clinging onto anything and anyone.

The creature swooped downward, again, but only for show. Its claws, black and curled, stayed tucked under its body, though it could have snatched any of them from the boat.

The rocking slowed, and Branimir pulled himself to his feet. "Tell us what do you want, *Lahmia*? I am not a child to be eaten." He was not sure what being child-like had to do with anything, but Dorofej said to convince the three-headed dragon as of much.

Adamus stumbled across the boat to stand in front of Branimir protectively.

"Wolos must be freed from the Netherworld," she rustled back. The voice had a hint of sweetness under the gurgled tone, like a myriad of voices uttering the same words at the same time.

Branimir looked to see his companions on the boat gripping their heads, covering their ears, as though pained by a sound he could not hear.

Branimir looked intently at the white dragon. With *Ojenek* in his pocket, he quickly solved the riddle of understanding the dragon's tongue. "Then, it is not a rumor; Wolos was killed. What does freeing the God of the Dead have to do with us?"

"Erzebeth sends for the stone you carry, Branimir," *Lahmia* hissed. "Give it to me so I may deliver it to those who venture forth. It will aid them in completing their charge."

"*Ojenek*," Branimir whispered, gripping the moonstone in his pocket. He had never thought he would be asked to part with his trinket.

He pulled it out and looked at the glowing stone within the palm of his hand. For a thousand years, the gem had been in his possession, found at Illuard within the Hall of Gravels, the *Eevaltti*. If he gave away his stone, he may never be able to talk to dragons, or centaurs, or the *old-dark*.

"How did you know I had it?" Branimir asked. "How did you find me?"

Each dragon head snapped its cone-shaped mouth, revealing the sharpened teeth. The nonverbal threat could not be missed. "Give it to me!"

He was certain the dragon would take it by force if necessary. Half-heartedly, he pulled his arm back and flung the moonstone into the air toward dragon.

"Branimir!" Dorofej cried.

Lahmia snatched *Ojenek* with her center mouth, and spun northwest instantly. Her white, leathery wings spread wide, and she soared through the sky at an unmatched speed.

"What has happened?" Jelena demanded, holding herself against the side of the knarr. "Those beasts don't belong here."

"What did you give the beast, Master Branimir?" Sefton interrogated, his voice booming in the night air. "First, you speak of following Marheena, and now, we watch you aid the Frozen Witch's servants."

"A bad omen for our voyage," Jelena curled her lip, "to aid Marheena."

"The creation of Wolos, dragons are, and not Marheena," Dorofej corrected, looking at Branimir with bewilderment, "but I say, why did you give *Lahmia* the *Ojenek*?

"Wolos is dead—" Alden started.

"Your argument makes no sense, Master Dorofej," Sefton sustained. "It is well known Zyem safeguards the Kalinov Bridge leading into the Netherworld. The monstrous Lord of the Dragons is controlled by Marheena, not Wolos."

"Understand the gods, you do not. Tired of trying to explain it, I am," Dorofej attested with a curt snort. He emphasized his question. "I say, Branimir, why?"

"Did you not hear, *Lahmia*? Of course, you would not have when I held *Ojenek*." Branimir gazed off into the distance. "Erzebeth sent for *Ojenek* to free Wolos. If we fail, perhaps her plan will help balance what has been unbalanced."

"You mean the *Gal of Garain'l*?" Adamus pulled at his beard. "What in the Nine Lands is going on?"

"But—" Dorofej started.

"And, if I had not," Branimir faced Dorofej with fortitude, "*Lahmia* would have frozen us solid with her icebreath. Better to live another day than not live at all."

Dorofej folded his hands. "Your wisdom, I do not question, Branimir. A way to save us from ourselves, I pray Erzebeth has found. Save us yet, she might."

Chapter XXIV

The Lilitu metropolis, Talastein, was incredible, sitting on the southeastern coast of Maharia. The city was positioned south of the Dyndaer, on the mouth of a river, which Branimir did not know the name. The longships lined in the harbor were twenty times larger than the knarr with white sails reaching toward the heavens. But the stunning city beyond, built layer upon layer, surrounded by red brick, took Branimir's breath away.

Towers and edifices, which Branimir could not identify, stretched well above the walls, overlooking the tops of the trees of the nearby Dyndaer. Reddish-brown Lilitu scaled and scrambled across all areas of the city. Even from the knarr, Branimir could see them marching along the walls, conducting business within the harbor, and walking atop the towers. Though, everything about their movements appeared ordered and systematic.

The Lilitu walked with their chins elevated and backs straight—each and every one—wearing different colored clothes and sashes. Branimir's mind raced back to Hanna with her red sash, then the Lilitu at the Ariadnean port with the blue clothes. The Lilitu at Talastein primarily wore blues and yellows. He noticed a few wearing a red sash like Hanna, and a couple fully dressed in white. It had to mean something.

No matter what they wore, each Lilitu spoke with precision, dipping their heads when beginning and ending their orations, paying mind only to their task. At simple glance, from the harbor, Branimir guessed the numbers of Lilitu within Talastein to be in the thousands. He remembered Drak talking about the Lilitu having cities all along the coast and Haemus Mons. The possibility of a population so large was unfathomable.

"The city is so big," Branimir said, gazing up at the fixtures.

"Ho," Jelena laughed. "Wait until you see that the depth runs as deep as the elevation. The Lilitu do not waste any space, scurrying like beetles beneath the surface and spreading like ants above."

"You mean to say this city is twice as large as what I can see," Branimir said, eyes widening.

"If not more," Jelena granted.

"We can talk about the Lilitu all day if need be, but someone tell me why are we towing into the harbor?" Alden asked. "We have enough supplies to continue for Melkorka."

"Inspection," Sefton said, shifting his eyes back and forth across the bay. He dropped the sails, and signaled Gaewl to line the knarr up with the docking. "No one passes through Talastein without inspection unless they wish to be run down by the Sirens. I promise we will be drifting toward Melkorka shortly enough."

"Sirens?" Branimir asked.

"An elite, Lilitu warrior class of women," Gaewl stated, guiding the boat as instructed. "They say their blades can cut through any blade made by Northmen, taken from the Uvil in the south."

Branimir scratched his head. The world had grown.

Gaewl must have noticed the confusion because he clarified, "Their weapons were collected from the desert people through trade. Surprisingly enough, at one time the Lilitu and Uvil had warred against each other in Haemus Mons. But the day after the war was done, the Lilitu were in the Uvil cities trading again. The buggers never miss the opportune chance to make coin."

"And, their best fighters are women?" Branimir asked with disbelief.

"Not all fighters are men, Kras," Sulanna huffed.

"Oh," Branimir said sheepishly, as the boat slowed in the harbor. "I am not saying they are, or should be, but I have never seen a place send their women to war."

"Might be what is wrong with the world, considering the Lilitu win nearly every war they have been a part of," Gaewl winked. "Truth be told, the *Rudhira* are not just women. The Lilitu have fighters that are male and female. It is just the Sirens who are women. I must say I am surprised you have not heard of them, Master Branimir. The Lilitu society is governed by females; it only makes sense their best swordsmen are also women. I have seen them fight. I'd put my money on a Lilitu Siren against any man, any day."

Branimir dropped his jaw. The *Rudhira* was the name of the warrior class in the Lilitu society. He was starting to put the pieces together, and understanding why Hanna had worn the red sash. The colors must indicate what part of the society each citizen belonged.

"What of the inspection?" Dorofej redirected the conversation back to Sefton. "The Lilitu are searching for something of value, yes? Looking for what, exactly, are they?"

"Precious wares," Jelena replied for Sefton, pushing her thick hair behind her ears with bony fingers. "Gems, jewels, or trinkets. Anything which might be considered rare, or they can use to elevate their status further with."

"Shouldn't be a problem, then," Sulanna mumbled. "With the moonstone and dagger gone, we are as empty-handed as a beggar."

"Dagger?" Sefton cast an eye over them, while he used an oar to help steer them toward the dock.

"Nothing to worry about anymore," Branimir said.

"Be sure not to mention any of such things, we should be," Dorofej reminded. "The *Kadari* may have ears, even here in Talastein."

Adamus rumbled his mustache and beard with his breath. "We are not fools, Dorofej."

The Stuhia adjusted his hood. "Better to say I said to say nothing than something be said and we all lose our heads, yes?"

The boat rocked against the wooden deck, settling into the port.

"Indeed," Branimir garbled, watching the two Stuhia clerks, wearing blue sashes, approach the knarr as Gaewl tossed the rope to the dockman to be tied off.

"Welcome, *Winds Rising*," the first clerk said, holding a piece of parchment in hand. "Who here is the Captain of this vessel?"

Sefton, already moving forward, waved his hand, introducing himself, "Sefton Jegger, at your service. We are only passing through, voyaging for northern waters."

"You are the Captain of the *Winds Rising*?" the look of skepticism was plain on the Lilitu's face. The bulbous eyes expanded to the point of popping out entirely.

Sefton shifted, shoulders relaxing. "Certainly."

Before the shipmaster could say more, the second Lilitu extended his hand. "Let me see your manifest, Captain Jegger."

"Gentlemen, I am afraid there is no manifest," Sefton answered. "Our shipment from…er, the Ariadnean port…was voided."

"Surely, you have been through Talastein before, Captain Jegger. Is the *Winds Rising* not a cargo vessel?" The first Lilitu said mockingly, glancing over the several Anshedar, outfitted for war.

Branimir did not blame them for their concern. He could only imagine what they looked like with Adamus with his axe, Sulanna in her breastplate, Dorofej in his darkened robes, and Alden, who looked like he had stepped straight off the battlefield.

"Yes, quite," Sefton smiled, jingling the rings on his wrists. "but the hamlet at the Ariadnean port was overrun by pirates, and so we…turned back, you see?"

"Pirates, you say?" the second said with a flat affect, motioning his hand off to the side. "You are certain about that?"

Sefton gulped, "More than certain." The man put his hands on his extended belly, shifting as though he might turn back toward Dorofej, or even Branimir, to confirm his story with the clerks. Instead, he simply dipped his chin. He repeated himself, voice quivering, "I am quite certain. See, the Northmen were hanged and the town raided."

"Let me see your papers," the second clerk demanded.

"I told you, I do not have my manif—"

"Not your manifest, Captain Jegger. Let me see your registration papers for this vessel."

Sefton faltered, conclusively twisting toward Jelena, who gawped back with a dumbfounded expression. She shook her head and finally lowered her eyes from the shipmaster.

From up the docks, a handful of Lilitu briskly walked towards them. The cluster was dressed in red tunics, covering their armor, fitted to their slender frames. Each held two long swords dual sheathed on their left side, one sword strategically placed over the other. Branimir eyed the decorated hilts with the black lace wrapped around each handle. He lifted his eyes to the hooded, crimson cloaks covering their faces, hiding their features.

"Just our luck," Gaewl whispered. "Sirens."

"Let me educate you," the second clerk said, "Your flags have the colors of the *East Point Traders* from Badsehra, *Captain* Jegger, which if you are not aware, is a Lilitu settlement. According to our registrar, the captain of this particular knarr is Margya Corran.”

Branimir’s chest stiffened with every word, but upon hearing the name, his knees buckled. He fell back onto the planks within the ship. The truth of the matter sunk in.

Sefton, Gaewl, and Jelena were the pirates.

“No,” he murmured.

He had cut the throat of the Lilitu named Margya in the longhouse at the port.

“Branimir, get up,” Dorofej insisted, grabbing him under the arm.

“He lied to us,” Branimir felt tears surfacing. He glared at Sefton, who cautiously peered at Branimir over his shoulder. Branimir snarled at the so-called shipmaster. “He lied to us.”

The Sirens arrived next to the clerks, uniformly, facing the troupe on the boat. The first clerk stepped back. “The punishment for piracy in Talastein is death.”

In fluid motion, one Siren reached across her body with her right hand and pulled a sword from the top scabbard.

“Wait!” Sefton stepped on the deck toward the clerks, hands raised and bracelets jingling. “Hear us—”

The Lilitu Siren was swift, the slanted, silver blade flashing level through the fat man’s neck. It cut clean through flesh and bone. Blood misted. The frame suspended for only a second before the head toppled off, and the body collapsed.

Branimir recoiled. The Lilitu would kill them thinking they were all the pirates.

Adamus wrenched his axe free. “This is madness!”

Sulanna reached to grab Adamus’s arm. “Hold on—”

Alden interrupted the noble woman, jerking his spear from his back. “It is not the time for diplomacy! They will not hear it.”

The other Sirens unsheathed their swords and advanced.

The old warrior sprang to the edge of the boat, swiping the spear in a wide flowing arc, the bladed edge slanted for the first Siren's head. The Siren was quick, tipping backwards, dodging the attack. Alden, balanced on the knarr's perimeter, did not hesitate. He rocked back, continuing the movement, and thrust the spear. The blade caught the Siren as she sprung back up from the initial attack.

The Lilitu cried out as the spearhead tore through her midsection, the shaft ripping through her back and then yanked back through as Alden retracted the weapon.

He bellowed, "For Svarog, the Kingdom and victory!"

The clerks tumbled away from conflict as the other Sirens advanced. The first broke Alden's guard, knocking the spear sideways with her blade. Another entered his space with her weapon raised.

Adamus rushed into the aggressive Siren with his shoulder, causing her to lurch sideways. With a cry, she was sent sprawling over the edge of the knarr. A splash sounded as she fell head first into the water.

A second, who had deflected the spear, swung her blade down toward the Ariadnean. He speedily met the blow with his weapon hand. The silver against silver reverberated, causing the Siren to stagger; perhaps, surprised her blade did not cut through the Uvil-crafted axe. Adamus took the moment to reach across Alden's weapon and pummel the woman in the face with his closed fist. The wallop knocked her flat on the dock, stock-still.

Branimir sunk against the opposite end of the boat.

"Untie the rope," Dorofej shouted, scanning the city beyond the bay. "Set sail, we must."

Alden shouted at Gaewl and Jelena. "Help us row this thing out of here, and we might let you live."

Jelena's tensed her jaw. "Killed by the Lilitu, by you, or by the *Kadari* at Melkorka. I'll take my chances." With a shake of her head, she sprang sideways off the boat into the water.

Gaewl clicked his tongue, looking to Alden and then Branimir. His hand inched toward the oars before he finally said, "I'm sorry."

He fell overboard after Jelena.

"Cowards!" Sulanna screamed after them.

Branimir twisted about on the boat, wondering if the water was the better option. He raked his eyes across the choppy water contemplating if he knew how to swim or not. After a short time, Gaewl and Jelena surfaced several yards away, swimming for the shore.

From the look on their pale faces, the water had to be freezing. There was little chance of them surviving, even if the Lilitu did not catch them.

Shouts from the dock brought Branimir back to the fight.

Red-clad Lilitu carrying bows began trotting down the docks in thick branched columns. He could not have guessed how the Lilitu had become so organized so quickly, as though they had an entire army waiting on standby.

Branimir barely caught sight of them before the remaining Sirens rushed the boat. Sulanna joined Alden and Adamus at the threshold of the knarr, struggling against the Sirens. In moments, the other Lilitu were positioned across the docks.

Arrows fired across the gap, dipping toward them with deadly accuracy.

Branimir shrunk back as Dorofej swiped his hand through the air, using *Koldovstvo* to direct the arrows away from the knarr. The projectiles plunged into the water harmlessly.

Sulanna cried out, oblivious to the archers, and charged pass Branimir. She held her long belt knife, her noble features rigid, attacking the Lilitu warriors. Her weapon sliced and stabbed while swords flashed toward her in rhythm. She stepped lightly, dancing back and forth, evading the quick blades. A blade nipped her shoulder, and her thigh, but she held her ground.

Alden's spear turned and rung through the ranks of the Sirens. He kept them back, extending and withdrawing the pole with immeasurable precision. The spear was quick, in the flesh and back before the eye could catch its movement. Yet, he too, was decorated with cuts and nicks on his face and arms.

Adamus held the left of Alden. The stocky man was a brawler, his axe rising and falling, hacking through skin and bones, and ignoring the cuts he attained. He had no fear of death, meeting every Siren with an abysmal growl of savagery.

"The rope," Dorofej shouted, again, over the din, using another blast of *Koldovstvo* to steer Lilitu arrows from hitting their mark.

Branimir disappeared, hurdling to the rope that fastened them to dock. He wasted little time slicing through the threads, ignoring the Lilitu who could not see him work.

"Dorofej!" Branimir yelled when finished.

The black-mage, who had been withholding his power, unleashed *Koldovstvo* on the Lilitu.

Ice shards exploded through the dock dismantling the ranks of warriors. Bodies were flung in all directions and screams resounded. Battle cries echoed in some throats, and screams of pain and anguish were found in the throats of others; some throats were no longer intact.

Branimir gripped onto the boat, shutting his eyes. The world was full of chaos; the cacophonous cries were devastating to his ears.

Seawater splashed around them and the *Winds Rising* was swept out of the bay, steered by a massive tidal wave, guided by Dorofej with his magic.

Branimir looked over the hull of the boat again. More Lilitu surged from the depths of the city. They were thick. Many sprang to their ships with the intent to give chase.

"No!" Sulanna's distorted cry sounded over the clashing waves, and commotion from the harbor. "Alden. Alden!" If a heart were ever to be blackened in fervor, this sorrowful sound spoke of such a darkening.

Branimir cringed.

He gripped onto the boat as it rushed away, looking for the holy warrior, who must have fallen over board when the waves jerked them to sea.

"Alden!" Branimir merged his voice with Sulanna, bawling with dissent.

In the distance, the old man was briefly spotted, overwhelmed by the rolling waves, sinking from sight.

Adamus, his eyebrows angled in temper, also caught sight of Alden crumpled under the sprung waves. "He is gone!"

Chapter XXV

Branimir carved another notch into the side of the knarr to mark their forty-sixth day on the ocean. They had stayed in the deep waters to avoid the coastal cities of the Lilitu, sparingly using *Koldovstvo* to outpace those who had given chase from Talastein. Branimir had not seen any ships following them for nearly two weeks. He dared to think they were safe for the remainder of the journey.

The wind blew strongly for most of the journey, carrying them briskly across the choppy waters. Even now, the springtime breeze filled the sails. With only days into the Season of Warmth, Bran was surprised by the tepid feel.

Branimir returned his dagger to his belt, watching the Ariadnean. The boat rocked and creaked under Adamus's weight as he moved to hang the lantern. The glow radiated like a small, bright beacon to Branimir.

"Branimir," Sulanna waved at him from near the mast, gesturing toward his dried meat and cheese, "come get your supper before it gets cold."

He stepped away from the stern, glancing past Adamus to the golden orb falling below the skyline. Its golden rays glistened off the endless waters, sparkling against the dark blues and whipping whites of the distant waves.

"We are lucky to have lost the three pirates," Adamus said while Branimir reached for his supper. "It has given us enough rations to make the journey without looking for another port."

Branimir took his first bite, hesitant to say anything. It was true that without Gaewl, Jelena, or Sefton, there had been more than enough food for them. If anything, Branimir had become plumper over the past month than any other time since he had returned from the Netherworld. Though, the three *pirates* who had previously procured the *Winds Rising* were not all that was lost.

He could not forget Alden.

Adamus found his seat between Sulanna and Dorofej, who already had their supper, and continued, "Sefton had gotten what he deserved after his show at the port. You really think they hung all those men?"

Branimir detected Sulanna drawing away from Adamus, unresponsive. Her hair was disheveled and eyes darkened at the edges. Branimir knew she had not slept well since leaving Talastein. He was certain the woman had been affected by Alden's disappearance more than any other.

"Speculated over this many times, we have," Dorofej said, chewing. "Some of the dead must've been a part of his regular crew, yes? I say, overrun by the Lilitu from the *Winds Rising*, they likely were, before we arrived."

Branimir partially listened. Again and again, the two had deliberated how Sefton and the others had ransacked the port, and then had been captured by the Lilitu.

"The Lilitu should not have attacked us," Adamus replied. He pondered for a moment, and then added, "Just like them to strike first. The *Rudhira* tend to ask questions after the fact."

"I am sure they thought we were with Sefton," Branimir assumed, looking away from Sulanna. "We might have done the same."

A moment passed, and Adamus continued, unable to let the topic go. "If there had only been *Nili*, we could have talked, but I know the *Rudhira*. Hanna was *Rudhira*. If they felt threatened, they would fight. And the Lilitu do not bother with prisoners."

"The *Nili*?" Branimir asked.

"The ones in blue," Adamus clarified. "They are the traders and merchants. They don't fight; they aren't allowed to. I have met a few, but I know more from what Hanna had told me."

Branimir garbled in response, signifying he did not need to know anymore. He remembered the blue worn by the two he had murdered in the longhouse. One of the Lilitu had held a weapon, even when the other had said to forego it.

He did not like this conversation, or any talk about the Lilitu. The banter generally ended with Adamus bringing up Hanna, which reminded Branimir of the Lilitu goddess, the Mother. In turn, this led to recalling Dorofej was faithful to Marheena. The black mage said the Frozen Goddess had given *Koldovstvo* to the Stuhia, the same magic which had saved Branimir's life more than once.

The correlation made his stomach uneasy and his head spin.

The details were so convoluted. Branimir's only reprieve came from considering what he was doing had to be done, no matter the discomfort. He had to keep Bohumir from being sacrificed and protect the Ash Tree from the *Kadari*.

"How much closer to Melkorka?" Adamus asked. He scooped up another bite.

Dorofej ran a hand through his red strands, eyeing Adamus. He chewed his food slowly with an aura of stubbornness. The Stuhia seemed bent on using his manners, savoring each bite. As if making his point, he gently placed another piece of meat into his mouth and finished it entirely before responding. "Ask me each and every night, you do."

The Ariadnean chuckled, holding his food between his teeth. "There is little else to talk about."

"Yesterday, passed beyond Salahan, we did. A few hours ago, the Hrani Highlands made their appearance on the western shoreline, yes? I say, shift our heading northeast in the morning, and soon find Melkorka on the horizon, we will."

"And, what of Drak?" Sulanna asked with as much composure as she could achieve. She had scarcely touched her own food. "How much further has he made it today?"

Branimir dug into his bowl while Dorofej received his nightly interrogation.

"Spent time in *Klukas* today, I did," Dorofej confessed, rubbing his chin. "On a boat north of us, he is. I say, exceptional progress, we have made. With enough luck, we might reach the Seven Islands before him."

"And Alden?" She mumbled, turning her head back to her bowl.

"You need to let him go," Adamus cut in. "I told you, the Lilitu do not keep prisoners."

"He hasn't been killed yet," she snapped back. Then, resting her gaze, turned to Dorofej again, "Has he?"

Dorofej's eyes glinted, as blue as the northern snows. "Comforted, you will be, to know he lives, yes? Still alive at Talastein, he is."

Adamus turned his head. "It makes no sense why they would keep him this long?"

Dorofej looked to Branimir for a moment and back again. "No certainty in anything, there is."

The growl in Sulanna's throat started before she could speak. Her chin quivered, elevating her eyes to meet those of Adamus. "Alden does not die so easily."

Adamus, as if recognizing his error, stared into his bowl for a moment. "I am not questioning his fortitude. By all means, not having him with us at Melkorka makes our road all the more difficult. I am only saying, we must focus on what lies ahead. Not behind."

Sulanna screamed out, throwing her entire meal off the *Winds Rising* and into the water. She stood, glaring at Adamus. "I know my duty. But I will not forget Alden."

Branimir jumped back from the eruption.

"I did not say to forget," Adamus softened his gaze.

"Sulanna," Branimir reached out with his hand to comfort her.

"Quiet," she said through clenched teeth, shaking, "all of you."

Branimir pulled back, while she stared at Adamus for several minutes. The only noise was Dorofej, who continued to chew, twisting his neck back and forth to look at the two deadlocked.

Finally, she half-stumbled, half-crawled to the other side of the boat, near the steering mechanism. She flopped against the side, throwing her hood over her head, staring back toward Talastein.

"Adamus," Branimir uttered.

"I am alright, Bran. She knows I did not mean anything by it." Adamus sighed. "I've seen grief a hundred times on a battlefield."

"She will be alright," Branimir said.

Adamus pushed the last of his supper into his mouth, grunting in agreement.

Branimir turned to face Dorofej. "What else have you found? Have you found Falmagon in this shadowy place you talk about—*Klukas*?"

"Told you, I did, at Ariadne that I lost track of Falmagon some time ago. While we traveled the Netherworld, he disappeared from my view," Dorofej adjusted his robes, and sighed. "Dead, I think he is not; but instead, hidden, I believe he is. I say, if I could have seen Falmagon, I would know for certain whether the Ash Tree was at Melkorka, yes?"

Branimir rubbed his nose. Admittedly, he did not know enough about *Klukas* and how it worked to understand what the black mage was trying to explain. "How could he be hidden, Dorofej?"

"Secret ways of manipulating *Koldovstvo*, there are. I say, such ways were once recorded in an ancient codex called the *Varkolak*. Many things, a wandering mind would learn within the vellum. See, within its bindings, it shows a Stuhia, not only how to find a person, but also how to conceal oneself from the scrying eye within *Klukas*." Dorofej rubbed his chin roughly, then threw his hands together in his lap. "To not be able to find the Highborn Long-Walker…makes sense to think he has found a Stuhia to hide him, and who has learned the secrets of the *Varkolak*."

"Could he not have learned the skill and hidden himself?" Branimir guessed.

"No," Dorofej spoke softly. "Like any Highborn—or *Kadari*—who has mixed blood between Anshedar and Stuhia, does not have the power to manipulate *Klukas*."

"Then it must be Eisliev?" Branimir suggested unnervingly. His stomach tightened at the thought of the red mage, who had controlled his mind at Cavell. If he never saw the Stuhia again, it would be too soon.

"Maybe," Dorofej replied. The black mage looked off into the distance, seemingly captured by his thoughts.

Adamus, unaware Dorofej's lost look, asked, "Who else could it be?"

Dorofej tilted his head. "Questions, I have been asking myself. I say, there are more than a handful of Stuhia in the world, yes? Remember, Branimir might, that Falmagon once had a crooked staff, called *Habërmani*, whence had once come from the Stuhia city, Lairhein. Knew of it before he had it, I did. Such peculiarities, I have considered for some time. Yet the Likhyi gave me a greater answer at *Garain'l*."

Adamus took his turn, asking the clear question. "What did it say? All I heard was gibberish speak within the catacombs."

Branimir's mind raced back to the riddled words of the *old-dark*. Faintly, he recalled learning Dorofej's true surname from long ago: Kaligula.

The black mage had the same surname as this mysterious Dagmar Kaligula. Branimir kept himself from mentioning the name, from which Dorofej had insisted on keeping secretive.

Thinking of *Garain'l* also remind him of having *Ojenek*, his moonstone. He turned his hand into a fist almost hoping it would magically appear, or even press against his leg within his pocket. Wishing it to him was useless. The three-headed, white dragon, *Lahmia*, took the shiny stone for Erzebeth. Brave, daring Erzebeth, who thought she could bring Wolos back to life.

He wanted to know how Erzebeth would see it done.

Dorofej answered Adamus, and confirmed Branimir's assumption. "I say, the Likhyi alleged my bloodline assisted in the destruction of the Ash Tree, yes? Clear, the *old-dark* was, that my bloodline, and not myself, it spoke of."

The Ariadnean fit the pieces together. "You are saying someone from your lineage is helping Falmagon destroy the Ash Tree and free the *old-dark*. You think he or she is using this *Varkolak* to hide what they are doing?"

Branimir gazed at Dorofej, who shuddered against the warming ocean breeze. The black mage dipped his chin to his chest.

"Surprised, I would be, if Falmagon or any of the *Kadari* are aware of what they are doing," Dorofej responded with a grunt. "Pray they act in ignorance and might be swayed to help save the world, we must. For now, too many things are unknown. Who brought *kaelandur* back from the Netherworld? Did this person from my lineage only recently act, and what is their motive?"

"What of Bohumir?" Adamus wanted to know. "Have you seen him in *Klukas*?"

"I did," Dorofej said, "before he, too, disappeared from sight. Studied the *Varkolak* well, someone has."

"Has he been sacrificed?" Branimir said worriedly.

Dorofej shook his head. "I think not, or turn this vessel around, I already would have."

Branimir gripped his trousers, swaying with the rocking knarr, asking one more final question. "How do you know so much about the *Varkolak*, and what it teaches?"

"Transcribed it, I did."

Chapter XXVI

Branimir sat next to Sulanna as she guided the knarr eastward through the water. Settled beneath their blankets, Dorofej and Adamus still slept, snoring in harmony.

Rubbing the sleep from his dried eyes, Branimir yawned. Morning had come quicker than he would have liked. Fog hung above the surface of the ocean, hovering in threaded mists, while the *Winds Rising* lobbed toward the distant Seven Islands.

Appearing to be lost in thought, Sulanna gazed into the distance at nothing, and Branimir gazed at her. She held the mechanism for the boat loosely in her hand, piloting in the great body of water. Sulanna's long knife had been in her hand from the time he had woken and found her operating the knarr. Her brown hair whisked against her cheeks, threads striking her in the nose and eyes; and still—as stagnant as a stool—she sat, staring at nothing.

"How are you, Sulanna?" he prodded with a tender tone.

The woman did not answer right away. He almost feared the wind had taken his words, but finally, with a long enough lapse of silence, she lifted her chin and faced him. "Why would you ask me such a thing, Kras?"

"Because," Branimir said, "last night was hard. I know Alden was…*is* your friend, and if you need to talk, I would listen to you."

At first, Sulanna did not change her sullen expression. "I am fine," she murmured. She closed her eyelids for a moment and took a deep breath, swelling her chest. When she opened her eyes, she spoke louder, "I don't think talking will help, but I will say this. I am not angry at Adamus. I know he meant well."

Branimir paused, searching for the words to fill the void between them. He and Sulanna had not spoken much while together, and it was only now he realized how awkward he felt with her. He should have started with small talk.

After bouncing across several waves, she said, "I know Alden and I have had our disagreements, but he is my friend." She fiddled with her dagger, running her fingers along the flat of the blade. "I was born in Eldhaft, a city of liars and thieves. I learned there to not treat friendships daintily," she continued. "Nothing in the world demands we have friends."

"No, there really isn't, is there?" Branimir glanced at the black mage thoughtfully. Branimir weighed on the many disputes he and Dorofej had come across over the years. In the past months, he learned Dorofej worshipped Marheena and created *kaelandur*. He added, "We choose who we keep close and who we push away. Finding good friends is difficult. You should hold on to the ones you have. I think they help us see what good there is in the world."

Sulanna twisted to look to where Talastein would be, hundreds of miles away. "An interesting thought, Branimir. I have often debated how *good* of a man Alden is, despite all his sermonizing. Sometimes I wonder why I love him at all."

Sulanna gasped at her own admittance, turning her face from Branimir, reddening. The response had come so fast, Bran struggled to find an appropriate reply.

Instead, he fought the smile from forming on his face as they bounded through the fog. He was uncertain what she meant by *love*—whether friendly or more—but the sentiment softened him. When Sulanna slipped her long knife back in its scabbard, he said, "I have come to find I can control how I feel pain, hate, or even fear—but not love. It is the one feeling that reminds me I am alive."

Sulanna looked back to Branimir, visibly moved by his words. At the same time, his mind wandered to all he had seen in Aenar and the Netherworld.

He added, keeping his grin, "Even living among the dead for a little bit will show you they can't know love or friendship."

Sulanna mirrored his expression. It was the first time he had seen her smile since leaving Maharia. She said with amusement, "Tell me, how did you come to be alongside Dorofej and his scheming?"

Branimir scratched his head. "A long time ago, he was my Master at Melkorka."

"So, you are as old as him?" Sulanna reasoned. "Is that where your wisdom comes from?"

"No, not quite," Branimir eyed the Stuhia, who still snored, wrapped up in his robes. "I really do not know how old Dorofej is; I do not think he knows either. At one time, I thought he was a crazed, old man, but he has shown there is more sense in his head than most would dream to have. Sometimes, tidbits of what he knows trickles out, but it is hard to find in all his hubbub."

Sulanna laughed out loud, throwing her head back with a snort. "When I first met him, I thought he was a smart boy, who had read too many books. I would have never thought his knowledge came from somewhere else." Her tone shifted, becoming more serious. "It makes me question a lot of what I had known."

Branimir scratched his head.

Sulanna exhaled, recognizing his confusion. "There has to be some reason why you and Dorofej came back to Aenar. Why now?"

"You think it was fate?" Branimir asked.

"No, I don't believe in fate," she said, "but I admit this quest is more telling than anything I have experienced. All this talk about the Ash Tree and the gods sounds like something out of legends."

"I thought you did not believe in the gods," Branimir said, scrunching his face.

"I never said that," Sulanna said. "I just don't have a need to kneel to them as others might." Sulanna lifted her finger to her lips, thinking. "The Kras were subjugated at one time. Wouldn't you prefer to be free than be a slave?"

Branimir parted his lips with amazement. The ridiculous question had but one obvious answer. "Of course. No living being wants to be caged, even if it is the only thing known."

Sulanna said, "That is what keeps me from bowing to any god, or at least any god which men teach other men about. The simplest of creatures know freedom is righteous, and superior. I would think a grander being—a god—would uphold such a thing for all living creatures. Gods should be nobler, more honorable, and full of humility. If they cannot be virtuous, they are not worthy of my reverence."

He admired her. "Most would not dare to question the gods."

"From what I can tell, there is little to lose in thinking for myself. If the God of the Dead has been killed, as we believe, I will suffer the same fate as countless others in the Netherworld." Sulanna turned the mechanism to the knarr to keep it on course.

Branimir asked the same question Dorofej had presented to him months ago. "At the end of the day, what do you want out of life?"

"The same thing anyone wants, I imagine," she raised an eyebrow, blue eyes widening. "I want to be happy."

"How do you do that?"

"I think if the answer to happiness were that easy, we would all easily find it. Though," she looked south toward Talastein. "I would not be surprised if the answer is found in friendship."

Chapter XXVII

Adamus called from the rear of the knarr. "Land." He gestured to the north, where a dark sliver contrasted against the light surroundings.

Branimir joined Sulanna in covering his eyes to see into the distance. The brilliant light of the sun reflected against the sleek, blue waters.

"Change course, we should not," Dorofej said, sweating beneath the heavy wool. "The cape of Kalamaar, you see there. I say, upon the Seven Islands, we will be, within the hour."

"I cannot believe we will see the Islands of Forghar again," Branimir said, feeling his chest tighten with excitement. "If I recall, the first island is called Cyreus. The boldest Anshedar were said to live there. What was the main hamlet? Mjovadalsa?"

"An unparalleled memory, you have, Branimir," Dorofej agreed. "Brave, the men from Mjovadalsa must've been, lest death they would have found, yes? Hordes of rusalki once gathered near the reefs, yes?"

Sulanna, who had been tugging at her hair, folded her hands and addressed Dorofej. "Rusalki? You mean to say the tales of the half-fish women are real?"

"Quite," Dorofej whistled between his teeth. He tensed his jaw, rubbing the stubble of his red beard. "I say, it could be the rusalki were slayed over the years. Heard of them much since returning to Aenar, I have not."

Branimir nodded half-heartedly.

"You have been around the wrong type of folk then. Tis something talked about often enough," Adamus spoke in his deep baritone. "Tales of fish people are spoken of frequently at any seafaring town, and even in Ariadne. Cannot say I have ever crossed one, but," Adamus winced, "even Hanna spoke of them. She said they were real."

Branimir deterred his eyes from the hero-warrior. He did not want to get wrapped up in another conversation about Hanna or the Lilitu. He veered the conversation. "Let's not risk getting too close to the reefs."

"I agree," Adamus said. "I hear the rusalki first kiss you, and then eat you. Though the first sounds pleasing, especially after bouncing about on a boat, I have no interest in being fish food."

"Impossible to avoid the reefs, it will be," said Dorofej with a shake of his head. "Covers the entire area, it does."

Sulanna snickered, blocking the sun from her eyes and scanning ahead. "Let's just stay in the boat then, and keep an eye out for any watery tarts."

Dorofej leaned back against the mast, and said, "Until then, let's get what rest we can, yes?"

A bit more than an hour had passed and the sun had barely moved above them. Kalamaar had grown in its breadth to the north. Green trees outlined the bank and the mountainous Crags of Kazimir swelled in the far distance. Branimir guessed he may have seen an animal or two along the coastline, but could not say for certain for they sailed miles away from the shore. His eyesight was superb, but still, it had its limitations.

When the toothed cliffs of Cyreus crested from the waves ahead, Adamus marveled and called to Sulanna to look upon the isle.

The red rock that colored Cyreus was the same as the Crags of Kazimir. The sight pulled at Branimir's heartstrings, reminding him he was nearly back to the place he might call home. Trees, olive-colored and far-reaching, darkened the tops of the cliffs and sides of the mountains, scaling five-hundred feet above the surface of the water.

"I do not see anything, not even a hamlet," Sulanna said, "but the sight of solid ground reminds me how much I dislike the look of water."

"I, too, am ready to be back on land. Though, I can only imagine what this is like for Branimir," Adamus responded, gawking at the bluffs.

Bran turned to him with a questioning gaze.

Adamus acknowledged him with a nod. "You had once said Melkorka was the one place you might call home. What is it like to almost be back?"

"Unbelievable," Branimir replied. "I feel excited and scared at the same time. When I left, I had looked back for what I thought was the last time. Coming back again is unnatural…I almost feel like I shouldn't be here."

Adamus shifted in his seat, manipulating the steering mechanism to sail between the mainland of Kalamaar and the island. He gave Branimir a knowing look. "'Tis the same anytime I have gone to war. I leave and think I'll never see my home again, and I return with mixed feelings."

Branimir looked at the cliffs. He thought of those he had traveled among, who were stronger, wiser, or gifted in ways he was not. He said faintly, "I wonder why I lived and others could not."

"The answer is not difficult really," Sulanna said, "and, it has nothing to do with the gods, or skill, or luck."

"Why then?" Branimir asked.

Sulanna said, "Men spend all their years trying to figure out why they are here. They explore the world, wage wars, and write laws as though it may give them a grander sense of themselves, or help them conquer their charge. But there is a truth buried within each of us, and it is meant to be shared with those whom we cross paths."

"You pay no reverence to the gods, but gives a lecture on fate. You are a strange mystic," Adamus laughed with astonishment.

"I am not speaking of fate," Sulanna frowned. "I am talking about balance."

"How can you say there is balance when there is clearly so much evil?" Branimir scrunched his nose.

"There is not more evil, Bran," Sulanna explained, tucking her hair behind her ears. "We simply notice the wrongs in the world without seeing the good. See, there is no value in *knowing* what good looks like, but when you *know* evil, you can recognize what dangers to avoid. Those who have some sense about them *know* evil because they have no interest in dying."

"I don't know how this relates to why I survived when others have failed," Branimir said.

Sulanna shrugged. "Maybe you have something the others did not."

Branimir paused. He did not think himself to be special.

"'Tis something to think about." Adamus cleared the smile from his face, but still joked. "Though, our skulls must all be cracked to be here. There can be nothing more waiting for us at Melkorka than death, and yet, here we are sailing toward it. No matter what Dorofej says, the four of us cannot hope to defeat the *Kadari*."

Branimir practically fell over. "If you think that, why did you come, Adamus? Do you want to die?"

Adamus laughed. "Of course not. I am here for loyalty and friendship, Branimir, or have you forgotten?"

He returned the smile. "No," he said, pressing his hands together, "but facing death…" He trailed off.

The Ariadnean picked up where Bran stopped. "I face death every day whether I am fighting on the battlefield or sleeping in a bed. I rather have a choice in how I depart from this world."

"I agree with Adamus," Sulanna answered, dipping her chin at the other Anshedar, "and to die for something meaningful holds value to me. Not for the sake of glory, or riches, but because I believed in what I fought for, and I believed it would make a difference." Sulanna's blue eyes twinkled. "We may die at Melkorka. It is true, the odds are not in our favor, but if we succeed in the task, our lives will not be wasted."

"Our death would not be in vain to protect something as sacred as the Ash Tree," Adamus nodded back at Sulanna. "Perhaps, Sulanna is right. Maybe there are no gods, and no fate, but it is hard to believe our crossing of paths in Cavell was simple happenstance. No, I am meant to be here with you, Branimir."

Branimir glanced back and forth at Adamus and Sulanna, hearing his inner voice secretly hoping neither would die in the days ahead.

"I just hope we can save Bohumir from whatever evil Falmagon has planned for him," he said.

Suddenly gray webbed hands sprung over the shoulders of Sulanna, yanking her backwards over the knarr and into the water. She cried in alarm, flailing her hands as she went.

"No, no!" Branimir screamed, rousing Dorofej from his sleep. The black mage bumbled, sitting up from his plank, crying out questions among the uproar.

Adamus's bawl joined chorus with Branimir, ignoring Dorofej's shouting. The hero-warrior lunged forward, letting loose of the steering tool and reaching for where Sulanna had been.

His hands grasped at air.

The knarr whipped forward, still pushed over the waves by the sail. Dorofej and Adamus sprung to the back of the boat to look where they had come from, while Branimir leapt to where Sulanna had been.

"Sulanna!" Adamus roared. His muscles tensed. He reached over and loosened the sail to slow their speed.

"What has happened?" Dorofej asked, grabbing his arm.

"She was taken by something," Branimir said swiftly.

"Taken by what?"

"Cannot say," Adamus answered, pulling away and slackening the cloth, "but we cannot leave her."

Dorofej's blue eyes looked back across the expanse of the water hopelessly.

The knarr slowed, bouncing along in the water, drifting away from the place where Sulanna had disappeared. Time inched along, but only after a moment, Branimir heard a weak voice whimper from the side of the knarr. It was soft beneath the colliding waves.

Branimir leaned forward, raking the side of the boat, when his eyes caught sight of Sulanna. She moaned, eyes closed, with blood oozing from her neck. Miraculously, her fingers clung to rope moored to the side of the boat. She drooped in the water, the waves washing over her shoulder as she bumped against the knarr, half-conscious.

The Kras opened his mouth to yell for the others when he saw a golden-haired woman bob up from the surface of the sea. His mouth was dry.

Her two round, golden eyes sparkled beneath the yellowish strands of hair, locking onto his own with a mesmerizing intensity. Her thin lips were pressed closed, spreading wide to the edges of her jawbone, beneath a small, flat nose. She almost looked human with her pale, pink flesh, but her features were just bizarre enough to distinguish her apart from the Anshedar.

In a weird way, Branimir thought she was rather sweet-looking. His heart pulsated in his chest. He felt light and had to grip the edge of the boat to steady himself, or likely would have tumbled overboard.

The melody that touched Branimir's ears weaved through the wisps of air. The song sounded both distant and against his eardrum, rocking his senses, unbalancing him. He tilted frontward while the girl swam nearer to him. The rusalki did not spread her lips, but Branimir swore the music came from her.

'Come here to me, in the sea,
Crawl on the ocean floor,
I'll show you shining, splendid things,
You've never seen before.'

'Swim here with me, in the sea,
Forget about your lore,
Fill your pockets with shiny things,
You've never had before.'

Bran gawked at the golden hair, his eyes catching sight of sparkling scales beneath the surface of the water. The gal swayed drifting closer to the knarr, water dripping from her drenching skin. He reached out to touch her. His small, red fingers wavered over the edge, past Sulanna, toward the rusalki.

He could almost touch her. A little more.

Her webbed fingers lifted from the water, and between her long-nailed fingers, she held a glowing moonstone. The *Ojenek!*

'Fill your pockets with shiny things,
You forever had before.'

Without thinking, he sprung forward for his shiny stone. "Branimir!" Adamus's voice sounded a lifetime away.

He lurched, suddenly hindered by the Ariadnean's quick hand. Immobilized, Branimir hung, for the briefest of moments, suspended in the air. The moonstone in the rusalki's hand—an illusion—dispersed into nothingness. Her pink skin turned a steely gray, spreading her wide lips and exposing sharpened fangs.

The rusalki suddenly sprung from the water, clawed hands extending for him.

Branimir shrieked as Adamus jerked him backward into the belly of the boat. The hero-warrior kept his eyes on the rusalki, arcing his axe at the beast. His silver blade sliced her up the gut and ripped through her leathery chest. Blood splattered. The rusalki spluttered mid-air, gasping, and splashed back into the seawater.

"Sulanna." Branimir wheezed, pointing to the side of the knarr. "Sulanna."

Adamus guardedly followed Branimir's finger. With a lifted eyebrow, he peered over the edge of the *Winds Rising*. He cried out with surprise, "She lives, Dorofej!"

"Be quick, Adamus, and bring her aboard," Dorofej stood over Branimir, surveying the ocean. "Done with the rusalki, we are not."

Branimir pulled himself to his feet, scrambling behind Dorofej. The water swirled and churned as hundreds of half-fish, half-women, circled beneath them. Colored scales glided across the surface and vanished over and over again.

Branimir said, "Lift the sail and let us flee."

Dorofej did not respond. He seemed lost in thought, staring at the waters and the rusalki beneath.

"There are too many, Dorofej," Branimir reasoned, holding onto the mast to support himself. Something about the rusalki's singing had left him feeling lightheaded.

"Branimir is right. Better for us to run than fight these wenches." Adamus heaved Sulanna into the boat. She crumpled into a distorted heap, eyes closed and mouth gaping open.

"Is she dead?" asked Branimir.

Balancing his axe in his grip, Adamus narrowed his eyes at the rusalki who spun beneath them. "She is unconscious is all. The rusalki took a good chunk from the side of her neck. How she managed to grab hold of the side rope is beyond me with the thing chewing at her face. She is lucky her arm was not torn right off."

"Heal her, Dorofej," Branimir said, peering over the edge for more fish women.

The black mage hurried to Sulanna, stretching out his hands to her wound. "Be at the ready, Adamus."

The hero-warrior grunted in response.

The steady glow of Dorofej's healing power swelled against Sulanna's wound. As he had done with Branimir after being attacked by the myling, Sulanna's skin stitched itself back together, mending back together. Adamus had hardly crossed the span of the small knarr before she was sitting upright, gasping for breath.

"Dorofej," she grabbed a hold of his black robe. His features had barely changed, indicating the little *Koldovstvo* he had used.

The shrieking of a rusalki jumping from the water silenced Sulanna. The golden hair of the beast flowed over its grayed skin, golden eyes bulging, and arms outstretched. Adamus spun and ducked away from the rusalki. The half-fish, half-woman flew over him. Branimir gawked in amazement at the long fishy body, sparkling red and blue, like gems, down its length before splitting off into a filmy tail.

A second rusalki, with a golden and olive-colored tail, leaped for Adamus from the other side of the knarr. Dorofej struck the rusalki with a blast of *Koldovstvo*. The small whirlwind propelled the screeching creature back into the seawater.

More and more sprouted from the water, grasping for them. Adamus swung wildly at the rusalki, focusing on dodging their hands than killing them.

"Get the sail up," Adamus said.

Sulanna, revived with energy, sprung from the depths of the boat. Her clothes were stained with blood, but her skin was vivid with color. She moved with the grace of a warrior fresh to the battlefield.

Branimir sprung to and fro on the boat, tying off the ropes to hold the blue and gold sail in place while Sulanna worked the crank.

As they rushed about, Branimir noticed the rusalki had stopped springing from the waters. A moment later, the white sail raised across the ship's mast.

"Hold," Dorofej whispered. "I say, the water has stilled, yes?"

"I noticed, too. What happened?" Adamus rumbled, balancing himself. The sail caught wind and the knarr grated against the surface of the ocean.

"There." Sulanna pointed to the north. "It is another knarr sailing this direction."

"But why would that stop the rusalki?" Branimir rubbed his pointed hose with the back of his hand, keeping low.

"Wondered, I had, if we would cross paths," Dorofej grunted. "The rusalki must be frightened by the vessel, which can only mean one thing, yes? The *old-dark*, it is. I say, set a course to intercept, and make haste, yes?"

"Drak," Branimir gasped. "Are you going to kill him?"

"Drak is no more, and retrieve *kaelandur*, we must. At any cost."

Chapter XXVIII

"He will not be able to disappear and flee from the boat," Sulanna said, "not like he did in Ariadne. He has nowhere to go, if we can only reach him before he reaches land."

"We will," Dorofej assured.

The knarr bumped and bashed against the waves, angling to catch the other boat slightly ahead. The blue and gold sail stretched with the wind, slightly pressed to its limit with calculated surges of *Koldovstvo* from Dorofej.

The red rock cliffs of Cyreus grew next to them as they neared. Drak's vessel loomed ahead, looking to be the same size as the *Winds Rising*, powered by red and black sails. Though, without the power of *Koldovstvo*, it was only a matter of time before the distance was closed.

Adamus buckled down against the front of the ship, the wind blowing back his beard and long black hair. "Stay between him and Cyreus. We do not want him fleeing to the shore."

"He could still turn north for Kalamaar," Branimir said as they entered the channel between the islands and the mainland.

"Pray, he does not," Dorofej said, sneering at the boat ahead of them. "Sink his boat before letting him reach land, I will."

Branimir gulped. He called out to Dorofej over the wind. "Tell me, why did the rusalki stop attacking us?"

"The Likhyi," Dorofej answered, nodding at the knarr ahead. He closed his mouth, thin lips pressed together as though his answer was satisfactory. Though, he added, smacking his lips, "A blessing and a burden, it is."

Branimir grimaced, refusing to give up. He ignored the anger that swelled in his chest, considering Dorofej insisted on referring to Drak as the Likhyi, or some variation thereof, and no longer seemed to recognize him as a Kras. The Stuhia seemed intent on killing Drak. "But why, Dorofej?"

"Sensitive to the power of the *old-dark*, some creatures of this world still are," Dorofej shouted back. "Rusalki have been in this world since time before time, yes? Dragons, too, I would say. Know that chaos and death, the Likhyi brings to all living creatures. I say, its presence, the rusalki likely felt, and fled in fear of its supreme power."

Adamus spun around to look at the Stuhia. "What *supreme* power do you speak of? Tis no mystery an *old-dark* is within poor Drak, but the Kras is hardly a threat."

Branimir squinted at the Ariadnean. He supposed in comparison the Kras did not rival the hero-warrior from Ariadne, much less an ancient god.

"Indeed," Dorofej said, "but a month has come and gone since Ariadne, yes? With every day, the Ash Tree is further destroyed, the Likhyi grows more powerful and poisonous. Already touched by the mystical and weird, Drak has been. I say, more has come from him being connected with the Likhyi, yes?"

"What are you saying?" Branimir asked, feeling as though he were picking at straws. Trying to find the right question to ask with Dorofej was tiresome. "Speak plainly."

Dorofej bellowed over the din of their sailing, "I say, Drak knew the knowledge of the rune staves, practicing the primordial craft of the *old-dark*, called the *Runista*, the same magic as the desert people, yes? The act of his dark magic left him vulnerable to the Likhyi at *Garain'l*, yes? Control of his body, the Likhyi then took. A funnel, he is, to the hoary dark magic, the *Runista*."

"Can you defeat him?" Branimir yelped. "What power would the Likhyi possess?"

"See, we will," Dorofej flared his nostrils, eyes locked on the knarr ahead. "Weak, still, he may be."

"'Tis clear that some quests require more prayer and hope than others," Adamus said unnervingly, looking toward Drak's boat.

Once they were a few hundred feet away, Drak's boat start to veer toward Kalamaar. Bran could see the Kras at the back of the boat, watching them with his coal-colored eyes. His crimson-colored head and pointed ears barely poked above the edge of the knarr.

A handful of men, around a dozen humans, moved around the boat, directing its course at the command of the Kras. Who knew what the sailors thought of Branimir and the others? Or, the better question was how did Drak convince them to give him passage to Melkorka?

He supposed it mattered little in the moment.

"They have weapons," Branimir said. He pointed at several who held longbows with arrows. "Likely waiting for us to draw near."

Dorofej curled his lip, "See them, I do."

Two hundred feet.

"Dorofej!" Sulanna yelled with warning as Drak's boat entered shallow waters. The *Winds Rising* heaved forward with another blast of *Koldovstvo* to the sails.

One hundred feet.

The mainland stretched in either direction, covered with sandy beaches. Branimir could almost smell the pine of the trees amid the salty water of the ocean. The Crags, which held the ancient ruins of long-abandoned Kras cities, reared toward the heavens beyond the trees.

Branimir was only leagues from Melkorka. He had left Kalamaar in the midst of fighting, and was returning again on the brink of battle. Drak had said it best back at Ojenir. Bran would never know peace in his lifetime.

Nearing Kalamaar and the other vessel, Dorofej held to his promise of stopping the boat. The Stuhia cast *Koldovstvo* pulling at the other knarr's sail. The cloth swiftly ripped free from the binding ropes, flailing and flapping into the waters uselessly.

The other boat slowed considerably, drifting towards the beach.

"Overrun them," Dorofej bade as arrows were released from the sailors on the other boat. The black mage huffed, swiping his hand, and ripping the weapons free from hands of the attackers and the arrows off course. The entirety of their arsenal was flung into the ocean.

The sailors shouting warnings of the *Kadari* echoed across the spread.

Sulanna yelled from the steering mechanism. "Hold onto something!"

Branimir wrapped his arms around the mast, watching Dorofej duck down and cling to the side of the knarr. In an instant, the *Winds Rising* collided into the back of the other vessel. Voices split the air as wood splintered. Branimir grunted, his hold broken from the shock. The world spun as he flew through the air and knocked into the planks on the other boat.

Pain surged through his back. He flinched, lungs burning for air. With his vision blurred, he sat up against the planks on the opposite boat. Several sailors around him, ignored him, launching themselves overboard. He watched them swim awkwardly toward the beach.

The impact had sent waves reeling out in all directions, thrusting the swimmers closer to the shore. The *Winds Rising*, surprisingly still intact, bounced backward, bobbing up and down.

Branimir stood, legs wobbling. He looked back at the *Winds Rising* feeling dazed. Dorofej struggled to his feet, stumbling to reach Bran. Adamus and Sulanna groaned as they, too, tried to regain their footing.

Then, Drak stood in front of Branimir. His black eyes looked lifeless, empty of the joviality Branimir had once known in the Kras.

"Drak," Branimir murmured.

A hoarse, harsh sound emitted from Drak's mouth, speaking in a language Branimir could not understand. He instinctively reached for *Ojenek* in his pocket, and remembered he did not have it any longer. The noise grated inside his head. He reached to cover his pointed ears.

This is what the *old-dark* sounded like; this is what Adamus had heard in the catacombs of *Garain'l*.

Dorofej crashed to the planks next to Drak with a loud thump. His frame shadowed the Kras, causing the Likhyi to stop speaking. *Kaelandur* flickered in Drak's hand.

"Dorofej, watch out!" Branimir screamed.

Dorofej vaulted backwards as Drak spun, tearing the dagger through the empty space. Drak vanished, toppling over his own feet to get away from Dorofej.

"Stop him, Branimir!" Dorofej shouted back plainly, his icy blue eyes darting around the boat warily, and to the water, looking for a splash.

Branimir, who could see Drak clearly, even though invisible, saw him scooting toward the threshold of the knarr. He hurled himself at Drak, pulling him back by his cloak.

Drak lashed out with *kaelandur* again, slashing the top of Branimir's hand. Pulling back with a yowl, Branimir winced, blood trickling from the cut. Branimir turned his scream into a roar, steadying his feet. He pulled free two of the daggers from his belt.

Watching Branimir's movements, Dorofej flung fire in the direction he thought Drak to be standing. The Kras shifted sideways to avoid the flame, and turned toward Branimir.

Even concealed, Branimir could see the darkness in Drak's gaze. The Kras lunged with *kaelandur*, and Branimir winced as the blade cut the side of his arm. He ignored the sting, and swiped his own blade forward, followed by a second blow with his offhand.

Drak eluded and evaded each strike seconds before Branimir struck. If he did not know any better, he would have guessed Drak could see seconds into the future. Branimir quickened his pace with the daggers, drawing at the skills he had mastered while traversing the Netherworld.

He twisted and plunged, pitching the blades forward over and over again. When the opportunity presented itself, Dorofej continued to fling fire from nothingness. In spite of everything, Drak moved as though he had spent a lifetime on the battlefield, dodging every attack. He ducked the fire and shirked Branimir's blades. Worse yet, Drak hastened his own actions, leaving nicks across Branimir's forearms with every counterattack.

Branimir stumbled back, exhausted, his own blood oozing down his thin arms. Behind him, he could hear Dorofej saying something about torching the entire boat. He also could hear the *Winds Rising* rocking, slapping into Drak's knarr. The boat rocked as Adamus eased onto the ship.

Sulanna shouted at him to come back.

Cackled words escaped Drak's mouth again.

"He is no longer a Kras," Branimir said to himself, his knuckles ached from squeezing his daggers.

Branimir snarled, throwing a dagger from his left hand, quickly followed by the dagger in his right. The Likhyi dodged each as expected, but Branimir kept coming, tugging the two remaining weapons from his belt. He threw another straight downward, striking the *old-dark* in the foot, pinning it to the wooden planks.

Drak screamed, falling backward onto his buttocks, and Branimir dove onto him. The other Kras struggled against Bran, swinging his arms, but Branimir had the advantage.

"Please, no," Drak screamed, raising his hands defensively, becoming visible once more. "Alack! Branimir."

"Drak?" Branimir stooped over the Kras, holding him to the ground with one hand. The other was raised with his last dagger, ready to plunge into Drak's skull.

"Stone the crows! What happened? Where am I?" Drak moaned. He quivered in Branimir's hands.

"Finish him, Branimir," Adamus shouted.

"A trick, it is," Dorofej cried.

The warning came too late as darkness percolated from Drak's mouth and eyes, silencing the voice of the Kras. The Likhyi jabbed *kaelandur* into Branimir's side without hesitation. Branimir pushed his own dagger downwards, but it was swiped away by the *old-dark*. Scoffing, Drak's thin lips spread into a wicked smile beneath him, displaying his crooked teeth.

"No," Branimir choked, overcome with grief. Ripping *kaelandur* from his flesh, he slammed it down at Likhyi. Red hands flailed frantically upwards to stop him, but there was no stopping the copper dagger from sinking into Drak's skull.

The next minutes were distorted. Branimir pulled the weapon free, clung it to his chest and toppled over. The black mage embraced *Koldovstvo*, touching the ancient healing magic in his blood. Yellow glowed opposite side of Branimir's eyelids. All the while, he cringed sensing his body restoring itself.

"Dorofej, stop," he mumbled. "You will need your strength at Melkorka."

"Patch the greater injury, I must," Dorofej replied with kindness. "Wear the scrapes and bruises for a while, you will, yes?"

"Is it over?" Adamus's voice sounded from nearby. "Is the *old-dark* defeated? Is it dead?"

"Doubtful," Dorofej answered, "but dead, its host has become. I say, where the darkness has fled, I do not know, yes?" Branimir fluttered his eyes open to look at the black mage, slight grey now lining his beard. He could see wrinkles at the corner of Dorofej's eyes.

"Oh, Dorofej," Branimir shook with emotion at what the black mage gave others at the expense of his own life. He avoided Drak, lying dead only feet from him.

"Here," Dorofej stretched out his hand, "hold *kaelandur*, I will, and keep it safe, yes?"

Branimir twitched his hand, surprised he was still holding the copper dagger. Eagerly, he handed it to the Stuhia having no interest in holding the dastardly weapon.

"Ahhh!"

As the hilt was pulled from his hand, Branimir screamed in pain. His entire body burned from the back of his skull to the base of his feet. He writhed and convulsed, throwing his head against the baseboards of the boat with hope it might end the torture. Tears flowed from his eyes, and through his soggy vision, he found the strength to jerk *kaelandur* back from the stunned Dorofej's trembling hands.

"What has happened?" Adamus reached for Branimir for a moment, before pulling back. The Ariadnean had fear in his eyes.

Dorofej's face fell to gloom. "The darkness has enveloped *kaelandur*, it seems, and bound itself to Branimir, yes?"

Branimir whimpered, the pain subsiding, clinging the copper dagger to his chest in alarm. "What does this mean, Dorofej? Nine Lands, what does it mean?"

"When and if *kaelandur* is destroyed," Dorofej shivered, looking toward Melkorka, "it may be, you will be, too."

Chapter XXIX

Adamus and Sulanna had stayed behind to drop the anchor to the knarr. Branimir observed them wading through the water and making their way back to the light brown sands of Folkmar. The four of them had done it. At last, they reached the island of Melkorka.

Branimir inhaled the stale air and twisted around to gawk at the familiar red rocks. They were named the same as the mountains on Kalamaar, the Crags of Kazimir. Except, these mountains had birthed the demonic Bukavac, along with the undead *Eretik*, Nedezhda Mager. The monsters had slaughtered nearly every Highborn and Kras who had been at Melkorka. The casualties had been great, including Jhar, Katerina, and Faina. And then, there had been Mojmir, who had died at the hand of Kinhar Sayan.

Poor Mojmir.

This is the place where *kaelandur* had been created, within the walls of Melkorka. Branimir knew with certainty that Dorofej had created the copper blade using the magical craft of *Koldovstvo*. The black mage had endowed it with the ancient power which brought Nedezhda back to life, and ultimately led to the Ash Tree's current state.

Now Branimir had come back to this dreadful place, and the circumstance had worsened. He worried for Bohumir,

Nedezhda's kin, who had been kidnapped by the *Kadari* to be sacrificed. Though having *kaelandur*, the cursed dagger, bonded to him concerned Branimir all the more. Dorofej said he would die if the dagger were taken from him or destroyed.

Branimir did not believe he would live to see the end of this tale. He simply hoped he was on the side of good, and would be remembered as a hero.

"Returned, we have," Dorofej said tenderly, standing tall in his robes next to the Kras. "Just beyond the ridge is Melkorka, yes?"

The black mage dipped his head toward the hill ahead of them. Trees sprung from the top of the hill where the sands of the coast ended and patched greenery began. Branimir was not sure he was ready to see Melkorka again.

"I have asked you many times, Dorofej," Branimir said, "and I would still like to know. Why have you kept me alive all this time? At Melkorka? In the Netherworld? In the Dyndaer? Why do you keep saving me from death?"

"Told you, I did," Dorofej said. "The option to give life, I have, and choose to wield it, I do."

Branimir responded with some heat. "I don't believe you. A long time ago, you claimed you told Kinhar to keep me alive."

Dorofej abruptly chuckled. He pulled at his beard, seemingly comforted by the hair hanging from his chin. "After the demons attacked Melkorka, it only stood to reason to have you on the journey, yes? Agreed, Kinhar did, that a Kras's talents could not be overlooked. And proved your worth and your heroism, and your friendship, at each juncture, you did. Yet, wanting to hold you for accountable for Nedezhda's return from the Netherworld, he did."

"But you were the one responsible for her return by creating *kaelandur*," Branimir said. He blinked several times and looked away from Dorofej to keep himself from tearing up, knowing the accusation may have cut wounds in his friend. Maybe, they could remain the heroes.

Footsteps interrupted them.

"What are we to do?" Sulanna approached, adjusting her belt knife with Adamus stepping lightly behind her.

Dorofej's eyes sparkled in the dying light of the day. Fog had begun to settle above the sea about an hour ago, and for the first time in days, clouds gathered in the skies.

"Rescue Bohumir, we must," Dorofej said, "and then, flee from Melkorka, we will. I say, an eye for the Ash Tree, we will keep, but a battle with the army of *Kadari*, we should avoid."

Adamus said, "Are we not here to also save the Ash Tree? If the *Kadari* are destroying it, we must stop them, Dorofej."

"I agree," Sulanna said. "Alden and I have made sacrifice after sacrifice for the sake of this fabled Ash Tree, and named ourselves enemies to the *Kadari* as a result. I do not want to spend the rest of my days running when I could end this here and now."

"And the end of all things tonight may bring," Dorofej licked his lips, "but there is much to risk, yes? Besides, changed, the situation has. Bound to *kaelandur*, Branimir undoubtedly is, yes? I say, what if he is slain in battle or is captured? The *Kadari* had also been seeking *kaelandur* to use on the boy, yes?"

Sulanna argued, "So, let Branimir stay here, or back on the knarr, while we venture forward to investigate. If we catch Falmagon, we will take his head and watch the *Kadari* fall to pieces without their fearless spearhead to guide them."

"If opportunity presents itself, I would welcome it," Dorofej granted with a nod of his head. "Though, recommend the opposite, I would. Sneaking and cunning is Branimir's trade, yes?"

"You mean," Branimir paused, "you want me to go tiptoeing around Melkorka while the rest of you stay here?"

Dorofej arched his eyebrows, looking back at Branimir with an unmistakable expectation.

"That's madness!" Adamus shouted.

"No," Sulanna looked at the black mage for a moment, and then turned to the other two. "Dorofej is right. Branimir can vanish from sight, and moves lighter than any of us can on our best day. The mages would not even know he had come, and then he could return to tell us the full of it."

Adamus's hand touched the axe at his belt. He grumbled.

"We can hardly make a plan without knowing anything of the place, Adamus." Sulanna perched her nose. "Be reasonable."

"I know what you are saying," Adamus said, twisting back, face reddened, "but tis hardly reasonable to send Branimir into the last place he should be, especially when he cannot be separated from the dagger." With emphasis, he stepped to Branimir's side.

Dorofej folded his arms, grimacing. "I say, what else can be done? Better chance for survival, we will have."

Branimir touched *kaelandur* on his belt, and shifted his hand to the one remaining dagger he had retrieved from Drak's vessel. If there was ever a time to be brave, he supposed this was the moment.

"Okay," Branimir consented, looking up at Adamus, "but if I am not back by morning, you best be coming for me."

"Ha!" Sulanna grinned, wrinkling her small nose. "You won't tell us to save ourselves?"

Branimir wiggled his eyebrows. "Sulanna, you wouldn't do it, even if I did. None of you would."

"Wouldn't even cross our mind," Adamus said, touching Bran's shoulder.

Gathering his courage, Branimir scampered off toward Melkorka, scanning the environment, while staying hidden in his realm of invisibility. Dorofej, Adamus, and Sulanna remained on the shoreline, hiding from sight with the knarr.

He raced across the terrain. The night fell and the white moon peaked in the heavens. The broken pebbles mingled among the few strands of grass, barely munching under Branimir's feet. His sensitive ears could scarcely pick up the sound. With each step, he encouraged himself to press forward and ignore his fears about being captured. He reminded himself the *Kadari* could not see him or hear him.

He was safe.

Melkorka sat on the same tall, flat hill Branimir remembered, but the castle had changed radically over the past millennia. The earliest stone walls had almost doubled in size and the keep towered higher yet. The stone looked fresher, newer, and even sturdier than it had a thousand years ago. The walls had battlements built across the tops with spacing between chiselled stones. Branimir remembered the Bukavac, the frosty demons from the Netherworld, who had attacked Melkorka when he had stayed here. The giants had no trouble assaulting the castle a thousand years ago. He believed it would be much more difficult if it were to ever happen again.

Additional curtain walls had been built beneath the hill and around the original structure, outlining what looked to be a small hamlet of houses and other buildings. Soft glows blended in the Kras's vision, telling him either lanterns or torches had been lit for the evening. From where Branimir walked, the addition looked to stretch almost half a mile around the hill. Falmagon had expanded the size of the stronghold considerably.

He shuddered to think of the numbers of *Kadari* residing in Melkorka. Finding Bohumir may not be as simple as he had hoped.

Branimir sneaked closer, clinging to the base of the outer curtain wall. He could hear the murmurs of the *Kadari* pacing back and forth, visible through the embrasures, on the wall walk above him. He could see the mages clearly, leaning forward, scanning the open grassland and scattered trees beyond the castle.

Ahead of him, a brown horse pulled a cart through the main gate. Several mages, dressed in light leather armor and carrying wooden staves, walked on either side. One of the *Kadari* led the horse by a rope.

"How much longer can we can keep this up?" one uttered. "The Bukavac weren't any weaker in the winter, and now with the Season of Warmth upon us, the numbers have almost tripled."

Branimir's ears tilted at the sound of Bukavac, but only half-listened. He quickened his pace to walk behind the cart in order to get through the gate. Additional *Kadari* guarding the iron doors stepped wide to let their brethren pass through.

No one detected Branimir slinking invisibly behind them. Though, he regretted the decision to follow the moving cart once the smell of decaying skin filled his nostrils. He shielded his nose with both hands, lifting his eyes to a decomposed arm sagging over the side of the cart. It was chock-full with dead bodies. Dead *Kadari*.

"Falmagon and Dagmar will think of something," answered a female voice. "You have been going on about this since we left the field. It is exhausting, Beryl."

Dagmar? Branimir's heart quickened. The stranger named Dagmar Kaligula was somewhere within these walls.

"I don't mean to be exhausting, but our friends are dying" Beryl said sheepishly. "Furthermore, the Ash Tree will not last. Someone has to ask these questions. The Bukavac armies have grown stronger and our numbers are dwindling."

The *Kadari* leading the horse interrupted, "Listen to Kerra. Neither Falmagon nor Dagmar would appreciate your gainsaying. The Ash Tree is not yet gone, and the rest of

Aenar is safe because of our sacrifice. What would you do differently?"

Branimir strained to see Beryl's reaction from the back of the cart. He was not surprised to hear the *Kadari* talk like they were at war with demons. He had heard the rumors throughout Maharia about their battles against the undead.

Beryl pulled at a yellow sash around his belt and drooped his shoulders.

The *Kadari* leading the horse noticed the gesture, and snorted. "If you do not have a solution, I suggest you stop your snivelling."

The flapping of a banner on the opposite side of the gate, above Branimir, stole his attention. He twisted his neck to see a familiar golden emblem with dancing swirls. The markings, the sign of Dahz the Lightbringer, had been sewn on white and blue fabric. As expected, and aligned with what he had heard back on Maharia. The *Kadari* still worshipped the Sun God.

The *Kadari* continued to discuss the Bukavac and the Ash Tree, but Branimir barely heard their words. Instead, he gawked at the sight within the walls. The spread of stone buildings and wooden houses formed a much different Melkorka than he had remembered, but it was the massive tree in the center of the courtyard that took his breath away.

He mouthed its name, "The Ash Tree."

The tree held many fruits and massive leaves as large as the Kras, but the wide base, roots, and branches had partially wilted in many sections. The blackened limbs gave Branimir clarity as to why the Likhyi were gaining power. The *Kadari* had more or less sapped the Waters of Life, and thus, the Ash Tree was fading. The prison for the *old-dark* had weakened.

Indeed, the Ash Tree was dying.

Even though he had told Dorofej the Ash Tree might be here, he could not believe his eyes. Dorofej had once said the Ash Tree changed its placement in the world from time to time, but what were the chances of appearing at the stronghold of Melkorka.

He pulled away from the cart and wandered nearer to the Ash Tree within the small pool of dark water, the Waters of Life. The tree had lost its full magnificence since the last time he had stood before it, but it still was breathtaking.

The Kras shuddered. He and Dorofej had thought the *Kadari* had been regularly consuming its resources for selfish reasons. But from what Branimir had gathered, the *Kadari* used its power to fight demons on the Seven Islands.

Branimir, staying unseen, leaned forward and scooped a handful of water to his mouth. Despite his assumptions, he could not miss the chance to be rejuvenated. The healing process of the Ash Tree coursed through his body, soothing his aching muscles and restoring the slight injuries that Dorofej had been unable to mend. Branimir sensed his youth return to his body. Instantly, he felt lighter on his feet, and filled with a sprightly energy.

With a light bounce, he skedaddled beyond the Ash Tree, contemplating which structure may have Bohumir within. The main keep caught his eye. He could only presume a prisoner would be kept in the old dungeon beneath Melkorka, the place which once held Nedezhda the *Eretik*.

The wooden doors on the former walls had been replaced with iron doors like those on the outer curtain. The entrance stood open, giving Branimir clear passage to the keep. He passed by more and more *Kadari* while he roamed nimbly through the dirt streets.

The white moon hung halfway to its apex by the time he skulked up the stone steps adjacent to the keep, and slinked through the unguarded, wooden door.

Melkorka's keep had been completely redone. Dirt flooring and rotting beams had been replaced with chiselled rock and fresh timber. Lanterns lit the great hall, leading to a hearty throne on a dais, with long tables for feasting along the sides. Wooden chairs lined the tables, and behind them were tapestries with the symbol of Dahz.

Branimir started toward the spiralling stone staircase, once leading to Kinhar's quarters, and stopped. It had been reformed, the sleek and smooth red stone cut and stacked to perfection. Branimir could only think the keep had been renewed with the power of *Koldovstvo*.

He shifted toward another staircase, once an angled dirt pathway to the dungeon. As he started down the narrow stone path, he could not help but wonder if the dungeon were still located at the base of the stronghold. The voices echoing from an open door below robbed him of the thought.

"Falmagon—" a woman pleaded. The sound of skin slapping against skin exploded in Branimir's ears.

"You will call me Patrician Sej," responded Falmagon's memorable timbre, "or, by *Mulafell*, a hundred times over I will strike you until you bleed."

Branimir quaked, shuffling slowly, down the stairs. The profane reference to *Mulafell*, Dahz's mystical hammer, was too familiar to Bran; there was only one man Branimir had ever heard speak in such a way. The Highborn Long-Walker lived. Despite all he had heard, Bran had not dared to think he would see the infamous man again.

Sobbing resounded from the depths below. "Please, I don't know anymore."

"She lies," grumbled a deep voice. "She knows where her brother hides. The question is how the boy came to be in Cavell without him or *kaelandur*?"

"Alyona," Falmagon said, "you served well in retrieving the dagger, but your subversion cannot go unpunished. Tell me where your brother has gone. Tell me where Artemiy has taken *kaelandur*!"

Alyona? Artemiy? The names sounded familiar, but Branimir could not place them. He stepped through the widened door into the shimmering lantern light, still hidden to those within the room.

Bran saw the dungeon had been extended. Hanging from the walls were linked chains with metal bindings. Above each set of shackles was the indention of an eye scraped with a moon and cross. He had seen a similar symbol above Nedezhda years ago, preventing her from touching *Koldovstvo*.

"I do not know," the woman whimpered, hanging weakly, straining against her bindings. Her chin tilted upwards, purplish eyes watering under the piercing gaze of Falmagon and the other redheaded man. Her mouth was bleeding, eyes swollen and black, and red marks streaking each side of her face.

Upon seeing the woman, Branimir had to cover his mouth with recognition. Of course. Alyona had been one of the *Kadari* at Shayol Domier a millennium ago. She was the only person he had met with purplish eyes. And Artemiy, her brother, had been the so-called Highborn, who had killed Asgrim, the centaur, who had accompanied them from Sorod. How had she survived this long? How could either of them have survived so long?

Falmagon clenched his fist, as if considering whether to strike the woman again. Leisurely, he raised his fingers and pulled at his thick mustache. "Dagmar," he shifted his head, long brown locks of hair shifting against leather armor, "we are wasting our time with her. Let's *speak* with the boy again."

Branimir's old master had plainly used the Waters of Life to maintain his youth. Falmagon looked as young as he had at Shayol Domier before the final battle with Nedezhda.

The redheaded man pursed his lips, scowling hatefully at Alyona. The man called Dagmar looked remarkably like Dorofej with scraggly red hair and bright blue eyes, filled with incomparable knowledge. He made Branimir's skin crawl.

Dagmar said, "The boy is useless. The immature brat thinks Artemiy is his father, and knows nothing about *kaelandur*."

"The boy told us about the black mage and Kras at Cavell," Falmagon contested. "He might know more."

"He also said the *Kluk* had killed them." At mentioning the last name of Eisliev, the red mage, Dagmar's face contorted with fury. "Yet you talk about Dorofej like he is still alive."

Falmagon frowned.

"Forget the boy," Dagmar said. He dipped his head at Alyona, slumped against the wall. "I know her type. She will tell us everything. I will pick her apart—piece by piece—and we will see how much she knows when her insides are scattered out in front of her."

"Patrician Sej, please," Alyona begged. "I have been a faithful servant…to the *Kadari*. I tracked Branimir and the mage…like you had asked…I've given so, so much…let me go…"

She heaved against the wall, tears falling down her cheeks.

Branimir squeezed his hand tighter over his mouth. Alyona had followed them through the Netherworld. How had he and Dorofej not known?

Falmagon backhanded her, jostling her body against the fastenings. She cried out in pain as the skin of her wrists cut against the iron. "And, you were supposed to bring me the dagger! Instead, you hid it from me!"

"I have done…what you wanted. I kidnapped the Mager boy when I returned," she said.

Falmagon sneered. "And, left him with your maddened brother on the other side of the world."

"I did not know Artemiy had *kaelandur*," she wept. "I did not know he would hide the boy from you."

"Liar!" Falmagon screamed, hammering his hand into the side of head again.

"I—" she tried, "I—"

Dagmar enunciated his words, speaking with a slow cadence. "Where is Artemiy? You risk everything with your secrets."

She struggled to raise her head toward the imposing man, and when she could not hold herself up, she slouched without strength. Still, she spoke clearly, "We are all dead anyway."

With a sigh, Dagmar lifted his hand toward the woman, giving permission to Falmagon, who readily struck her once more. The simple gesture caused Branimir to deliberate whether Falmagon or Dagmar was in charge.

Alyona fell limp in the chains, unconscious.

"Worthless swine," Dagmar muttered. "Ages and ages pass and nothing changes. When she awakens, we will start over."

"It is futile, Dagmar." Falmagon turned away from Alyona, addressing the redheaded man. "We are running out of time. Dorofej must have *kaelandur*. You must look for him in *Klukas*."

Branimir's heart stopped.

Dagmar reached into the pocket of his red robe, pulling out a miniature book. Using *Koldovstvo*, the book with its leather casing, enlarged in the man's hand. "I cannot simply find anyone I want. I have to personally know who they are," the man said, placing his hand on the book. "I have to know the essence of their spirit."

"Then, teach me," Falmagon demanded. "I know him. We must be certain he is dead."

"You are not a Stuhia," Dagmar barked. "If Dorofej is like me, as you presume—and for some reason knows the mysteries of the *Varkolak*—I have kept us from being found in *Klukas*. No more can be done. If he comes, he comes."

"You do not know him, Dagmar," Falmagon sniffed, pulling at his mustache again. "Dorofej will be difficult to defeat. I saw the way he fought at Shayol Domier. And you have heard Alyona. If he endured the Netherworld, he surely survived Eisliev Kluk."

Dagmar grinded his teeth. He shrunk the book again and placed it in his pocket. "Our focus is to find the dagger and sacrifice the boy. The ritual with his blood will restore the Ash Tree, keeping the *old-dark* at bay."

Falmagon snorted. "The Bukavac will continue to bleed from the Crags. The Ash Tree will weaken again. Destroying *kaelandur* is the only way, and I am telling you—Dorofej will have it."

Dagmar's face turned red, turning to Falmagon. Though, before he could say anything, footsteps echoed down the stone path leading to the dungeon.

"Lord Kaligula. Patrician Sej." A short girl burst through the doorway, panting. She did not even look in Alyona's direction. "A knarr has landed on the shore."

Falmagon glowered. "Gather a scouting party. Let's see who has come to Melkorka."

Branimir backed out of the dungeon, and ran.

Chapter XXX

Branimir slipped through the streets toward the outer gate, the stale air of early summer filling his lungs. He had to return to the coast before the *Kadari* discovered the others in hiding. Melkorka was only about six hundred paces from the shoreline. If he was quick enough, Branimir might just outrun them. That is, as long as the main gate was open at the outer curtain wall.

He repeatedly looked over his shoulder, at his flank, fearing that Falmagon might bolt from the keep at any moment and give chase. Branimir did not think he had been discovered, but he could not be certain what tricks Falmagon, or Dagmar, would have at their disposal. If Dagmar could enter *Klukas* like Dorofej, he may have other secrets, too.

His hand touched the copper dagger at his belt. The risk of being caught by the *Kadari* was too great. He could not forget what was at stake. If Falmagon retrieved *kaelandur*, they would kill Bohumir. He wanted the Ash Tree saved, and the Likhyi stopped, but not at the cost of a child. Besides, he could not be certain Falmagon told the truth. Dorofej said Bohumir's sacrifice would give the *Kadari* more power. Did he mean by giving life back to the Ash Tree?

The unanswered questions pounded against his skull, while he looked back at the towering keep of Melkorka. Why had Alyona and Artemiy followed him and Dorofej to the Netherworld? Did Alyona hide the dagger and boy from Falmagon? Did Artemiy? What was their fear? And who exactly was this Stuhia named Dagmar Kaligula?

His mind raced while he ran.

With a grunt, Branimir hit something solid and fell back on his haunches. He flickered into sight for a half-second, before gaining control of his invisibility once more.

He lifted his gaze to the figure in front of him, attached to the oversized leg in which he had collided. The tan skin of the giant looming over him was dreadfully familiar. The piercing blue eyes of Tyr Og were cock-eyed, looking down, examining the ground in confusion.

"Bah! What in the Nine Lands was that?" he bellowed.

The Ispolini stood next to Eisliev. The Stuhia's red robes covered him from head to foot, including his red hair. He stopped in his tracks to glare at Tyr. "What in the Nine Lands was what?"

Branimir's heart stopped at the sight of Eisliev. The scene at Cavell replayed in his head. The magic-wielding Stuhia had somehow manipulated his mind, causing him to attack his friends. He could not allow Eisliev to gain control of him again.

Tyr clenched his six-fingered hands into fists, nostrils flaring. "Ah! I've been hit by something right beneath the knee. With all you foul mages running about, who knows which fool cast what."

Eisliev snorted. "No *Kadari* is going to waste time prodding at the ankles of an oversized pile of sheepdip."

Tyr growled, reaching back slightly as though he might grab the massive battle axe from his back. He stopped, however, and turned to Eisliev. "Then, what do you suppose it was?"

Eisliev taunted the giant. "I think you tripped over your gargantuan, donkey feet. Now, can you stop your drivel so we can get on with this?"

Breathing again, Branimir realized neither had noticed him. He twisted his neck to check the courtyard. The *Kadari* nearby either ambled about carelessly or huddled near the Ash Tree. None raised an alarm.

Branimir scowled, catching sight of the gates. The iron doors were closed shut.

The giant stressed the visible muscles in his arms and chest. Branimir stood while Tyr responded. "I did not sign up to kill the boy. The Crimson Sun hired us to deliver him and then be gone."

"I don't care two hoots what the Crimson Sun hired us to do. You know I came here with my own agenda. I have spent years finding Dagmar, and now that he is within my reach..." Eisliev clenched his fists, his voice trailing off. He glared towards the keep.

"I don't understand why you hate Dagmar the way you do," Tyr said.

Eisliev said, "You wouldn't. The blood feud between the Kaligulas and the Kluks is old. That covetous swine ruined my family."

Tyr rumbled. "Then use your fancy, little ring on Patrician Sej. Force him to take you to Dagmar."

Eisliev started at Tyr with wide eyes, crossing his arms with irritation. "The *Faegrim* only lets me control those who cannot touch *Koldovstvo*. The Patrician may be a half-breed," the Stuhia paused to sneer at the *Kadari* in the courtyard, "but he can still touch *Koldovstvo*."

Branimir raked his eyes over Eisliev, searching for the so-called *Faegrim*. A silver band on the red mage's left hand—the smallest finger—stood out. The *Faegrim* was the secret to Eisliev's mind-altering magic.

"You can't use it on me either," Tyr said, "and I have nothing to do with your magic."

"That is because the Ispolini are too thick headed."

"Or too smart."

"Don't flatter yourself," Eisliev said, waving his hand for Tyr to follow. "Bottom line, if Patrician Sej won't let me have an audience with Dagmar," Eisliev hissed through clenched teeth, "he will not have the boy."

Tyr growled under his breath. "You speak of doing a dark thing. We don't even know why they wanted the boy."

"I don't care," Eisliev said. "If he wants to thwart my plans, I'll do the same to him."

Branimir clenched his crooked teeth to hold back a scream. They could only be talking about Bohumir. He could not think of a worse situation. The two were heading to murder Bohumir! All the while, the *Kadari* prepared to scout the shore, where they would find Dorofej and the others. Once Falmagon learned they had arrived at Melkorka, they would be hunted.

He had to hurry, but he could not let poor Bohumir be slaughtered by the red mage. The whole reason they had come to Melkorka had been to rescue the boy. Being here in this moment could not be any more perfect.

Tyr and Eisliev walked down the road.

Without devising much of a plan, Branimir trailed behind the two. They headed for a common house built among the many other wooden homes.

"How are you gonna do it?" Tyr asked, slowing his step so the mage could keep pace.

"Me?" Eisliev shook his head. "I am not doing it. I come from a respectable bloodline. The Kluks do not take innocent lives. You must be mistaking me for a Kaligula."

Branimir flinched as Eisliev continued to say Dorofej's surname with a negative undertone.

Tyr glanced at the home ahead of them. He said, "And, you think since I am a barbarian I will snap the boy's neck and not think twice about it?"

"Thinking is not your strong suit, Tyr. You are the brawn," Eisliev grabbed a hold of the knob to the door of the home. "It is more in your job description than mine."

The giant put a meaty hand over Eisliev's. "You misjudge me and my people. I have no interest in killing the boy, Eisliev. He has done nothing wrong."

"He has outlived his purpose. He was nothing more than a bargaining chip for Dagmar."

Tyr scowled. "Could just as easy set the boy free, you know? He doesn't have to be killed."

Branimir crouched behind them.

"For them to simply capture the boy all over again? I don't think so," Eisliev's voice was grating, derisive. He mocked the Ispolini. "If you want to forever be known as a coward, I will do it."

Tyr tightened his face, unable to make eye contact with the mage. After a moment, he finally nodded. "It's your revenge. Not mine."

He released Eisliev's hand, curling his six fingers back at his side. He looked away while Eisliev gaped at the massive man.

"Fine," Eisliev said. "Stay out here."

Tyr repeated his question, scanning the courtyard. "How are you going to do it?"

"In a way that assures there is nothing left," Eisliev said, twisting the knob. "Whatever they have planned for the boy will not be done."

Chapter XXXI

Eisliev pushed the wooden door open, flooding the street with white light. He pulled his hood back and stepped through the opening.

Branimir, sprang into action, bounding around Tyr and diving through the doorway. He landed behind Eisliev and then scurried into the corner of the room.

Eisliev slammed the door shut behind him.

"What do you want?" Bohumir squeaked from where he sat cross-legged near an open hearth. The flames flickered near his skin, spindly arms folded in his lap. The room held nothing but the three of them, layered with mildew and dust.

Branimir's mouth dried seeing the boy. Bohumir looked as though he had hardly eaten in weeks. He sat scrunched over, almost too weak to raise his head to Eisliev. He coughed into his hand, spraying droplets of spit onto an empty plate and a waterskin by his ankles.

The red mage squinted at the boy, fidgeting with his fingers. Bohumir glared back at Eisliev with round eyes.

Sliding the dagger soundlessly from his belt, Branimir's skin tingled with anticipation. Even if he killed Eisliev, he did not have a clue how he could escape Melkorka with Bohumir. Tyr stood guard outside the door and the main gate was shut.

Branimir squeezed the dagger's hilt, feeling the weight of the weapon in his hand. He was not a stranger to killing, but he did not take it lightly. At one time, he had been called a warrior among the Kras. The defeat at Cavell haunted him as well as his mistake when killing the Lilitu at the Ariadnean port. Though, he had slaughtered many demons in the Netherworld, and defended Dorofej against the undead at *Garain'l*. And now, he would be forced to protect Bohumir by sinking this dagger into Eisliev's skull.

His chest tightened, glaring at Eisliev, who had brought him so much grief.

Bohumir cringed, saying, "I already had my supper."

The red mage did not pause. The red mage propelled the wooden plate with *Koldovstvo* from the floor with the potency of an arrow, embedding itself into Bohumir's neck. The cascade of blood showered down the boy's shirt and the floor. Before Bohumir could gurgle, let along raise his hands to grab the projectile, Eisliev used *Koldovstvo* to fling the boy's lithe body into the flames.

The murder was quick.

Bran gagged at the sight. Bohumir wriggled and thrashed on the coals, the flames searing through his skin, eating away at his clothes and hair first. The blood waned in the blaze.

The smell of charred meat infused Branimir's nostrils.

The red mage said, "There would be nothing left of the boy to recognize, let alone use for a ritual."

Eisliev shifted his weight to the back of his heel to turn around.

Branimir chucked his extra blade into the back of Eisleiv's head. The pointed weapon—quick as lightning—bore through flesh and bone until nothing remained but the handle.

Eisliev did not so much as flutter an eyelid. The red mage, the Stuhia, tarried in a standing position while the flames crackled and then collapsed face first into the wooden planks of the home.

Branimir bawled. With tear-filled eyes, he pounced on Eisliev Kluk's back, gripping his dagger with the intent to pull it free. He tugged it, heaving with all his strength, but the blade was stuck. His mind reeled.

Branimir should have separated from Dorofej at Cavell and pursued the boy. Instead, he had abandoned him. And now, his reluctance against Eisliev left the boy dead.

The red robes beneath him were as colorful as Eisliev's blood seeping from under his red strands. Branimir could not help but look to the shriveling corpse of Bohumir once more. He balled his hand into a fist in attempts to stop himself from trembling.

Branimir quaked with fury.

He jerked the other dagger from his belt, *kaelandur*, and jabbed it into Eisliev's back. He stabbed the red mage over and over again. In his head. His neck. His shoulders. His backbone.

He hated the red mage. He hated himself.

Droplets of blood disgorged from the skin with every repetitive assault. Crimson liquid wetted his face and soaked his trouser legs. He did not care.

He did not hear the door creak open behind him, but he heard the thundering voice of Tyr Og. "No! Foul half pint?"

Branimir coiled his body to meet the blue eyes of the Ispolini, realizing in his rage, he had forgotten to maintain his hiddenness.

The giant barreled through the door, reaching for Branimir.

The Kras crumpled away from Tyr, disappearing once more. Behind him, Bohumir's remains cackled in the flames.

Tyr faltered, stopping in his tracks. Branimir followed Tyr's gaze to the shredded body of Eisliev. Even the Ispolini would second guess fighting an enemy he could not see. Bran thought him wise to hold back. He had fought plenty of Bukavac in the Netherworld. Brute strength did not contend against his stealth.

From the corner of the room, Branimir watched the giant look to the Ash Tree in the courtyard behind him and then back at Eisliev's body. His eyes reflected his deliberation before he scooted backward from the home.

Seeing the Ash Tree gave Branimir an idea. He acted fast, snagging the waterskin from the ground and dumping its contents onto the ground.

"Killer!" Tyr roared from the doorway. "Killer!"

Branimir slinked around the giant and ran for the Waters of Life. From the corner of his eye, he noticed the gates had been opened, and were slowly being closed again. Either someone had recently returned to Melkorka or someone had just left.

Tyr roared from the doorway of the house at any *Kadari* who would hear him. "Come quick," Tyr continued with intensity. "Hurry! Eisliev has been slain. There is a murderer within the walls."

The nearest *Kadari* rushed toward Tyr. Branimir dodged them in the road, sliding to the dark pool with the waterskin outstretched. The liquid flooded into the opening.

Kaelandur, secured in the scabbard at his belt, pressed against his side while the skin filled. He ignored the tension in his muscles, the feeling of wanting to curl into a dark corner and weep. The sense of self-loathing had not left him, but he had his sense of duty.

The *Kadari* behind him shouted questions at Tyr, screaming for someone to fetch the Patrician.

Unwilling to waste any more time, he gathered up the waterskin and peddled his feet toward the closing doors. As it was said, the Kras were quicker than any human, and Branimir made full use of it.

He bolted around the many scattering *Kadari*, immobilized carts, and random obstacles. In seconds, he had scampered through the gate, and was darting along the stone wall. Behind him, he heard the iron doors cling shut.

The shadow of Melkorka grayed behind Branimir. He fled toward the shoreline, overlooking the thinning grasses, broken pebbles, and glistening moon which had caught his eye before. There was nothing pleasant about being back home.

He wanted to be gone from Melkorka.

Chapter XXXII

The coast came into sight about the time the first raindrop struck Branimir on his hooked nose. Fitting for the rain to come when their deaths were nigh.

Branimir first saw Adamus. The hero-warrior was humming to himself while testing the weight of his silver axe. Sulanna stood near him, watching the hills leading to Melkorka. The black mage lay between them.

Dorofej exploded up from the sand, pointing in Branimir's direction. "Returns, he does." Dorofej climbed to his feet, pulling at Adamus. "Flee, we must. I say, the *Kadari* are coming."

Branimir materialized several feet from them, causing Sulanna to jolt.

"Branimir," Sulanna gasped, "you are covered with blood!"

"What has happened?" Adamus stormed forward scanning the world behind Branimir, looking for an army to follow.

"You were with me, Dorofej?" Branimir asked with confusion, hearing only the black mage.

"Up until leaving the dungeon, I was, yes?" the black mage responded. "Be with you physically, I could not, but in *Klukas*, watch you, I could."

Branimir could not hold back his sadness any longer, falling to his knees. Tears streamed down his red cheeks. "I killed him, Dorofej. I…I killed him."

"If a man you had to kill, a choice, you did not have."

"I had to kill Eisliev, but I am not speaking of him. I mean Bohumir. The boy is dead because of what I could not do," Branimir cried.

"The boy is dead," Adamus said incredulously. "Our journey has been for nothing then. We have failed!"

Branimir sunk his hands into the sand, dropping his head. He repeated the words solemnly, "We have failed."

Raindrops started to fall more frequently, spattering around him.

"Know whether or not we have failed, we do not," Dorofej said, looking ominously toward the night's sky. "A blessing in disguise, it may be. Without the boy, the *Kadari* cannot perform their ritual, yes?"

"They only wanted him to strengthen the Ash Tree, Dorofej," Branimir said. "I heard it clear enough. They want more power to fight the demons."

Adamus took a step backwards, his face rigid with confusion. "That hardly sounds like an evil scheme."

Sulanna dipped her chin. "I agree. Did we not come here ourselves to save the Ash Tree? It sounds like the *Kadari* had found a way."

"I say, sacrificing the boy would have only bought them time, yes? Saved the world from the Likhyi and stopped the demons from coming, it would not." Dorofej raised his finger with a sense of urgency. "Best to focus on escaping, yes? Find a better solution, we will not, if we are captured."

Sulanna, keeping her forehead crinkled, spoke with insight. "Dorofej is right. We cannot worry over the things which have already come to pass, but only what we can now do. If the boy is dead, there is nothing to be done."

Adamus exhaled loudly, seemingly perturbed by the outcome. Considering the hero-warrior's dark magic displayed at *Garain'l*, Branimir wondered if the Ariadnean would have sacrificed Bohumir if he thought it was needed.

Branimir gripped his head in his hands. "Falmagon is determined to find *kaelandur.*"

Sulanna shifted her weight, shooting Adamus a worried glance. "All of us? What good is the dagger if the boy is dead."

"He may not want it anymore," Adamus said.

"True, Adamus. Though, risk letting them have *kaelandur*, we cannot, yes? For now," Dorofej continued, "we must flee before the *Kadari* come. Coming with the scouting party, Falmagon and Dagmar are."

Sulanna's irritation came across in her tone, demanding a clearer answer. "They are coming *right* here?"

Branimir demanded, at the same time, "Dorofej, who is Dagmar?"

"How do they know we are here?" Sulanna said immediately after.

"They saw the knarr," Bran explained, waving off Sulanna. He repeated his question to Dorofej. "Who is Dagmar?"

"Let them come," Adamus said. "I have been at sea for far too long and would welcome a battle."

"The time to be brave or stupid, it is not, Adamus," the black mage glared. "The *Kadari* wield immeasurable magic with access to the Ash Tree, yes? I say, Dagmar holds the *Varkolak*, yes?" Dorofej shuddered, looking west momentarily, and then said, "Won, this battle cannot be."

Branimir scowled, being ignored again.

"Those are gruesome words, Dorofej," Sulanna said, the rain now coming in a downpour. She looked up warily at the visible moon, and then reached out to touch the rain with disbelief. "What is this *Varkolak*?"

"A book," Dorofej said. "I say, every time I beseech you to make haste, a hundred questions I then receive, yes? The time for questions is not in this moment. Come."

"Who is Dagmar!" Branimir shrieked.

"My grandson!" Dorofej cried, and then mumbled in a softer tone. "He is my grandson."

Branimir gasped. "Your grandson?"

"Yes." The black mage grimaced. "All the same, leave from this place, we must."

"We aren't going to get out of here without a fight," said Adamus, gesturing to the opposite side of Branimir with his head.

Branimir spun on his knees, soaked by the wet sand. Even through the rainfall, the Kras could see a troupe of *Kadari* striding toward them. At the forefront of the group marched Falmagon and Dagmar.

"Dorofej," Branimir howled, pressing the waterskin into the dark mage's hands, "the Waters of Life. Drink."

With a look of wonderment, Dorofej took the pouch from Branimir and restored what he had lost since Ariadne.

Thunder crashed in the heavens. Lightning danced behind the circling dark clouds, and still the moon shined above them.

The next moment hastened. Dorofej screamed for them to gather close to him. Branimir nosedived to the black mage's feet while Sulanna and Adamus hung close to his side. Dorofej's hands flung upward, using *Koldovstvo* to create a blue shimmering orb. It encompassed them all, forming from nothing, and expanding wide.

On cue, fire and stone hailed from all directions, cast by the *Kadari*. The magic slammed into the bluish ball of energy, but held every physical element at bay, including the rain.

"Outside this orb is certain death," Adamus said with bewilderment. He pulled free his axe, looking for a moment to move to the offensive. There was none.

Sulanna said, "You cannot hold this forever, Dorofej."

The black mage, aging gradually responded, "For as long as I must, I will."

"I can fight them," Branimir said. "They will not be able to see me, but I only have *kaelandur* for a weapon."

"No!" Dorofej took a step back, empowering the orb as magic struck it again and again with more ferocity. "Strike the copper blade against human flesh, dead or alive, you must not. Saw what happened to Nedezhda, you did, yes?"

Branimir's eyes widened. Eisliev. *No!*

Dorofej truly had not been with him when he killed the red mage.

Adamus, missing the significance of the conversation, said, "Tis a fine plan, Branimir, I have my dagger you could carry. Or, perhaps you could carry Sulanna's knife?"

Sulanna pulled her long knife from her belt, and held it out to him. "It will do better in your hands than in mine, if you can hurry."

Branimir, filled with uneasiness, took the weapon from Sulanna. He could not carry Adamus's dagger again. In his hands, he may as well have been carrying a longsword. The heavy weapon felt strange to him.

"Hurry, Branimir," Dorofej said, flinching as more magic struck the orb. "Weaken their numbers, and join the battle, we will."

Vanishing from sight, Branimir stepped out from the protective globe.

Precipitation pelted his body while he sprinted at the *Kadari*. He held the long knife to his side, gripping the handgrip with two hands to manage the mass. Branimir swept wide, avoiding the whirlwind of lightning, wind, stone, and fire. The *Kadari* in their leather armor were aging, dark strands collecting shimmers of gray. As he circled to the rear of the horde, more than fifty, he could hear Falmagon commanding the troupe.

"Hold nothing back," Falmagon bawled. "We are the stronger. Remember, youth awaits you in Melkorka. Leave nothing to question."

Dagmar walked steadily next to Falmagon. The Stuhia had not touched *Koldovstvo*. His words were faint in the din of battle, but Branimir's ears could hear the words. "The black mage will not last against us, but we should not kill him until we have *kaelandur*. We must know whether he created it."

"Don't be foolish, Dagmar," Falmagon said, twisting his head forcefully at the man. "Dorofej must die. Now!" He screamed at the *Kadari* force. "Destroy him. He cannot hold his shield forever."

The rain slapped against his face, picking up speed over the short spans. Horrid bile, sour and dry, burned Branimir's throat. Ahead, the first *Kadari*, a girl in light armor hurled fire at his friends. Her eyes, likely once innocent, were filled with wrath, unquestionably following Falmagon's orders.

Branimir loathed killing.

He slowed and repositioned himself behind her and briskly sliced the blade-edge across the back of her knees. She crumbled to the side with a startled scream and he silenced her, stabbing the sword into her chest.

While she choked on the blood in her throat, Branimir could only see Eisliev's dead body. And then, Bohumir. And then, Hanna. The death never ended.

He would never get the images from his head.

Yanking the long knife free, he avoided her dimming eyes. Battle was not a time for thought; he knew that. He had caused enough damage by thinking too much. He did not have time to contemplate what needed to be done.

Another woman, directly ahead of his first target, caught his attention. She turned around and gasped at the dead *Kadari*.

Rushing the woman head on, Branimir pushed off of the ground, holding the weapon at waist level. Sulanna's knife was too heavy to hold over his head. As he fell into the woman, he jabbed it forward, the blade sinking into her midsection. She fell backwards with him landing on top of her, hanging desperately to the weapon.

Her scream echoed as she scrambled to grab her invisible assailant. He stayed nimble ducking away from her flailing hands. He hurriedly hopped away from her while pulling the sword free. Fire seared the space he had been in from her hands. Right away, he rotated around her, thrusting the sword into her neck.

The flames shooting from her hands ceased, but the harm had been done. Cries of alarm cultivated across the *Kadari* ranks, and attention turned to the two dead women within feet of each other.

"Sara?" one yelled.

Another shouted, "Who did this?"

The rain turned to ice, forming into balls the size of a man's skull, and slammed into several *Kadari* near Branimir. He dived clear of the ice shards. Many of the *Kadari* fell, bleeding from the scalp.

Falmagon, several paces away, shouted throwing stone back toward Dorofej, who had plunged the ice boulders. He, again, raised his cerulean shield to block Falmagon's attacks.

Branimir pushed wet strands of hair from his forehead and ran in the sludge of muddied sand. The rain soaked into his tattered cloak, weighing down his movement. He loosened the string at his neck, and let the fabric fall away from him. It was better to be chilled in the rain than to carry the extra weight of wet wool.

He worked his way toward Falmagon, gathering the courage to strike down the spearhead of the *Kadari*. He noticed the mages regrouping and marching quicker towards Dorofej, Adamus, and Sulanna.

He picked up his pace, using Sulanna's long knife to slice the tendons of another *Kadari*, a male this time. He cut the throat after the mage had fallen. He repeated the maneuver on another. And another.

While invisible, Branimir could not be touched. He might be able to kill them all, if he remained undetected. He did not think he could hold up against a single magic user, especially Falmagon or Dagmar, unless he stayed out of sight.

A blast of earth behind him sent him spiraling through the air, the long knife sailing from his hand. Branimir squealed, hurtling into the sodden dirt. He heard the crack of his arm as it twisted beneath him awkwardly. He howled in agony over the racket of the battle.

"Branimir!" Adamus clamored, tearing out from the protection of Dorofej's simmering shield. The Ariadnean's action told Branimir all he needed to know. He was obvious to the world.

He did not have to turn his head far to see Adamus's breastplate gleaning. The hero-warrior barreled into the first mage, sending the man sprawling, and then sliced his axe into the torso of a second. A third raised its hand, but moved slower than the Ariadnean. Adamus grabbed the *Kadari* woman by the scruff of her robe, jerking her forward, and head-butted her. Blood spurted from her face; she staggered backwards, but he had already let loose of the woman, sprinting for Branimir.

Sulanna, on his heels, grabbed the bloodied *Kadari* with the broken nose, and snapped her neck. She, then, dived into a roll toward another, who hastily flung fire at her. She sprung up beneath the flame, striking the mage in the arms, veering the attack into one of their brethren. Her target wailed in fury. Sulanna did not flinch, snapping his arm and then his neck.

Her hands moved with untold speed in close combat.

Branimir tried to stand, but felt too dazed and wobbly from the pinpointed blast. Pain coursed up his arm and into his shoulder. He winced and sunk back the mud.

"So, you are the Kras," Dagmar sneered, leering over him. "Where is this *dagger* called *kaelandur*?"

Branimir inched back from the Stuhia's intimidating gaze. Again, the man looked uncannily like Dorofej, except for the hate radiating from his icy eyes.

"Tell me where it is and I may let you live," Dagmar threatened, quailing his hand.

"No," Branimir said meekly, trying to stand on his feet.

A fist half the size of his face struck him. Branimir fell hard, spitting a mouthful of blood.

"It will not do you any good," Branimir said, looking at Dorofej's so-called grandson. "Bohumir is dead."

"So, you do know where it is," Dagmar jeered. He pounded Branimir again, hitting him in the temple. A memory of Falmagon beating him grated his memory. The Stuhia whacked him again, shouting at Branimir to give up *kaelandur*. "Give me the location and this will stop!"

Dagmar hit him until his jaw swelled and his cheek felt numb. Blood trickled into his eye, and slid down the side of his face. Branimir kicked back, but his feet were feathers in comparison to the man's fists.

Kaelandur pressed against his side. His fingers inched toward the dagger.

In the shadows, in the shield of the rain, Adamus pitched himself into Dagmar. The impact sent the Stuhia roiling across the ground. Adamus pursued the man until he stopped rolling, and then stooped over him. Adamus struck the man with a heavy fist. Dagmar grunted against the blow, his head slamming back into the dirt.

Adamus lifted his silver axe when a rock slammed into him, sending him spiraling away from Dagmar. He twisted mid-air and landed with a thud. He sprung to his feet and was pressing forward again before Branimir could say anything.

Falmagon emerged from behind Dagmar, throwing another stone at Adamus. Before the rock struck the bulky hero-warrior, a blue shield shaped in front of him. The boulder shattered and crumbled harmlessly.

Across the expanse, Dorofej had his black hood pulled over his brow. The lengthening gray beard growing from his chin and down his front was unmistakable. Yet his hands worked meticulously through the air. He cast his craft back at the remaining *Kadari* while protecting Adamus.

"It is time to end this," Dagmar said, stumbling back to his feet. He stampeded forward, but instead of advancing toward Adamus, he aimed for Dorofej.

"Get up, Branimir," Adamus shouted, eyeballing Dagmar as he ran past him. The Stuhia blurred as he slithered through time and space. Dagmar wielded *Koldovstvo* like Dorofej. Branimir remembered the black mage saying he held the power of the void within *Koldovstvo*; he said it had been in his blood.

Branimir lost sight of the Stuhia, glancing across the field, and instead, saw Sulanna struggling against another *Kadari*. The side of her face was bloodied and burned. Another blue shield from Dorofej hovered around her.

"Branimir!" Adamus yelled again.

The Kras whimpered, holding his arm to his chest. He stumbled several steps towards Adamus and crumbled back to a knee. The world gyrated; his stomach churned.

A foot smashed into his back. "You are not going anywhere, Branimir," Falmagon scoffed, kicking him a second time. "You will tell me what I need to know. I will save this world."

Falmagon continued to wield *Koldovstvo*, casting stone and fire at Adamus. The hero-warrior sneered at the Patrician of the *Kadari* and marched forward, protected by the blue shield.

Branimir's insides felt broken, blood oozing over his gaping mouth. His chest burned like fire; his focus hazed. He fought against the blackness, keeping his sight on Adamus, who closed the distance. Branimir wriggled and thrashed to break free, but Falmagon pressed down with more weight.

Branimir convulsed against the pain, his broken arm trapped under his body. He tried to lift himself upward. He tried again. Nothing.

A heavy grunt sounded and the pressure on his body disappeared. He barely saw Falmagon fall as Adamus's fist connected across the man's jaw. An arm wrapped around Branimir's waist with more ferocity than intended. Adamus pulled Branimir to him.

"Come on. Dorofej needs us."

Branimir's feet wobbled as he tried to stand on them, searching the ground for Sulanna's long knife. He could not see anything but sand, but he noticed Falmagon writhing against the ground. The Patrician would not stay down for long.

"I am not sure I can, Adamus," Branimir coughed up blood, nearly collapsing again.

The *Kadari* were closing on them. In the distance, he noticed more mages advancing over the hill from Melkorka.

"You must get away," Branimir begged.

Adamus sheathed his axe, lifting Branimir fully from the ground. "No, I will carry you, my friend."

From the chaos, Sulanna approached them, contorting her face in pain. She was bruised and bleeding, but she stood. Branimir forced himself to look away from her burnt face.

Again, a vision of Bohumir clouded his head.

Sulanna heaved. "Get Branimir to the knarr if you can, or further up the coast. I will help Dorofej."

"Sulanna," Adamus started to contend, but she ran ahead of them without another word.

Dorofej, with his whitened beard, battled Dagmar, his red hair graying. Fire, ice, and stone erupted as the two of them altered through space and time. The movements were so quick, Branimir could hardly follow the two Stuhia. Their battle raged, a personal war of masters of their craft.

When Dorofej could not move quick enough, the blue orb—a substance like honey—would gel around the black mage and absorb the magical energy. From the rear, the rest of the *Kadari* hurtled unimaginable bright rays and lightning at Dorofej. He maintained another cerulean wall to block their attacks, but the abjuration had begun to fade.

With a boom, Dorofej finally hit Dagmar with a burst of wind. The Stuhia revolved through the air toward the other *Kadari*.

Adamus, who had ignored Sulanna, approached Dorofej with Branimir in his arms seconds after the noble woman.

"How do we escape, Dorofej?" Adamus asked.

The Stuhia looked to Adamus, Sulanna, and then finally Branimir. His voice sounded ancient and troubled, "Make a way, I will."

Falmagon could be heard behind them, back on his feet, screaming like a madman. The Patrician wielded his own craft against the magical shield. Each strike caused Dorofej to wince as he tried to hold the glistening wall.

"Keep *kaelandur* away!" Dorofej cried, leaving one hand to hold the wall and raising another to the side. "Save yourselves!"

"We all will go," Sulanna said.

Behind her, the fabric of reality was ripped away before their eyes. Where shoreline met water, there was suddenly a gaping hole, large enough for a man to slip through. It led to another place. Low rolling hills were faintly lit by a crescent moon. No rain fell opposite of this gateway.

"Flee!" Dorofej screamed, his arms trembling. It took all his strength to craft this wonder. Branimir feared this was beyond his skill.

"Where is this?" Adamus asked.

"Gaetana," Dorofej said. "Now, go!"

Branimir wept, reaching for him. "We need you, Dorofej. You must come with us!"

"I cannot follow. I can…not…"

Adamus dipped his head, too familiar with the casualty of war. He seized Branimir tighter, in spite of his pleas, and carried him through the gateway.

Sulanna gripped Dorofej's shoulder and with a final look. She stumbled away hesitantly.

Branimir cried, gripping Adamus. He struggled to see Dorofej until the pathway shut. The battle of Melkorka was over.

The black mage was lost.

MAHARIA

Book 3

The Kaelandur Series

Thrice Nine Legends

Month of Blossoming

Second of Warmth

1351 CE

Prologue

Dorofej Kaligula angled his eyes to gaze at the iron manacles binding his arms to the stone wall in the lower levels of Melkorka. He shuddered at the sight of his pasty, white flesh, prickled with gooseflesh, hanging exposed against the dry air. His thin legs were also fixed to the floor, keeping him rigidly hooked in place. His brittle bones ached; his strength was ever-fleeting.

He chest tightened with despair—not from the arduous position—but from knowing how *Koldovstvo*, the ancient magic, had once again gifted him with old age. Only weeks ago, he had been young and vivacious; but now, his wrinkled skin hung loose from muscle, and his body twinged as though his insides no longer had the resolve to function another day. His organs were likely as frail as the white hairs dangling over his eyes.

The black mage kept his knees locked to prevent the metal above from digging into his wrists. The blood from past captives staining the metal clasps spoke clearly of the antagonizing pain that would come if he allowed himself to simply hang. He questioned how long any man could hold this position before his wits were broken along with the finite body.

Dorofej did not know how long he had been standing in this irregular position. It may have been days, possibly a week. No light entered Melkorka's dungeon, only shadows. The room changed considerably since he had last been within its confines twelve-hundred-years ago. Where dirt paths and rickety cells once stood, rarely used, Dorofej now saw chiseled red stone, fresh timber, and twice as many chains for prisoners.

With a strained breath, he twisted his neck, where he knew a carved symbol of the eye, scraped with the moon and cross, hung over his head. The magical marking prevented him from touching the craft, *Koldovstvo*. He whispered its ancient name. *"Znaki."*

He drooped his head in defeat. Even if the symbol were erased, Dorofej was not certain he had enough life in him to wield *Koldovstvo*. Another trickle of magic through his fingertips may very well end his life.

He had no interest in dying. Not yet.

He suppressed a cough. The odor of urine and feces clung to the air as closely as a hero might cling to honor and glory. Sadly, his own filth was among the filth beneath his feet. Rats and unmarked pests screeched and scraped across the stone floor. Over and over, the creatures neared him to nibble at his wrinkled toes, checking for decay.

With a shudder, shout, or twitch, Dorofej indicated to the vermin he was not dead. But the rodents were patient, accustomed to the unwritten process of the underground, hollowed chamber. No doubt, in short time, there would be no resistance, no shuffling or screaming, and then they could feast on his flesh.

Across the room, the latch clicked and the oak door creaked open. Air from beyond the dungeon circulated into the room. Dorofej could not hold back his cough this time, and hacked harshly, the ashy dust filtering up to his nostrils and into his throat.

The flickering torchlight danced across the dungeon, nearly blinding him. Twisting his neck, his long white hair fell away from his face, providing a faint image of many shadowed figures slinking into the room.

"Careful," said a man in white robes. "Do not loosen the binds until the giant is chained."

The *Kadari* paid no attention to Dorofej. Their attention stayed on the Ispolini, the giant, who was being dragged across the floor with magical strands of *Koldovstvo*.

Dorofej recognized Tyr Og. The giant had helped kidnap an innocent boy, Bohumir Mager, for the *Kadari* to sacrifice here at Melkorka. Though, none would have guessed the plan would have been thwarted by the red mage, Eisliev Kluk, who slaughtered the boy first.

Tyr growled, having the ability to do nothing more but speak. "For the hundredth time, I did not kill the boy. Eisliev killed him, and the half pint killed Eisliev with a dagger."

"Hold your tongue," Falmagon Sej spouted, following Tyr and the other *Kadari* through the door. The Patrician of the *Kadari*, once known as the Highborn Long-Walker, was easily distinguishable. "We will hear your so-called truth when it is time."

"Listen to me. I helped you," Tyr shouted. "There is no reason to hold me here. Please!"

Falmagon responded to the Ispolini, but lifted his blue eyes to Dorofej, mockingly. "I will be most interested to hear more about this dagger in very, very short time."

Dorofej strained to keep his head elevated to maintain eye contact with the Patrician. The muscles in his neck and upper back ached. He tried to focus on breathing through his nose to forget the pain.

It was a mistake. He coughed harshly again at the rotten smell.

Falmagon maintained the smirk on his face. "Yes, the truth will be revealed soon enough. Won't it, Dorofej? Say, why don't you give up your little charade and tell me what I need to know?"

Dorofej wheezed, desperate for a drink. "Oh, tell me—you must—what needs to be known, yes?"

The demeanor of the Patrician changed as soon as Dorofej opened his mouth. "Do not play your games with me. Where is *kaelandur*? Does Branimir have it?" Falmagon flared his nostrils, blowing air through his thick mustache. He advanced, holding himself inches in front of Dorofej's face.

Dorofej lingered, stone-faced. Indeed, his friend, Branimir Baran held *kaelandur*, the copper dagger, the hourglass of Dorofej's life. Though, he would never tell Falmagon such a thing.

"I say, why do you care?" Dorofej said. "Dead, the boy is. Sacrifice him, you cannot."

"Answer the question," a deep voice demanded from behind Falmagon. The man, called Dagmar, ambled forward from the shadows. Dorofej fought the man on the shores of Folkmar before being imprisoned. At the time, Dagmar lost years of his life casting *Koldovstvo*. But now, the Stuhia regained his youth. He had a head full of red hair and smooth, scarless skin. Seeing Dagmar reminded Dorofej the Ash Tree and the Waters of Life were just beyond the castle's dungeon. His salvation was less than a hundred feet away.

Dagmar gripped a thick book under his arm, and continued, "Someone has broken the old laws by creating this dagger with *Koldovstvo*. If you are truly Stuhia, you know the maker must be killed to abolish the dagger."

"Know the law of the Stuhia, I do," Dorofej said, eyeing the leather book. He knew its name: the *Varkolak*. "I say, why are you eager to destroy *kaelandur*?"

Falmagon huffed with superiority, seemingly offended by the question. "Because demons have continued to come from the Netherworld and it must be stopped. They are intent on destroying the Ash Tree. This started with the creation of the dagger, and it will end with the dagger's destruction."

"That is why you sent Alyona and Artemiy after the dagger, yes?" Dorofej contemplated. "Want the dagger, you did, to stop the demons?"

"Why else?" Falmagon squinted at Dorofej, likely questioning how he would know of Alyona and Artemiy. Yet he said nothing of the two *Kadari*. Instead, he defended his reason. "It was not until I met Dagmar that I learned you were a Stuhia, and I had to kill you to destroy *kaelandur*. Everything I do is for the saving of this world, Dorofej."

"Misinformed, you are, Falmagon Sej. Proof, you are, there are worst things in this world than demons," Dorofej said, coughing again. He unsuccessfully tried to find saliva in his mouth. "And come, the demons will, whether *kaelandur* exists or not."

"Do not insult me with your lies," Falmagon said haughtily. "You are trying to save your own skin."

"My own skin?" Dorofej said, lifting his eyebrows with as much innocence as he could muster.

Dagmar fell into the façade. "Did you not create *kaelandur*, Stuhia?"

"Of course, he created it!" Falmagon cried, glaring at Dorofej. "Don't bother entertaining this pile of piss with such a question. He is talking in his riddles to buy his time, hoping someone will come and save him. Listen, it was only him and Jhar who crafted the dagger, and Jhar is dead."

The black mage snorted, looking to Dagmar. "The law of the Stuhia, I know."

Dagmar tilted his chin to Falmagon, and then back to Dorofej. "Humor me."

Dorofej swiftly stated, "Familiar with the *Varkolak*, I am." He bobbed his head in acknowledgement of the book under Dagmar's arm.

The redheaded man in front of him stepped backwards in sheer shock, mouth gaping and eyes widening. "How do you know the name of this codex? How does he know this, Falmagon?"

"Because passed it to my son, Mihael, I did, after the fall of the Carian Council?" Dorofej kept his eyes from Falmagon, who he could hear breathing heavier and heavier. He locked eyes with Dagmar. "Scribed it, I did."

"What!" Dagmar roared, his voice echoing in the dungeon. "Mihael? You gave this codex to my father?"

Dorofej lowered his head.

"You are my grandfather?" Dagmar asked shakily.

"He is deceiving us, Dagmar. Let us kill him and be done with this. His death will save Aenar," Falmagon demanded.

Dagmar hurriedly grabbed Falmagon's arm, pulling him away. His eyes never moved off Dorofej hanging from the chains. "No. If he did not create *kaelandur*, killing him will do nothing but have Dahz find disfavor in you."

"One way or another, the world is better without him. I would rather watch him burn than reach Thrice Ten Kingdom," Falmagon proclaimed.

"If he is my grandfather…if he knows the law of the *Varkolak*…"

Falmagon interrupted. "Wouldn't you know if he was your grandfather? He is lying."

"I never knew my father's father," Dagmar sluggishly said. "You do not understand the significance of what this man is saying. Whether he is lying or not—even to know the name of this codex—speaks of the knowledge he holds. We cannot kill him," Dagmar said while Falmagon stared incredulously back, "yet."

"Your logic is the same as my predecessor, Kinhar Sayan," Falmagon whispered, "and he is dead. The *Kadari* cannot fight an endless war against Marheena's demons and lead the people of Aenar to redemption. We can kill him now and end this."

Dagmar shook his head. "The only way to destroy *kaelandur* is to kill its maker *with* the weapon."

"What?" Falmagon sneered.

"You cannot simply kill him. His life is bound by the life of the dagger," Dagmar explained. "And you need the weapon and creator to complete the deed. Without *kaelandur*, you are powerless. You would not be able to kill Dorofej if you tried."

Falmagon bawled in frustration, folding his hands into fists. "Fine, Dagmar. Then we must find Branimir Baran."

Dagmar curled his lip. "I can find him."

"If you won't tell me where *kaelandur* is," Falmagon turned back on Dorofej, staring hard into the black mage's icy eyes, Branimir will. Even if I must tear him limb from limb, he will talk."

Dorofej hung his head in defeat.

ABOUT THE AUTHOR

Joshua Robertson was born in Kingman, Kansas on May 23, 1984. A graduate of Norwich High School, Robertson attended Wichita State University where he received his Masters in Social Work with minors in Psychology and Sociology. His bestselling novel, Melkorka, the first in The Kaelandur Series, was released in 2015. Known most for his Thrice Nine Legends Saga, Robertson enjoys an ever-expanding and extremely loyal following of readers. He counts R.A. Salvatore and J.R.R. Tolkien among his literary influences.